F
Griffin

Griffin, W. E. B.

The last witness.

DATE			

THE LAST WITNESS

ALSO BY W.E.B. GRIFFIN

THE
LAST
WITNESS

W.E.B.
GRIFFIN

AND WILLIAM E. BUTTERWORTH IV

G. P. PUTNAM'S SONS
NEW YORK

PUTNAM

G. P. PUTNAM'S SONS
Publishers Since 1838
Published by the Penguin Group
Penguin Group (USA) Inc., 375 Hudson Street,
New York, New York 10014, USA

USA · Canada · UK · Ireland · Australia
New Zealand · India · South Africa · China

Penguin Books Ltd, Registered Offices: 80 Strand, London WC2R 0RL, England
For more information about the Penguin Group visit penguin.com

Library of Congress Cataloging-in-Publication Data

Griffin, W. E. B.
The last witness / W.E.B. Griffin and William E. Butterworth IV.
p.   cm.—(Badge of Honor series; Volume 11)
ISBN 978-0-399-16257-2
1. Payne, Matt (Fictitious character)—Fiction.   2. Police—Pennsylvania—
Philadelphia—Fiction.   3. Philadelphia (Pa.)—Fiction.   I. Butterworth,
William E. (William Edmund), author.   II. Title.
PS3557.R489137L37   2013   2013016782
813'.54—dc23

Printed in the United States of America
1   3   5   7   9   10   8   6   4   2

BOOK DESIGN BY EMILY S. HERRICK

Fic.

This is a work of fiction. Names, characters, places, and incidents either are the product of the
author's imagination or are used fictitiously, and any resemblance to actual persons, living or dead,
businesses, companies, events, or locales is entirely coincidental.

ALWAYS LEARNING   PEARSON

IN FOND MEMORY OF

SERGEANT ZEBULON V. CASEY

Internal Affairs Division
Police Department, the City of Philadelphia, Retired

"There came a time when there were assignments
that had to be done right, and they would seek Zeb
out. These assignments included police shootings,
civil-rights violations, and he tracked down fugitives
all over the country. He was not your average cop. He
was very, very professional."

HOWARD LEBOFSKY
Deputy Solicitor of Philadelphia

I

"Stop yelling, Krystal, and listen very carefully to me," Maggie Mc-Cain ordered evenly, hoping her tone did not betray her deep fear. "He can track you with your cell phone. Turn it off. Then take out the battery if you can."

Maggie, at the wheel of her eight-year-old Toyota Land Cruiser, was twenty-five years old and, standing five-six and weighing one-thirty, slender and fit. She had pale skin, intense green eyes set in a pleasant face, and shoulder-length chestnut brown hair that she mostly wore up, as now, brushed smooth against her scalp and tied in a tight, neat ponytail. She had on elegant dark woolen slacks and a heavily woven black sweater.

Her work cell phone in hand, Maggie heard her personal phone begin ringing in her purse. When she quickly dug it out and saw that the caller ID read MOTHER, she pushed a key to silence the ring, then let the call roll into voice mail.

Oh, damn it, Krystal! she thought, as she heard Krystal starting to cry.

And damn this traffic!

A sea of glowing red brake lights reflected on the rain-slick Center City street. It was a cold, dreary night, the rain occasionally mixing with wisps of snow. She stared out past the swishing windshield wipers, anxiously awaiting the signal light to turn green.

"Did you hear what I said?" Maggie went on. "Use my house phone to call me back. But first make sure all the doors are locked and stay away from the windows. Try to be calm. I'm just minutes away."

The image of a desperate Krystal Angel Gonzalez—a curvy five-foot-one, nineteen-year-old Puerto Rican—frantically pacing the stylish living room of Maggie's Society Hill town house flashed in her mind.

That was exactly what Krystal had done two days earlier, when she banged on Maggie's door at four in the morning. Then she dropped onto the leather couch and lay on her side. Under crossed arms, she tugged her knees tightly against her chest and, off and on, sobbed uncontrollably for hours.

Krystal had finally escaped from Ricardo, the twenty-seven-year-old Fishtown strip club manager she briefly had been calling her boyfriend. But at a brutal cost. Her short dark hair was matted with dried blood, her face bruised and swollen. Raw welts had formed on the back of her thighs where he had whipped her with a pair of wire coat hangers folded together.

She promised me she'd never go back to him, Maggie thought, watching the traffic light finally cycle to green. *I warned her over and over that he really didn't love her.*

"Please hurry!" Krystal said hysterically. "Ricky said the beating was nothing like what he'd do if I told! He'd make me disappear, like Lizzi and Brandi. Then . . . he tore my clothes off and . . . and . . ."

Krystal Gonzalez's quivering voice trailed off.

And you did tell, Maggie thought, shaking her head.

Oh my God . . .

"I'm almost home," Maggie said, and then, raising her voice to be heard over Krystal's sobs, added, "Now turn off your phone!"

Maggie broke off the call. She stuffed the phone in her pocket as her silver SUV rolled up to the intersection. She hung a fast right, pressing harder on the accelerator as she followed Pine Street toward Society Hill.

As a rule, and Maggie devoutly believed in rules—"A place for everything and everything in its place," she often said—she did not like talking on the phone while driving. She also did not like speeding. And she really did not like breaking her own rule of anyone connected with Mary's House being prohibited from coming to her residence.

But seeing Krystal throwing away what might be her last chance to get her life straight . . . I just can't stand that.

We were accomplishing so much.

And now this . . .

Mary's House, in nearby South Philadelphia, served as a temporary residence for young children and teenagers waiting to be placed in foster homes by the city's Department of Human Services. The facility actually was composed of two four-bedroom row houses sharing a common wall. With no signage announcing its existence, Mary's House looked no different from the neighboring well-kept duplexes that lined the street across from Girard Park.

The charity was one of the many ministries of the Church of the Assumption of the Blessed Virgin Mary, the century-old Roman Catholic parish on Philadelphia's affluent Main Line, where Maggie McCain's family had worshipped since before her birth.

At Mary's House, Maggie, with a master's degree in social work

from the University of Pennsylvania, wore many hats. Her biggest
was that of chief administrator. She dealt with the detailed—and
often obscure—requirements of the Department of Human Services
while overseeing the two other social workers who day to day kept up
with the twenty-plus female residents ranging in age from five to
seventeen.

If allowed—especially as compassion for the kids' lot in life
chipped away at any wall of professional detachment—it quickly
could become an all-consuming job.

Maggie knew the City of Philadelphia had its challenges—
perhaps more than its fair share in terms of struggling families. It
was the fifth-largest city in the United States, with one in four of
its 1.5 million residents living in poverty, a third of them under
age eighteen.

And the tragic result of that meant an annual caseload of some
twenty thousand—from infants to teenagers—moving through the
overburdened bureaucracy that was the city's Department of Human
Services.

DHS's role, with hundreds of millions in annual funds, was to
protect the abused and neglected. This meant investigating and overseeing broken families—and, when necessary, immediately removing
children from a potentially dangerous environment. Thus, at any
given time thousands found themselves in temporary care while
DHS evaluated if it was safe for them to be returned to their family—
or placed with a foster family.

And Mary's House was but one small charity among dozens in
Philly providing help—temporary shelter that included food, clothing, health care, and more—until permanent foster care, or adop-
tion, could be secured.

The thick, well-worn file labeled "Gonzalez, Krystal Angel" had been among the first cases that Maggie McCain had reviewed after arriving at Mary's House.

That had been two years earlier, when Krystal had just turned seventeen. It had taken Maggie nearly half a year to earn the confidence of Krystal, who since age ten had suffered the revolving doors of various homes. The last time at Mary's House had been her third to live there.

What Maggie found in her file was, while without question horrific, sadly common.

"DHS, after notification by an anonymous source, confirmed through the various utility service providers that the address of the Brewerytown row house where the mother and her five (5) children lived did not have gas, water, or electricity. On-site inspection by caseworkers found that there was trash littering every room, as well as evidence of rodents and human feces. Said conditions—'clear and convincing evidence of parental inadequacy'—thus meet the Pennsylvania standard for terminating parental rights."

The file further stated that the anonymous source alleged that the mother and her new boyfriend were selling crack cocaine—when they were not using it.

With a court order, and backed by two Philadelphia Police officers, DHS caseworkers came and took the children away.

Krystal—at ten the youngest sibling—and her four sisters were placed in Mary's House and from there into their first foster home. All against the objections of their maternal aunt, who wanted them in her Kensington home with her three children.

Relatives wanting five more mouths to feed? Maggie had thought incredulously, reading the file. *Or just five more checks from DHS?*

These situations are so desperate . . . no matter how much money gets thrown at the problem.

After two years, a DHS caseworker discovered evidence of abuse of the oldest Gonzalez sibling by the foster parents—and suspected there was more—and the girls returned to the safety of Mary's House.

It would be a brief stay.

The aunt lobbied DHS to the point that she finally won court-approved custody of them. The file notes stated that all was more or less okay for the following three years—until the driver of a stolen car hit the aunt in a Kensington crosswalk, killing her. DHS, due to limited space, then split up the six cousins—the eldest two, almost eighteen, had run away and not been heard from since—between three temporary homes.

Krystal, who'd just turned fifteen, wound up back at Mary's House with no real hope of ever living again with her sisters and cousins.

Caseworkers, as much as they wished to oversee each and every child without fail, knew that the system, frustratingly flawed, was anything but perfect—and that there were those who invariably fell through holes in the safety net that was DHS. The younger kids, particularly infants, understandably commanded the majority of attention. At high risk were the teenagers, who constantly tested the patience of caseworkers. They would talk back, lie, and sneak out at night, violating Philadelphia's curfew. Alcohol and drug use, particularly among those who'd been abused, wasn't at all uncommon.

Maggie McCain herself had added ample notes in Krystal's file, most often in connection with the twins Lizzi and Brandi.

Krystal had met the attractive, blonde sixteen-year-olds at a West

Philadelphia facility serving DHS, where they'd lived for almost a year. Not church-affiliated, it was two miles from Mary's House, and twice its size. The girls had found the rules there were fewer, or not strictly enforced, or both, and being opportunistic—if not cunning— teenagers they took advantage of that.

A year after befriending Krystal, Lizzi and Brandi had introduced her to an older girl, all of twenty-one, who impressed them with the money she said she earned serving cocktails at a couple of Philly nightclubs.

Krystal had been so awed that she'd dropped her guard and gushed to Maggie McCain: "She has the latest everything—her hair, her nails, her clothes! And her own place! 'Ya gotta use what ya got to get what ya want,' is what she said. She's going to help find Lizzi and Brandi jobs, and let them share her place until we can get our own."

"*We?*" Maggie had blurted.

"I mean them. Lizzi and Brandi."

But Maggie had understood exactly what she meant.

The girls had led tough lives, ones that most people could not— and, truth told, really did not want to—begin to try to comprehend. The closer the girls got to eighteen, the odds of them being adopted into any family, let alone a stable, loving one, were about as good as the chance they'd be taken bodily into heaven. And the promise of a new, exciting life on their own simply was too tempting.

Maggie at first couldn't compose a reply.

"Use what you got to get what you want"?

That could not be any clearer. . . .

Then, even as she began saying the words, Maggie knew they were falling on deaf ears: "You girls must be very, very careful, Krystal. You have to understand that there's a price, sometimes a very steep one. . . ."

Maggie McCain sped through the tree-lined cobblestone streets of Society Hill, a posh section of Center City overlooking the Delaware River that dated back to the 1700s.

The knot that had formed in the pit of her stomach at the mention of Lizzi and Brandi felt like it was getting worse.

If those poor girls aren't dead, they probably wish they were, she thought.

And Krystal may have just missed the same fate.

She turned down a brick-paved alleyway, then thumbed the button of the garage door opener clipped to her sun visor. Approaching the back of her three-story town house—in the last year she'd spent a small fortune renovating the hundred-year-old structure—she saw that the wooden door of the garage was almost completely open. The interior was brightly lit.

Glancing up, she saw that there were no lights in the windows of the second and third floors.

Krystal didn't call back on my house phone, she thought, nosing the Land Cruiser inside the neat, orderly garage. *Maybe she went to bed?*

Or she's hiding in the dark . . . ?

Maggie put the SUV in park and turned it off. As she opened her driver's door, she heard a heavy *thump* upstairs and what sounded like glass shattering and, a moment later, the rush of air.

Maggie jerked her head, struggling to hear as the garage door closed.

Maybe she fell? But what was—?

The smoke alarms suddenly went off with a steady, ear-piercing squeal.

She got out of the vehicle and ran up the staircase. Reaching the top, she grabbed the doorknob—and instinctively yanked back her hand when she felt the heat. She tugged her thick sweater cuff over her hand, then quickly grabbed and turned the knob.

The door opened onto the kitchen. When she pulled on it, flames flickered out of the crack. She slammed it shut.

What's that smell? Gas?

She waited for a long moment, then tried again.

This time the flames were not quite as intense—and now she could see Krystal. She was lying on the kitchen's hardwood floor. What looked like a beer bottle with a rag tied to it lay in a pool of blood beside her head. A second one was shattered on the marble countertop. The wooden cabinetry was burning rapidly.

The room reeked of gasoline.

"Oh my God!" she whimpered, her green eyes tearing.

I need to call nine-one-one!

No—I don't. The alarm system does that.

She pulled her sweater over her head and ran to Krystal and knelt. Krystal's face was coated in blood. Her eyes were glazed. Maggie touched her neck to feel for a pulse, found none, then grasped her shoulders and shook her.

"Krystal!"

There was no response.

When she had shaken her, her head had moved—and Maggie now noticed a small brass object, then a second one, in the blood pool. She immediately recognized them as spent bullet casings.

She looked back at Krystal—and now followed the trail of blood on her neck to the small round entrance wound the bullet had made behind her right earlobe.

You poor thing . . .

Maggie quickly looked around the kitchen, then down the hall that led to the front of the house. At the end, she could see that the front door was wide open.

Did she not lock the door?

Or did she let in whoever did this?

The flames on the cabinets suddenly grew stronger and hotter.

She ran back to the door to the garage, went through it, and slammed it shut. She slapped at the wall to the left of the door frame until her fingers found the control button that opened the garage door.

The light on the opener in the center of the ceiling came back on. The motor hummed as the big wooden door clunked upward.

She could hear the sound of sirens, faint but clear. They were coming from the direction of the firehouse not quite a half dozen blocks away at Sixth and South.

Maggie ran down the steps.

She pulled from the front passenger floorboard of the Land Cruiser a canvas sailing bag—its neat stitching read YELLOWROSE SPRING BAY RESORT & SPA, VIRGIN GORDA BVI—then took it behind the enclosed stairway. She opened the narrow door there. A single bulb above automatically came on, and she crouched as she entered the small enclosure.

A heavy rug covered most of the concrete floor. Tugging back the far corner, she uncovered a false floor that was a three-foot square of sheet metal.

She slid the square aside to reveal a fireproof safe that had been set in the concrete floor. Its door had a readout and a digital keypad for its combination, and she quickly punched in a string of numbers. The keypad beeped as each number was pushed.

Suddenly there was a rapid series of three *beeps*. A tiny bulb beside the readout lit up red. The screen flashed ERROR.

"Damn!" she said, breathing heavily.

She punched the CANCEL key, then held her breath and again rapidly keyed in the combination's string of numbers. When she finished, she hit the pound symbol key.

Simultaneously there came a single *beep*, the tiny bulb glowed green, and the readout flashed OPENING. That was followed by the whirring sound of the door tumblers disengaging the insets of the door frame.

She exhaled heavily, then swung open the fireproof safe's heavy door.

Maggie reached inside and pulled out a stack of folders and notebooks. She quickly stuffed them into her shoulder bag. She then reached back into the safe, found a bulging brass-zippered cloth bank pouch with the silk-screened logotype KEYSTONE FINANCIAL SERVICES, and a heavy black plastic bag imprinted in gold with LUCKY STARS CASINO & ENTERTAINMENT, and added them to the canvas bag.

Finally, she extracted a black molded plastic clamshell case. She flipped open its silver latches and swung back the top. She looked for a long moment at its contents—a Baby Glock Model 26 9mm semi-automatic pistol with two extra fully charged ten-round magazines—then grunted and shook her head. She racked the slide back and a shiny round ejected, landing inside the safe.

Damn it.

She then let loose of the slide, chambering another round. She stuck the pistol and extra magazines into her bag with everything else, then dropped in the plastic case, slamming the door shut.

———

Maggie McCain climbed into the Land Cruiser and with effort put the now heavy canvas bag on the front passenger seat. Tires squealed as she quickly backed out of the garage.

When she slid to a stop in the alleyway and looked up through the snow that now fell steadily, she could not believe her eyes. The entire second floor was engulfed in flames. And the flames were quickly spreading to the third floor.

The sirens were getting louder.

It's all too little too late.

Poor Krystal . . .

Her thoughts were interrupted by her work cell phone ringing. She tugged it out of her pocket, looked down—and gasped.

The screen read KRYSTAL G.

That's impossible!

She's . . . she's . . .

After a moment, the call went to voice mail, and a moment later Maggie touched the message icon that appeared on-screen.

Over the speakerphone, a Latin male's voice, with a siren growing in the background, growled: "I told those *putas* to keep their fuckin' mouths shut. Now I'm tellin' you, bitch—"

Her heart raced. She dropped the cell phone as if it also were on fire.

She put her hand over her mouth, staring at the phone on the floorboard until its screen dimmed and went dark.

She looked out the windshield, her mind starting to spin as she watched the flames.

That was the guy . . . Ricky?

He's here! And knows my number!

He has to know about Mary's House. . . .

What else is on Krystal's phone?

Her mind flashed with the scene of the burning kitchen and the girl, lifeless on the floor in a pool of her own blood.

The sirens screamed closer.

She shook her head, trying to clear it.

She jerked the gearshift into drive and floored the accelerator.

She frantically slapped at the door panel, finally finding the window switches. The right front and rear windows both went down at once. Bitter cold air blew into the SUV.

She felt as if she were going to start shaking, from both the chill and the fear, and forced it back.

She then reached down to the floorboard, grabbed the cell phone, and threw it. It went out the front window, disappearing into the thick snowflakes. Then she hit the switches again, putting the windows up.

As she skidded to a stop at the end of the alleyway, an enormous red fire truck filled the windshield. Engine 11 flashed past, its siren wailing and emergency lights pulsing in the falling snow.

Crying, she dug the Baby Glock out of the bag while watching the fire truck make a right turn onto her street.

She then spun the steering wheel left. And again floored the accelerator.

[TWO]
Latitude 23 Degrees 32 Minutes 64 Seconds North
Longitude 81 Degrees 92 Minutes 77 Seconds West
North of the Republic of Cuba
Sunday, November 16, 1:35 A.M.

"Damn it, Miguel, that's got to be them!" First Mate Raúl Alfonso announced, peering through binoculars as he stood beside the helm of the *Nuevo Día*. "Those Pangas are right on the GPS coordinates they sent. But why two boats? Is one a backup? Or what . . . ?"

The sky was clear, the winds calm, the sea almost flat. The thin crescent of a new moon hung near the horizon amid a blanket of twinkling stars. The humid air was thick, its salty smell heavy.

The *New Day* was a faded black, rusty steel-hulled cargo vessel 280 feet in length. In addition to a regular schedule of calling on ports around the Bahamian Islands, she and her sister ship made staggered once-a-week trips to Havana from their home port of Miami. The vessels delivered items deemed by the Communist government of Cuba to be of humanitarian value—for an outrageous import tariff paid by the Cuban exiles in the States who sent them—and thus permissible to enter the sovereign island nation.

Months earlier, in another humanitarian shipment, handheld Motorola two-way radios and Garmin GPS units, possession of which Cuban law considered treason and would result in the bearer's immediate imprisonment and likely torture, had been smuggled to Cuban fishermen inside fifty-pound bags of dried *frijoles negros*. Black beans, a Cuban staple, were in almost as great a demand as rice.

A chunky round-faced thirty-year-old Cuban-American, Alfonso stood five-five. He wore a mussed tan uniform, the shirt untucked and his ample belly straining its buttons.

Even with the high-powered optics and the clear weather, he could make out no more than the silhouettes of the two Pangas in the predawn darkness. The narrow, low-profile, twenty-five-foot-long fishing boats, each powered by a single outboard motor, were designed more for calmer inshore waters than for the open sea.

"Perhaps God is with us," Alfonso said, as he passed the binoculars to the ship's master.

"Don't speak too soon, *mi amigo*," Captain Miguel Treto replied.

Treto also was Cuban-American. At thirty-three years of age, he looked like a slightly older version of Alfonso, though not nearly as chunky. His tan uniform was much neater.

Alfonso pointed out the pilothouse window.

"Near one o'clock," he added helpfully, "about two hundred yards out."

"Got 'em, Raúl," Captain Treto said, almost immediately after putting the rubber cups to his eyes. "But, like what happened last month, they could just be other fishermen. Or, worse, even a trap. Radio the code to confirm that's really them."

The previous day, the *Nuevo Día* had made the run from Miami to the Port of Havana. The Cuban capital was only ninety miles due south of Key West. Alfonso and the four-man crew had unloaded the cargo of forty-foot-long corrugated metal intermodal containers in just under two hours. Immediately thereafter, with paperwork complete—and none of the crew, including the captain, having been allowed ashore—lines were cast off and the ship headed back to the States.

When south of the Gulf Stream, particularly during the ten-mile approach and departure of the island, it was standard operating procedure for the captain to keep the speed of the twin diesels at a fraction of the usual twenty-knots-an-hour cruise speed. This accomplished a number of things, beginning with better fuel consumption. But more importantly it also bought extra time for the captain to locate any rendezvous target and, during a pickup, for the ship not to draw attention when suddenly slowing or stopping.

Since clearing the breakers at the mouth of the Port of Havana, the *Nuevo Día* had been making just over five knots per hour. She now, after four hours, was approximately twenty miles east, not far from Santa Cruz del Norte, the small fishing town (population thirty-two thousand) where the Río Santa Cruz emptied into the Caribbean.

The lumbering vessel—in addition to her red, green, and white navigation lights burning—had small clear lights on either side of the bow. They illuminated the thirty-six-inch-high rust-stained white letters that spelled out NUEVO DÍA on the faded black hull.

If they have binocs, Alfonso thought, *they won't be as good as mine.*

And if I can't make out their details, who knows what they can—or can't—see?

Alfonso thumbed the handheld's PUSH TO TALK key three times. That caused three clicks to sound on the speaker of any radio within ten or so miles that shared the frequency. They knew that it was possible that someone in the Fuerzas Armadas Revolucionarias—Cuba's Revolutionary Armed Forces—could be monitoring radio traffic and would somehow interpret the clicks as being a signal. But, being a very common frequency and not maritime specific—not to mention the laxness of the Tropas Guarda Fronteras, especially at such an early hour—their experience had been that it also was equally entirely improbable.

TGF, the Interior Ministry's Border Guard, used aging Soviet-built patrol boats to interdict Cubans fleeing the island and anti-Castro agents infiltrating it. But, with failing assets and regular shortages of fuel, they managed to do so only sporadically.

"Nothing!" Captain Treto said unnecessarily, as they both strained to see out into the dark distance, Treto still using the binoculars.

Then, a long moment later, a beam from a flashlight on the closest Panga lit momentarily, then lit again, and again.

"There!" Alfonso said.

He keyed the radio twice more, and after another moment the light flashed twice more.

"Good enough?" Alfonso said.

Treto grunted.

"Not really," he said, putting down the binoculars. "Anything is possible."

"So then what do you—?"

"Here," Treto said, interrupting him.

He reached under the helm and came out with a dull stainless steel Remington twelve-gauge pump shotgun. Instead of a long wooden stock, it had a compact black polymer pistol grip. And its barrel had been cut short.

"Prepare to take them aboard, Raúl," Treto ordered, racking the foregrip back then forward to chamber a round of double-aught buckshot. He handed the shotgun to Alfonso. "Be quick. But take no chances. If it goes to shit, we open fire, then scuttle the boats with the bodies."

"And if it's just Castro's TGF goons trying to lure us into a trap?"

"Same as always. We say we thought that any small boats way out here had to be in distress—'We know nothing about anyone seeking exile in the States!'—and were following the United Nations Convention that rendering aid is the ship master's legal and moral obligation. And I'll let them hear me call Miami on the satellite phone and repeat that. If that fails . . ."

His voice trailed off.

"If that fails—what?"

"Then we pray, *mi amigo*. We pray."

He patted his back. "Now go, Alfonso."

"Aye-aye."

Ten minutes later, Captain Treto had the *Nuevo Día* sitting dead in the water, her diesels idling. He stood just inside the open door of the pilothouse, using the steel wall to conceal himself as he covered Alfonso and the crew working almost immediately below. The butt of a stainless steel Ruger Mini-14 semiautomatic carbine with a thirty-round magazine of .223 caliber hollow points and ten-power scope rested on his right hip, muzzle pointed skyward.

The crew tied up the two battered gray Pangas alongside the ship almost at her stern, where the deck dropped closest to the water. Alfonso had the shotgun and a flashlight trained on the boats, the barrel following the beam as it bounced from stem to stern and illuminated those aboard. He and one of the men in the first Panga exchanged greetings in Spanish.

Those boats are packed! Treto thought. *But why am I surprised?*

Alfonso turned, looked up to the pilothouse, and gave Treto a thumbs-up.

The only damn sure thing we've learned to expect is the unexpected.

One guy was all they said to pick up. And now there's got to be more than a dozen people in those boats. Must've paid off the TGF—or took 'em out.

What the hell. The more the merrier.

Singuense un caballo, Castros!

The long, narrow Pangas bobbed and rocked as the men and women aboard moved anxiously, making it difficult for them to transition to the twenty-foot-long ladder hanging over the side of the more stable ship.

But slowly, one by one, they managed.

At the gunwale, two crewmen stood on either side of the top of the ladder. They shone flashlights on the ladder rungs, helping the passengers aboard as they reached the top. Two other crewmen then led them to a bunkroom below deck.

Fifteen minutes later, Captain Treto heard the starter on the engine of the first Panga grinding, and after a moment the outboard finally fired up loudly. Two of the ship's crew then untied the Panga's fore and aft lines and tossed them over the side. They went to the lines of the second Panga and prepared to repeat the process as the first boat quickly pulled away and disappeared into the inky dark.

A moment later, its engine running and lines retrieved, the second Panga followed.

One pickup down, one to go, Treto thought, glancing at his wristwatch.

Should make it in under two hours.

He sighed audibly, then stepped back inside the pilothouse and stuck the carbine in its rack by the helm.

He put the *Nuevo Día*'s engines in gear, set a due north course, and gradually ramped up her speed to twenty knots.

At just shy of four A.M., right at the southern edge of the Gulf Stream, First Mate Raúl Alfonso oversaw the securing of a Bahamian-flagged forty-five-foot cabin cruiser alongside the cargo ship.

The cabin cruiser was far more stable than the Pangas had been, and almost as soon as the boarding ladder was put over the side, someone was quickly coming up it, followed by another and another.

Captain Miguel Treto lit a fat cigar as he again watched the boarding process from the pilothouse door.

The cigar barely had an ash ready to fall as he smiled appreciatively at the last of ten young women stepping aboard. Then two of his crew went quickly down the ladder and reappeared minutes later, each struggling under the weight of an enormous black duffel bag on his back.

Just as we were told to expect, he thought. *Will wonders ever cease?*

[THREE]
Off Islamorada, Florida
Sunday, November 16, 2 P.M.

It was a *Greetings From Paradise!* picture-postcard day in the Florida Keys. An occasional puffy white cloud floated in the deep blue sky. The wind and sea were calm, the temperature a comfortable 85 degrees.

Matt Payne stood at the flybridge helm of the sixty-one-foot-long yacht. The tropical sun warmed his face as the Viking Sport Fisherman cruised right at thirty knots, the gleaming white vessel smoothly slicing through the clear blue water.

The twenty-seven-year-old, who was six feet tall and a solidly muscled one hundred seventy-five pounds, had a chiseled face with dark, thoughtful eyes. He kept his thick dark hair clipped short. A homicide sergeant—Philadelphia Police Department Badge Number 471—he was now off duty and on holiday. Accordingly, he was barefoot, wearing only a pair of bright red surfboarding shorts, a Phillies ball cap, and Ray-Ban aviator sunglasses.

He tilted his head back to drain his beer—then casually crunched the can and tossed it into a plastic bucket by his feet. He belched loudly.

Ahhh! he thought, reaching down and setting the autopilot on a compass heading of 220 degrees. *I can't think of a more perfect and relaxing way to spend a day.*

He glanced down to where Amanda Law was reclined on deep cushions arranged in the middle of the yacht's long, sleek nose.

Especially being on the water with my angel goddess.

Sublime . . .

Amanda wore a black bikini and black flip-flops. A broad-brimmed straw hat, white with black piping, shielded her head. A thick, glossy copy of *Modern New Mom!* magazine was fanned open facedown on her lap.

She was gesturing in an animated manner with her left hand as she spoke on her cell phone, which she held in her right.

Matt smiled as her platinum gold engagement ring—encrusted with tiny diamonds that he'd told her reminded him irreverently of so many very shiny and very expensive barnacles—twinkled in the bright sunshine.

Dr. Amanda Law, the chief physician at Philadelphia's Temple

University Hospital Burn Center, had recently turned twenty-nine. She was extremely intelligent, with a bright face and eyes—and an air of complete confidence. She stood five-foot-five, weighed one-ten, and had the lean, toned body of an athlete. Her thick, luxurious blonde hair she'd woven into a pair of heavy braids, each now resting on a shoulder.

As Matt started to turn his attention back to the helm, he saw Amanda putting down her phone. She then reached over to the small control panel between the cushions and turned up the volume of the high-fidelity audio system.

Playing throughout the boat were tunes from Matt's portable digital music device. He had compiled more than five hours' worth of tropics-themed tracks in a file he had, with tongue firmly in cheek, labeled "Pirate Playlist."

The sound of Caribbean steel drums had just faded out on Jimmy Buffett's "Changes in Latitudes, Changes in Attitudes," and now began Michael McCloud singing "Just Came Down for the Weekend."

They could really be singing about me, Matt thought, grinning broadly. *A guy flees the frozen North for the warm tropics, embraces island time—and winds up staying a quarter-century.*

That'd be just fine with me.

We're a world away from Philly—and the damn insanity of me dealing with murders.

His grin faded.

Do we have to go back to that?

Matt saw the screen of his cell phone, which he had placed in a cup holder in front of the wheel, light up. A text message box appeared:

```
305-555-1254 2:05 PM


IT'S CHAD. WE STILL ON FOR TONIGHT?
```

Guess he got a new number down here.
Or had to borrow someone's phone.
Bet he dropped his in the drink again!
Matt picked up the phone and texted back:

```
TRIED TO TEACH ANOTHER PHONE TO SWIM, HUH?


YUP. WE'RE EN ROUTE TO LITTLE MUNSON NOW. ETA 2
HOURS.


SEE YOU AT 7. BRING $$. YOU ARE BUYING.
```

Growing up on the upper-crust Main Line, known for Philadelphia's old money, Chadwick Thomas Nesbitt IV and Matthew Mark Payne had been buddies since they wore diapers. The friendship of the Nesbitts and Paynes—Chad's father and Matt's stepfather were best friends—went further back than that.

Matt put his phone back in the cup holder and pulled a water bottle from the built-in cooler. He looked back over his right shoulder, then over his left, making his regular scan of the area for boat traffic and other possible obstacles. He thought he heard the music getting a little louder again and glanced back down in time to see Amanda pulling her hand and its twinkling diamonds away from the control panel.

Well, she clearly likes my music mix.

Maybe cranking up the songs is her way of hinting she could get used to this, too. . . .

Matt and Amanda had arrived in the Keys two days earlier, exactly a week after he mentioned over dinner in Philadelphia that he finally had found in Florida a year-old Porsche 911 he wanted to buy. It would replace his 911, which had been riddled by shotgun blasts as he'd chased a pair of robbers in a restaurant parking lot, one that happened to be a dozen blocks from the police department's headquarters.

"Now that I've finally finished up the last case's paperwork, I can take a little time off and go get it," Matt said, then took a swig of red wine.

Amanda knew he was referring to what the news media had been calling the "Halloween Homicides," a series of murders involving a vigilante shooter taking out convicted sex offenders and drug dealers who were fugitives.

In the end, Matt had become involved in a shoot-out and then a chaotic foot chase across the massive Interstate 676 suspension bridge—the Benjamin Franklin—that had been broadcast live. Images from that—all invariably showing Matt running and dodging cars with his Colt .45 semiautomatic drawn—soon appeared in every local media outlet from television to print to the Internet with headlines that, in one sensational phrasing or another, screamed: "Bullets Fly as the Wyatt Earp of the Main Line Solves Serial Murder Mystery." Various national media ran with the story, too.

"You're being disingenuous, sweetie," Amanda had replied, pointedly but with a smile. "What you mean to say is that your Uncle Denny ordered you to take the time off so you would be out of sight and mind of the media, not to mention the ACLU. Playing up the story of the wealthy hometown hero with a growing history of shootouts sells newspapers—and creates friction for City Hall."

Matt's "Uncle Denny" was First Deputy Commissioner Dennis V. Coughlin. The fifty-six-year-old wasn't a blood relative, and thus not actually Matt's uncle. But he was his godfather—having been best friends with Matt's biological father, who was killed in the line of duty while Matt was still in the womb—as well as second in command of the Philadelphia Police Department.

And it was the mayor himself who had ordered—through Coughlin—that Matt take another "cooling-off period." With all his shootings having been thoroughly investigated by Internal Affairs and judged to be righteous, the time off wasn't meant exactly for Matt's benefit. The periods were instead designed to give the media and the American Civil Liberties Union time to find something else on which to focus their seemingly boundless energy.

Careful, Matty, he thought. *Don't need to pick the scab off that conversation now.*

No question Amanda would like for this cooling-off period to become permanent—for me, as she says, "to quit playing cop and get a job where no one shoots at you."

Her being newly pregnant can't help but bring that up again.

"I stand corrected," Matt said, smiling and raising his wineglass. "Either way, I'm off-duty and going toy shopping."

"And I've been waiting to hear what you were going to do with your time off," Amanda had then enthusiastically announced. "Let's go together to get your toy!"

"Really?" he said, almost dropping his glass. "You can get away from the hospital?"

"Of course. You need a break from the city, and I personally need a saltwater fix. Diving is out of the question for me right now. But maybe we could get some fishing in. Certainly we can enjoy some nice long walks on the beach."

Matt's initial plan was for them to fly from Philadelphia to West Palm and check into the Breakers or the Four Seasons on the beach there. The sports car—which he had already had professionally inspected and the sale paperwork completed by overnight courier— would be waiting when they arrived at whichever hotel Amanda chose. They would watch the Atlantic Ocean's waves go up and down for a week or so, then drive the 911 back to Philadelphia.

But when Matt outlined that to his stepfather, Brewster Payne offered another idea.

"As I was having lunch at the Union League," he had said, "Steve Whittings stopped by my table to say he had news that might take the sting out of the storm having sunk the boat."

The Union League of Philadelphia, with the motto *Love of Country Leads*, was founded as a patriotic society during the Civil War. It enjoyed an exclusive membership—well heeled and well connected— including such luminaries as the founding partner of Mawson, Payne, Stockton, McAdoo & Lester, which was the city's most prestigious law firm, and the president of Franklin National Bank. The Union League's impressive brownstone covered an entire Center City block, a brief walk from City Hall and many other political and corporate power addresses.

"He always was partial to the Hatteras," Matt said, having a mental image of them fishing aboard the fifty-five-foot *Final Tort IV*.

"That's because he almost always caught the biggest fish on her."

Matt chuckled. "He certainly likes beating the Nesbitts. I'm beginning to think Chad gave up fishing and went to those high-performance offshore boats because of that."

"Would not surprise me. The Nesbitts have always been very competitive. Anyway, Steve told me that his bank was having trouble getting rid of a Viking they'd repossessed after its owner went to jail last summer. He said it really is a buyers' market, and that if I were interested, the bank was damn tired of having the boat on their books. He said he'd almost intentionally sink his own boat so he'd have an excuse to buy her."

"She must be nice. Are you interested?"

"Of course. We've never been without a boat. I just don't have time to go there and check her out. And now that you're planning on being in the area . . ."

Matt nodded thoughtfully. "A *Final Tort IV*. Why not?"

Two phone calls later—one from Brew Payne to Steve Whittings to explain the situation and get details on the boat, and another call from the banker to the yacht broker, whom Whittings instructed to give Matt a familiarization cruise, then hand over the keys for however long he wanted them, having made the point, "I've watched Matt run his father's boats since he could stand and hold the wheel, he won't so much as ding the boat"—it was a done deal.

"Matt," his stepfather reported back to him, "you can get your car in West Palm, then meet the broker in Islamorada. Captain Clyde has the boat next to his at Bud and Mary's Marina. Take Amanda down to Little Palm and put it on my account."

[FOUR]

Matt scanned ahead of the Viking with his binoculars as he—off-key but with gusto—sang along with Buffett about a modern-day pirate. After leaving Islamorada, the big boat had been running almost two hours on a southwesterly course, following along the chain of islands and the bridges of the Overseas Highway connecting them. Matt could easily make out Seven Mile Bridge, which ran south of Bahia Honda to Big Pine Key. He saw what was easily a score or more of other vessels, mostly powerboats but some under sail, crisscrossing the area. And, just out at the edge of the Gulf Stream, a cruise ship was headed east, passing a rusty cargo ship riding high with an empty deck and slowly making its way northward.

Matt heard Amanda playfully clear her throat behind him as she approached the helm. He felt her hand reach around him, finding the volume control.

"I hope you're not planning to use those singing skills to provide for your new family," she said as she turned it up.

He put the binoculars on the console and turned to her. She had pulled back the front brim of her floppy hat, revealing her face dominated by a pair of big round black sunglasses and an even bigger mischievous smile.

"Thanks a lot," he said, smiling back. "You know how that part of the vow goes, the 'for richer, for poorer' one . . . ?"

"I think not," she said, and kissed his neck. "You took advantage of me, and got me in the family way. You're obligated to make it right."

His hand slipped to her bikini bottom and gently squeezed her right cheek.

"With pleasure," he said, then added, "So you like my Pirate Playlist, I hear."

"Very much. I love all of this down here," she said, making a grand sweep of the horizon with her left hand. "And I adore what I read about Little Palm Island. How did you say you discovered it?"

"In Scouts. And we really did discover it."

"Boy Scouts?"

He nodded and pointed toward shore.

"Off Big Pine Key there are a couple of small outer islands once owned by the guy who made a fortune selling wood-refinishing products. The undeveloped one is called Big Munson, which he donated to the Scouts after some government agency wouldn't let him build on it. Thirteen or fourteen years ago, Chad and I camped out on it for a week with a bunch of guys from our troop. We played castaways, like Robinson Crusoe, diving the reef, cooking fish on driftwood fires, that kind of thing. Our second day, we were paddling sea kayaks around a tidal flat of mangrove trees when we came out the other side of the island—and almost ran into an enormous yacht. It was moored at a lush little island that was ringed with an immaculately groomed sandy beach. The irony wasn't lost on us. There we were, a bunch of nasty-smelling sunburned city boys living in mosquito-infested tents next door to a really swank resort accessible only by boat. We didn't think our kayaks counted."

She laughed. "Little Palm?"

He nodded. "I like to call it by its old name, Little Munson, just to remind the staff I lived next door before I even knew the place existed. You know, back in the day, Harry Truman and John Foster Dulles stayed there."

"How nice. And now the soon-to-be Mr. and Mrs. Payne."

"Huh," Matt grunted. "I don't know, baby. I was thinking we'd go native. When was the last time you were in a tent?"

"Enjoy yourself. I'll be getting room service and a massage in one of those thatched-roof cabanas oceanside that I saw in the photographs."

He chuckled. "Fine. Be high maintenance. Dinner with Chad is at seven. He texted earlier to confirm."

He then pointed to a pack of maybe ten high-performance boats that had appeared to the south of them. The boats, moving fast, were kicking up tails of white spray. A helicopter kept pace with the pack, then picked up speed and moved up the coast.

"That's probably him playing with his buddies in their go-fasts," he said. "He's running the company's new boat."

Chad Nesbitt was being groomed to one day take over Nesfoods International, just as his grandfather had groomed Chad's father. Chad recently had been promoted to vice president and put in charge of developing new brands at the Philadelphia headquarters.

"Oh, yeah," Amanda said. "The boat you said that's promoting their NRG! drinks."

Matt nodded. "That caffeine-packed sugar water is making a helluva lot of money. He told me his new NRG! boat cost a cool million—and that's for a forty-two-footer that only seats maybe eight. Its twin Mercury Racing engines pump out more than two thousand horsepower. Top speed is around one-thirty."

"A hundred and thirty miles an hour? That's insane. Why?"

"'Healthier—*Faster!*' That's the marketing slogan. The boat's been wrapped in custom vinyl to make it look like a giant can of the stuff. But simple answer? Chad's come to love go-fasts after hanging out with Antonov. And because he's got a big hand in the promotion, he gets to pick where they throw money. He said there will be race car promos, too. Guess I'll have to change his name from the Soup King to Speed King."

"Antonov? The casino guy?"

Nikoli Antonov was general manager of Philly's year-old Lucky Stars Casino & Entertainment, an enormous five-story complex that offered cavernous areas for gambling—2,500 slot machines, 100 gaming tables—fine dining, and performances by top music artists. Despite the competing casino that was nearly next door, Lucky Stars was said to sell the highest volume of alcohol in all the Commonwealth of Pennsylvania. Both casinos were just off the I-95 Delaware Expressway and overlooked the Delaware River, not far from Amanda Law's luxury high-rise condominium building in Northern Liberties.

Matt nodded. "Nick Antonov has a couple of boats promoting the casino. One is supposed to be out there with Chad and the others. But I think Chad said someone other than Nick is running it."

"And they're doing this why?"

"Some children's charity. I forget which one. Entry fee is maybe fifty grand, a drop in the bucket considering the cost of feeding a go-fast. But the quiet big money, just like with college and pro ball, is bet in Vegas and on the side. There are guys at Lucky Stars right now watching these boats on the betting TVs in between pulls on the slots. Not to mention the mob bookies in South Philly are running the odds. Which reminds me: the guy who was head of the Philly mob and just got out of the slam after ten years, Tony the Fixer?"

"What about him?"

"He now lives in Palm Beach. Says he's just working on his tan."

"I take it you don't think so?"

Matt shook his head. "A condition of his release is that he can't associate with any wiseguys—which is all he knows in Philly. Otherwise he's back to jail. But it's all BS. Fact is he can run the mob from down here, from anywhere, just as he ran it from the slam. And there were plenty of mob hits while he was in there."

"Do you think he's involved with this race?"

Matt shook his head again. "Not directly. Only with those South Philly bookies taking bets. There's no racing involved here. It's a Poker Run. Basically, the boats make five stops, drawing new cards at each one. They started this morning from a marina in the Conch Republic—"

"Key West?"

He nodded. "The whole thing is filmed—that was what that helicopter was doing. At each stop, other cameras show the hands as they get played. Then the boat with the best hand wins something like a new Mustang that's donated by the local Ford dealer. Meantime, the charity gets a fat check."

Amanda considered that for a moment, then said, "I think I'll settle for just writing a check directly to the Shriners while sitting on this nice boat and watching the scenery drift by."

In Philadelphia, Amanda could see the Shriners children's hospital across the street from her office at Temple University Hospital.

Matt smiled.

"That's the woman I love," he said, as his cell phone began ringing.

Amanda saw that the caller ID read THE BLACK BUDDHA.

"What do you think Jason wants?" she said, looking at Matt. "I thought you were off-duty."

Lieutenant Jason Washington was Matt's immediate boss in the Homicide Unit. He was enormous—six-three, two-twenty-five— articulate, impeccably tailored, and had very dark skin. He also was one of the best homicide detectives on the East Coast, from Maine to Miami, and did not take any offense at all to being referred to as the Black Buddha.

"No disputing the fact that I'm black," he said, "and a Buddha by definition is a venerated and enlightened individual."

Amanda grabbed the phone, smiling at Matt as she put it to her ear.

Matt shook his head, but he was grinning.

"Well, hello, Jason!" she said. "I do hope this is a social call. How is Martha?"

Amanda's father, before being offered retirement while recovering from a bullet to the hip from the robber he'd ultimately shot dead, had worked with Washington in Northeast Detectives a decade earlier. Charley Law and Jason Washington had become close, and Martha Washington long had served as a sort of protective aunt toward Amanda.

It was no secret to any of them that Amanda—who said she'd grown up worrying that every day she saw her father leave for work would be the last she'd see him alive, and then he did get shot—would be the polar opposite of upset if Matt were suddenly to find an occupation that did not involve hazardous duty.

After a pause, Matt heard Washington's sonorous voice. Then he saw Amanda's eyebrows go up behind her big round dark sunglasses.

"Thank you. Of course. Here he is," she said, and handed the phone to Matt.

"Hey, Jason," he said, watching Amanda watch him. He smiled. "Is the department falling apart without me?"

"Matthew, my apology for interrupting your romantic getaway," Jason said, his deep tone sincere.

"Always happy to hear from you. You know that. What's up?"

"This is delicate, but I need you to do something for me. Discretion is paramount."

"Anything."

"I'm going to mention a name, and I do not want you repeating it during our discussion right now."

"Okay . . ." Matt said, reaching down to adjust the autopilot as an excuse to turn his face away from Amanda.

"As soon as absolutely possible—and without it triggering further questions—I need you to figure out a way to work Margaret McCain into a conversation with Amanda, asking if she has heard from her lately. And, if you can manage it without her becoming suspicious, also ask if any of her other friends or associates have."

Maggie McCain? Matt thought, fighting the automatic urge to glance at Amanda.

What the hell is that about?

"You got it, Jason. Can I ask why?"

"No, you cannot. I'm sorry. Call me when you have an answer, Matthew."

[FIVE]

Latitude 25 Degrees 44 Minutes 71 Seconds North
Longitude 81 Degrees 58 Minutes 58 Seconds West
The Straits of Florida, Southeast of Key West
Sunday, November 16, 4:15 P.M.

"Lucky One, Lucky One. Tin Can, over," Jorge Perez's handheld Motorola radio crackled with the voice of Miguel Treto as he maneuvered the sleek fifty-foot Cigarette Marauder at the back of a pack of ten other high-performance boats.

A wiry, tall thirty-four-year-old, Perez had been born in Miami of Cuban parents six months after they fled the Communist island-nation. He was deeply tanned and had short black hair and a goatee.

His intense brown eyes were shielded by dark polarized sunglasses. He wore khaki shorts, a dark blue linen shirt with a white tropical flower motif, and tan leather deck shoes.

The open cockpit had seven high-back deeply padded leather seats. Perez was at the helm. The other six seats were filled with stunning blondes and brunettes with bronze tans, the girls all in their twenties, all more or less clad in the tiniest of bikinis. Two were sunning themselves topless.

On both sides of the white Marauder's long hull and on its foredeck were images of a giant pair of rolling red dice and the wording:

```
             MORE WINNERS, MORE MONEY!

        LUCKY STARS CASINO & ENTERTAINMENT

   PHILADELPHIA, ATLANTIC CITY, NEW ORLEANS, BILOXI
```

The boats in the pack were of a variety of sizes and styles—but all designed for speed. A few had simple solid-color hulls. Most, though, like the Marauder, featured wild graphics covering their enormous decks and hulls—everything from stylized U.S. flags to skull-and-crossbones to racing motifs with black-and-white checkered flags and circled numbers. The boat running directly ahead of Perez's resembled a giant can of the energy beverage NRG!

As the pack of go-fasts—most of which also had attractive young women aboard—followed the island chain northward, Perez had the Marauder running not even at half throttle. The speed readout in the corner of the Global Positioning Satellite screen indicated forty-six miles an hour.

With three 1,075-horsepower Mercury Racing engines, the

Marauder could hit a cruise speed of seventy-five miles an hour and a top speed of 124. In addition to the cockpit seats, the area below deck had room for another eight passengers. The nicely furnished cabin, heavily insulated and air-conditioned, resembled what one would expect to find aboard a private jet aircraft, complete with plush leather couches, a high-end entertainment system, and a flat-screen television.

In the cabin were two sunburned, balding, olive-skinned, middle-aged men, both wearing khaki shorts and baggy Cuban guayabera shirts that didn't conceal their paunches. Each sat with an attractive twenty-something bikinied blonde in his lap. They all were watching the Poker Run on the TV as a bikinied redhead poured them more frozen piña coladas from a blender.

Perez grabbed the handheld and keyed the mic.

"Go, Tin Can."

"Just saw your first wave of boats pass. Over."

"Roger that. I'm running near the middle of it. And L-Five is about ten minutes back in the second wave. Over."

"Got it. I'm tracking your positions on GPS. We just started the first off-loading. Should be complete in twenty. What about the Red Stripe? Over."

Perez sighed, then keyed the mic again.

' "Stand by, Tin Can."

Jorge Perez then said impatiently into his Motorola radio: "Lucky Five, Lucky Five. Lucky One. Did you copy Tin Can? Over."

Lucky Five was Perez's cousin Carlos, a diminutive thirty-year-old who Perez occasionally taunted by accusing him of having a Napoleon complex. He was at the helm of a forty-eight-foot Fountain Express Cruiser, one of the Poker Run boats without any graphic design. Its low-profile deep blue hull practically blended in with the sea.

Riding with Carlos was just one twenty-something, an amazingly attractive brunette whom Perez said he was sending along "so you won't look like a fucking *maricón*—despite your *pingita*."

Carlos had wondered if the girl spoke, or at least somehow understood, Cuban—she had smirked at Perez's accusation that he might resemble a homosexual with a tiny prick—and that was only compounded as she wordlessly spent the day sunning and sipping the French champagne she found in the galley of the luxurious cabin.

Being ignored really pissed him off.

"L-One, L-Five," Carlos replied, sounding annoyed. "I heard it. No problem hooking up with Tin Can in twenty."

"But will you be alone?" Perez said pointedly, letting his Latin temper slip. "What the hell is up with Red Stripe? *Over . . .*"

Red Stripe, the beer brewed on the Caribbean island of Jamaica, was one of Perez's favorites. He had a case of it iced down, along with a variety of other imported *cervezas*, in the aft cooler. But "Red Stripe" also was the code name that Perez had picked to mean any United States law enforcement asset, in this case particularly that of the U.S. Coast Guard, which emblazoned its boats, helicopters, and airplanes with its crossed-anchor logo within a crimson-colored forward-slanting stripe.

Fifteen minutes earlier, Lucky Five had radioed—somewhat hysterically—that just as his pack of ten go-fasts droned past an idling Coast Guard SPC-LE—a thirty-three-foot-long aluminum-hulled "Special Purpose Craft—Law Enforcement"—the boat had immediately throttled up and begun chasing the pack.

And chasing him. Or so Carlos had feared.

Lucky Five was running at the back of the pack, which was some fifteen minutes ahead of the third group of ten that brought up the rear of the entire line of thirty-one Poker Run boats.

Perez really had had no choice but to order that Carlos keep the Fountain at the back, because there it would attract the least attention. But it also made Lucky Five the easiest to cull from the herd if, for example, the Coast Guard wanted to perform what Perez derided as a "courtesy inspection."

Enforcing maritime law on the high seas—from looking for drug smugglers to counting life jackets—was a mission of the Coast Guard. Captains whose vessels were stopped and found to be in compliance would suffer only a short delay, generally from a courteous but professional boarding crew.

Perez more or less sneered at the thought of the Coast Guard SPC giving chase. Powered by three 300-horsepower outboards, the lightweight SPC would have to run hard to catch the fast Fountain. And the Marauder, with triple 1,075-horsepower engines, would easily leave the SPC in its wake.

But not for long.

Perez was acutely aware that all that the Coast Guard had to do was call in for support—including scrambling aircraft, if necessary—and there would be nowhere for anyone to run.

Perez had made sure that, like his Marauder, Carlos's Fountain was completely in compliance with all laws.

If only for the moment, he thought.

It was common knowledge that if the cops really wanted to stop him—or, for that matter, any vessel operating in U.S. waters—they only had to declare that the vessel was operating in an unsafe manner.

The Coasties could easily board his boat with any excuse. They could say they saw the shitter discharging overboard, then tell him, "Guess it's okay after all. Better safe than sorry. Have a nice day."

But if they pick up on his nervousness, and keep an eye on him, we're totally screwed.

"L-One, L-Five," came Carlos's reply after a moment, his tone sounding relieved. "All clear. Red Stripe turned toward shore. Looks like he's headed for Looe Key." He added, "Maybe some tourist got a snorkel full of water on the reef. Over."

Perez grunted. He shook his head as his eyes scanned the speedboats in his pack, then the waters beyond the pack where the coral reef was. He did not see the Red Stripe.

Looe Key? You better hope not.

That's close to where we're headed, you fucking idiot!

"Stay focused!" Perez snapped. "L-One standing by."

Perez dropped the handheld into its holder beside where the in-dash VHF radio was mounted. Wedged in the lip of the VHF faceplate were four playing cards, a pair of diamonds and a pair of kings. The readout screen on the faceplate cycled, showing the radio was monitoring channel 16—the international frequency for distress and general calls—and channel 79.

The display then locked on 79, and the loudspeaker came to life with an excited young female voice.

"Attention all Poker Run captains," she announced, her tone over-the-top chipper. "Headquarters station calling. Wave one is about to arrive at our fifth stop, Lost Key Resort, where boats get their last playing cards. Wave two is approximately ten minutes behind, and wave three, the last wave, left Key West fifteen minutes ago. So far only one boat's dropped out, due to a mechanical problem. Keep safe out there! HQ headed for Lost Key and we're standing by on channel 79. . . ."

Perez sighed, then reached to the helm and turned down the volume on the VHF. He looked back and watched the lumbering cargo ship fading into the distance.

———

Ten minutes later, Carlos picked up the handheld radio and said: "Visual made. Coming up on my two o'clock. Should overtake in five—repeat five—minutes. Over."

"L-Five, Tin Can. I see you on-screen. Understand five minutes."

Carlos glanced at the gorgeous brunette as he reached for the Fountain's throttles. She was napping, her empty champagne cup tipped over in her lap.

He retarded the three big diesels slightly. The speed indicator on the dash and on the readout on the screen of the Global Positioning Satellite receiver both dropped from fifty to thirty-five mph.

The pack quickly pulled away from the Fountain. When he was about a hundred yards back, Carlos looked over his right shoulder, saw no other boats, and turned the wheel to the right. Then, lining up the cargo ship with the tip of his bow, he bumped the throttles up until the speed indicators read sixty-five.

He glanced back to his left. The high-performance boats cut across the water, their frothy white V-shaped wakes scoring the deep blue surface.

No one seemed to notice that their pack now numbered nine.

Six minutes later, Miguel Treto's voice crackled over the radio: "L-Five, Tin Can. Approach at the stern, starboard side. No lines. My crew will hold you alongside."

"Got it."

Carlos saw a white thirty-foot-long center console fishing boat come out from the far side of the *Nuevo Día*, crossing in front of her bow. There looked to be maybe ten aboard—young men and women—plus a burly, shirtless captain with dreadlocks.

The passengers were quickly moving under a cover at the front of the boat as it picked up speed and headed toward land.

Carlos deftly maneuvered the Fountain into the shadow of the *Nuevo Día*, nudging up against four rubber bumpers hanging on either side of the boarding ladder. A pair of long aluminum poles with hooks reached down and held the boat secure against the bumpers.

Carlos glanced at the brunette, who now craned her neck looking up to the top of the ladder. He did, too, and saw that an attractive young blonde in a sundress had already started down the rungs.

He crossed the cockpit, preparing to help her step from the ladder onto the Fountain. He looked up again and grinned. He had a perfect angle right up her dress—and saw she wore no panties.

The brunette led the last of the girls into the cabin as the long aluminum pole next to Carlos started being pulled upward. About a minute later, it reappeared with the handles of an enormous black duffel bag looped around its hook. The pole lowered the stuffed duffel to the deck of the Fountain, then pulled back up and lowered a second one.

Carlos dragged them to the transom, opened a hatch there in the deck, and dropped the bags into the dry-storage hold below.

As the Fountain began drifting away from the cargo ship, Carlos spun the wheel and gave the port engine about twice the throttle of the others, causing the Fountain to turn clockwise almost in its own length. He then started to straighten up the wheel as he added more throttle to the other two engines, balancing out the rpm's. Then he pushed all three throttles at once. The Fountain practically leapt forward, and in almost no time was hitting sixty-five mph.

Five minutes later, as a few of the girls were coming out of the cabin and sipping champagne from clear plastic cups, he spotted the last pack of boats in the Poker Run. He made turns to put his bow a little ahead of the pack, then bumped up the throttles to wide open.

Carlos pretended not to notice that the wind with the higher speeds was causing the brunette's champagne to slosh all over her.

[ONE]
Office of the First Deputy Commissioner
Philadelphia Police Headquarters
Eighth and Race Streets
Sunday, November 16, 3:05 P.M.

"Yes—to answer the question that I'm sure has been on everyone's mind—I'm damn well aware that this is a highly volatile situation," the Honorable Jerome H. "Jerry" Carlucci, mayor of Philadelphia, all but growled. "To a large degree, the department has been lucky to keep quiet and compartmentalized the disappearance of the first two caseworkers. But with the McCain girl now gone missing, it would

appear that that luck just ran the hell out." He waved his right hand
in the direction of the muted flat-screen television that was tuned to
a local newscast. "Especially when the goddamn media gets wind
of it."

Five men, all standing, watched Carlucci pacing along the curved
wall of bookshelves in the large third-floor office. Built in a circle
design, the decades-old four-story "Roundhouse" was said not to
have a straight wall anywhere, including in its elevators.

The men were First Deputy Commissioner Dennis V. Coughlin,
whose office it was; Captain Francis Xavier Hollaran, Coughlin's assistant; Chief Inspector Matthew Lowenstein; Captain Henry
Quaire, the head of the Homicide Unit and who reported to Lowenstein; and Quaire's number two, Lieutenant Jason Washington. All
were in plainclothes.

Carlucci was a massive—large-boned and heavyset—sixty-two-
year-old with intense brown eyes and dark brown hair graying at the
temples. He wore the suit he had put on for church that morning, a
pin-striped gray woolen two-piece with a light blue dress shirt with
white French cuffs and collar, and a red silk necktie with a matching
silk pocket square.

Before becoming mayor, Carlucci had spent twenty-six years in
the Philadelphia Police Department, holding, he was quick to an-
nounce, every rank but that of policewoman. He spoke bluntly and
did not suffer fools—period. When he reached across the proverbial
political aisle, it usually was with an iron fist. That certainly had
made him more than a few enemies, but he didn't give a damn. He
enjoyed the respect of far many others—ones who appreciated his
ability to not only confront seemingly impossible problems but, more
times than not, to effectively fix them.

Carlucci stopped at the window near the big wooden desk. He

turned to Coughlin, who stood behind the desk, next to the high-back black leather chair that showed years of use. Coughlin, tall and heavyset, with a full head of curly silver hair and eyes that missed nothing, projected a formidable presence.

"Denny, where the hell did you say Ralph was?"

"He's the keynote speaker at the National Chiefs of Police convention."

"Which is where?"

"Vegas."

Carlucci's eyebrows went up. "Of course he gets to go to tony Las Vegas. I think the nicest place—and I use that loosely—that I went as commissioner was Newark."

There were a few chuckles.

Police Commissioner Ralph J. Mariana was the department's top cop—the last position Carlucci had held before his retirement and being elected mayor. Both the commissioner and the first deputy commissioner served at the mayor's pleasure, although they were appointed to their jobs by the city's managing director. The seven thousand policemen they commanded—the country's fourth-largest force—were all civil servants.

Carlucci was neither surprised at Mariana's absence nor was he angry. It was no secret that Mariana—a natty, stocky, balding Italian with four stars on his white uniform shirt—served as the face of the police department, while it was his three-star, Denny Coughlin, who effectively saw to the day-to-day running of the department.

And it was His Honor the mayor who ultimately called the shots.

The brass in the room had a long history—certainly professional but also to varying degrees personal—with one another. When young Philadelphia police officers showed promise, a "rabbi" quietly mentored them as they rose in the ranks, preparing them to take on greater responsibilities. Jerry Carlucci, for one example, then a captain and head of the Homicide Unit, had been Denny Coughlin's rabbi.

Carlucci looked from Coughlin to the others.

"The department has run out of luck because Margaret McCain's father . . . you are aware of who the McCains are?" he said rhetorically, continuing before anyone could answer: "For everyone's edification, allow me to share. They're among the Proper Philadelphians—the founders—right up there with the Whartons and the Pennypackers and the Rittenhouses. There's the story that Michael McCain, one helluva clever lawyer who later became governor, banged heads with Ben Franklin over the way various parts of the Declaration of Independence were worded. And Will McCain, Margaret's father, is a chip off that old block—the old man also was six-foot-something and had a hot Scottish temper. Would not surprise me if, like the old man, Will carries a gun everywhere. Hell, the McCains once owned the land that's now the Radnor Hunt Club. So, understanding that background explains why Will does not take no for an answer. He's like General George Patton—also a Scot—in that he gets what he wants. And what he wants right now are answers about his daughter."

"I sympathize with her father and his frustration," Chief Inspector Lowenstein offered. "The McCain girl has gone to great lengths trying to become untraceable—and done so remarkably quickly. His fear is grounded, and that is without the benefit of knowing anything about the other missing caseworkers."

The ruddy-faced Lowenstein, who was Jewish, had a full head of curly silver hair. He was barrel-chested, large, and stocky.

"The damn fact of the matter," Carlucci said pointedly, "is that *we* essentially don't know a thing about what happened to those two women."

The room was silent for a long moment. Then Coughlin came to Lowenstein's defense.

"It's certainly not for lack of effort," Coughlin said evenly, the frustration in his tone evident. "Since those first two went missing last week, Matt has had an entire unit in Special Operations quietly running down every lead."

Carlucci nodded.

"I of course understand that, Denny. As well as the frustration. Yet now we're looking for three." He turned to Lowenstein. "It sounds as if you've decided that Margaret McCain is a willing participant in her disappearance."

"I don't know if the word 'willing' is entirely accurate," Lowenstein said, waving a sheaf of papers. "But it is looking like she could be the one making the decisions. What she's doing seems almost planned."

"What're those papers?" Carlucci said.

"The initial responses to our electronic queries. I'm thinking that because of her job keeping track of the kids at Mary's House, she became quite knowledgeable about electronic tethers—credit and debit cards, cell phones, E-ZPass, et cetera. She's being careful. There's been no signal from her personal cell phone, which could mean she has intentionally turned it off or that it has a dead battery. Her Land Cruiser's GPS unit either is not working or has been disabled. When we queried the Pennsylvania Turnpike Commission, her E-ZPass account came up with no active travel through any toll-booth in the last forty-eight hours." He paused, then went on: "And there were only two charges on any of her half dozen credit cards. Both to the same PNC MasterCard. One was for forty bucks and change at a Gas & Go near the airport. The other was made a half hour later, at two o'clock this morning, at a Center City pharmacy for more than three hundred dollars."

"Anything on their surveillance cameras?"

"We got a look at images at the Gas & Go, but they were too dark and grainy to tell if she was alone or not when she pumped gas. The pharmacy's system was inoperable."

"Okay, so it sounds like she topped off her gas tank, suggesting she's hit the road—and is avoiding tolled ones. And the other's probably for prescriptions? They aren't cheap."

Lowenstein shrugged. "Could be. If I were leaving town for a while, I'd want my meds. We should know shortly—we are waiting for a response from the store as to what its computer system says the itemized receipt shows she bought. But that's the end of the trail. After that, there is nothing. It's like she pulled the plug on everything."

"What about that stuff they're all doing on the Internet?" Carlucci said.

"Social media activity?"

"Yeah. That produced a number of leads with the other two caseworkers. Is she in touch with anyone through that?"

"It produced leads," Coughlin put in, "but none went anywhere. The caseworkers themselves never posted anything on the Internet after they went missing."

"And it's worse with the McCain girl," Lowenstein added. "We asked everyone—friends, family, neighbors, coworkers—and every single person said Margaret never really embraced social media. She tried one or two, then gave up on them. Her mother said she didn't think that they were worth the time, that they took away from her privacy."

Carlucci looked deep in thought.

"Okay. Back up," he then said. "When was the last time she was seen?"

"As far as we know at this point," Jason Washington picked up, as he pulled a notepad from his jacket, "the absolute last contact that any family or friends had with her was last night when she left dinner." He paused and looked at his notes. "That was at Zama Sushi near Rittenhouse Square about ten-fifteen. She was with her cousin, twenty-year-old Emma Scholefield, who is a junior studying dance at University of the Arts."

"And did this cousin have anything to offer?" Carlucci said.

Washington shook his head. "Not much more than Mrs. McCain had already told us she'd told her. The cousin stated that Margaret appeared absolutely normal, upbeat, her usual self. They talked mostly about her sailing trip in the British Virgin Islands and their plans for the upcoming Thanksgiving and Christmas holidays. When they left the restaurant, the cousin said that, as she started walking up the block toward her apartment, she saw Margaret get in her Toyota SUV and drive off toward Walnut Street. Margaret had told her she was looking forward to a good night's sleep so she could hit the gym first thing in the morning."

"Which never happened."

"Right. Gym records show she hasn't been there in three days."

"Okay. Then what?"

"Mrs. McCain said that, at exactly ten thirty-one, she called Margaret's personal cell phone, got no answer, and left her daughter a voice-mail message. At that time, according to telephone records, Margaret's work cell phone had been connected for four minutes to the cell phone number that we believe to be the Gonzalez girl's. It is a pay-as-you-go phone, and we do not know who purchased it."

"Gonzalez is the dead girl?"

"Yes, sir."

Carlucci considered all that, then said, "And the McCain woman's fire alarm automatically called in at what time?"

"Precisely at ten forty-two. That was eight minutes after the call between the work cell phone and the go-phone ended. At ten fifty-one, nine minutes after the firehouse got the call, there was one last call from what we believe was the Gonzalez go-phone to Margaret's work cell. There have been no other calls on Margaret's personal cell phone—as noted, it's off for whatever reason—and none dialed on the work cell phone. The Crime Scene Unit guys found the latter, broken, in a puddle in the alley. It looked as if it had been hit hard, maybe dropped."

"And that go-phone?"

"Phone company records list at least two dozen different numbers the Gonzalez go-phone dialed or texted since last night, including Margaret's work cell phone three times in a row today just after twelve noon. We traced its signal to West Philly, to the Westpark high-rise at Forty-fifth and Market. That's of course a Housing Authority property, one in fair shape and full. So, no way for us to pinpoint in which apartment the phone could be. Then Anthony Harris had a great idea. He drove over there and began calling the phone over and over. Some miscreant with attitude finally answered, and when Harris told said miscreant that he had the money he owed him and was waiting with it outside the gate, the miscreant hung up. Then the phone went dead, the signal turned off."

Carlucci grunted. "Damn. But that was worth the attempt. Has to be pretty good odds that someone owes that punk money. And, even if not, he would have taken the cash off Harris's hands—even sending some surrogate to get it, in case he smelled it was a setup.

Not grabbing the easy money must mean he's really running scared, and that doesn't suggest anything good."

"We've got an unmarked sitting on the Westpark high-rise, in case the phone goes live again and he hits the street," Lowenstein said. "We also have one keeping an eye on her business, Mary's House, and one at the residence."

"On the chance that the doer will return to the scene?" Carlucci asked, but it was more of a statement.

"It's a long shot but we've all seen it happen before."

Mayor Carlucci looked at Jason Washington.

"What else did they find at the scene?" Carlucci said.

"To begin with, the front door was wide open when the firefighters arrived," Washington said. "The door showed evidence of forced entry—it'd been kicked in. But whoever did it, if they left any other fingerprints, footprints, whatever, we'll never know. The fire department did their job quite thoroughly—drowning the blaze *and* trampling the crime scene. They got the fire out, and who the hell knows how much evidence. Neighbors we questioned immediately began calling it a home invasion, and repeating that to the media. We did not go out of our way to disabuse anyone of that."

"But?" Carlucci interrupted.

"But here's the problem: Who tries to cover a home invasion with Molotov cocktails? There was one broken on the kitchen's marble counter, the other intact in the middle of the floor. Most robberies are in-and-out jobs. They don't bother destroying the scene." Washington pulled a folded sheet of paper from his coat and went on: "The medical examiner wrote that the Gonzalez girl did not die in the fire. The autopsy this morning found that her lungs had no fire smoke damage—and that there were two mushroomed .22s inside her cranium." He mimed a pistol with his thumb and index finger and pointed behind his right earlobe. "Entrance wounds here. Putting a .22 behind the ear is not exactly the hallmark of a home invasion, either."

Glances were exchanged as they nodded agreement. They knew that a .22 caliber round, due to its low mass and velocity, was not powerful enough to penetrate the bone of a skull. But it could enter through soft tissue at the ear—then bounce around, effectively scrambling the brain and causing death more or less instantly.

"It's more the mark of a professional hit," Denny Coughlin said.

Carlucci grunted and nodded.

"Questions then become," Washington went on, "Why the girl? Or were they targeting Margaret and the girl got in the way? And of course if they were targeting Margaret, why did she just disappear?"

"Who is this girl?" Carlucci said. "Gonzalez, did you say?"

"That's right," Washington said. "Krystal Angel Gonzalez, age nineteen. She had an EBT card in the pocket of her blue jeans."

He paused, and Carlucci then nodded, affirming that he knew it was an Electronic Benefits Transfer card, which looked and worked like a plastic debit card.

"Food stamps," Carlucci said.

"Now called SNAP," Washington went on, "for Supplemental Nutrition Assistance Program. We ran the card, got off it her name and Social Security number, and that pulled up a hit with CPS. She'd been in and out of foster homes since age six. Before turning eighteen, her Last Known Address was in South Philly, at Mary's House. She also had twenty-two bucks cash in her jeans—all singles, one rolled up and containing cocaine residue—and two orange fifty-dollar poker chips from Lucky Stars."

Washington motioned with the sheet from the medical examiner.

"The autopsy also found evidence that she was healing from

rough sexual activity," he said. "Most likely that she'd been sexually assaulted, especially considering the welts on the back of her legs that the medical examiner believes were from a wire coat hanger."

Carlucci made a sour face as he shook his head.

"Such a damn shame," he said. "But the sad fact is that if I had a dime for every time some trick in Philly got whipped with a pimp stick, I could be living the high life like our boy Matty." He paused. "Which reminds me, Denny, where the hell is he?"

"To use your phrase," Coughlin said, "he's living the high life. They're in the Florida Keys. Jason was just in touch with him."

"They?"

Washington nodded, and explained, "Mrs. McCain gave us a list of Margaret's friends. Amanda Law was on it. She said Amanda and Margaret had spoken since she returned from her vacation. Amanda is with Matthew, so I called him and requested that he discreetly inquire if Amanda had heard from her."

"Charley's daughter, the doctor? Any truth to the rumor I heard that they're getting married?"

Washington nodded. "Indeed there is. They are."

For the first time, Carlucci's face brightened. "Good. Her old man, like Matty's, was as solid a cop as they come. Maybe since she understands cops she can keep ole Wyatt Earp out of the headlines."

"Jerry," Coughlin put in, "I wouldn't mind having him on the case. He runs easily in those social circles—"

"No," Carlucci snapped, making eye contact. Then he sighed. "No, Denny, not right now. Maybe later—"

His cell phone began ringing. He made a look of annoyance, then glanced at its screen, muttered, "Damn, McCain," then put the phone to his head and answered in an authoritative, even tone, "Carlucci."

All eyes were on him as he said: "*Who* just heard from Maggie?"

[TWO]
Off Big Pine Key, Florida
Sunday, November 16, 4:02 P.M.

Matt Payne double-checked the lightly laminated NOAA navigation chart, then picked up the binoculars, scanned ahead of the Viking, and after a moment located what he was looking for—the outer markers of the channel that led to Big Pine Key, Little Torch Key, and Little Palm Island.

If he had wanted, he could just as easily have looked at the screen of the GPS unit, which would have pinpointed the exact location of the markers and the entire channel, and the boat's exact position relative to them, then dialed in the autopilot. But Matt, as much as he appreciated technology, liked to practice his map and compass, dead reckoning, and other navigation skills—believing that it wasn't a case of *if* technology was going to fail but *when* it would crap out on him.

As wise ol' Murphy made law, "If anything can go wrong, it will— and at the worst possible damn time."

Only a fool tempts fate at sea. . . .

The dark blue of the deeper water now gave way to a glistening aqua green. The depth sounder, confirming what he read on the chart, showed they were running in sixty feet of water. Closer to shore, and the clear, shallower water there, the white of the bottom could easily be seen.

When he put the optics on the console, he saw his cell phone screen light up and a text message box appear:

MICKEY O'HARA 4:03 PM

CALL ME ASAP. I'M CHASING DEADLINE AND NEED INFO.

Michael J. O'Hara, a Pulitzer Prize–winning reporter, and Matt had developed an interesting—if unusual—close friendship over the years. The wiry thirty-seven-year-old, of Irish descent and with a head of unruly red hair, was unorthodox but uncompromisingly fair—and thus had earned the respect of the cops who walked the beat on up to the commissioner himself.

It was O'Hara who, when Payne had been grazed in the forehead by a ricochet bullet in his first shoot-out, photographed the bloodied rookie cop standing with his .45 over the dead shooter, and later wrote the headline: "Officer M. M. Payne, 23, The Wyatt Earp of the Main Line."

I'm not working any cases, Matt thought as he texted back: "OK. ASAP."

What could I know that he wants for a story?

Matt turned to Amanda, who was reclined on a long cushion beside him, reading a book titled *Cruising Guide to the Bahamas.*

"Almost there," he said.

"Great!"

She put down the book and went to stand beside him.

He pointed to a long narrow outer island.

"That's Big Munson. It's about a hundred acres of little more than mangroves and mosquitoes."

"The one where you and Chad reenacted *Lord of the Flies*?"

He looked at her. She was grinning mischievously.

"Maybe Chad. He's never shied away from power grabs. For me it was more like *Treasure Island* mixed with Crusoe, thank you very much. Anyway, Little Munson, which is all beach and palm trees and dripping with creature comforts, is next to it."

As he made a slight course correction to the north, putting the Viking on a compass heading of 310 degrees, another pack of the go-fasts appeared ahead. It was headed for the same channel, and after the first boat began slowing to idle speed for the approach, the others a moment later dropped their speed almost at the same time. Matt counted nine boats.

He then eased back on the Viking's throttles. As the big boat slowed, her hull settling lower in the water, he thought he heard the faint sound of a police siren.

Immediately, he muted the music, looked back over his shoulder, and exclaimed, "What the hell?"

There was in fact a siren. And it clearly was coming from a Florida Marine Patrol boat, its emergency light bar flashing over the center console's aluminum tube T-top roof.

About two hundred yards ahead of the police boat was a twin-engine, thirty-foot-long center console fishing boat. Matt grabbed the binoculars. He could make out a lone, shirtless, dark-skinned man aboard, his dreadlocks flying almost straight back as he stood with a death grip on the steering wheel.

"What's that boat doing?" Amanda said.

"Not to sound like a smart-ass, but I'd say he's running. He's got to have that thing at wide-open throttle. There's little more than the props in the water. But why? You can't outrun the cops here."

"Looks like he's headed for those Poker Run boats."

The go-fasts now were beginning to form a single-file line as they approached the channel's first outer marker.

In no time, the fleeing boat caught up with the back of the pack of go-fasts, the police boat in hot pursuit. It began weaving in and out of the line, coming dangerously close to colliding with the first two that it passed. The captains of some of the other boats, realizing what was happening, quickly maneuvered to get out of the way. A few lay on their horns, shouted, and, fists pumping, made obscene gestures as the boat flew past.

The police boat broke off its high-speed chase but still followed.

The burly man with the dreadlocks, not slowing, then entered the channel.

Matt saw that a thirty-three-foot Coast Guard boat with triple outboards and its emergency lights flashing had appeared farther up the channel near the end of a small island. It turned sideways, effectively shutting down the channel.

"See? Nowhere to run," Matt said, his tone incredulous. "He's headed right into the hands of the Coast Guard."

The boat then made a hard turn to the right, leaving the channel.

"I'll be damned! He's trying to cut across the shoal at Big Munson!"

The boat's propellers began churning up sea grass and sand as it entered the shallow, maybe two-feet-deep, water. Another center console police boat—this one with a large golden badge and the words MONROE COUNTY SHERIFF on its white hull—then appeared ahead of it, at the far end of the thickly treed key.

The speeding boat started to make a zigzag course, the man with the dreadlocks clearly trying to come up with some evasive course.

Then he suddenly made a hard 90-degree turn to the left.

"He's going to run ashore!" Amanda said.

The boat was headed directly for the sandy white beach and thick vegetation that edged Big Munson.

Just as the boat got close to the beach, the driver throttled down.

The boat appeared to settle softly in the shallow water—then shot up onto the sandy shoreline and suddenly pitched up. It went airborne briefly before landing in a more or less cushion of mangrove trees, stopping with the bow pointed skyward. The impact had thrown the man with the dreadlocks to the deck.

The boat's twin outboard engines, their exhausts no longer submerged and muffled, made a deep pained roar. After a long moment, the stunned man was able to get up and, one at a time, shut them down.

Matt could now see that the area forward of the center console had some sort of cover. And people had started scurrying out from under it.

Then, from the tree line twenty yards away, one, then two, then a half dozen more boys in T-shirts and dark green shorts suddenly ran out onto the beach, then turned and went as fast as they could toward the boat. Slung on the shoulder of the last one in line was a medium-sized white duffel bag with a red cross on it.

"Well, how about that," Matt said. "Here come the real first responders—Scouts in action."

The burly man with the dreadlocks hopped down onto the beach. The others began to follow quickly, one by one sliding over the side of the boat and landing on the sand.

A couple of them began limping. The man with the dreadlocks helped them to a spot on the beach, then directed the others to sit with them. They more or less made a line paralleling the shoreline.

"Oh my God!" Amanda said, shocked. "They're okay after that? It's amazing they weren't killed! I should see if they need a doctor."

"There's no way to get you there—even if I thought they'd let you."

The Boy Scouts arrived at the scene and immediately began checking the injured and performing first aid.

The police and Coast Guard vessels came in as close to the island as possible without running aground.

"Why aren't the cops rushing ashore?" Amanda said.

"Why should they? Those people aren't going anywhere. They're on an island surrounded by what looks like ten levels of law enforcement."

Five minutes later, Matt lined up the Viking to follow the Poker Run pack through the outer markers of the channel.

He heard more sirens, these coming from the Overseas Highway. All the action on the water had caused the heavy weekend traffic to slow to a crawl. Weaving through it were two Mobile Intensive Care Unit ambulances, their sirens screaming. They came to a stop beside the water's edge at the foot of the bridge.

"And here come the paramedics."

From the corner of his eye, Matt noticed something moving quickly. He looked to his left and saw a big blue-hulled Fountain speedboat overtaking the Viking. It roared around them, then cut its speed and smoothly dropped in behind the last boat in the pack.

Lucky for him it really isn't a race, Matt thought. *He'd have come in dead ass last.*

But what a beautiful boat. I wonder if they're going to screw it up with some stupid shrink-wrap design like those other go-fasts.

Clearly it doesn't need them to attract hot women. Look at all of them!

Amanda did not notice. She was looking through the binoculars and watching the police. They now were wading ashore and approaching the accident scene.

"Well, that's curious," she said.

"What?"

"The people who were on the boat are smiling at the cops like they're long-lost friends."

[THREE]
Little Palm Island, Florida
Sunday, November 16, 7:15 P.M.

The resort's intimate dining room featured warm wooden floors, a high-pitched ceiling, and a wall of windows that offered a picturesque view of the pristine white beach—lined with tall, leaning palm trees—and beyond it the vast Atlantic Ocean. The room, which was maybe half full, held only twenty-five round tables, each with seating for four. They were nicely separated so that the guests—and their conversations—would not be on top of one another.

Amanda Law, wearing a simple but elegant linen dress and sandals and with her thick hair now unbraided, sat between Chad Nesbitt and Matt Payne, who looked almost like twins—Chad was a little shorter and stockier—both dressed in khaki slacks, cotton knit shirts, navy blazers, and deck shoes.

Matt had his stainless steel Colt .45 Officer's Model tucked inside his waistband at his right hip.

"Even if you had broken bones, you'd be smiling, too," Chad said, stirring his second Myers's dark Jamaican rum and tonic cocktail. "Goodbye, Communism. Hello, Land of the Free and Home of the Brave."

"And that happens all the time down here?" Amanda said as she delicately squeezed a slice of lime into her glass of club soda.

Chad shook his head. "There are far more quiet landings than a wild running aground like today. I heard someone today say it's up to eight thousand people so far this year—and that's just here, not counting coming up through Mexico. The Cubans are willing to do anything for freedom. You've heard of the wet-foot, dry-foot policy?"

Matt shook his head.

"What—" he began, then stopped as he saw the waiter approaching with a full round tray.

"If you'll please pardon the interruption," the waiter said, placing an enormous bowl before Amanda. "For the lady, our coconut lobster bisque to start."

"That looks wonderful," Amanda said. "Thank you."

He put a plate in front of Chad and said, "The seafood seviche with crisp plantain chips."

And then he put two plates in front of Matt, who was taking a sip of eighteen-year-old Macallan single malt whisky.

"Crab fritters, sir," the waiter said. "And this, of course, is the tuna and oyster sashimi you called about earlier."

Matt looked at the waiter and was about to ask a question when he saw another waiter coming toward them with an enormous round plate piled high with finely crushed ice, on top of which were two dozen oysters on the half shell. The waiter put it on the table at the empty place setting.

"Enjoy," the second waiter said, then both left.

"Can anyone tell me," Matt said, looking between Amanda and Chad, "whose brilliant idea it was to instruct servers to say, 'Enjoy!' Is that an order? The entire purpose of why we came is to enjoy the meal. It's not like we need to be told to."

"Want to explain why you're about to *enjoy* two dozen raw oysters?" Amanda said. "*And* oyster sashimi?"

"I thought you knew, my love, that these mollusks have a special, shall we say, *romantic* effect," Matt said, smiling as he held up one of the half shells with an oyster. "Please *enjoy* one . . . and by one I mean help yourself to a dozen, of course."

"Really, Matt?" Chad said, shaking his head and grinning. "You're absolutely shameless."

"I think, Romeo, that you've already caused enough trouble being overly romantic," Amanda said playfully, picking up her soup spoon. "And thanks to the condition you put me in, I have to be careful about not eating high-mercury fish. I really wanted some tuna."

"Well, suit yourself," Matt said, then put the half shell to his lips and slurped the oyster out. Hand on his chest as he chewed, he looked at Amanda with an exaggerated face of extreme gastronomical satisfaction. Then he swallowed, exchanged the empty shell for a full one, and looked at Chad. "What were you saying about that dry-wet policy?"

"Wet-foot, dry-foot," Chad corrected, as he piled seviche on a plantain chip. "It's U.S. immigration policy, unique to Cubans trying to come to America. If a Cuban national can step on U.S. soil, he or she can stay, and a year and a day later becomes nationalized. If, however, they get intercepted at sea—anywhere on the water, even if it's a foot deep, that's the 'wet foot'—they get shipped back to the Castro Brothers' Happy Havana. Which they just risked their lives to flee— maybe for the third or fourth time—because the Castros don't exactly welcome them home with a brass band."

Chad ate his seviche, and began piling more on another chip.

"And the cops try keeping them from reaching land?" Amanda said.

"As you saw, that can get almost comical, a real cat-and-mouse catch-me-if-you-can game. But they have to. Otherwise, if word got to the Cuban masses that everyone could just step ashore and begin enjoying the bounty of America, Florida would be flooded. I mean, c'mon, they're not exactly rushing to Haiti, which is half the distance. It'd be worse than during the Mariel Boatlift. Remember that, Matt?"

"Yeah," Matt said, after washing down another oyster, "when Castro let something like a hundred thousand leave in 1980. And it happened again in '94. The luckier ones landed packed in boats barely able to float, carrying little more than their Eleguá."

" 'Eleguá'?" Amanda parroted.

"The West African–Caribbean Santería god that they believe controls their paths, their destiny. Eleguá is represented by a clay disc that's the face of a child. Castro cleverly cleared out his jails and loony bins, forcing them onto the boats. The more desperate lucky ones used rafts smaller, and less seaworthy, than a bathtub. Little more than tire tubes and blocks of Styrofoam lashed together. God only knows how many did not survive the trip."

Amanda considered that for a moment and, sadly shaking her head, said, "And you acquired this vast knowledge how?"

"Next door, around the campfire when we were kids camping on Big Munson. And, later, on family trips to the Caribbean."

"So now," Chad went on, "out of Miami's Little Havana, the exiles there have created a cottage industry of sorts. They charge Cuban-Americans upwards of ten grand to have a relative snuck out of Cuba and snuck ashore here."

Matt nodded thoughtfully. "Which explains why that guy was

determined to get those refugees onto land. A dozen people at ten grand each comes to a hundred and twenty thousand reasons."

"What happens to the guy running the boat?" Amanda said.

"Likely nothing," Chad said. "Often he's a Cuban, too. They don't earn even a dollar a day—and that's in pesos, which are worthless anywhere but Cuba. So, he's broke. But if he produces a Cuban national identity card, he's home free—literally. Even if he gets locked up, he probably won't serve any real time, and when he's released, wouldn't surprise me that someone slips him a nice cash payment. And maybe puts him and his Eleguá in another boat for another run."

"Frightening," Amanda said.

"Yeah," Chad said, then drained his drink. "But I'll tell you what's really becoming frightening."

"What?" Matt said.

"Philly. Just when you think it's bad enough, things get worse."

Matt grunted. "No argument there."

"I mean it's something new every day. Did you hear what happened to Maggie McCain's place? Daffy drove by it this afternoon. I just heard about it shortly before that."

Daphne Elizabeth Browne Nesbitt was Chad's wife and the mother of Matt's toddler goddaughter. The Nesbitts lived minutes away from Maggie in Society Hill, at Number 9 Stockton Place, one of three enormous (four thousand square feet) units built behind the facades of a dozen pre-Revolutionary brownstone buildings.

What the hell is up with this? Matt thought.

Everyone knows but me? Damn it!

"Maggie?" Amanda immediately said. "Is she okay? What happened?"

"A home invasion," Chad explained. "At least that's what we think it started as, but then her place caught on fire. Luckily the fire station is close by. I didn't want to bring it up at dinner, but . . ."

"Her house was invaded and burned? When?" Amanda said, then muttered, "How come I didn't hear?"

"Happened late last night. She wasn't home, as far as anyone knows. But word from the neighbors is that a Crime Scene van was there long after the fire truck guys left." He looked at Matt. "I'm surprised you don't know anything about this."

No shit. Me, too, Matt thought.

But now I know why Jason called. They must be treating this as a homicide.

How exactly does Maggie fit in? Clearly she is missing. . . .

"I don't know about a lot of Killadelphia cases that are working," Matt said. "Don't forget that our City of Brotherly Love averages a murder a day."

He felt Amanda looking at him and met her eyes. He could see sadness in them—and that her mind was in high gear.

Amanda then pulled out her cell phone and placed a call. A minute later, wordlessly, she hung up.

"Maggie didn't answer," Amanda said matter-of-factly, looking at her phone as she thumbed the screen. "I got one of those canned mechanical messages saying that her voice-mail box is full. And then it hung up on me."

She slid the phone back in her purse.

"I just texted her to call me. I wonder if Sarah has heard from her . . ." she said, pulling her phone back out to send another text.

And that just answered part of the Black Buddha's question.

Why the hell is Jason keeping this so secretive?

Well, she gave me my opening . . .

"When did you last hear from her, Amanda?" Matt said.

"Maybe a week ago, after Maggie got back from her sailing vacation in BVI. I forget which day."

"She was okay?"

Amanda shrugged. "She seemed to be. Why wouldn't she be? I didn't notice anything out of the ordinary. But then I was pretty caught up in my own world, making plans to come here and all."

"Daphne," Chad offered, "didn't even know she was back from the islands."

"I wrote Maggie a letter of recommendation for when she applied to UC-Berkeley," Amanda said suddenly, wistfully.

"You mean Bezerkly?" Matt said derisively. "Home of Peace, Love, and Anarchists."

Amanda shook her head.

"There are also normal people there, Matt. She was simply looking for a different environment. And boy did she find it. She'd followed a girl friend out for undergrad, then realized she really wasn't a West Coast type. So she then decided, after two years, that it wasn't for her. She said she came home to make a difference in Philly. And then I wrote another recommendation for when she went for her master's degree at UP."

"No good deed goes unpunished," Matt said. "She could have gone and made a difference anywhere."

"Yes, she could have. Someone else we know has similar resources and options."

Matt met her stare—*she doesn't have to say what those glistening eyes are screaming, "Stop playing cop . . ."*—and after a moment raised his eyebrows.

"Touché," he said.

She made a thin smile and nodded, then cocked her head and said, "What did you mean by that, Matt? 'No good deed . . .'? You don't know something bad has happened to her."

Well, I cannot tell her that Jason asked.

But after she gets over the initial shock of this, she's going to put two and two together. . . .

He shrugged. "You're right. I don't know. Just a gut feeling."

Amanda nodded thoughtfully, then put her napkin beside her plate and said, "Excuse me. I'm going to get some air."

Matt immediately got to his feet and put his hand on her chair, sliding it back as she rose. Chad stood, too, absently wiping his hands on his napkin.

I shouldn't have said that, Matt thought, looking at her sad face.

And so much for the oysters—nice job, Romeo.

If I knew it wouldn't upset her more, I'd tell Jason I'd help.

Damn it . . .

[FOUR]

As they watched Amanda walk toward the entrance to the restaurant, three men—one fit and tanned who looked to be in his thirties and two middle-aged and sunburned—entered. Young blonde women, in tight dresses and high heels, were on their arms.

Amanda, seemingly oblivious to the group, squeezed past and went out the door.

The blonde with the younger man, who evidently was leading the group, giggled and grinned as she leaned into him. She was trim and tall and tanned, with a beautiful face featuring bright emerald eyes that seemed to miss nothing.

The younger man scanned the restaurant. He and Chad made eye contact, and Chad nodded once. Then he turned to the group and gestured for them to go into the bar.

Matt studied the guy as they left, and did not like what he saw.

"Who was that?" Matt said as he and Chad settled back in their chairs.

"Nick Antonov's guy. He's local, out of South Beach."

"Looks like an ABC."

"SoBe?"

"Okay, a SoBe ABC. South Beach American-born Cuban."

Chad nodded. "Right. Forgot that one. Well, Little Havana is right next door to South Beach. Anyway, I met him yesterday at Key West International. The FBO put Nick's small jet next to my Lear. Something Perez, I think."

" 'Small jet'?"

"It's a Citation. His bigger one is a Gulfstream, a G-four, I think."

"You mean Tikhonov's G-four," Matt said.

Yuri Tikhonov, forty-eight, had significant investments in Philadelphia, as well as other cities in the U.S., in Europe, and in his homeland of Russia. He was worth billions, having made his first thousand million dollars shortly after the age of thirty-five. Many of the skills that made him a highly successful businessman, it was said, he had honed in the Sluzhba Vneshney Razvedki, Russia's agency for external spying and intelligence gathering.

Others suggested that it had more to do with his close relationship with high-ranking politicians in the Kremlin—men he had served under in the SVR, once known as the KGB.

"Okay, I take your point," Chad said. "The planes are the casino's. And since Nick works for the casino, and it's Tikhonov who owns a huge chunk of the casino, they're his. I just never see him on them."

Matt speared two oysters from their shells as he said, "I don't have to guess why those Florida hotties are hanging with older guys."

"That's the curious thing. They're not from Florida. The girls are Russian. They work at the casino. Casinos plural—I heard that they rotate the girls. That one on Nick's arm, Star, she's a twenty-one-year-old Ukraine."

"What about those older guys?"

"I dunno. Maybe Nick's clients from Philly or Jersey?"

Matt was quiet for a long moment, clearly lost in thought. Then he made a face and drained his single malt. Putting down the glass, he looked at Chad.

"How tight are you with Antonov and his crowd?" Matt suddenly said, somewhat sharply.

"What do you mean?" Chad shot back, his tone indignant. "I don't fuck around with those girls—or any girls—if that's what you're implying. The mother of your goddaughter would have my nuts served to me on the tip of the dull rusty knife she used for the castration."

"And the girls on your boat?"

"Screw you, Matt! They're hired by the PR firm. They're legit."

"No shit?" Matt said, pushing his chair back to stand. "How can you be sure?"

"I'm sure, damn it," Chad said, working to keep his voice low. "Why are you even suggesting otherwise? What's gotten into you?"

"Well, it wouldn't be the first time you got conned into some shady deal."

Chad tossed his fork and knife onto his plate and crossed his arms.

"You're not going to let that thing with Skipper go, are you?"

Matt shrugged. "'That thing'? I've told you that I don't begin to blame you at all for his death—the dipshit was going to get himself killed one way or another all on his own. I've been told that I shouldn't speak ill of the dead, but it's one thing that he ruined his life—and it's something entirely worse that he almost got Becca killed. As I've said, my point is that you didn't walk away from Skipper when you could have."

Matt and Chad had grown up with J. Warren "Skipper" Olde, whose history of booze and drug abuse had begun when they all attended Episcopal Academy prep school. His father made a fortune building McMansion subdivisions across the country. While the twenty-seven-year-old Skipper had a few legitimate—if questionably successful—real estate projects in development in Philadelphia, it turned out that he supplemented his cash flow by being actively involved in the manufacture and sale of methamphetamine.

Skipper, on September ninth, had been in a seedy motel room at the Philly Inn, one of the properties owned by the company that Chad Nesbitt had invested in. It was on Frankford Avenue, which had come to be known as the Boulevard of Broken Dreams. They had planned, when the timing—and tax break—was right, to demolish and replace the two-story motel with upscale condominiums. At about two o'clock that September morning, with Becca Benjamin, Skipper's twenty-five-year-old girlfriend, waiting right outside the room in her Mercedes SUV, the meth lab in the room exploded.

The motel became consumed by the chemical-fueled inferno. Two illegal aliens who had been cooking the methamphetamine were killed. Skipper was critically burned. Becca suffered burns and a severe head injury.

Ambulances rushed Skipper and Becca to the advanced Burn Center at Temple University Hospital. There, Matt met the head of the burn unit, Amanda Law, MD, FACS, FCCM.

The bodily injuries had been bad enough. But the next day one Jesús Jiménez, sent to permanently settle an ongoing disagreement over drug money, snuck into the Intensive Care Unit and pumped thirteen rounds of 9mm into Skipper.

Amanda had confided to Matt that it was her brutally cold professional assessment that Jiménez had done Skipper a favor. There was no question that if he was not going to die from his burns, he would've suffered a long and painful recovery from them and never been the same again.

Meantime, Becca, recovering from her injuries, battled with Survivor Guilt, and Amanda had arranged for her to be treated by Dr. Amelia Payne, who had been her suitemate at the University of Pennsylvania. The surname was no coincidence—Amy was Matt's sister, and had long held the same opinion as Amanda vis-à-vis the Wyatt Earp of the Main Line hanging up his gun belt.

Chad looked out the dining room windows at the Atlantic, then turned back to Matt and said, "I thought I was doing the right thing investing in Skipper's project. And when it all blew up, so to speak, especially after learning about the damn meth, I admitted I'd made a mistake—a *huge* mistake, okay?—one that I've been lucky has not caused any fallout with Nesfoods. As you just said, 'No good deed goes unpunished.'" He paused, then added, "So, that said, I am not making any damn mistake with Antonov and whatever he and his South Beach Cuban are up to."

Matt met Chad's eyes for a long moment, nodded, then exhaled audibly.

"Okay. Sorry," Matt said, not sounding completely apologetic. "It's just that something about that SoBe Cuban rubbed the cop in me really wrong. It triggered my Don't Believe Anyone mode. That, and I'm suddenly ten kinds of really pissed off. I brought Amanda down here to have a pleasant time away from Philly—and we're not here forty-eight hours and the shit has followed us. Now she's upset . . ."

Chad nodded. "I understand, man. No apology."

"Thanks," Matt said, and looked over his shoulder. "If Amanda returns, tell her I'll be right back."

"Where are you going?"

"To hit the head. Mother nature calls."

And to make a call so maybe we can get this shit behind us and get back to having a good time.

Right. Dream on, Matty.

Unless we find out that Maggie has suddenly popped up safe somewhere, her missing is going to keep weighing on Amanda. . . .

Matt crossed the dining room and entered the gentlemen's facility that was between the dining room and the bar. When he exited, he turned in the direction of the bar. He expected to see the men with the young women as he entered, was surprised they weren't there, then went through the bar and outside. He followed the path lined with flickering tiki torches down toward the immaculately groomed beach, pulling out his cell phone as he went.

When he looked at the screen, he saw that Mickey O'Hara had texted three times and, in the last hour, called twice and left voice-mail messages.

What the hell is up with him?

Well, first things first . . .

He speed-dialed Jason Washington.

"Good evening, Matthew," Jason answered on the first ring.

"Sorry to have taken so long. It's been a very interesting day since you called."

"What do you have for me?"

"I'll tell you about the other later. To answer your question about Maggie McCain, Amanda said she has not spoken with her in about a week. She doesn't recall exactly which day. But it's been since Maggie came back from a trip to the Caribbean."

"We're aware of the trip. Did she say if she understood it to be business or pleasure?"

"We"? Matt thought. *That certainly sounds official.*

" 'Vacation' was the word she used. Amanda has spent the last half hour trying to call and text her, since learning about her house catching fire—"

"How did she hear that?" Washington interrupted.

"Not from me, obviously," Matt said. "Chad Nesbitt told us just now at dinner. Said it started as a home invasion. Any truth to that?"

"Your friend whose family owns Nesfoods?" Jason asked, but it was more of a statement and effectively evaded Matt's question.

"Yeah. He's down here on business. Actually, it seems like half of Philly is down here."

"Did he say how he knew? Did he have any other information about her?"

"No, not really anything else. Only that his wife had driven past and seen the damage and crime-scene tape—and said that she hadn't known Maggie was back from her trip."

There was a moment's silence before Washington said, "Okay, got it. Thank you."

"What the hell is going on, Jason?"

"Let me know if Amanda hears from her. I will get back to you, Matthew," he said, dodging the question as he broke the connection.

Matt stared at the glowing screen.

If she hears from her?

Then if someone did die in Maggie's house, it wasn't her.
She's simply missing.

He shook his head, then speed-dialed Mickey O'Hara.

[ONE]
Hacienda Gentlemen's Club
Northwest Highway near Lemmon Avenue, Dallas
Sunday, November 16, 7:45 P.M. Texas Standard Time

The two-year-old dark gray Chevrolet Tahoe, coated in road grime
and with mud caked to its wheels and fenders, sat in the parking lot
of Juanita's Tex-Mex Cantina. The lot was adjacent to the Hacienda
strip club, the building of which in a former life had served as a Sears
& Roebuck home appliance store. The restaurant, despite its garish
colors and Spanish-language signage, still somewhat resembled the
Burger King that it originally had been.

The Tahoe wasn't the only vehicle in the parking lots lining
Northwest Highway that looked as if it could have just driven in
from the sticks. There were plenty of dirty cars and trucks, some of
them farm and ranch pickups, but most advertising some type of
service—plumbers, electricians, welders.

Odds were heavy, however, that the Tahoe was without question
the only one with red-and-blue emergency lights behind the grille, a
fully automatic Heckler & Koch UMP .45 ACP submachine gun in

a concealed lockbox in back, and, in a rack mounted in the headliner, a Remington 870 Tactical twelve-gauge shotgun.

Sergeant James O. Byrth, of the Texas Rangers, sat behind the wheel, his right elbow on the armrest as he held a cell phone to his ear. In his left hand, at the knuckles, he repeatedly tumbled a small white pinto bean from pinkie finger to thumb, then back again.

Byrth was thirty-one years old, six feet tall, a lithely muscled 170 pounds. His thick dark hair was neat and short. He had on gray slacks—the cuffs breaking over a pair of highly polished black ostrich-skin Western boots—a white cotton dress shirt with a striped necktie, and a navy blue blazer, single-breasted with gold buttons. Pinned just above the shirt pocket was his sterling silver badge, a five-point star within a circle engraved with DEPT. OF PUBLIC SAFETY—TEXAS RANGERS—SERGEANT. A white Stetson rested brim-up on the passenger seat.

As he listened, Byrth's dark, intelligent eyes stared out the wiper-smeared windshield, intently watching the traffic at the Hacienda's front door. The façade of the strip club had been painted a bright canary yellow and had posters of half-naked girls in suggestive poses stapled to it. Above the black door, which was swung completely open, a red neon sign flashed ENTRADA. A bouncer, a swarthy rough-looking Hispanic, sat on a backless stool in front of the door, his arms crossed as he eyed the cars circling the parking lot and the approaching customers.

"Hold one, Glenn," Byrth said into his phone as he heard the growing whine of twin turbofan jet engines. "Here comes another damn plane."

He looked across the street to where an elevated line of airport runway approach lights blinked into the distance. A moment later a Boeing 737—the medium-range passenger jet's bright orange belly

illuminated by its landing floodlights—flashed overhead with a deaf-
ening roar. He watched it descend over the runway lights, then land
at Love Field, Dallas's municipal airport.

After a moment, Byrth said, "Okay, Glenn, give it to me again.
What's the kill count up to?"

Texas Rangers Sergeant Jim Byrth had spent most of the day with
Hunt County Sheriff Glenn Pabody, after Pabody had put in the call
around seven o'clock that morning. Since the founding of the legendary Rangers in 1823—making them the United States' oldest state
law enforcement organization—the relentless lawmen had earned a
reputation for taking on extraordinary cases that others didn't have
either the resources or the authority, or often both, to handle. Such
was its importance that Section 411.024 of the Texas Government
Code stated: "The Texas Rangers may not be abolished."

"I ain't sure what exactly this is, Jim," Pabody had reported. "But
it ain't just another Hunt County meth lab. It's a helluva lot worse.
Definitely some kind of organized crime. Maybe cartel? You need to
see it to believe it."

Byrth had headed toward Lake Tawakoni, an hour's drive east of
Dallas. As he drove along Interstate Highway 30, the city gave way to
suburbs, then that turned to large spreads of horse and cattle ranches,
some of which were dotted with towering rigs drilling for natural gas
in the vast shale. Exiting the freeway, he picked up two-lane farm-to-
market roads, following them through country that became increasingly rugged and heavily wooded.

Near the lake, finding the entrance to the property had not
proven a problem. It was just past a wide spot in the road—the tidy
little town of Quinlan, population a thousand or two—and had a

Hunt County Sheriff's Office patrol car parked on the shoulder of the road. The white Ford Crown Victoria Police Interceptor, even with its emergency lights dark, stood out in the middle of nowhere.

A uniformed deputy sheriff, who looked to be maybe thirty and apparently hadn't missed a meal in all those years, stood in the middle of the dirt road, his thumbs dug into the black leather Sam Browne gear belt just below his well-rounded gut.

Byrth hit his wig-wags and the enormous deputy, now recognizing the Tahoe as an unmarked vehicle, stepped aside.

"It's a ways back, sir," the deputy sheriff said with a pronounced drawl, after Byrth introduced himself. "But you sure as hell can't miss it. And it is hell—I ain't seen nothing like it. Ever."

Limbs from bushes and trees scratched and thumped at the Tahoe's sides as Byrth navigated the narrow dirt road. It was muddy and deeply rutted, and he was convinced the SUV might at any moment slide into one of the oak trees that edged the road.

He then passed open fields with barbed-wire fences. And, after a good ten minutes of bouncing down the road from rut to rut, the Tahoe bottoming out twice, the narrow road turned sharply.

Around the bend there was an iron pole, rusty and bent, pushed to the roadside. It had a sign wired to it, a wooden board crudely hand-painted PRIVATE! DONT ENTER!

He rolled past and saw that the road now widened, opening up onto a sleepy ramshackle property that looked to have been hacked out of the wild by hand.

The first thing he saw, also standing out in the middle of nowhere, was a white Ford F-150 four-door pickup truck with the same HUNT COUNTY SHERIFF'S OFFICE markings as the Crown Vic. It was parked beside a beat-up Chevy Malibu and an old moss-covered fifth-wheel camper. The boxy aluminum-sided trailer, its four tires long ago gone flat, leaned sharply. To the right of it, ringed with barbed wire, was a small corral, at the back of which he could make out a two-stall stable that had been patched together with mismatched boarding.

Jim Byrth rolled to a stop beside the pickup and got out. He saw Sheriff Pabody, in his tan uniform, stepping out from behind the trailer.

Pushing sixty, Pabody was tall and fairly fit, with weathered skin and a bushy head of white hair. He had his right hand on the grip of an almost new matte black .30 caliber Springfield Armory M1 carbine. It hung by a black nylon sling from his right shoulder, next to the older Springfield Armory tactical 1911-A1 .45 ACP holstered on his hip. His left hand held a folded red bandanna over his nose and mouth.

As the two men approached each other, Byrth called out, "Glenn, I thought I told you that cutting out those greasy fried mountain oysters would stop that foul gassy problem of yours."

Pabody grinned as he stuffed the bandanna in his back hip pocket. He let the carbine dangle, and held out his hand.

"Sure good to see you, Jim," he said sincerely, meeting his eyes. He then nodded in the direction of the corral and added, "It's pretty damn nasty back there."

Byrth knew that Pabody, once an Army reserve major, had seen his share of gruesome scenes as a Green Beret fighting the Taliban. He recognized that for the understatement that it was, and nodded.

"So, what the hell do we have here? You said a game warden found it?"

Texas game wardens, like the state troopers under the Department of Public Safety, were peace officers with the power to enforce laws statewide, on and off the pavement.

Pabody nodded. "Luckily not just any game warden. I thought you knew Gerry Bailey."

Byrth shook his head. "Should I?"

"There's good guys in the business"—he pronounced it *bidness*—"and there's really good guys."

"Don't tell me. Another of you Green Beanies?"

Pabody nodded. "Fifth Special Forces Group. Led assault sniper teams in Afghanistan and Iraq. Put in his twenty years, then figured he was pushing the odds of meeting his maker after four long tours in the Sandbox. Good ol' country boy. Nothing makes him happier than hunting and fishing—and, okay, to hear him tell it, that and fucking."

Byrth grunted and grinned.

"And now Bailey gets paid to be around it," Pabody went on. "The hunting and fishing, that is." He paused in thought, then went on, "I meant that crack about fucking as a joke, but maybe that, too. Man, this was the last thing that he—hell, any of us—expected to find out here."

He sighed audibly, then went on: "Anyway, Bailey was making a routine patrol early this morning looking for poachers. He was on his all-terrain vehicle when he crested a hill not far from the lake and came across the guy. This Mexican was big and beefy, maybe thirty. He was dressed all in black and carrying a nice Mossberg pump, a twelve-gauge. He took off running. When Bailey ordered him to stop, then pursued him, the guy stopped and took two shots at him."

"Hit him?"

Pabody nodded. "Got grazed by some pellets. Birdshot. Nothing bad. I made him go to the ER—he was able to drive himself." He paused, shook his head, then added, "But wouldn't that be a bitch?

Do four years dodging raghead bullets and IEDs only to get blown away by an illegal Mezkin damn near in your own backyard?"

"Yeah, a real ironic bitch. Did Bailey bag him?"

Pabody nodded again. "So the guy takes off into the bush. Bailey gets off his fancy four-wheeler, grabs his Car14, and takes off after him. Bailey gains ground on him, shouts for him to stop. Fucking idiot then tries to take another shot—and it's game over. Bailey says it wasn't intentional—blames not hitting center mass on his heavy breathing, but that's bullshit because he's such a good shot he could drive nails at a hundred yards with a .22, and he had the selector on single, not full auto—he puts a round right above the bad guy's right eye. Top of his head explodes like a ripe cantaloupe."

"Nice shot. You said he was an illegal. Any ID, background?"

"Not a damn thing on him—just my gut feeling that he's illegal. We're running down property records to find who owns this place. Anyway . . . when Bailey comes up on the guy, he gets a whiff that's overwhelming. Since it's not Bailey's first rodeo around a mess of gray matter, and he knows that that's not what he's smelling, he can't figure it out. So he recons the area—and bingo." He nodded toward the corral. "Hell, come here. I'll show you."

Jim Byrth smelled it before he saw it. The combination of odors was that of rotten eggs and putrid meat. It was oddly familiar to him, in an unsettling way.

"Behind the stable there," Pabody said, pointing to what was the edge of an eight-foot-tall open-air shed. "That's where Bailey found the drums."

Pabody put his bandanna to his face as they stepped back to it. Byrth fished out a handkerchief from his pants pocket.

The shed was roughly twenty by thirty feet, with a floor of bare earth and, atop what looked like four old telephone poles, a low, flat roof of rusted sheets of corrugated metal. It held eight fifty-five-gallon high-density polyethylene drums more or less in two lines of four. The blue plastic—with SULFURIC ACID CAUTION! HIGHLY COR-ROSIVE! stenciled in white—was faded and stained.

Six of the drums were covered with blue plastic lids. The lids for the other two were missing, and when Byrth looked in the nearest one, the disfigured face of a teenaged girl stared grotesquely back.

"Jesus!" he said from behind his handkerchief. "You never get used to seeing something like that."

The flesh on her cheeks and chin and forehead—all the parts above the surface of the murky fluid in the drum—was blue-black. What little hair she had left was ragged stubs of blonde along the top of her forehead.

Under the fluid's surface, the body was simply bony skeleton. And what was left of the skeleton—there was nothing below the waist—was in various degrees of disintegration.

Byrth felt Pabody's eyes studying him.

"*Pozole,*" Byrth said, shaking his head and turning to look at Pabody.

"What?"

"South of the border, that's what they call this process of getting rid of bodies," he explained. "Pozole is actually a Mexican stew. Apparently, the Cártel del Golfo has its own gallows humor. I first saw this in Nuevo Laredo, then outside Juárez, a couple years back. Those Zetas are ruthless sonsofbitches. They're literally liquefying anyone in their way—the cops and soldiers and reporters they can't buy off—just making anybody they don't like disappear. Their rivals they behead and stack 'em in town like cordwood to intimidate everyone else."

Los Zetas was made up of deserters from commando units in the Mexican army—units that were trained and armed by elite U.S. forces in the war against the very drug cartels they joined. Los Zetas had acted as the enforcement arm of the Gulf Cartel before breaking off on their own. Battles over routes for the trafficking of drugs and guns and humans across the United States border—the areas leading to Interstate 35 at Laredo being highly prized—became an endless bloodbath.

"Juárez is the murder capital of the world," Pabody said. "Six thousand killed in the last two years."

"That's just counting official deaths," Byrth said. "No telling how many more get murdered. The Mexican government acknowledges that almost thirty thousand of its citizens have simply disappeared. Cases get opened when family members report someone's gone missing. Someone who just never comes home, or was abducted from their home, or even 'arrested' by uniformed police or military."

"There's a lot of cops on the take."

Byrth nodded. "Theirs and ours. Then there's also the fact that Zetas and others not only got trained as cops or soldiers before joining the cartels, they kept the uniforms and weapons. How the hell is the average *abuela* going to know that the 'official' hauling off of her son or grandson in front of her very eyes ain't legit?"

"And when she goes down to the police station asking questions, there's no record of arrest."

Byrth nodded again.

"No body means no murder, no nada," he said. "That's very effective intimidation."

Pabody's eyes grew. "It's not just girls here, there's evidence men were also . . . liquefied. You figure this is some of Zetas's work?"

"For lack of better words, it damn sure smells like it. But out here?

It could be someone copying them. Sinaloas, Knights Templar, any of them. Fucking cartels and their splinter cells can be anywhere."

Pabody's eyes went back to the drum. "It looks like he just stood the dead bodies in there."

Byrth nodded. "And as the acid ate away at them, they slowly sank lower."

"Until they were completely gone," Pabody added.

"In Juárez, they did the same with sodium hydroxide, potassium hydroxide—"

"What's that?"

"Lye. Caustic soda. Much easier to get than acid."

"At least a couple of these barrels have got labels that show they were sold to Tyler Oilfield Services," Pabody said.

"Probably stolen from an oil- or gas-drilling site," Byrth said. After a moment he added, "Lye requires heat. And it's not as thorough. This acid, however, dissolves it all, including dental fillings and such."

"How quick?"

"Tissue's gone away in about half a day, bones and everything else in two."

Byrth looked around the immediate area.

There was a fire pit that had a scorched black metal ring about four feet in diameter. Byrth recognized that it was part of a wheel from a big-rig tractor trailer. Inside the ring were smoldering ashes and the remnants of charred logs. Just outside the ring was a swath of partially burned fabric from a pair of blue jeans.

"The guy was pretty sloppy about getting rid of evidence," Pabody said. "That is, if he even cared."

Pabody reached into his shirt pocket and pulled out a small plastic zipper-top bag. In it was a business card.

"This is just a tip of what I saw when I stuck my head in the door of that shithole of a RV."

He handed the bag to Byrth. He saw that it was a cheap generic business card, white with black type, for the Hacienda Gentlemen's Club. It showed its address and a "hotline" phone number. Under that was a box with flowery handwriting that read: "April. In town Nov 11–15 only!!! Call me to reserve my dance room!!! 561-555-4532." The "i" in April, instead of being dotted, had a heart drawn over it.

"That's a South Florida area code," Byrth said.

"Yeah, and when you call it, the auto voice-mail message says her box is full." He grunted. "So to speak."

Their eyes met. Byrth smirked.

"Sorry, Jim. More of that gallows humor. This girl—none of these girls, hookers or whatever—didn't deserve whatever happened to get them here. Anyway, I called in this April's phone number to the office. They got the process started on getting her records from the phone company. And I'm having a flatbed tow truck come fetch the trailer so forensics can go through it after they're done doing the scene here."

"Good idea."

"With the exception of what's left of this body, we ain't getting any DNA off any dissolved bodies. There's nothing left but acid in those covered drums. But there's a shitload of panties—those string ones? 'thongs' mostly—and some bras in the trailer that could give us something. And Lord knows what they'll find on the mattress."

Byrth pulled out his cell phone and, using its camera function, took a close-up picture of the business card through the clear plastic bag.

"November eleven through fifteen?" Byrth said, handing the bag back and checking the date window on his wristwatch. "Today's the fifteenth."

"You reckon April was missed at work last night? Or if she's expected tonight?"

"One way to find out."

"Well, it's entirely possible she could have a cell phone with a Florida number," Texas Rangers Sergeant James O. Byrth said into his phone as he looked through the Tahoe's windshield at the front door of the Hacienda. "But it's a Pennsylvania ID you found?"

"Yeah," Hunt County Sheriff Glenn Pabody said, "a DOT non-driver ID issued to one Elizabeth Cusick, age twenty, five-one, one-ten, blonde, blue eyes, a Hazzard Street address in Philadelphia. That's Hazzard with two z's. Last name spelled Charley Umbrella Sierra India Charley Kilo. What kind of name is that?"

Byrth was writing that down as he heard the turbine engines of another jet approaching.

"Maybe Polish?" he said. "Lots of Poles in Pennsylvania. And Italians and Irish and Germans and Latinos . . . Would you pop a shot of it and send it to me?"

"Sure thing. Didn't you say you were just up there? In Philadelphia?"

"Yeah. Running down some mean bastards who thought they were going to be the next Zetas."

"Maybe you can pull a few strings then, get some answers quicker."

"I'm damn sure going to try." He paused, then, his voice rising, added, "Here comes another jet. I'll call you back later."

Byrth broke off the call as the roar overhead drowned out whatever Sheriff Pabody had begun to say. It wasn't as loud as the 737 had been a few minutes earlier. He looked up to the approach lights and saw that this aircraft was a corporate-sized jet, white with elaborate red artwork.

Nice. Are those gambling dice painted on it?

His eyes then went back to the Hispanic bouncer at the front door of the strip club.

That boy looks friendly as fire ants.

Wonder what my odds are of getting any answers in there—a million to one? Worse?

Byrth's cell phone then made a *ping!* sound. He looked at it and saw that Sheriff Pabody had sent him the photograph he'd taken of the girl's Pennsylvania Department of Transportation identification. He tapped the image and the ID filled the screen of his phone. He dragged his fingers on the screen, enlarging her head shot.

"Wow," he heard himself softly say aloud. "What a beautiful girl."

Framed in rich chestnut brown hair, the energetic, youthful face with a bright sensual smile seemed to stare out right at him.

Then his mind flashed with the horrific image of the blue-black blotched flesh of the face that stared back at him from the drum of sulfuric acid.

Could it be the same girl?

That one was blonde. Or maybe bleached-blonde.

And Glenn said the toll is at least ten.

God help them . . .

Byrth, as was his ritual, reached down and double-checked his .45s—the full-frame Model 1911-A1 in his hip holster and the smaller-framed Officer's Model on the inside of the top of his left boot. Then he grabbed his Stetson and stepped out of the Tahoe.

[TWO]
Society Hill, Philadelphia
Sunday, November 16, 8:57 P.M.

"I'm sure the police will solve this soon, Mrs. McDougal," Michael J. O'Hara said after shaking hands with the sad-faced silver-haired elderly woman and stepping to the sidewalk in front of her townhome. "Thank you for taking the time to speak with me. Nice to see you again."

The woman nodded wordlessly, glanced up and down the narrow tree-lined cobblestone street, then quickly shut her front door. He heard a solid *clunk-clunk-clunk* as she locked the three new dead bolts she'd had a handyman install only hours earlier.

O'Hara looked six doors down the street to where yellow CRIME SCENE DO NOT CROSS tape roped off the sidewalk in front of Margaret McCain's fire-damaged home. Arranged against the wall under a soot-covered window was a small makeshift memorial. It consisted of more than a dozen long-stemmed flowers and a bouquet of balloons floating above a pair of plush two-foot-tall teddy bears embracing each other.

The night air had a heavy acrid burned smell to it, and that clung to his nostrils and the back of his throat.

O'Hara felt his cell phone vibrating in his pocket. He pulled it out.

"Where's my cameraman?" he said into it, answering without introduction. "I'm going to do my live shot here at the scene."

The phone began vibrating again.

"Hold on a sec, damn it," he said.

He looked at the caller ID. It read MARSHAL EARP.

Finally! he thought.

O'Hara put the phone back to his head, snapped, "Just get him here now," then touched a key that broke off that call and answered the incoming one.

"Matty!" O'Hara said into the phone. "You really must be embracing island time if ASAP means four hours. Just how the hell is life as a beach bum?"

"Well, it was fucking great, Mickey," Payne said, his tone bitter, "until Philadelphia raised its ugly head down here."

"Whoa! What do you mean?" He paused in thought, then added, "This wouldn't have to do with the McCain girl, would it?"

Payne was quiet for a long moment, then said, "What do you know about that?"

"Screw you, buddy. The question is, What do *you* know about it?"

"Not a damn thing. I wish I did, though."

"Oh, come on! Matty—"

"I'm out of the loop, Mickey. Even Jason Washington won't tell me what the hell is going on. All I know is what Daffy Nesbitt told Chad: that it was a home invasion. Amanda has been trying to reach Maggie for the last hour."

"The Black Buddha—the best homicide detective on the East Coast—is working a home invasion case? I don't buy it."

"I agree. And I didn't say that. Because I don't know. I just got off the phone with him. For whatever reason, he says I can't ask about it."

"That's interesting."

Payne grunted. "That's one way to put it. All I know for sure is that it's starting to screw up what began as an amazing trip down here." He paused, then added, "Why are you playing journalist? You're supposed to be the boss now."

"I am the boss. But once a journalist, always a journalist, Matty. Write that down. It's in my blood to chase a good story, just as it's in your blood to chase bad guys. And when the home of a scion of a Philly family is firebombed and she's missing, I'm personally going to cover the story."

"Did you say firebombed?"

"Yeah. The accelerant was gasoline. One of the guys in on the crime scene—you can guess who—quietly told me Molotov cocktails."

"No shit . . ."

"And I've got the scoop on whose house it is because my so-called competition hasn't figured that out. It's listed on the property records under a generic named trust, and neighbors aren't talking to the media for fear they might be next. Old Lady McDougal just had three—count 'em, three—new dead bolts put on her front door. She said she wouldn't have opened her door if she hadn't known I was 'a nice laddie.' So, I know it's Maggie's, and I like Maggie and want to help."

"How do you know her?"

"I can't believe you just asked that. I know damn near everyone. It's my job."

Matt grunted again. "Point taken. So, how?"

"About a year ago she called me about my CPS stories, and said because of Mary's House she wanted to continue our talks. . . ."

When Michael J. O'Hara had been the lead investigative reporter at *The Philadelphia Bulletin*, he wrote "Follow the Money," a series of articles that blew open the City of Philadelphia Department of Human Services. O'Hara had spent months digging, and uncovered gross incompetence and graft. His front-page reports led to a whole-sale revision of the department, including the resignation of long-entrenched top administrators.

It also won O'Hara a Pulitzer Prize for public service.

Curiously, his winning the prestigious award had been the beginning of the end of O'Hara's long career in newspapers.

The owners of the *Bulletin* had put their public relations flacks to work overtime, boasting that the Pulitzer proved their newspaper offered the highest caliber of reporting anywhere. Mickey's redheaded mug was plastered on the sides of Southeastern Pennsylvania Transportation Authority buses and practically every billboard in town. But all that—and the perception of the PR having gone to O'Hara's head—had created more than a little animosity among certain colleagues in the newsroom.

A great deal of the friction was the result of petty jealousy on the part of the managing editor, Roscoe G. Kennedy, who took enormous pride in having earned a master's degree from the University of Missouri School of Journalism. Kennedy knew that O'Hara was equally proud of having, as Mickey put it, attended the School of Hard Knocks.

Mickey's first job with the *Bulletin* was at age twelve, when he pedaled his rusty bicycle on a West Philly newspaper route, slinging copies of the afternoon edition at row house after row house.

By the time Mickey was sixteen, one of his best buddies at West Catholic High School convinced him to add a sideline to his route—running numbers slips for Francesco "Frankie the Gut" Guttermo.

That had worked out reasonably well, until Monsignor Dooley, who had made absolutely clear that he would not tolerate any immoral act, caught Mickey with the slips at school. The monsignor offered to go lenient on him if Mickey would confess his sins—and assist the monsignor in cleansing the school of the unholy filth that was gambling.

Mickey, embracing the code of silence that was *omertà*, refused to rat out his buddy. And he damn sure knew better than to even mutter the name Frankie the Gut.

Accordingly, the monsignor booted Mickey to the curb, telling him not to come back until he was repentant and prepared to make amends.

Mickey, turning to his *Bulletin* job to fill his now extra time, discovered that a newsroom copyboy position had opened. He was told that it was little more than a gritty gofer job, but it sounded like the best job on earth to someone who was looking at another bitter winter throwing papers from a worn-out bike.

Against all odds—including being evasive about his proof of having graduated from high school early—he got the job and survived the ninety-day probationary period.

Mickey had found the newsroom a fascinating environment. He not only did the lowly tasks thrown at him, he made sure he was conveniently in the line of sight when the assistant city editor looked around for someone to do last-minute work no one else wanted— research, fact-checking telephone calls, et cetera.

Proving himself competent and reliable, he soon was given small writing assignments.

Everything was going beyond his wildest expectations until, days shy of his eighteenth birthday, he was called into the managing editor's office.

The assistant city editor was there, and Mickey was convinced that this was the end of his run. But when he was shown the front page of the edition just off the presses—and the byline *Michael J.*

O'Hara at the end of a very short article he'd researched and written—
he found himself accepting a job offer as a very junior reporter.

Then, twenty years later, looking at his proud mother seated at
the front table in the ballroom of the Waldorf Astoria in New York
City, O'Hara found himself giving an acceptance speech after being
awarded the Pulitzer Prize.

He did not think life could get any better—he was being paid to
do a job he loved, and one he did damn well, while helping those
who couldn't help themselves, such as the orphans and the abused
stuck in the morass of Child Protective Services.

Then, mere days after returning from New York, he was told in no
uncertain terms: "Face it, Mickey, those bastards are screwing you."

The giant of a black man delivering this news—one Casimir J.
Bolinski, Esquire—happened to serve as legal counsel and business
agent to heavy-hitting professional athletes.

Casimir "the Bull" Bolinski had also been Mickey's coconspirator
at West Catholic running Frankie the Gut's numbers slips.

If Mickey had given in to Dooley the Drooler, Casimir would
have found himself also booted out of school—thus ending the Bull's
path to a Notre Dame scholarship and, more critically, his career
playing for the Green Bay Packers. And without that high pay of pro
ball, Casimir would not have been able to afford to study law in the
off-seasons, then become a sports agent after retiring his helmet and
shoulder pads.

A highly successful agent, he represented the best of the best. He
was ultimately earning far more off the field than he'd ever been paid
to play.

And for all that, the Bull said, "I can never adequately repay you,
Mickey."

The Bull, however, did try—by taking him on as a client. And the post–Pulitzer Prize employment contract that Bolinski negotiated for O'Hara with "those bastards" at the *Bulletin* was far beyond anything Mickey thought possible. It included compensation consistent with, the Bull announced, what he found other winners of the Pulitzer were being paid, as well as a fat expense account, a new company vehicle, and more vacation days than Mickey thought he could ever use.

The contract also included language for an exit clause—one that would prove critical.

Roscoe Kennedy and Mickey O'Hara had been having what euphemistically could be described as "creative differences" over the treatment of Mickey's exclusive that was about to be the *Bulletin*'s lead story. It was about Sergeant M. M. Payne having shot two robbers after they almost killed a couple in a restaurant parking lot. It was accompanied by a photograph O'Hara had taken of Payne— wearing a tuxedo, cell phone in one hand and .45 in the other— standing over a dead robber.

Kennedy had written a snide "Wyatt Earp of the Main Line Shoot-Out" headline, defending it by saying that the photograph made Payne look like the bloodthirsty gunslinger he really was. O'Hara called him out for twisting the moniker Mickey had given Matt as a compliment, then for using the story in an attempt to publicly ridicule a cop who was doing his job.

And then he punched Kennedy.

Bolinski, who happened to witness the whole incident unfold, carried Mickey out as Kennedy yelled before the whole newsroom unflattering descriptions of O'Hara—and that he was fired.

The contract, however, proved solid. It provided Mickey with a paid thirty-day break, one he decided to use by traveling to France. A fugitive from Philly—Fort Festung, who'd been found guilty in absentia for murdering his girlfriend and leaving her body to mummify in a trunk—was enjoying the French's refusal to extradite anyone sentenced to death. O'Hara felt that the outrage warranted a book. He needed research, and dragged along Matt Payne, who after the shooting also found himself with time on his hands.

When the Philly courts allowed Festung's sentence to be reduced to life behind bars, France gave in to the extradition—and Mickey O'Hara got a picture of Sergeant M. M. Payne arresting the fugitive Festung.

While Mickey wrote his book, the Bull found him new employment as the publisher and chief executive officer of an Internet start-up venture—CrimeFreePhilly.com—backed by very deep pockets. It not only allowed O'Hara to be in charge of doing what he did so well, it also gave him a platform and an audience far greater than anything the *Bulletin* ever could have. And it had allowed him to develop other news reporting properties.

"Okay, Matty, I'll give you the journalist's Who, What, Where, When, and Why. Here's the lead of my story tonight: 'Margaret Mc-Cain, the twenty-five-year-old scion of one of Philadelphia's founding families, remains missing tonight following what Philadelphia Police are calling a home invasion that left her Society Hill town house engulfed in flames late last night.'"

"That's pretty straightforward."

"Wait. There's more. Last sentence of lead: 'Police are withholding comment as to whose body was secreted from the scene after the medical examiner's van was parked in the closed garage of the Mc-Cain residence.'"

"Really? I hadn't heard that detail either. That's curious."

"Yeah. Curious. My source did say it was a female."

"Okay, look, Mickey, that reinforces something I thought. Which is (a) I agree with you that if Jason is on the case, it's being treated as a homicide—if it walks like a duck, talks like a duck, et cetera, et cetera—and (b) because Jason wants to know if we hear from Maggie—and is being quiet about it—then he's saying that she didn't die in her home. Other than that, I have nothing."

There was a long moment's silence, then O'Hara said, "Okay. Thanks." There was another pause, and he added, "Then who do you think it is the ME bagged and tagged?"

"I have no idea, Mickey. I wish I did. I could call Dr. Mitchell— he has to have finished the autopsy by now. Or even Javier, his tech. They might tell me. But then that'd probably get me in hot water with Jason. He specifically told me no questions."

"When the hell did you start caring about getting in hot water, Matty?"

"Hold one. I've got a call coming in. It may be Amanda."

O'Hara listened to silence as Payne checked his phone screen, then heard him say, "When it rains it pours." O'Hara then saw movement across the street. When he looked he saw Detective Anthony Harris leaving a town house. Mickey knew Tony well, including that he'd worked in the Homicide Unit years longer than Matt's total time with the police department.

Bingo! Mickey thought.

Then he heard Matt back on the phone: "Okay, Mickey, where were we?"

"More proof it has to be a homicide," O'Hara announced. "Harris just appeared down the street, coming out of a residence."

O'Hara started walking in that direction.

"Tony!" he called out, then said into the phone, "I'll call you back, Matty."

No sooner had O'Hara ended the call and slid the phone into his pocket than he saw a glow from the phone in Harris's hand, and then Harris putting it to his head.

O'Hara heard him say, "Hey, Matt. What's up?"

I'll be damned, O'Hara thought.

Harris made eye contact with O'Hara as he said, "That puts me in a tough position, Matt. Jason said everything goes through him. Everything. Period."

[THREE]
Little Palm Island, Florida
Sunday, November 16, 9:12 P.M.

Matt Payne looked at the phone number of the call that had just rolled into his voice mail. It was from area code 713. He tried to place it as the voice-mail message began to play.

"Howdy, Marshal . . ."

Jim!

". . . If you can break free from that beautiful better half of yours, I'd appreciate you calling me. I'm following a lead in the Miami area right now, then another up your way." He paused, and there came an overwhelming whine, what sounded like a jet aircraft passing nearby. He then went on: "I'm giving you a heads-up, Matt. It's gotten worse—beyond CATFU. Call me."

Beyond Completely And Totally Fucked Up? Payne thought.

What the hell could that be?

About two months earlier, Texas Rangers Sergeant James O.

Byrth had come to Philadelphia—with his huge white Stetson that Payne had dubbed The Hat—hunting a vicious drug-cartel member who was trafficking in young girls, guns, and illicit drugs. Deputy Police Commissioner Coughlin had assigned Payne to work with Byrth.

Juan Paulo "El Gato" Delgado and his ring had left a trail of dead bodies from Texas to Philadelphia—and there kidnapped Dr. Amanda Law, not knowing she was in any way connected to Payne—before a shoot-out that found Delgado dead and Amanda rescued.

Payne regularly recalled one of the last things that Byrth had said when Payne dropped him at Philadelphia International Airport: "Come visit us in Texas, Marshal. We've got plenty more bad guys like Delgado. And it's only going to get worse."

Payne pushed the key on-screen that read CALL BACK.

Jim Byrth answered on the first ring.

"Howdy, Matt. Thanks for getting back so quick. You must be sitting around bored to tears. How are things in Philly?"

"Hey, Jim. On the contrary, I wish I was bored. Look, I may have to break off this conversation, but I wanted to at least return your call. What's going on?"

"I just walked out of a titty bar—"

"Lucky you. Congratulations," Payne interrupted, sharply sarcastic. "You called to tell me that?"

Byrth was quiet a moment, then said, "What's crawled up your ass, Marshal?"

"Sorry. I am a little pissed right now."

"Want to tell me about it?"

"Not right now. I have to get back to dinner. You go."

"Okay, I'll make this quick. Can you run some Philly names and addresses through your system for me?"

"Sure. What's it in regard to?"

"I reckon it'd be a long shot if I asked you if you knew what Pozole was," Byrth said, and before Payne could reply, he added, "It's a Mexican stew."

Payne grunted. "So you called to talk about food?"

"You remember your buddy El Gato?" Byrth said, ignoring that. *The Cat.*

Payne's memory flashed with an image of a defiant Delgado, his hands and feet taped to a chair in a hellhole of a Philly row house.

Having just found Amanda captive there and cut her free, Matt had put the muzzle of his .45 between Delgado's eyes. He wrestled with the impulse of blowing Delgado away, if not as payback for kidnapping Amanda, then to honor all the young Hispanic girls he had raped and tortured—including cutting off the head of one teenaged Honduran. In the end, Payne had decided against "shooting them all and letting the Lord sort them out," and allowed the Cat what turned out to be at least his ninth life.

"Where's this going?" Payne said. "The bastard's dead. You saw to that."

You tossed a black bean at Delgado's bound feet—then turned a blind eye when our informant put a bullet in his head.

Not that the sonofabitch didn't deserve what he got. Especially considering what he no doubt was going to do with Amanda, whether or not he got a ransom for her.

You're probably tumbling another bean across your knuckles as we speak.

Is it white—or black?

Byrth had told Payne, also on their way to the airport for Byrth's flight back to Texas, about the Mier Expedition, led by Texas Ranger John Coffee Hays in the 1840s.

Hays and Big Foot Wallace had pulled together a group to invade Mexico. South of the border, however, they found that they'd severely underestimated their target.

They were captured.

"The order came down to execute every tenth man," Byrth explained.

Black and white beans were put in a pot to determine who lived and who died. A man drawing a black bean was shot. Those who drew the white beans lived to carry the tale back to Texas.

Byrth had then explained why he had no remorse for the informant's "self-defense" killing of Delgado. Beyond the unspoken fact that it had been what Payne considered payback for all those whom the brutal Delgado had harmed, it also eliminated paying for courts and prisons.

"El Gato getting himself killed saved taxpayers at least a million bucks."

"Los Zetas," Byrth now explained, "makes El Gato's little gang look like choirboys. And I may have just found evidence here in North Texas of their handiwork that I've witnessed in Mexico."

"Zetas? The former enforcers of the Gulf Cartel?"

"Yeah. Now on their own and worse than ever. If it's Zetas or someone copying them, it gives new meaning to 'Don't go digging up more snakes than you can kill.' Ergo, CATFU."

"What's worse?"

"Liquefying young strippers-slash-hookers."

"What? How the hell does that happen?"

Byrth began, "In the woods by a lake we have found a ratty camp with more than a half dozen fifty-five-gallon drums of sulfuric acid. . . ."

"And," Byrth finished five minutes later, "Sheriff Pabody, a really good guy, showed me this titty bar's business card he found in the trailer. It's got a girl's handwriting that says when quote April unquote would be working and her phone number. I'll send you a shot of it and forward the shot that Pabody sent me of her DOT ID."

"That'll work," Matt said. "So, you went to the strip club and—"

"Yeah. The card said she was supposed to work there just these last three nights."

"And let me guess—nobody knew nothing."

"'Nada,' as it's said in ol' *Ess-pan-yole.* It took me some time to get anyone to even admit they could speak English. Finally I was handed a napkin with a phone number written on it. When I called, sounded like a white guy who answered. Identified himself as Todd Lincoln and said that he was the owner of the club. And he of course offered to cooperate completely. He might have some local Dallas cops bought to look the other direction but knows that I can really bring in the heat."

"And?"

"And what else? I got the usual BS runaround. Anyone can get ahold of those cards and write whatever they want on them. He said he would ask his managers about any girls named April. 'But it's probably a stage name, if she exists at all.'"

"And since you don't know what she looks like . . ."

Byrth's mind flashed with what was left of the face of the girl in the barrel.

"Not unless she's the one pictured on the ID. Even showing everyone in the titty bar that image blown up on my phone I came up with zilch."

Matt felt his phone vibrate once.

"Well," he said quickly, clearly trying to wind up the conversation, "send those to me, and I'll get them right up to Philly."

"'Up to Philly'? Where are you?"

"In the Keys with Amanda. But some shit's just hit the fan, so I don't know what's next."

"Is she okay?"

Matt could hear genuine concern in the Texan's deep voice.

"Thanks, man. She's fine. Someone we know is missing after her house was firebombed last night."

"Damn. I'm sorry. I won't hold you up any longer. Get back to me when you can."

"Will do."

"Good luck, Marshal."

"You, too, Jim."

Matt broke off the call, then checked the screen:

```
AMANDA 9:22 PM


WHERE ARE YOU? WE NEED TO TALK.
```

Oh shit, he thought as he typed: "Meet in bar?"
Is this good or bad?

Either way, I'll need a drink.

Then maybe we can get back to dinner . . . and everything else.

He hit SEND, and another message box popped on-screen:

```
BYRTH 9:23 PM


GOOD HEARING YOUR VOICE. IMAGES FOLLOW.


GIVE AMANDA A KISS FOR ME. TAKE CARE OF HER . . .
LADIES LIKE THAT ARE RARE INDEED.
```

As Matt smiled and nodded appreciatively, his phone vibrated twice. Each of the messages contained only an image. He studied the Hacienda business card, then the girl's Department of Transportation ID.

Beautiful girl . . .

Hazzard Street? That's in Kensington.

He hit the FORWARD key, found Tony Harris's phone number, and typed: "Our brother-in-arms the Texas Ranger needs whatever we can find out about this girl. Can you have someone run it ASAP? Maybe Kerry Rapier can crack it open beyond the obvious. Thanks."

The girl's bright eyes seemed to stare out at him as his finger touched the SEND key and the image went away.

He then looked out past the palm trees and the groomed white sand beach to the Atlantic Ocean, and the majestic moon and blanket of stars above it. The wind was picking up. He inhaled deeply, enjoying the cleansing feel of the salty air, then exhaled and shook his head.

So much beauty in this world. And so much hell.

You never know what's coming next.

As Amanda's friend Carl Crantz said just before his lungs gave out:
"Live every day like it's your last."

He turned and started to walk up the tiki-torch-lined path toward the bar. Another message came in with an image.

A third?

He read it:

```
BYRTH 9:23 PM


MATT, THIS IS IT FOR NOW. FIGURED YOU NEEDED TO SEE
WHAT WE'RE DEALING WITH. GOT THIS FROM THE SCENE.


FWD: GLENN PABODY 8:03 PM


JIM . . . HERE'S THE LAST IMAGE.
```

And then he tapped the image.

"Oh shit!" he blurted.

He stopped and stared at the photograph of the acid-burned teen-
age girl's face looking up from inside a blue barrel.

[FOUR]
Love Field Airport, Dallas
Sunday, November 16, 8:55 P.M. Texas Standard Time

The manager of Lone Star Aviation Services—a tall man in his late thirties, with almost a military buzz haircut and dressed in slacks, well-shined brown loafers, knit shirt, and a brown leather A-2 flight jacket—walked with purpose over to the medium-dark-skinned man who stood stiffly, hands on his hips, staring out the bank of windows that overlooked the busy airfield.

Lone Star was a fixed-base operator—an enormous limestone-faced steel building that was the hangar, and a limestone two-story building that served as its corporate offices and lobby reception area, and a concrete pad that could hold fifteen to twenty jet aircraft and two big red fuel trucks—in the northeast corner of the airfield, in the general aviation section. It was separate from the airport's main terminal building, visible in the distance with orange-bellied 737s lined up at the gates.

"Tango Romeo is on the ground, Mr. Badde," the manager of Lone Star Aviation Services announced.

H. Rapp Badde, Jr., thirty-two years old, was a city councilman-at-large with a well-earned reputation in his native Philadelphia for being alternately arrogant and charismatic. Somewhat fit—he had a bit of a belly rounding out the fabric of his white silk shirt—Badde stood five-eleven and two hundred pounds. He wore a custom-cut two-piece black suit and his trademark narrow black bow tie. A brand-new roller suitcase, a cheap counterfeit Louis Vuitton, black with pink accents, stood at his feet.

"Tango Romeo?" Badde automatically repeated. "What the hell is that? Sounds like some kind of Roman lover's Latin dance."

He flashed his politician's bright cap-toothed exaggerated smile, his belly shaking as he chuckled at his own wit.

"My apology, sir. I should have said Mr. Antonov's aircraft has landed."

"Then what's Tango Romeo?"

"The aircraft's identification number is N556TR. In the language of aviation, 'T' is said 'Tango' and 'R' is said 'Romeo' for clarity, to avoid confusion in radio communications."

The look on Badde's face suggested anything but clarity.

The manager pointed out the window at a Cessna Citation X.

"There it is now," he said.

The twin-engine jet aircraft was turning off the runway onto the taxiway. On the side of the engine that was visible Badde saw: N556TR.

The aircraft's paint scheme featured a pair of undulating bright red ribbons. They ran along its gleaming white fuselage, ending on the T-tail, which had two bright red dice, the face of each showing two rows of three white pips.

"Railcars," Badde automatically said aloud to himself.

He had been more or less studying the various games of gambling since becoming involved with the ongoing development of the new Lucky Stars casino, and was quietly impressed with himself for re-membering.

"Excuse me, Mr. Badde?"

"Those dots on the dice," he then said loudly, with authority, "those are called railcars when there's twelve of them."

The manager hesitated before replying, "If I'm not mistaken, I believe, sir, that it's boxcars."

Badde turned his head in thought, then said, "That's what I said. Boxcars."

"Of course. My mistake."

"Wonder if there's any significance to their being boxcars?" Badde went on. "It's not a train, it's a plane. Guess it probably just looks good."

The manager didn't reply.

"What kind of plane is that?" Badde then said. "One of those Boeings?"

"Boeings are much bigger, sir." He pointed toward the 737s at the main terminal gates. "Those are Boeing airliners."

"I came here on that." Badde pointed to the nearest business jet parked on the pad with eight others, a couple at least twice its size. "It's a what?"

"A Hawker."

"And this one coming in?"

"Tango Romeo is a four-month-old Citation Ten, the latest version. It's a midsized jet, a little bigger than the Hawker."

"And faster?"

"Yes, sir. A little. At flight level four-nine-zero it cruises around four-sixty, four-seventy knots." He paused, then added, "That's an altitude of forty-nine thousand feet, and speed just over six hundred miles an hour. With the headwind light tonight, it made the trip from Key West in right at two hours. And that included a stop, a brief one, in New Orleans."

Badde nodded as he wondered, *What did they do in New Orleans? Their casino downtown is at least a half hour from the airport.*

"Had to stop for gas?" he said.

"They weren't on the ground long enough for that. Besides, the Citation's range is around thirty-five hundred miles. Depending on winds, that's New York City to Los Angeles and halfway back again."

"You're just full of interesting flying facts," Badde said. "How do you keep up with it all?"

"It's my job, of course. But aviation is addictive."

"Yeah. So I'm seeing! This Citation, how many can it hold?"

"In addition to the two crew, up to twelve passengers, depending on the cabin configuration."

"What's one worth?"

"New, around twenty million—"

"No kidding?"

"—but there are plenty of nice older ones to be had for eight, ten. We have a couple for sale in that range in the hangar, as well as others."

Badde nodded, impressed. There had been plenty of general aviation airplanes at the fixed-base operator at Northeast Philadelphia Airport when the Hawker arrived that afternoon to pick up Badde. Most of the ones he'd seen, though, had propellers, not jet engines, and were much smaller than the Hawker.

There had to be some.

Maybe, like the Russian's here, they're gone somewhere.

The giant doors on the hangar began sliding open. The interior was brightly lit, and Badde could see even more aircraft inside. Enormous red, white, and blue flags—one of the United States of America with its fifty stars and one of the State of Texas with its Lone Star paying homage to when it was its own sovereign nation—hung in the middle from the steel beam rafters. A tractor tug drove out and connected to the Citation's nose gear.

Looks like what they say about everything being bigger in Texas is true!

And this place is cleaner than the one today in Philly. That glossy floor looks clean enough to eat off of.

"Well, Mr. Badde," the manager said, "welcome again to Texas. And please let me know if there's anything else that we can do for you and the City of Philadelphia. Particularly if you're in the market for a fine aircraft."

"Now, that would be a very nice thing to get!" Badde said. "And none of that TSA security nonsense. Just hop onboard and go. I can get used to this kind of lifestyle."

The manager smiled, then left.

H. Rapp Badde, Jr., watched with almost childlike fascination as the impressive Citation rolled up to near the limestone-faced hangar and was wanded to a stop on the well-lit pad. He heard the whine of the engines winding down.

Idling nearby was a highly polished black Cadillac Escalade ESV with darkened windows and shiny chromed wheels. The big SUV's Texas license plate read Y-ROSE-5. It began moving slowly, then stopped alongside the aircraft as the jet's stair door opened and rotated downward. The driver's door swung open and a clean-cut brown-skinned young man in a two-piece black suit and collarless white dress shirt stepped out. He opened the door behind the driver's.

Jan would like this kind of living large, too, Badde thought.

It's a shame she already had the meeting set up for tomorrow and couldn't come. But Santos assured Jan there would be more opportunities.

On paper, Janelle Harper, a graduate of Temple's Beasley School of Law, was Badde's executive assistant. In reality, the curvy, full-bodied (five-six, one-forty) twenty-five-year-old with silky light brown skin was his paramour.

Although Badde adamantly denied that they had a relationship that was anything but professional, the truth of the matter was not exactly a well-kept secret in Philadelphia. Months earlier, for example, a photograph of them on a Bermuda beach had appeared in the local media. Thus, it was known—though mostly ignored—by Wanda Badde, Rapp's wife of six years.

He had spent the previous night with Jan, in the luxury Hops Haus twentieth-floor condominium he provided for her, after a furious Wanda had thrown him out of their house.

When Jan got the call that the Hawker would pick up Rapp at Northeast Airport that afternoon, he'd had enough clothes at the condo for the trip. But he'd found it necessary to borrow the counterfeit Louis Vuitton suitcase he had bought on the street in New York City for Jan as a surprise, not expecting she could tell it was a fake.

She had never touched it.

[FIVE]

Talk about things being bigger in Texas! Badde thought when he saw the first person appear in the open doorway of the aircraft.

The nicely tanned, long-legged blonde had a full figure with impressive breasts. She wore a short, tight white dress and glittering silver high heels. He guessed she was around Jan's age.

With all the skill and ease of a runway model, she smoothly descended the steps and went across the pad. As she hopped into the backseat of the Escalade, swinging in one long leg at a time, her dress rode up her thighs, and Badde watched with great interest as she rotated her hips and tugged it back down.

My God! That is a good-looking creature!

Badde then heard the peculiar ring tone of one of two cellular phones that he carried. He had selected the sound of a klaxon, thinking the annoying repetitious note was appropriate for what he called his Go To Hell phone. He gave out that phone's number—listed as belonging to Urban Shelters LLC—only to his accountant, his three lawyers, and a select few others who were friends or business associates. When any of them called it, the odds were that something was going to hell—or about to.

He pulled it from his coat pocket. The caller ID showed 3040201.

Last time a weird number like that came up, it was Yuri.

And I don't want to talk to him now.

He waited for the call to go to voice mail. When there was no message left, he quickly turned off the phone.

Whoever it was, I can blame the phone being off from still being in flight.

He looked back to the aircraft. A second passenger had appeared in the doorway.

Another stunning woman!

She started down the stairs and was followed by four more fashionably dressed, long-legged women, all but two of them blondes. They also climbed into the Cadillac.

Is there a mold that these girls come out of, or what?

The clean-cut brown-skinned young man got back behind the wheel as the shiny black Escalade's doors closed. The SUV began to move toward a gate that was being opened in the chain-link fence that surrounded the airfield.

Wonder where they're going?

He looked back to the aircraft. Next off was a tall light-brown-skinned man who looked to be in his thirties. He wore crisp slacks and a white dress shirt and a navy blazer. With the exception of a neatly trimmed goatee, his head was almost cleanly shaven. He waved once toward the Escalade. The driver waved back as the SUV began pulling away.

Now, Baldy here looks like someone important.

A tall black Ford F-150 four-door pickup with six-inch-high chromed badges on the front fenders that read KING RANCH EDITION then drove onto the pad. It pulled to a stop at the aircraft's wingtip. Its driver, a beefy Hispanic with wavy black hair and wearing faded blue jeans, black pointed-toe Western boots, a snug black T-shirt, and a dark blazer, hopped out. He looked younger, maybe in his mid-twenties. He was talking into his cell phone, gesticulating angrily with his free hand, as he went to the foot of the stair door.

I wonder who the chunky cowboy is?

And why didn't that important guy go with the hot girls?

As the tall man came down the steps, the cowboy broke off the call, then held out his right hand and smiled broadly. They shook hands and then walked toward the pickup, talking and nodding as they went. The cowboy then glanced toward the building where Rapp stood watching, then started in that direction as the tall man went to the pickup.

Well, Santos's executive assistant called Jan about the airplane picking me up and told her that I'd be met here.

Guess Cowboy's the guy.

There was a pair of plate-glass doors on tracks next to the reception area. They had a motion detector, and when the chunky cowboy approached, the pair slid open. The cowboy looked around the lounge and found only a black man standing there.

"Excuse me," the cowboy said. "You're waiting for Santos, yes?"

Badde was expecting to hear a strong Mexican accent. It was, instead, surprisingly American.

Well, like my old man made a point of teaching me when he was mayor, immediately establish the power structure.

"Yes, I'm Rapp Badde, and I've been waiting for a Mr. Santos." He nodded toward the suitcase. "You want to grab that?" Then he looked out the window toward the important man. "I assume the boss is expecting me."

The cowboy glanced toward the pickup and chuckled.

"Excuse me. Did I say something funny?" H. Rapp Badde, Jr., snapped.

"Oh, no. Meeting El Jefe is always the highest priority. I'll fetch your"—he paused, looking at the bag—"is this a knockoff? I've never seen pink Louis—"

"I don't know what it is," Badde interrupted, clearly annoyed his luggage would be called into question by anyone, much less a cowboy. "I had to borrow it out of necessity, not that it's anyone's business."

"It happens, I suppose . . ."

Badde, not knowing what to make of that, ignored it and walked toward the automatic door, leaving the cowboy to tend to his suitcase. The door whooshed open, and Badde started for the tall Ford pickup.

As he approached the bald, natty Hispanic, the man turned and had what to Badde looked like a somewhat surprised look.

"I'm Rapp Badde," Badde announced formally, offering his hand.

The man shook it as he wordlessly looked beyond Badde. The cowboy was quickly approaching. The plastic wheels of the suitcase had seized up, and they were grinding noisily across the concrete.

Badde glanced back, then ignored it.

The cowboy said, "Hey, Jefe, you want to put this in the back? Is there room for it?"

"I'll get it," the man began, looking at the cowboy curiously. Then he looked at Badde and said, "I'm Robert Garcia, Mr. Badde."

What? "Garcia"?

"I expected to see Santos," Badde immediately said, as they broke their grip.

Garcia looks like he's a twin of that Wop who's head of the Center City business district.

Well, Jan did tell me that they call Italian immigrants WOPs because it means With Out Papers. And illegal beaners don't have papers.

But this guy's accent doesn't have any Mexican in it.

The man nodded in the direction of the cowboy.

"I thought you did meet Mike."

Badde looked at the cowboy, who was holding out his hand.

"Mike Santos," he then said, grinning as he firmly squeezed Badde's hand. "Pleasure."

He's the one in charge? Damn it!

"I didn't know," Badde began, his arrogant tone making it more a statement than an apology. "I thought Mr. Garcia here . . ."

"Completely understandable. Happens to us all one time or another," Santos said evenly. "Please call me Mike. And this ol' Tejano is my lawyer. You can call him Bobby."

"Tay-hawn-oh?" Badde repeated.

Santos nodded. "A Texan of criollo Spanish descent. His family was here when they still called the place *Tejas*."

Spanish descent!

That explains why he looks like the Center City Wop's twin.

"Me," Santos went on, "I'm just a wetback. I set foot in Texas only after swimming across the Rio Grande."

Badde stared back.

Garcia laughed out loud.

"Don't believe that bullshit," Garcia said. "He was a snot-nosed thirteen-year-old. The real hardship of his arrival here was having to fly coach on Delta Airlines from Rio de Janeiro. Then, after prep school, he spent four years at TCU chasing ass while pretending to be a business major."

Rapp looked between them.

Prep school?

I don't know what to believe.

They're treating me like we've known each other for years.

But I know enough to be damn careful—they didn't get around all this money by being stupid shit kickers.

And what about those women? I want to ask what that was about, but they haven't said a word. . . .

"TCU?" Badde said.

"Texas Christian," Garcia explained. "In Fort Worth, thirty miles from here, aka 'Cowtown, Where the West Begins.' And, Rapp, for the record, I know that about Mike because I was there every step of the way. We were even in the same fraternity. Then I came to Dallas for law school. Southern Methodist is, if it's possible, probably more out of control than TCU."

Santos then laughed, and slapped Badde on the back.

"Oh, hell. It's true. I was in the ranch management program."

"Ranch management?"

Santos nodded, then gestured at the pickup.

"Let's get rolling. I need a drink. We can talk on the way."

The gate in the chain-link fence rolled opened, and the tall black Ford pickup truck roared through it. Mike Santos was behind the wheel.

"My family," Santos explained, "has spreads in Argentina, Brazil, and Colombia. Cattle, mostly. My father wanted to get something going here, so he sent me to boarding school in San Antone—where Bobby and I met in eighth grade—then college. Big ranches are big business, and that ranch management program is like an MBA—an MBA in cow shit."

Santos, grinning, glanced over at Badde, who was in the front passenger seat. Bobby Garcia had taken the seat behind Santos, so that he could see Badde when he turned to talk.

Badde was impressed with the truck. It rode surprisingly comfortably, and its interior had heavy leather and wooden panel accents throughout, giving the cabin the rustic feel of a lodge. There was stitching in the leather that, like the badge on the front fender, read KING RANCH EDITION and had the "Running W" brand that had been, among other things, seared into the hides of countless herds since the ranch's founding in 1853.

"Like this King Ranch?" Badde said. "What's up with that?"

"King's is one of the biggest spreads in the world. Takes up damn near all of South Texas. My father wasn't looking for that—just something big enough down along the border. I oversee my cousins who run it."

"So how did you go from that to what you're doing now?" Badde said. "The private equity?"

Santos grunted. "You ever smell cow shit, Rapp?"

Badde, looking out the windshield at the dramatic colorful skyline of downtown Dallas in the near distance, had to think about that. After a long moment he shook his head, then looked at Santos. "Maybe once, as a kid, out in Pennsylvania's Amish country. If I did, I don't really remember it."

"Well, you're not missing a damn thing."

Badde then snorted.

"What?" Santos said.

"I just remembered I did. It was in Lancaster County. In a tiny town called Intercourse."

Santos laughed.

"I'm calling bullshit on that," Bobby Garcia said from the back-seat, but Badde saw that he was grinning.

Badde turned on his politician's big toothy smile and shook his head. "No. And get this: Intercourse actually isn't far from a place called Blue Ball."

Garcia now laughed.

"You'd think it would be far the hell away," he said.

"They were dairy cows," Badde said. "It was a long damn time until I drank milk again after that trip."

"There you go," Santos said. "I decided that I didn't want to spend a lifetime smelling shit—especially back home. But because I was still a Colombian national and my student visa was all but expired, I had to find something fast so I could legally stay in the States. I wanted to go into venture capital and that got me—got Bobby and me, after starting OneWorld Private Equity Partners—introduced to the Fed's EB-5 green card program."

OneWorld funded a huge part of the casino, Badde thought.

And is funding part of the new sports complex.

Each of those to the tune of a hundred million.

I'd like to get more than the crumbs I'm getting. . . .

"Speaking of that," Garcia said, "Yuri says you're doing good things in Philly with PEGI."

Hearing the Russian billionaire businessman's name always made Badde uncomfortable. Especially in the same sentence as PEGI.

And he just pronounced "Peggy" right.

How much do these guys know about Yuri's involvement? That is, the intimidation beyond the money. He's made it clear that there are conse-quences for failing to meet his high expectations.

"PEGI is working," Badde said, trying not to overplay it.

It's been a pain in the ass. But it is looking like it will work.

If no one pokes their damn nose in it. . . .

The Philadelphia Economic Gentrification Initiative was a special program developed—and solely administered—by the city council's Housing and Urban Development Committee. Specifically by its chairman, one H. Rapp Badde, Jr. He had conceived it after attending an urban-renewal conference with Jan in Bermuda.

PEGI was helping pave the way for new projects—including those of Yuri Tikhonov. The first had been the Lucky Stars Casino & Entertainment. And soon to begin construction was a new indoor sports and live music coliseum that could fit sixty thousand fans under its retractable roof. It was owned by Diamond Development, forty-nine percent of which was in the hands of Tikhonov. The rest, the fifty-one percent majority, belonged to minority-owned companies such as Urban Ventures LLC, of which Badde quietly had a piece, one much smaller than he preferred.

"And," Santos added, "that as mayor, you will make even better things happen. But first you have a hotel to build, yes?"

Badde met his eyes and said, "I certainly hope so. About being mayor, I mean. And I'm definitely going to build the hotel. Just takes money."

And I'm not going to deal with Yuri having a piece of this project.

"I don't think there'll be any trouble finding that money," Garcia said.

Santos slowed the truck. Badde saw that they were just shy of downtown proper. A towering stone-faced complex loomed ahead. Before it, centered in a large berm of lush green grass, was a block of granite the size of a city bus. Chiseled in four-foot-tall black roman lettering was: TWO YELLOWROSE PLACE. Badde then saw individual signage for street-level high-end retail stores and restaurants and for a hotel, clearly a luxury one, he'd never heard of.

Across the street from the complex was an equally impressive high-rise residential building.

Santos steered the truck into the high-rise's cobblestone driveway and pulled to a stop before the enormous well-lit front doors. Doormen on either side of the doors were swinging them open, and out marched three stylishly dressed women. One was olive-skinned, one cocoa-skinned, the third ivory-skinned—and all looking like stunning fashion models. They seemed to float across the walkway as they headed toward the revolving door to the bar of a chophouse next door.

Philadelphia City Councilman H. Rapp Badde, Jr., could not stop himself.

"Is there not a single ugly woman in this town?" he blurted.

Santos and Garcia laughed.

"It'll take a second to get you your room," Santos said, "then we can head over there for a little something liquid to cut the trail dust."

Their doors were opened by valets in red blazers.

"Welcome back, Mr. Santos, Mr. Garcia," one said, and to Badde added, "Welcome, sir."

"Yeah," he replied, flashing his well-practiced politician's smile.

IV

Matt, approaching the entrance to the restaurant's bar, could see Amanda through the big window that overlooked the patio deck. She was standing with Chad at the bar, and it took a moment before she saw him coming up the tiki-torch-lit path. She said something to Chad, who nodded, and then she walked outside to meet Matt.

Matt went up the short flight of steps to the deck, watching appreciatively as the ocean breeze blew her dress and hair. But then he noticed that there was something in her expression that he couldn't quite place.

I know she's upset. But there's more to it than just that. . . .

He reached the top of the steps.

"Hey, you okay?" he said, leaning forward to kiss her cheek.

"Chad is ordering our meals now," she said. "I don't think I can eat, though. I'm sorry, Matt. I've just been sick to my stomach over this." She paused, glanced out at the ocean for a long moment, then went on: "I know what it's like to be taken, to be powerless, and cannot get over that that might be happening right now to Maggie."

She was anxiously flipping the phone in her hand.

He looked at that and said, "I've been juggling calls, too."

"I imagine one was to Jason? Maggie is why he called earlier?"

I knew she'd pick up on that!

I'm not going to lie about it—I don't want to lie to her about any-thing.

"Yeah. Something strange is going on with Maggie's disappear-ance. He won't tell me what it is—won't tell me anything. But he did say he wants to know if we hear from her, which suggests to me that they believe she's alive."

"That's something, I guess," she said, with no enthusiasm.

"You have any luck with anything?"

"I talked with Mrs. McCain. This afternoon Maggie sent a text to her cousin Emma."

"They heard from her? That's good news."

"I don't think it helped. Especially since Mrs. McCain is more than a little upset that no one can reach Maggie. She used one of those websites that lets you send anonymous texts and e-mails." Amanda shook her head. "She may have meant well, but it really backfired with her family."

"What did she say?"

Amanda thought for a moment, then quoted: " 'Tell everyone I'm fine, I love them, and not to worry. Explain later. Will be in touch soonest. Hugs.' "

"That's all?"

"That was it."

Matt grunted. "Pretty damn vague. And doesn't begin to address what happened at her house."

Amanda nodded.

"Because the text was sent anonymously," she then said, "how would they know it's legit? Couldn't someone be forcing her to send it?"

"Yeah, there's always that possibility. But hard to say. What doesn't make sense is why, if she's okay, she's going out of her way not to be reachable. If there was a way to get to her, we could ask for proof of life."

"What would be proof?"

"A photograph of her holding, say, the front page of today's newspaper or even holding a laptop with Mickey's website on the screen with some current news story. Hell, with her story on it. Anything that shows her alive doing something that's recognizable as right now."

She thought for a moment, then in a hopeful tone said, "She did begin the text with 'Spider.'"

"'Spider'?"

"Mrs. McCain said it's the nickname Maggie sometimes calls her cousin. It alludes to Emma's modern dances, to how she moves. And to the spider rolls that are her favorite. They shared one Saturday night at that Rittenhouse sushi place, the one near your apartment."

Matt shook his head. "Not exactly proof of life. But that could help confirm the message is legit. Not many people know she's missing. And bad guys, even if they had the cousin's phone number, would have no reason to contact her, let alone know to call her by a nickname. They'd go right for the big money—her parents."

"So then that's probably why it's being considered legit," Amanda said. "But it's clear she's not 'fine.' Not being reached and only sending messages is anything but fine."

"And that's been the only communication, just the one text?"

Amanda nodded. "As far as I know. Mrs. McCain did ask me to see what you thought about the police asking if she had any knowledge of Maggie letting girls from Mary's House stay at her place. That's suggestive, no?"

Matt nodded thoughtfully.

So, that's who the ME bagged.

The questions, though, are still: Was she the intended target? Or was it Maggie? Or both? Or someone else?

"What are you thinking, Matt? One of them was there and started it?"

"What I'm thinking is about what Mickey O'Hara said. He was one of the calls I was juggling."

"What does he know?"

"Not much. He was calling to see what I knew, and I told him what Jason said. But what he did say was that one of the crime-scene guys quietly told him two things. One, that the place was firebombed—"

"Firebombed!"

"Molotov cocktails. Coke bottles filled with gasoline."

"Oh my God! Then it wasn't just a home invasion?"

"Doesn't look that way. At least I don't think so. And two, that the medical examiner's van was put in the garage, the door closed, then whoever died in the house was snuck out."

"A girl from Mary's House . . ."

"Or girls? But why was it done quietly? And why is Jason not talking?"

They were silent for a long moment. Then Matt exhaled audibly and blurted, "I've really had enough of this."

"What? Enough of what?"

"I'm sorry, baby, but I'm beyond frustrated. And mad. I brought us down here to have a good time. And we were doing that." He paused and ran his hands through his hair. "But now this has happened, and there's not a damn thing I can do, even if I knew it wouldn't make you more upset."

Amanda stepped toward him and ran her fingertips down his cheek.

She met his eyes.

"I understand," she said. "I'm torn, too. That's what I wanted to talk to you about."

Torn? So that's what I saw in her face but couldn't figure out.

"Torn about what?"

"We've been dodging the issue since we found out that I'm pregnant," she began softly. "I meant what I said that night at my place. That we're at a critical time in our lives. That we've both been given second chances. That I want us to get this next one right."

And, he thought, his mind filling with the image of them in the Hops Haus penthouse condominium on the leather couch, *I can see you saying it in that stunning sequined dress that shimmered like the ocean is doing right now. You were really in your cups.*

"Remember?" she said.

Matt nodded solemnly.

He would never forget her explaining, with uninhibited honesty, that she wanted them to have what Anne Bancroft had said was the key to her happy marriage of a half century to Mel Brooks. Amanda had quoted Bancroft saying that her heart still raced at the thought of her mate, just as it had at the start, because there was both love and excitement in their relationship: "When his tires crunch coming up the gravel driveway, I think, 'Now the fun begins.'"

Amanda now went on: "Thanks to my dad having been a cop, I deeply understand what it is you do. And why you do it. It's in your blood, and you do it well, which is a tremendous honor to the memory of your father and uncle. My dad knew them, and you know he speaks highly of them. As does everyone else I highly respect."

Matt felt his throat constrict.

Amanda inhaled deeply, then let it out slowly.

"But I have to be clear," she said softly. "You willingly put your life in danger. And you put it on the line for strangers. Damn it, Matt, if you die, the fact remains that it will destroy me. It will destroy our family—but it will really destroy me. And, yes, I know I'm being selfish with all this."

He cleared his throat and said, "It's understandable—"

"Let me finish, please," she interrupted softly. "I could be dead now from the kidnapping. And you have scars from being shot while on duty. . . . It's a miracle you aren't dead."

The door to the bar opened, and she went suddenly silent.

Out walked an attractive couple who looked to be in their fifties. They sipped at cocktails as they held hands. The husband, smiling broadly, quietly said something to his wife that caused her to laugh, then to move in closer and kiss his cheek.

Amanda forced a thin smile as she and Matt stepped aside and the couple passed and went down the steps. They watched them, still hand in hand, start walking the tiki-lined path toward the beach.

Matt then met Amanda's eyes.

You may know what she's thinking—"That could be us in twenty years, if you don't get killed"—but keep your mouth shut, Matty.

That way you won't have to spend the rest of the night trying to extricate your foot from it.

" 'Tis better to remain mute and thought the fool than to speak and confirm it. Again."

She gathered her thoughts, then went on: "I said I'm torn because I without question believe in what I said about us being given second chances. We can't lose that. I want a million days like we had today on the boat."

"Yeah!" he said. "And so do—"

She held up her hand.

Try it again, Matty: Mouth shut!

"I'm not finished. Matt, I never thought I'd say this, but I want you to go back to work. Not for strangers—for Maggie. Find her. But for God's sake"—she paused and placed his left palm on her dress over her belly—"and especially for ours, promise me that you will be careful."

Her belly rose and fell with her breaths. He felt its warmth through the soft linen fabric. He looked in her eyes as she squeezed his hand.

Tears were welling as she whispered, "Now the fun begins."

He leaned in, put his arms around her, and kissed her on the lips softly and slowly.

They had not finished when her phone began ringing. It wasn't until the fourth ring that she pulled back and glanced at its screen.

Then she handed the phone to him.

"Answer it," she said, wiping a tear from her cheek.

"Who . . . ?"

Matt took it and saw that the caller ID read: MRS. MCCAIN.

She knew this was coming. . . .

Matt cleared his throat, then spoke into Amanda's phone: "Mrs. McCain? Hello, this is—"

A male's stern, gravelly voice cut him off.

"Hello? Who is this?" he demanded. "Matt? Matt Payne?"

Matt looked at Amanda. She was watching intently.

"Yes, sir. Matt Payne speaking."

"Will McCain here," he went on, his tone impatient. "Listen, it's been one long, hellish day. I'll cut right to the chase. I want you to find my girl and get to the bottom of whatever the hell is going on. I'm not getting the answers in the manner I'm accustomed. I was about to hire the best private detectives my people could find. Then I overheard my wife speaking with Amanda tonight, and she mentioned your name. When can you get here?"

Matt was quiet for a moment.

How can I possibly do this outside of the department? Without its resources, I'm at a huge disadvantage.

"Matt? You there? Hello? Hello? Damn these phones!"

"Yes, sir, Mr. McCain. I'm here. I would do whatever I possibly could to help. But please understand that right now there are limits as to what I'm able to do. For one, I'm in Florida—"

"Not a problem."

"Yes, sir, I agree that's minor. But there's more. I'm assigned to the Homicide Unit, and I've been taken off the job—"

"I understand that you're on leave. I just talked to Jerry about that. If he doesn't have you put on this . . . this *situation* . . . I told him that I'll hire you privately."

No surprise he has a direct line to the mayor.

That's the way it works at that level. Call in a favor or a contribution—or, if necessary, a threat.

"Sir, as I'm sure Mayor Carlucci could tell you, there are very capable men, detectives with far more experience than I have, who can do a better job —"

"Matt, I'm not one for false modesty," McCain replied sharply. "Particularly right now, when I need results. Everyone knows you're not one who's afraid to get his hands dirty and get the job done. There's a reason that O'Hara character called you the Wyatt Earp of the Main Line years ago and it stuck."

"Sir, that's—"

He felt a nudge and looked at Amanda.

As she mouthed, *Say yes,* Matt felt his phone vibrating. He pulled it from his pocket, checked its screen, then held it up for Amanda to see. She nodded as she read: DENNY.

"What are you saying, Matt?" Will McCain's voice came over Amanda's phone.

"I was saying, yessir, Mr. McCain. I'll speak with Commissioner Coughlin right now."

Five minutes later, winding up the conversation, Denny Coughlin said, "Be aware, Matty, that Carlucci wasn't exactly happy with Will McCain's demand that you be put on the case. He even turned me down this morning when I asked if you could help work it. It's not that Carlucci doesn't have faith in you—he is at his core one helluva cop and knows another when he sees one—but he's also a savvy politician. I think he is worried that the perception of the Wyatt Earp of the Main Line is becoming a bit of a political liability."

"Yes, sir. I understand, Uncle Denny."

"Just keep your nose clean. Jason Washington is including you in the conference call tomorrow morning. Seven sharp."

"Got it. So that I don't come in completely ignorant, can someone send me what we have so far?"

"Jason is working on that. But for now get some rest. It's late. What did I tell you a long time ago about fatigue?"

Matt nodded. "That fatigue shuts down the brain when you over-work. 'Get rest and then you get results.'"

"We all want to get the McCain girl back. But let's be smart. And safe."

"Yes, sir."

"Good night, Matty."

The connection went dead.

Matt looked at Amanda as he dialed Tony Harris's cell phone.

"Well, that's that," he said to her, then into the phone said, "Hey, Tony. You awake?"

Matt listened for a moment, then said, "I'll be quick. I'm now in on the McCain case. Anything I should know before tomorrow morning's conference call?"

So much for me keeping my nose clean.

He listened for another long moment, and when he heard Harris say that they were coming up with nothing more on Maggie McCain than they had come up with on the other two missing women, Matt thought, *Two others? I can't let Amanda know that. No wonder Jason wouldn't tell me. He couldn't.*

Matt looked at Amanda as he said, "Thanks. Okay, Tony, now go on back to sleep. Don't you know what Denny says about fatigue and getting proper rest?"

Matt Payne heard Tony Harris then suggest "with all possible due respect" that Payne should perform on himself a sexual act that was a physical impossibility.

"Yeah, well, same to you, buddy," Matt replied, but he was smiling. "Sweet dreams."

He broke off the call. Amanda raised her eyebrows in question.

"Nothing new since Maggie's e-mail," Matt said.

Which is not exactly a lie.

But it's not the truth, the whole truth, and nothing but the truth, so help me God. . . .

"Nothing more to do now that's not being done," he said. "I'm on it first thing tomorrow."

"Well, that does make me feel a little better."

He held out his arm for her to take.

"Let's go grab dinner. You're eating for two, you know."

[TWO]
Players Corner Lounge
Front and Master Streets, Philadelphia
Sunday, November 16, 10:01 P.M.

"I can pull over there under the El and wait, Mr. Gurnov," the driver of the dark blue Audi R8 sedan said, stopping in front of the Fishtown dive bar. A dusting of snow had accumulated on the bar's dirty redbrick front. Its blacked-out windows, with silver reflective silhouettes of well-endowed naked women holding martinis and poker cards on them, practically rattled with the music system blaring the Jersey rock band Bon Jovi.

"This won't take long," Dmitri Gurnov said, meeting the driver's eyes in the rearview mirror.

Gurnov, tall and wiry, carried himself with a steel-like intensity. The thirty-year-old had pale skin, sunken eyes, and a three-day scruff of beard. He wore a black leather jacket, a black collarless shirt, blue jeans, and polished black leather boots. He could feel the weight of the compact Sig-Sauer 9mm he carried in the right pocket of his coat.

Gurnov glanced up and down the snow-covered street, then opened the right rear door. He stepped onto the sidewalk that was little more than crumbling concrete. He looked across the street, where an overflowing industrial dumpster sat in front of another old bar. The space was being gutted. A new sign on one of the boarded-over windows announced that a wine café was coming soon.

We can't keep this shithole bar here much longer with that going on.
Especially with the girls working.

The Fishtown section of Philly, bordering the Delaware River, was beginning to feel the benefits of the gentrification of neighboring Northern Liberties. In addition to NoLibs' many small independent businesses similar to the wine café, nearby were the two busy casinos overlooking the river and, a dice throw away across the expressway from them, the upscale Schmidt's Brewery apartments, movie cinemas, and the Hops Haus complex of high-rise condominiums and trendy retail stores and restaurants.

The deterioration of Fishtown had started decades earlier. With the loss of jobs went the loss of community, first the tight-knit families of Italians moving out and then many of the tough working-class Irish who had taken their place following. Some hung on, but the first wave of bohemian outsiders were moving in, buying at affordable prices and pushing the 'hood to rise up, mirroring the success of NoLibs.

With a wealth of new development being planned out on various architects' blueprints—including, Gurnov knew, ground finally broken on a Diamond Development entertainment complex just blocks away at Jefferson and Mascher—the clock was ticking on the old pockets of Fishtown that remained seedy.

A dive bar like the Players Corner Lounge was but one example of what the changing demographics would eventually push north into the harder hit areas of Kensington and Frankford, sections that long had been—and likely would continue to be—in a really bad way.

The moment the car door shut with a *thunk*, the Audi pulled a quick U-turn.

The dive bar's dented metal door was set back in what would have been the corner of the old three-story building. As Gurnov started toward it, a SEPTA train on the Frankford-Market El loudly rumbled and screeched overhead. He briefly looked up at the brightly lit railcars, then down at the Audi parking beneath the El and killing its headlights. He grabbed the metal bar that served as the door handle and pulled. The loud thrumming music poured out as if it had been trapped in the small confines of the dusky, dank room.

It took a moment for Gurnov's eyes to adjust. The lounge was mostly dark except for dimmed lighting behind the wooden bar that was along the left wall and a pair of bright red and blue floodlights harshly illuminating the stripper pole on the small stage to the right. An olive-skinned brunette, with obvious stretch marks on her pudgy belly, was hanging upside down near the ceiling from the chromed pole, pumping her arm to the beat of rock star Jon Bon Jovi belting out *It's! My! Life!*

Of the twenty tables filling the floor, only five or six had anyone sitting at them, the patrons all males except for one young female clinging to her hipster date at a back table. Near the stage, Gurnov saw a table of four who looked like they were college kids, probably fraternity brothers. Another stripper, a platinum blonde Latina down to only a T-back thong, was working their table, vigorously rubbing her ample hip against one of the drunken guys as she tried to sell lap dances . . . and more.

None of the customers paid the tall, wiry man any attention as he moved across the room in the direction of a half dozen electronic poker machines.

He came to a dusty gray curtain on the wall at the end of the bar. "Yo, bro, you call about a girl?" a rough-looking woman Gurnov hadn't noticed behind the bar called out loudly. "You can't go back there!"

She was in her thirties, short and dark-haired, wearing tight white shorts and a black low-cut T-top. Tattoos covered both arms and her entire chest. She was pouring vodka into a shot glass that was on the bar. Beside it a cell phone was lit up with an incoming call.

"The hell I can't," Gurnov snapped, pulling back the curtain.

She stared at him, tossed back the shot, and, pouring another, said, "Yeah? Fuck it, then. You deal with whatever happens."

Gurnov uncovered a swinging door with NO ADMITTANCE stenciled on it in large letters. He swung it open inward and entered a short hallway. It was lined with cases of cheap alcohol and mixers stacked along one side and led to another door at the other end.

He found that the second door, stenciled with ABSOLUTELY NO ADMITTANCE!, was shut. But when he tried the knob, it was unlocked.

Moron! Gurnov thought. *I've told him over and over the office stays locked!*

He shoved that door open—and was greeted by the sight of very large, very brown, and very hairy male buttocks.

He quickly looked around the small dirty office. With minor differences—the very large brown hairy buttocks notwithstanding— he noticed nothing had really changed since a week, if not a month, ago.

It held an old steel safe and a battered wooden desk, the latter's top strewn with various papers and forms, a couple of matchbox-sized clear plastic packets containing white powder, a black laptop computer, a small box holding used cell phones, and a small digital camera. There were two chairs, one with the seat covered in old newspapers. A dim light came from a lone bare lightbulb hanging overhead from a short length of electrical cord.

The large brown hairy buttocks were thrusting rhythmically with the mechanical moans of a skinny bleached-blonde teenaged girl. She had a young, pretty face, somewhat childlike, and was bent over the wooden desk, her black and white checked skirt hiked up, and a pair of high heels beside her bare feet. Her white shirt was unbuttoned, her tiny breasts pressing on the desktop. She licked at a white powder residue on her index finger.

"What the fuck, Ricky?" Gurnov announced from the open door.

Ricardo Ramírez—a chunky five-foot-eight twenty-seven-year-old Puerto Rican with a pockmarked face—quickly glanced over his shoulder as he continued the thrusts. His dark, hard eyes were glazed.

When he recognized who it was standing in the doorway, he stopped. He slapped the girl's left buttock.

"Want some of this, man? It's new."

Are you kidding me? Gurnov thought.

The teenaged girl jerked her head around. Her hollow eyes were also glazed.

"You done yet, Ricky?" she said, her voice sleepy.

Ramírez shrugged as he looked at the girl, and went back to thrusting.

Gurnov shook his head, more than a little disgusted and annoyed.

He felt the weight of his Sig in his jacket pocket.

I should pistol-whip the bastard—one good whack.

But then I'd have to get the blood off.

He crossed the dirty office to the chair that was stacked with tabloid newspapers. He saw they were old copies of *Philly Weekly*. He rolled up one, then marched over and smacked Ramírez across the back of his head.

"Knock it off! I have dogs better behaved than you."

Then Gurnov looked at the girl, who was looking over her shoulder to see what the loud noise had been.

"You," he ordered, "get the hell out of here!"

The girl then looked at Ramírez, who was backing away, shuffling his feet while reaching down to pull his jeans up from his ankles.

"Do what he says, Summer," Ramírez said, zipping his pants. "Go on up front. Talk to Ashley. See if any work's come in for you. Tell her the room in the basement's open."

Dazed, Summer stood, dropped her black and white checkered schoolgirl skirt back in place, and tied the front of her shirt in a knot. She grabbed one of the plastic packets of cocaine while working her feet into the high heels, then wobbled on them toward the door.

"And back off the blow, bitch," Ramírez said, taking the packet from her hand as she went through the door. "You need to start making money tonight to pay your bill!"

Ramírez closed the door.

"Lock that damn thing," Gurnov snapped. "I tell you that over and over." Then he added, "Another 'Summer'? How old is that one?"

"Eighteen," Ramírez immediately said, grinning at his automatic lie. "She's good. She'll earn her keep. She's already in the hole almost a grand, countin' her bed and rubbers and shit. Everything. And, yeah, Summer, April, whatever—you know dudes love bitches named that."

He reached for a black laptop computer on the desk. Its scratched plastic case was covered in liquor advertisement stickers. He opened it and pointed to the screen as it flickered to life.

"Here. Check out her ad I put online today," Ramírez said, trying to focus on the screen. "She's a 'private massage therapist' with 'best hands in the business.' I got really creative."

Photographs showed the body of the young girl. She wore the same schoolgirl outfit and high heels. The white top was tied up tight, revealing her midriff and accentuating her breasts. The black and white checkered skirt also was tight on her curves, and short enough to reveal the bottom edge of her buttocks. There were close-up shots of her youthful hands and thighs and chest. Everything but a photograph of her face.

"I wrote here 'I like what I do and so will you. In call, out call.' And that she loves to travel and to please. That's true, too." He grinned. "Anyway, she said she's from Bucks County, and out on her own. Tried to get in that flophouse up in Frankford. Lighthouse Life? They were full up and I got the call from Tony. Cost me a hundred bucks for that. Now, a little of Cuzzin Héctor's hydro, at worst some coke, and she's good to go."

Gurnov bristled at hearing Héctor's name and the hydroponic weed. He already regretted fronting Ricky any money. And he really was pissed when Ricky loaned Héctor—who really wasn't Ricky's cousin; he was a Ramírez from Cuba—the twenty-five grand to set up the house in Kensington. Growing pot indoors, using artificial lighting, guaranteed a steady nearby supply of the highly potent marijuana to move. Gurnov recognized that it also was one more thing that could blow up in his face. Héctor was already on the run after someone ratted out the grow house he'd worked near Miami.

"The girl looks sixteen," Gurnov said.

Ricky shrugged. "I got ID saying she's eighteen."

The bastard never learns, Gurnov thought.

This is what caused the problem in the first place.

They're too damn young—and too stupid to not talk.

He didn't say anything for a moment. Then: "What're you on? You look like shit, Ricky."

"A little blow. And some E to stay awake. Last night was rough."

Gurnov thought Ramírez looked like he'd need at least Ecstasy to have been up the whole time.

"Look, I'm serious. You need to be careful. Tell me what happened last night."

Ramírez's expression changed.

"I'm . . . I'm really sorry, man. I thought I had that fuckin' thing under control. Really!"

What?

"What do you mean by that?" Gurnov said, his tone ice cold. "You take care of it or not?"

Ramírez avoided making eye contact.

"I shot that *puta* Krystal, man," he said, nervously kicking his shoe tip against a desk leg. "In the back of the head, behind the ear, just like you said to."

"What about the other . . . ?"

Looking at his shoe, Ramírez slowly shook his head.

He then said: "Damon thought Krystal was it, man. So he threw the Molotovs. We had to get out."

"Damn it, Ricky!" Gurnov blurted. "Tell me you got the books back. I don't care about the other shit."

Ricky silently shook his head.

Gurnov inhaled deeply, then exhaled, trying to keep his composure.

"You know there's gonna be hell to pay for this," he said. "Mr. Antonov does not like surprises. Especially one like this."

And that's why I never told him about any of it.

I knew better than to let Ricky drag me into his running drugs and girls.

The damn money was just too easy to pass up. . . .

Ramírez looked up. There was terror in his eyes.

"I know! I know! I'm sorry, man. I'll find her. Promise. I'll get the books *and* the money back."

"You'll find her?" Gurnov exploded. "Where're you looking? Up some little whore's ass? What the hell are you thinking?"

Ramírez's hazy eyes were tearing. He rubbed them.

Gurnov shook his head.

Fuck! This cannot get back to Nick.

It's probably time to shut this place down. . . .

"No, Ricky. I'll take care of it. You . . . you get the girls out of town as planned."

[THREE]
Washington Dulles International Airport, Virginia
Sunday, November 16, 10:17 P.M.

"Just one more second and we should be done," the gray-haired, plump female American Airlines desk agent said helpfully, smiling as she tapped keys on the computer terminal. "You really should consider joining our frequent-flyer program. It keeps all your information handy to speed up this process. Plus you get miles toward trips, so as you zip right through the process, eventually you'll travel for free!"

The woman looked up and smiled broadly at the nicely dressed young woman with the pleasant face, intense green eyes, and, under a GEORGETOWN HOYAS ball cap, chestnut brown hair that fell softly to her shoulders. There was a backpack hanging by one strap over her right shoulder.

Will you please just hurry up and get me on the plane!

"Perhaps later," the young woman said.

The agent nodded, then turned her attention back to the computer terminal.

I wonder what she'd say if she knew I'm a platinum-level member and have enough miles banked in my account for probably ten first-class tickets.

"You also should seriously look at getting yourself a passport," the desk agent added helpfully. "It's not required for Saint Thomas— your valid driver's license is all the ID you need—but it does speed the process, too."

Got one.

But sirens would probably go off if you scanned it.

"You're just going to love the Virgin Isles," the agent went on. "Hurricane season is as good as over, and you're there right before the high season starts, mid-December, when it gets really expensive."

I know. I was just there for two weeks.

"Do you like living in Philadelphia? So much history."

And crime. Can't forget that.

Just like our nation's capital.

The young woman looked as if she were trying to be patient. But the talkative agent, who seemed to be attempting to single-handedly deliver friendly customer service for the entire airline, unfortunately was coming across as increasingly annoying.

Okay, I'll play along.

"I prefer living here on the Hill much better," the young woman said. "I don't know what I'll do when my internship ends, but Georgetown Law sounds like it might work."

"Politics. Now, that must be exciting. You know this airport was named for John Foster Dulles, who was secretary of the State Department."

Now she's giving a history lesson? Ugh.

Can I just get my ticket, please?

I guess she means well.

Well, except for when I told her I needed the card to sign declaring that I'm checking a firearm.

She about wet her pants. "You have a pistol? And you travel with it?"

Then it really made her mad when I corrected her by quoting the regulations, telling her it was okay to have both the unloaded gun and its ammo in the same bag, as long as they were in a locked case.

"I looked it up on the Internet."

She practically hissed, "Well, we'll let our friends at TSA clear that."

She wasn't quite so chatty after hanging up with them, having learned that I was right.

The American Airlines desk agent held out a paper ticket.

"Okay, you're all set," she said, her tone now professional. "Your first leg, I have you ticketed to Miami on flight six-eight-eight with a connecting flight, five-oh-four, the first flight out to Saint Thomas. I have your bag checked all the way through to your final, SST." She pulled back to show the back of the ticket. "I've stuck your bag tag here, on the back of your ticket. And your inbound"—she paused and glanced at the young woman—"that's your return flight, I have you booked for next Thursday."

"Thank you very much," the young woman said, smiling warmly as she took the ticket. "You've been most helpful. I do appreciate it."

The desk agent smiled back.

"And here's your ID and debit card," the agent then said, her tone again cheerful. "Have a nice vacation."

Well, that seems to have mended the bridge.

"Thank you again very much," the young woman said.

"Oh, and by the way: Happy birthday, Miss Stewart!"

The young woman looked up. "Excuse me?"

"That's okay. I see you're being shy. But celebrate life! Congrats on turning twenty-one last week. It should be a happy, exciting time!"

Yes, it should, she thought, carefully placing the ID and prepaid Visa debit card in her leather clutch near the zippered pocket that held the IDs and debit cards of two other young women.

I'd share that with Alexis Stewart, if she hadn't stumbled back to Mary's House and overdosed last month, having never gotten over those years of being raped in foster care.

And with Krystal and all the others . . .

"Well, thank you," the young woman said, forcing a smile. "It is. This trip actually is a birthday gift. I'm just a bit harried right now."

"Don't you worry. You'll figure out this travel stuff soon enough. You're young. Have a nice flight."

[FOUR]

Southwest Chop House

Two Yellowrose Place, Dallas

Sunday, November 16, 9:30 P.M. Texas Standard Time

"We can structure the funds, base them anywhere from Delaware to the Cayman Islands," Miguel "Mike" Santos, chief executive officer of OneWorld Private Equity Partners, said, looking between Rapp Badde and Bobby Garcia. "Our preference, of course, having the majority of our investment products there, is the Caymans."

They were in the posh high-ceilinged lounge of the five-star restaurant. It was about half full, but there was high energy coming from the lively crowd.

Ten white-linen-covered tables with deep, high-backed, U-shaped leather seating, each capable of holding six or eight comfortably, lined the walls on either side of a black marble-topped bar in the center of the room. A grand piano was in one corner. At the table nearest the piano, Santos sat opposite Rapp Badde, Santos with a view of the entryway between the bar and restaurant and Badde with a view of the nice-looking crowd—mostly women, including the three who had floated past the SUV—ringing the bar. Bobby Garcia sat between them, with a view of both.

Their waitress, young and attractive, had just delivered their second round of drinks.

Earlier, Badde had been first to order, requesting a Jameson Irish whisky and club soda, and then Garcia and Santos had said yes when the waitress asked if they were having their usual. Badde didn't know what that was, but both of their cocktails were clear liquid with bubbles and a lime wedge. He guessed vodka, or maybe gin, with either tonic or soda water.

"Politically," Badde now said, a bit arrogantly, "it would be a good idea to use Delaware. What with Wilmington being right down the road from Philly."

Santos and Garcia exchanged a glance.

"Well," Santos then said, turning to look at Badde, "you're right. There is good reason why so many—sixty percent, in fact—of Fortune 500 companies incorporate in Delaware. Their laws are better geared to corporations than most other states. But as friendly as Delaware can be, Cayman keeps everything quiet."

Garcia, who was stirring his drink, looked up and added, "That's why it's called the Switzerland of the Caribbean. Its confidential Relationships Preservation Law, Section Five, has criminal penalties—imprisonment and cash fines—for anyone who even attempts to offer to divulge confidential information. They don't so much as report who the officers of a company are, never mind where the money comes from or where it's going."

Santos nodded. "You can't accomplish that anywhere in the States. So we're not being political. We're talking business."

Badde met his eyes, then nodded.

Got it.

And maybe some money can find its way into a confidential account in my name.

"The Caymans have more than five hundred banks," Santos went on. "While financial markets everywhere have been melting down in the last few years, not a single one in Cayman went out of business. In fact, they were providing trillions of dollars in cash infusions to cash-strapped countries."

Badde nodded thoughtfully as he sipped his Irish whisky and club soda.

"Let me ask you this . . ." Badde then began.

"Of course."

". . . where does Yuri base his?"

Santos raised his eyebrows. "I'm sorry. But I'm sure you'll understand that we do not discuss anything about our other clients."

Then why the hell did you bring him up driving here?

"It would violate our client confidentiality," Garcia put in. "Which we're sure you can well appreciate."

"Not a problem," Badde said. "I can ask him."

I can . . . but I won't.

"What we *can* tell you," Santos said, "is that our Focused Investment Niche Strategies are Cayman-based funds. They're highly diversified, including many EB-5s. And, as your PEGI records will show, all OneWorld investment vehicles for Diamond Development are FINS."

Why the hell didn't Jan tell me that before I came down here?

I wonder if she knew.

He took another sip of his whisky, then nodded.

"I knew that, of course. That Diamond had FINS. I just didn't realize the fine print of FINS being in Cayman."

Listen to me. I'm already talking like them.

Not bad for the son of a South Philly barbershop owner.

But I'm not really sure exactly where Cayman is. Maybe near Puerto Rico?

Too many little islands down there.

"I know you've heard all this," Santos said, "but please let me just lay it all out."

"That's why I came," Badde said, smiling broadly. "Have at it."

"As I said, FINS is diverse," Santos then began. "We create vehicles—these specialized instruments known as funds—that invest in everything from oil and gas to cruise lines, resorts, restaurant chains, and much more.

"Some domestic money is there, but it's tight. There is, however, significant foreign money out there. For OneWorld, Asian investments right now are biggest, followed by Central and South American monies. Accordingly, that's where the EB-5 monies originate."

The what? "EB-5 Central and South American monies"?

So much for talking like them.

"EB-5?" Badde said. "Didn't you say you have one yourself, Mike?

Santos nodded. "Yes, as you know, the EB-5 is a visa designed for immigrants of serious means. It's nothing like the well-known specialty occupation H-1B and -2 visas, which the United States Citizenship and Immigration Service also administers."

Well, now I know.

And you don't know that I didn't.

"For starters," Garcia said, "while there're only ten thousand EB-5s available each year, the U.S. has never issued the entire lot of them. Compare that to 'specialty occupation' visas. Those are gone by mid-year, and they run in the six figures."

"The H-1B and -2," Badde said.

"Right," Garcia said. "H-1Bs are architects, doctors, engineers, university professors, all sorts of computer types—hell, even fashion models. Their stay is only good for three years, with a three-year re-newal. So, six tops. And if they quit their sponsoring employer, or get fired, they have to find another or leave the U.S."

"Not that they always do," Santos added. "Plenty overstay their visas illegally. But then if found, they can be deported. Same with H-2B visas, the seasonal jobs, like agriculture."

"But not EB-5. It's golden," Garcia said, then smiled. "No pun intended."

"You said 'serious means,'" Badde said. "How much we talking?"

"Each EB-5 requires at least a million dollars," Garcia said.

Badde nodded thoughtfully.

"That's the other main difference," Santos said. "You cannot buy an H-1B or 2. But, as long as you meet the requirements, a foreigner can buy as many EB-5s as he can afford."

"Up to ten thousand," Badde said, a little loudly.

He grinned, then took a long drink of his whisky.

Santos and Garcia chuckled, then exchanged a brief knowing glance.

Garcia drained his drink, and Santos discreetly motioned for the waitress's attention. Badde saw her look over, then smile and nod. She started toward them, carrying fresh drinks.

Now, that's service!

She was keeping an eye on us, and didn't even have to be told to have the bartender pour us another round.

"For the million dollars," Garcia said, as the waitress put the drinks before them, "the investor gets fast-tracked to permanent residency—a green card for himself, for his wife, and for his kids under twenty-one. In order to keep that status, the investment must create and maintain at least ten jobs for existing Americans, plus ones for himself and his family. These can be directly and indirectly created. For example, a hotel creates direct jobs—from the front desk to the restaurant staffs to housekeepers—as well as indirect ones— vendors who wash the sheets and towels, landscapers, valets. It's not hard to do."

"And it's extremely lucrative," Santos said.

"How so?" Badde said.

"These foreign investors mostly want to become permanent residents," Santos explained. "That's their focus. So while a typical investor would expect seven, eight, even ten percent return on investment, these immigrants are content with, say, two percent. Additionally, if you're the one borrowing the money, you're paying less interest, so your profits are higher."

"That's damn cheap capital, Rapp," Garcia said. "And it's capital that may have left the country and now has an avenue back to create opportunity here." He made a sweeping gesture around the lounge with his hand. "You're sitting in an example."

"How do you mean?" Badde said.

"Yellowrose is one of four significant companies in the hospitality market owned by China Global Investments. We packaged Yellowrose, then sold it to them and continue to help them expand it."

"The Chinese have all these new high-rises?" Badde said, his tone not concealing his surprise. "I thought the yellow rose had something to do with Texas."

"It does," Garcia said. "The Texas War of Independence. It's legendary. There was even a hit song in the 1950s about it. Mitch Miller's 'Yellow Rose of Texas.'"

"So then what's the connection with the flower?" Badde said.

Garcia looked toward the bar. "See that long-legged filly in the tight black dress? One of the three we saw earlier?"

Badde stole a look, then turned back to Garcia. "Oh, yeah. Beautiful woman. That creamy light chocolate skin is incredible."

"In the day, that was called 'high yellow.' Legend is that a high yellow mulatto by the name of Emily West—she was an indentured servant who got herself captured when the Mexican army took Galveston in 1836—seduced General Santa Anna. My mother's side of the family is descended from Santa Anna, which makes this story not one of our prouder moments."

"What was wrong with being seduced?"

"The problem was Santa Anna became so enamored with the beautiful half-breed that her distraction allowed General Sam Houston's Texas Army to win the decisive Battle of San Jacinto. And ol' Sam trounced Santa Anna. It was really an ass-kicking—the whole thing lasted only eighteen minutes. When the dust settled, six hundred Mexicans were dead. That's—what?—more than thirty killed every minute. Houston lost only nine men. Santa Anna was taken prisoner and, being president of Mexico, signed a peace treaty. And so began the Republic of Texas—thanks to the Yellow Rose of Texas."

"Damn!" Badde said, impressed. "The power of . . . women, huh?"

Garcia and Santos chuckled.

Santos said: "That the company name, as you note, Rapp, suggests local ownership doesn't exactly hurt, either."

Garcia nodded. "Right. And as I was saying, in addition to this development, there are twenty-five Yellowrose luxury hotels and resorts around the world. New York City, London, Paris, Tahiti, the Caribbean, Uruguay, Cabo San Lucas. This Dallas complex was in part financed with EB-5 funding that we at OneWorld put together. Every worker here counts toward the jobs needed to qualify."

Badde glanced around the room, nodding appreciatively.

"For securing the approval of Immigration Services," Santos said, "which designated OneWorld an elite regional center because of our history with them, we get a transaction fee of ten percent. Plus of course management fees for the investment vehicles themselves."

Rapp Badde picked up his drink and sipped as he started to do the math. Feeling the effects of the alcohol, he gave up calculating after coming up with a hundred thousand for each million dollars invested.

If a building gets a hundred million, their cut is a cool mil just in fees.

Who knows what they bring in for management fees . . . ?

"Rapp," Mike Santos said, "when Bobby here said earlier that we know where to find money, he wasn't kidding. We have a long list of investors in our various funds. Among them are those already preapproved by the Immigration Service for EB-5 visas."

"More than two thousand waiting," Bobby Garcia added. "And another thousand in the process leading up to preapproval. Our goal is to use up all those ten thousand available visas before anyone else."

"What's the holdup?" Badde said.

"We need approved projects. Immigration Services has to sign off on the investments to ensure that the jobs are in fact created. You happen to know anyone who might be looking to build something?"

Badde looked between Santos and Garcia, then grinned broadly, flashing his bright white-capped teeth.

I could tear down all of North Philly and build new!

"Like maybe a new hotel?" he said, then held up his cocktail glass. Garcia and Santos touched theirs to it.

"Rapp, assuming the project meets requirements," Santos said, "and from what I've seen, it does, we're prepared to put up a hundred mil, for starters. How does that sound?"

Badde looked between them for a moment, then smiled.

"I'd say it sounds like a deal."

"All right. Let's talk about something more interesting!" Santos announced, then glanced at the bar ringed with women.

Badde's eyes followed his, then he smiled and again held up his glass.

After they clinked, Badde drained his drink.

Garcia and Santos did the same with theirs.

These guys can drink! Badde then thought.

Screw it. I'm feeling good. What've I got to lose asking?

"Those beautiful women who got off the plane?" he said. "Where did they go?"

A busboy appeared at the table and whisked away the empty glasses. Immediately behind him was their waitress with fresh drinks.

Garcia and Santos exchanged glances.

"Interesting that you asked, Rapp," Garcia said, and pulled out his cell phone. He started thumbing a text.

"They went to join others at the hotel across the street," Santos said. "They're in the hospitality industry, usually working with the casinos and hotels. What's called Guest Services."

I knew it! Badde thought smugly.

The casino was why the plane stopped in New Orleans!

"Bobby's having a few who've been in town awhile come join us. Some are from the Ukraine, some from Belarus. They're all in the States as seasonal workers."

"They came on those H-something visas?"

"Yeah," Santos lied.

[ONE]
Slip F-18
Little Palm Island, Florida
Monday, November 17, 6:17 A.M.

Matt Payne was in the galley of the Viking Sport Fisherman, sipping coffee while standing before his laptop computer that was on the black granite countertop. Within reach were the coffeepot and a large bowl of fresh fruit. The peels of two bananas were beside the computer. From his digital music player, he had the sound system speakers overhead cranking out island tunes from his Pirate Playlist.

He yawned, then rubbed his eyes.

Almost two hours earlier, in Cabana Two, the spacious palm-thatched seaside room Amanda had chosen, Matt had suddenly awakened from a sound sleep. He stared at the ceiling fan, his mind spinning faster than the fan blades as he tried to make a complete list of everything he had to do before they were to board Chad Nesbitt's Learjet at Key West International around noon.

He had yawned then, and when he checked his watch, he was not surprised that it showed it was four-thirty.

I'm lucky I got that much sleep.

It had been right at midnight, after he and Amanda and Chad finally had had dinner, that Matt had stripped to his boxer shorts and crawled into the king-sized bed.

Amanda was taking her time in the bath. Considering how the evening had played out, especially with Amanda being upset, Matt decided that there was absolutely no chance in hell of there being anything resembling romance—not to mention carnal intimacy. He told himself that he would not be surprised if Amanda came to bed wearing worn-out sweatpants, a baggy wife-beater T-shirt, a towel wrapped around her hair, and her face, neck, and upper chest smeared with a thick therapeutic coating of eucalyptus-scented cream—plus maybe thick slices of cucumber to soothe her puffy eyelids.

Accordingly, he had set the alarm on his cell phone for five-thirty, then turned onto his side at the edge of the bed and, yawning deeply as he closed his eyes, buried his head in the soft goose-down pillow.

When some minutes later he felt behind him the bedsheet being raised, and then the weight of Amanda and her twenty gallons of face cream sinking in, he was surprised that she continued sliding across the big bed toward him, her gentle, wonderful fragrance torturing him.

And then he was even more surprised when he felt on his back not only the warmth of her body as she began spooning with him—he always grinned when she said she liked to sometimes be the "big spoon"—but also the warm soft touch of her completely bare skin.

Then, nuzzling her nose into his neck, she kissed him.

What she began next had not stopped for a solid hour.

It was amazingly passionate, he had thought, sitting up and admiring her peaceful form beside him beneath the sheet, *as if she was afraid it might be the last time it ever happened.*

I should stick around and see what happens later.

Should—but my mind won't stop racing.

Then, on the bedside table, his cell phone vibrated once but did not light up, which told him he had received an e-mail message.

He knew it would be futile trying to drift back to sleep. Not wanting to awaken Amanda by lying there tossing and turning, he'd decided to go to the boat and bang out on his laptop the list of things to do, then start knocking them out, with catching up on e-mails at the top.

He pulled on khaki shorts and a new T-shirt—an orange one that had stenciled in black: CONCH REPUBLIC CLUB FED, A GATED COMMUNITY, YOU MUST BE INDICTED TO BE INVITED—grabbed his phone and pistol, then, barefoot, slipped out of the cabana.

The sixty-one-foot Viking was essentially a floating mobile condominium, self-contained and self-supporting. It had four large staterooms, each with a queen-sized bed and its own private head that included a stand-up shower. Its heavy-duty generators ran everything from the vast array of electronics (TVs, microwave oven, communications equipment) to the hot water heaters and washer/dryer, the air conditioners, even the desalination machine that daily could turn a hundred gallons of raw salt water into drinkable charcoal-filtered freshwater.

Matt had been impressed that the Viking also had its own Internet system, including Wi-Fi. Like the television signal, the Internet signal was provided by a satellite antenna. It was a separate, portable antenna about the size of one of the Travis McGee hardback novels he'd found onboard.

But more like a science fiction novel, considering what all it does.

Connected to a computer, the antenna hooked up from almost anywhere in the world with one of a dozen space-age birds that Inmarsat—for International Maritime Satellite—had in geostationary orbit twenty-two thousand miles above earth. Connection to the Internet usually took about three minutes. It was remarkably fast, though depending on various factors, such as weather, it could deteriorate to, at best, half the speed of a normal land-based connection.

But when at sea or sitting at anchor in some remote island cove, Matt knew that it was a helluva lot better than nothing.

Now tied up at the dock, the vessel had everything provided by shore lines. There were ones for electricity and for freshwater and for cable television and the Internet and more, leaving nothing to want.

I think I really could live on this boat, Matt thought. *Maybe take up salvage work like Travis, which would be an interesting twist to what I'm already doing.*

Wish I'd given the boat the really good shakedown cruise I wanted.

But the sooner we find Maggie McCain, the sooner I can . . .

As the pot of coffee brewed, the first e-mail Payne read was the one that had come in right after he'd bolted awake. It was from Corporal Kerry Rapier, a twenty-five-year-old blue shirt in the department's Science & Technology section, which included Information Systems, Forensic Sciences, and Communications divisions. While Rapier was small in physical stature—some said impossibly so, causing doubt that he was actually old enough to be an officer, let alone a four-year veteran—Rapier was a genuine wizard with high tech.

Which explained why he had been given the reins of the multi-million-dollar war room—the Executive Command Center—on the third floor of the Roundhouse.

The ECC could hold nearly a hundred law enforcement officers representing—depending on what quantity of proverbial fecal matter was hitting the fan at the time—the PPD, the State Police, the FBI and DHS and Secret Service, *and* Interpol. Its walls of large flat-screen TVs were linked to computer servers that accessed the department's vast databases as well as tying into endless layers of real-time communication equipment, from the closed-circuit surveillance cameras mounted citywide to any digital device worldwide that could produce and send a video or audio signal.

The pop-up window filling Matt's laptop screen showed:

```
From: <rapier.k@ppd.philadelphia.gov>

Date: 17NOV   0434

To: SGT M.M. Payne <payne.m@ppd.philadelphia.gov>

Subject: MCCAIN, Margaret

Attachments: 4


Good morning, Marshal . . .
I got the amended e-mail from Lieutenant Washington
on who to patch in for the video conference call at
0700. Glad to see your name added to the list. Was
wondering where you were.
    Am sending you some backgrounder information on
the case.
    There's more, but it's really just more of the
```

same, and I can't send it right now because there
are technical problems with the ECC.

Had to get here early - trying to make sure the
bugs I'm working out stay out. I've learned the
hard way that electronics do not like budget cuts.

Anyway, be sure to link in via the department's
encrypted VPN Tier-1AA gateway. Maybe there's
enough money for the department to make the rent
on that.

Also, I got from Tony Harris that DOT non-driver
ID you wanted run. The Cusick girl only had two
hits, both fines for personal possession of less
than 30 grams of marijuana. She paid $200 for the
first bust last year, and $300 for the second a
couple months ago.

The Hazzard address in Kensington blew up with
all kinds of hits, though. Mostly drug-related. So
I drove past it on the way home last night, and
then the hits made sense. It's a flophouse called
New Hope. It was locked down for the night - the
roll-up steel doors over the windows and front door
closed so tight that a couple crackheads who'd
shown up too late were sleeping on the stoop.

I hate to think why a good-looking girl like
that would have to be at a place like that.

Anyway, I was going to go back by there today
and look around, then let you know.

                                           KR

Payne sipped at his coffee as he thought, *Because, sad to say, she was probably a hooker.*

He then went to the attachments. He scrolled through them quickly at first, then went back and read them more carefully, hoping to find what he thought he had missed by scanning them.

He didn't.

Mostly dead damn ends.

And Kerry saying there's just more of the same isn't exactly encouraging.

The crime-scene report was there. It detailed what he'd already learned, adding little. When he read Dr. Mitchell's report on the autopsy of the Gonzalez girl, he was surprised to learn something new: that the medical examiner had determined the cause of death to be from two .22 rounds fired into her brain from behind her ear.

That certainly means something—something beyond that she got whacked—but what exactly?

There's a rock under that rock to look under . . . just hope under it isn't another dead end. Have to see what, if anything, ballistics comes up with.

And the files on the two missing female case workers at West Philadelphia Sanctuary were as thorough as possible—though the investigations offered no clear clue as to what could have possibly caused their disappearance.

Short of the obvious: "I'm sick of dealing with a frustrating, thankless job—I'm never coming back."

They were just hardworking people putting in their time, hoping at the end of the day they made a difference in some kid's life.

And there really was no information on Maggie McCain, except for the blind text she sent saying she was fine. She really had left no trail to follow.

These could easily turn into cold cases. . . .

Shaking his head in frustration, he created a folder on his desktop, named it MCCAIN.CASE, then dragged all the files into it. Then he transferred from his phone to his laptop the images that Jim Byrth had sent him, created another folder that he named BYRTH.LIQUID. MURDERS, and dragged them into it.

He looked back at Kerry's e-mail, copied the paragraph about what he had found out on the ID, then went to his personal e-mail and created a new e-mail:

```
From: MP <w.earp.45@pa.blueline.net>
Date: 17NOV  0434
To: Tex <jim@tx.secure.net>
Subject: Update on CUSICK, Elizabeth


Jim . . .
Below is what I got from Kerry Rapier on your
mystery girl. Will send more when I get it.
```

Matt then pasted in the e-mail the short text, put it in italics, then clicked on the button that was an icon of a carrier pigeon.

Okay, on to what's next on the to-do list: arranging for what happens with this boat and my new toy.

As Matt was pouring more coffee not two minutes later, his cell phone rang.

When he saw the caller ID, he wasn't surprised.

He muted the music from the overhead speakers and answered the phone: "And how are things this morning in the Wild West?"

"Bigger in Texas and better than everywhere else," Jim Byrth answered. "I was going to say something about how impressed I was that you were getting such an early start, but it just occurred to me that your time zone is an hour ahead."

"I've been up for two hours."

"Okay. Then that makes us even. I can't speak for you, but first thing I did this morning was map out that Cusick girl's address. It's a shithole row house, almost identical to that condemned one we found El Gato holed up in—"

With Amanda tied up . . . but being a decent guy he's not going to pick off that scab.

"—which is not far away, the only apparent difference being this place on Hazzard is actually habitable."

"Depends on how you define 'habitable.' There's easily sixty, seventy flophouses like that in Kensington alone. They're moving up from Fishtown and NoLibs, pretty much following the outpatient drug clinics. 'The Bottom'—Frankford, in the Fifteenth District—is getting hammered. Twenty-fourth District is overrun. Just hundreds of them."

"No shit? Tell me what a flophouse is in Philadelphia. I know what one is in Texas—an old hotel packed with vagrants."

"Sort of the same thing here. If someone running a flophouse could find a hotel in Philly to turn it into one, they'd probably fill, too. They are cash cows."

"How so? Vagrants tend to be broke."

"Simple. There's a serious shortage of places for the really poor to live. The so-called luckier ones can get in with the Philadelphia Housing Authority. But there's easily fifty thousand people on the PHA waitlist. And you'd better be a married couple—or at least a single mom or grandmother—without so much as a parking ticket if you expect to be anywhere near the front of the line. For those who can't and are in Al-Anon and Nar-Anon, the city's Office of Addiction Services throws money at some licensed drug recovery houses. But those are few, and overflowing, too, leaving independent flophouses to fill the void."

"These flophouses actually offer Alcoholics and Narcotics Anonymous meetings?"

"They pretend to—so they can draw the addicts in with their welfare checks. The worst ones are basically no more than old row houses with a bunch of makeshift bunks—just nasty mattresses on frames of two-by-fours. They're supposed to get boardinghouse permits from L&I—the city's Licenses and Inspections Department—but most thumb their nose at that. They don't want to be on L&I's radar because they're shady operators to start with. So at four, five hundred bucks a month, it's a place to crash for those fighting a futile battle . . . and to eventually crash and burn."

"What about hookers?"

"Oh yeah. Ones who, if they're not trying to kick their habit then they're probably hiding from their pimps. Or all of the above. Hate to say it, but that's what this Cusick girl is looking like. Not the first, and not the last."

Byrth grunted. "Lots of pretty girls out there making poor choices."

After a long moment, Payne said, in a lighter tone of voice, "Well, the silver lining to pretty girls making poor choices is you've got a chance at a date. I suggest you not be too picky."

"*Great,*" Byrth said, drawing out the word, his tone sharply sarcastic. "Girls are being boiled down in drums of acid and you're a damn comedian." He paused, then exhaled audibly. "But, you know, you're right. All we can do is hunt down the bad guys, and try to find some humor somewhere." He paused again, then added, "Tell you what, Marshal . . ."

"What?"

"I think I'm going to make you my sexual adviser."

"Wait. Your *what*? That's BS—"

"No, really. You can be my sexual adviser—as in, when I want your fucking advice, I'll ask for it."

Payne laughed out loud. "Deal."

"Anyway, how long are you going to be in the Keys?"

"Unfortunately, we're headed back to Philadelphia today. In a few hours. One of the main reasons I was up early was to work on the missing person case that I mentioned to you last night. Maggie McCain is her name."

"Why unfortunately?"

"It's not looking like there's going to be a happy ending. Maggie runs a place for kids in Child Protective Services. I just found out two other women from another CPS place went missing last week. Anyway, if I can, I'll go with Kerry this afternoon and check out the flophouse."

Byrth was quiet for a moment, then said, "I haven't had one of those cheesesteak sandwiches in a while. I'll meet you there."

[TWO]
Over the Leeward Islands, Lesser Antilles
Monday, November 17, 6:50 A.M.

"Then Ricky, he showed up at the Sanctuary," Krystal Gonzalez was saying as Maggie McCain watched her pacing the living room of Maggie's Society Hill town house.

She stopped and began crying again.

"And then he grabbed Brandi, said she still owed him money, so that meant he owned her. Ms. Quan yelled for Ms. Spencer to call the cops. And Ricky, he said that that would be their last mistake ever."

The curvy, petite nineteen-year-old anxiously ran her fingers through her black hair. A very slender doe-eyed twenty-six-year-old woman of Asian descent, who stood about as tall as Krystal, appeared. She stroked Krystal's head and said meekly, "Brandi begged us not to call."

A tall, sad-faced twenty-seven-year-old black woman walked up, nodding. "Said he'd kill us all. Burn down the Sanctuary."

"Lizzi and Brandi were afraid of the cops, that they'd arrest them, too," Krystal said. She pointed across the room. "All they wanted was out."

Maggie looked to where Krystal pointed. The two attractive twenty-year-old blondes were standing there.

"That's why Lizzi said they went along with leaving town. She and Brandi thought they could get away on the road. But that didn't work. And then Lizzi and Brandi told Ricky again that they wanted out, that if he didn't let them out, they'd go to the cops. Tell them how he started giving them drugs and working them when they were underage. But then I never heard from them again"—she glanced across the room, and when Maggie looked, too, the blondes were gone—"so I told Ms. Quan and Ms. Spencer all that. And I told them about the notebooks he kept in the office and what was in them. They didn't believe me. 'All you girls do is lie.' So I stole two when Ricky passed out drunk in the office."

She held up the thick, well-worn spiral notebooks.

Maggie looked at them, then looked back at Krystal.

Now Quan and Spencer were no longer in the living room.

"I texted Ricky, said I was done doing that shit. Told him to leave me alone or he'd never get his books back."

Krystal, motioning with the books for Maggie to take them, said, "It's here. Now we can be safe."

Then she softly repeated it, "Now we can be safe."

Then Krystal was gone, and the notebooks sat in a pool of blood in Maggie's burning kitchen. . . .

"Excuse me," an insistent female voice said, causing Maggie McCain to slowly open her eyes. She felt someone shaking her, then realized that it was her seatback being pushed and that the nasal voice was that of a flight attendant, who added, "You're going to need to put this upright for landing."

As American Airlines flight 504 banked over the Caribbean Sea on final to land at Cyril E. King International, Maggie wiped tears from her cheek.

So, how long are the bad dreams going to go on?

She slid open the window shade and stared out.

Monsters like Ricky can't get away with this.

The sun was coming up, casting dramatic light across the verdant hills of the islands rising from the vast blue ocean. Bright colorful houses dotted the hillsides down to where the larger resort hotels spread out along the white sand beaches.

Normally, the beauty stirred a sense of excitement and adventure in Maggie. Now she felt neither, only a surreal numbness.

First thing I am going to do, she thought, *is get that bastard where it matters most to him—in the wallet. Let him worry and squirm.*

I know what money he's making, and the outrageous, disgusting way he's making it.

And I can use his books to get him, too.

He's going to learn you don't fuck with a McCain.

She watched out the window as the airliner settled toward the sea, coming so close to the surface that it looked like it might land on the water. Then at the last minute its tires finally chirped as they touched down on the runway, the threshold of which began right at the water's edge of the small island.

"Welcome to the tropical paradise of Saint Thomas, United States Virgin Islands," the flight attendant's nasal voice came across the intercom, her tone attempting to be perky.

Backpack slung over one shoulder and wearing sunglasses and the Georgetown Hoyas cap, Maggie deplaned and made her way through the concourse to Baggage Claim Two. She passed plenty of police. There were uniformed local cops, as well as federal agents, ones with their shirts lettered ICE or DEA. She kept telling herself that she had nothing to worry about from the Drug Enforcement Administration or Immigration and Customs Enforcement—or any other cop. And none seemed to pay another young American woman any particular attention, which she thought more or less supported that.

Then again, she realized, she really didn't know who might be looking for her.

She saw, not surprisingly, that a lot of women were talking on their cell phones, and wondered if she should pull hers from her backpack in order to blend in. She immediately decided against that, because the last thing she wanted to do was turn on the phone. If a cop noticed her pretending to converse over a darkened phone, one clearly dead, it would raise more flags than simply not having a phone out in the first place.

Near Baggage Claim Two, she found the man holding a clipboard so that it showed the YELLOWROSE logotype and TRADEWINDS ESTATE. He was a short, brown-skinned, potbellied, gray-haired islander with a friendly face. She walked toward him, and as she approached she saw that his name tag read MANUEL. Pleasantly addressing him by name, she introduced herself as Alexis Stewart, and after he had turned over the clipboard and confirmed she was indeed on his shuttle bus list, she went to the baggage carousel to locate her luggage.

It was there within minutes, and another twenty after that Manuel had all five of the newly arrived guests of the Tradewinds Estate aboard the turquoise open-air safari bus, an older Ford F-250 flatbed pickup converted with a thatch roof over passenger benches that could seat fifteen. He'd used up at least half of that time squeezing their luggage into a rear compartment.

Maggie decided the other four guests, judging by their rings, were married couples. They had found their seats in the first and second rows of the safari bus. They talked among themselves, their conversation animated and covering the usual small talk, beginning with, "The islands are just so amazingly beautiful." "Is this your first time to visit?"

Maggie, having seen the dynamic happen time and again, knew the odds were high that during their stay the women would become fast friends, with the men dutifully following suit.

Which was one reason Maggie discreetly had taken her seat on the second-to-last row, and proceeded to pretend she was reading a paperback. She was grateful the shuttle wasn't an enclosed van, which would have put her in closer proximity to the others and they likely would have attempted to draw her into the conversation. While she was prepared with stories of what she was doing there—starting with "a birthday vacation"—she really didn't want to lie if it could be avoided. And not talking was simply a way of doing exactly that.

The turquoise safari bus, merging with the traffic flow on the left side of the street, turned off the airport property and followed Veterans Drive along the coast. The rising sun was quickly warming the cool morning, the temperature, according to the flashing WELCOME TO SAINT THOMAS sign they just passed at the airport, already approaching eighty.

As the humid salty air blew through the open bus, Maggie breathed in deeply and thought that it felt good.

Or maybe it's that I'm out of Philly . . . and in a place that's far away . . . and feels far safer.

I've always felt safest in the islands.

Over the top of the paperback, Maggie watched as they passed the familiar sights of Frenchtown—Saints Peter and Paul Cathedral, at the foot of Frenchman's Hill, caught her eye, and the busy ferries at Blyden terminal—then the shops and restaurants lining the narrow, congested streets of downtown Charlotte Amalie.

It will be easy to blend in.

She looked across Veterans Drive. In the bay were fifty or more sailboats tied to mooring buoys. A couple of the big fifty-foot-plus catamarans were already under way, people moving about purposefully on deck as sails were hoisted.

On the far side of Charlotte Amalie, where two cruise ships towered over the docks, the safari bus turned off the main road. It made a series of sharp turns, Manuel grinding an occasional gear as he downshifted and followed the serpentine two-lane up a steep incline. After topping the tall hill, he left the bus in a low gear and it chugged down the other side.

The truck's engine then backfired—and the two wives shrieked, then a moment later laughed at themselves.

Maggie was surprised she hadn't jumped out of her skin.

Shortly thereafter, the brakes squealed as the bus approached on the right an eight-foot-high natural stone wall covered with thick flowering vines. There was an enormous gate that blocked any view of what was behind the wall. The only clue was on the gate—a wooden sign with hand-chiseled lettering: TRADEWINDS ESTATE, AN EXCLUSIVE YELLOWROSE ESCAPE.

The breeze carried the fragrance of the vine flowers, filling her head.

The gate slowly swung open, and Manuel ground the transmission into gear, then rolled the safari bus through.

Maggie caught herself sighing with relief.

"As you requested, we have you in our most secluded cottage," the young black hostess said, as she and Maggie stepped from the brightly painted electric golf cart. A bellman in a battered black cart that carried Maggie's luggage was pulling up behind them.

Maggie guessed that the hostess—her name tag read BEATRIX—was no more than eighteen. She had somewhat hard features but a pleasant, reserved personality. She spoke with a hint of a British accent.

"Being the farthest from the main house," Beatrix went on, "it also commands the best private view on the property."

They had just come from the "main house," a four-story mansion of quarried stone once owned by a rum maker. Five years earlier it had been converted into a quaint boutique hotel with twenty rooms. There was a large open reception area on the first floor, which led outdoors to the grand restaurant overlooking the sea. It had tables to seat sixty, and except for a thatched roof was completely open to the elements. Nearby, a large swimming pool with a waterfall had been sculpted into the hillside.

With the main house's conversion, a dozen cottages had been added throughout the property, as had the one-lane paths winding among them through the hills.

Maggie saw that her cottage, out on a point of the hillside three hundred feet above the small bay below, was built in a hexagon shape. Its walls were mostly large windows that could be slid together, completely opening three-quarters of the building to the cool, steady winds blowing ashore. A level down, tall palm trees framed the stone decking that contained a small swimming pool, an infinity style that appeared to flow into the ocean itself.

Maggie, slipping her backpack from her shoulder and placing it on a low couch, found herself admiring the elegant, comfortable furnishings and how everything seamlessly blended in with the natural surroundings.

"It really is quite lovely," she said, trying to sound more excited than simply relieved to finally be there.

"Your welcome package is over there," Beatrix said, motioning toward a low wooden table beside the pool. "We deliver a continental breakfast of fresh baked goods daily, or anything more at your request. There is a pot of our rich local coffee, as well as a pot of hot water if you should prefer tea. And fresh fruit."

"Perfect."

The bellman, having delivered Maggie's bags, stepped out of the cottage and slipped away without a word, disappearing behind the tall thick hedge of sea grape trees that shielded the cottage.

"Finally," Beatrix said, "I spoke with our marina manager, and he asked me to tell you that the dockmaster is seeing to your charter boat. You're welcome to call him or"—she gestured toward the section of hedge to the right—"just beyond there are steps leading to the marina, as well as the beach. It's a lovely walk down. Coming up, however, you may wish to take one of the golf carts. Even I find the hills to be a workout."

Maggie smiled. "Good advice. Thank you. Did you grow up here?"

"I recently came here to attend school. I grew up in Virgin Gorda." She pointed. "That's about ten miles away, in the British Virgin Islands."

Maggie was nodding as an image of the giant volcanic boulders on the beach at the Baths of Virgin Gorda came to mind.

"Do you know it?" Beatrix said.

"Actually I was just . . . I mean, just wondering if it was worth the effort."

"Oh yes. It's much quieter than here, fewer people. I shouldn't say that, but it's true. I take the ferry back and forth, but you could easily sail there. Just be sure to bring your passport."

"Not this trip. But that's good to know."

"Well, then. Anything else you need is simply a phone call away," Beatrix said, handing Maggie her business card. "Please contact me directly, or of course any of our staff."

Five minutes after Beatrix left, Maggie had made herself a cup of tea—denying herself a splash in it from the liter bottle of local Cruzan gold rum she found on the welcome tray. She took the tea into the bedroom of the cottage and began digging through her suitcase. She had bought the luggage and most of the clothes in it at the giant outlet mall just south of Baltimore the previous day.

At the bottom she found a pair of linen shorts and changed into them, then tried to flatten out the wrinkles as she carefully hung her blue jeans in the closet.

Then, back in the suitcase, under her canvas sailing bag, she found the hard plastic case and pulled it out. She worked the combination of the lock, then took out her Baby Glock. With a practiced hand, she loaded the pistol in between sips of tea.

She knew that having the pistol was illegal in the Virgin Islands.

God help me!

First it was coming up with fast lies. Then traveling on false IDs. Then bringing a gun, which I've never done.

Is there no end to what I'll do going down this rabbit hole?

But . . . at least I am still alive.

She dug again in the suitcase and pulled out the heavy canvas sailing bag. She made it a little heavier by slipping the Glock in it, then grabbed her tea and went out to the pool deck.

Beside the table holding the food and drink was a chaise longue in the shade of an umbrella. She put the bag on the chaise's thick blue cushion, then looked back to the cottage, shook her head, and retrieved her backpack from the low couch inside.

Finally, sitting cross-legged on the cushion of the chaise longue, she pulled her laptop from her backpack. She looked at the canvas sail bag and saw its neat stitching that read YELLOWROSE SPRING BAY RESORT & SPA, VIRGIN GORDA BVI.

Glad Beatrix didn't see that.

But then I could have just said it was Mother's, or anyone's, for that matter.

There I go again. Ready with the easy lie.

And, really, why does that bother me?

Because the girls always do it?

But to them, it must be a survival skill.

Which is what I've made it . . .

She reached in the sail bag and removed a square gray plastic-encased device that was about half the size of her laptop. It had a small face panel with a power on/off button, a battery-power gauge, three jacks, and two light bars, one vertical and one horizontal. It also had an adjustable folding leg that allowed the device to sit at varied angles. She placed the device at the foot of the blue cushion and plugged one end of a cable into one of the jacks and the other end into the laptop.

Okay, let's power on everything.

With the laptop booted up, she clicked on an icon shaped like a globe.

She leaned toward the foot of the cushion. Both light bars on the device's panel blinked yellow. Then the vertical one turned half yellow and half green. She slowly rotated the device left and the horizontal light bar blinked red. She reversed, rotating the device to the right. The red went out, then the yellow that returned was replaced with half green. She continued turning it right—and then both bars became a solid green.

She looked at her laptop screen, and in one window there was:

INMARSAT ACQUIRED. ANTENNA STRENGTH 98%.

Well, good. The subscription's not expired from last time.

No way I could renew it without a hit on my credit card.

Would have to rent one. Or steal one . . .

Then she opened a new window on her Internet browser and clicked on the icon that would take her to a secure server.

After she signed in, an icon that looked like a mailing envelope automatically popped up. On it was a small red circle with "109" on it.

Her throat constricted.

And fifty of those e-mails are probably from Mother.

She must be going bonkers. I feel awful.

But this has been my first chance to send anything since yesterday.

She opened a new e-mail message, typed "I'm fine!!!" in the subject field, then wrote in the body: "Hi!! I'm in a good place but on the move. More shortly. Promise! Love you!! Mag."

She then sent it to her mother, father, and cousin Emma.

Hang in there . . . so far so good.

She clicked again on the globe icon, and a moment later the screen read DISCONNECTED FROM INMARSAT. Then she powered off the antenna.

She poured herself some more tea.

Sipping it, she looked over the edge of her cup out at the Caribbean Sea, then thought of the dream she had on the airplane. She shook her head as she felt her eyes tear. She put down the cup.

Okay, you bastard . . .

She reached in the canvas sail bag, removed a thick spiral notebook, and flipped back its well-worn cover. She began to carefully study the first page—then suddenly began sobbing, and curled up in the fetal position on the cushion.

[THREE]
Little Palm Island, Florida
Monday, November 17, 7:10 A.M.

"Okay, it looks like we're finally all here again in one piece," Matt Payne said, looking at the laptop screen and everyone's images that were no longer pixelated.

Payne's screen was divided into quarters, four big boxes with individual images, all live feeds, of Jason Washington, Tony Harris, Kerry Rapier, and Matt.

"Sorry for that electronic burp, gentlemen," Corporal Kerry Rapier said, from his bottom left corner box.

Matt's image was in the bottom right box. He carefully had adjusted the laptop so that the pinhole camera centered in the upper lip of the screen captured him from the chest—just above the CONCH REPUBLIC CLUB FED stencil—up over his head. Behind him was nothing but black.

Twenty minutes earlier, right after getting off the telephone with Jim Byrth, Matt had had what he considered one of his better ideas of the already long morning.

He had gone down to the master stateroom and grabbed one of the black pillowcases off the big bed. He hung it from the ceiling of the galley so that it would mask anything behind him. That way there would be no distractions in the background—sunrise causing glare, for example, or someone walking past on the dock—to interrupt their videoconference.

Perhaps more importantly, it would also have the added benefit of saving Matt from getting his chops busted about what a tough life it must be yachting in paradise.

What they don't know, or see, won't hurt them . . . or me.

The top left box with the image of Jason Washington showed him wearing a crisp white dress shirt with a nice blue necktie. Behind him on the wall were framed photographs of Washington with his wife and ones with other police officers, clearly indicating to everyone that he was sitting at his desk in his office in Homicide.

Tony Harris also had on a shirt and tie and navy blazer—all

somewhat rumpled. He, too, was in his Homicide office, and holding a heavy china coffee mug just to the side of his head.

Matt had immediately recognized the mug. After tiring of trying to find who was swiping his personal plain coffee mugs in the office, he recently had had a dozen cheap ones custom printed with a representation of his Philadelphia Police Department Badge 471 on one side and, opposite that, also in gold, the words STOLEN FROM THE DESK OF HOMICIDE SGT M.M. PAYNE.

He had been convinced that that would stop his cup from disappearing.

He had been wrong.

Kerry Rapier, wearing his police uniform blue shirt with its three blue chevrons on the sleeves, was at the command console in the Executive Command Center. He also held what he called "a Wyatt Earp of the Main Line Collectible," which when word of that got around only had served to accelerate the cups' disappearance.

And they're holding them up now to quietly taunt me.

"Jason," Payne said, mock serious, "when we're finished here, be aware that I intend to be filing charges of petty theft."

Washington, who of course had the same images of everyone on his screen, in his sonorous voice intoned, "To what might you be referring, Matthew?"

Then he raised to his lips a "collectible" and took a sip.

Tony and Kerry chuckled.

Matt shook his head and snorted. But he was smiling.

Washington then said, his tone unmistakably serious, "I understand that Kerry had the foresight earlier to send you the files?"

"Yes, sir. I've gone over them. A couple times."

"That then makes you our set of fresh eyes. Anything in them jump out at you?"

Matt shook his head.

"Only that it's remarkable how little there is. Except for the Gonzalez girl being executed in an unusual fashion, there's next to nothing right now to go on."

"Unfortunately that appears to be the case," Washington said, nodding. "Tony, would you share what else we have?"

Harris grunted. "There's not a helluva lot to add, Matt. We were able to trace the anonymous text that Maggie sent back to the IP address of the computer she used. It was in an Internet café outside of Washington, D.C."

"So, assuming she sent it, she's no longer in Philadelphia," Payne said.

"It seemed a hot lead," Tony went on, "but when I interviewed the manager he said I was describing half the women who came in there. He did say he never noticed any female customer being there with someone who may have been holding her against her will."

"And there's no sense in hunting prints on the computer," Payne said.

Matt saw Jason nodding as Tony said, "Right. Even if we were able to find hers among—what? dozens? hundreds?—of others who used the keyboard, we're not going to find Maggie herself."

Matt watched Tony take a sip of coffee from his cup as Tony glanced at a notepad.

"I'm just going to rattle these off," Harris said. "Stop me if you want."

"Rattle away," Matt said, making a sweeping hand gesture at his laptop camera.

"One, we did get some prints lifted," Tony went on, "partials taken off the one Molotov cocktail bottle that did not break. Not great, but they're being run now. Two, Maggie has a current permit for concealed carry of a pistol. Three, the residue on that dollar bill rolled up in the Gonzalez girl's pocket tested positive for coke. Four, the Gonzalez go-phone went live again last night—"

"Stop," Payne interrupted. "When and where? At Westpark?"

Tony looked up from the paper. "No, not the apartments in West Philly. It was in the area of NoLibs and Fishtown. Just after midnight last night. Whoever had the phone redialed the last number—"

"Maggie's work cell phone," Payne said, remembering the report stating that. "Which was found broken in the alley. And the go-phone then dialed it three times in a row at noon yesterday."

Washington sat stone-faced, quietly impressed again with Matt's natural ability to absorb vast amounts of information and effortlessly produce it on the spot. But Washington wasn't at all surprised. That was more or less expected of those who graduated from the University of Pennsylvania summa cum laude and those who finished first on the department's exam for promotion—both of which Payne had done, the latter earning him the right to his choice of assignment, the Homicide Unit.

"Right," Harris said, "and then, for the first time since Maggie went missing, it dialed her personal cell phone, which was, and is, still turned off. Then the go-phone signal went dark again."

Payne sighed. "Well, that's *something*. At least we know the go-phone's still in play. We just need to find it."

"Yeah, and with luck, by the time you get here we should have more forensics on the data we took off her work phone."

"What about the other two dozen phone numbers and texts that her go-phone made between the time of the murder and when it went dark after you tried to trick whoever had it at Westpark?"

"Not a single one answered when we called. Not even out of curiosity. Which is odd."

"Maybe they were told to ditch their phones and get new ones?" Payne said, and thought, *They buy the damn things like they do drugs, in bulk.*

"That is entirely possible," Washington said. "Disposable cell phones being a cost of doing business. We're now waiting for the phone company to trace ownership of those numbers. I have a feeling Matt's right about the ditch-your-phones order, though, and that's likely to become a cold trail, too."

Payne nodded thoughtfully. "Makes you wonder why hers hasn't been ditched." He paused, then said, "What else you got on your list, Tony?"

"Just one last thing. All the neighbors I spoke with last night couldn't say enough nice things about Maggie. Said she was an extraordinary neighbor, nice and friendly, always taking care of her place. If she saw litter on the sidewalk, she picked it up. They were sick about the home invasion."

Matt looked away from the screen in thought.

"I can smell the gears burning all the way from here," Washington said. "What are you thinking, Matthew?"

Payne, rubbing his chin with his thumb and index finger, turned back to the screen.

"Nothing really. It's just that the go-phone went live in the No-Libs–Fishtown area."

"And?" Harris said.

"And that's where the casinos are."

"So?" ·

"I'm afraid that I'm not following you either, Matthew."

Matt shrugged and made a face. "That's because there's nothing to follow. Nick Antonov's name came up at dinner last night. Some SoBe ABC—"

"Now you're talking in tongues, buddy," Harris said.

"South Beach American-born Cuban, Tony. A guy named Jorge Perez. He was running Antonov's boat, the *casino's* boat, and entertaining a couple of middle-aged goombahs who looked like they could've just fallen off the pasta truck in South Philly or South Orange. Or, considering Perez, maybe closer to Havana on the Hudson. Just didn't smell right. And apparently it's still bugging my subconscious."

"You've really lost me, Matt. How does Union, New Jersey . . . ?"

"Like I said, Tony, there's nothing to follow. That go-phone could have been anywhere. Including the Hops Haus condo high-rise. And I'm not about to implicate Amanda any more than anyone else."

"All right, then," Harris said. "That's all we have for now. We should have more details in by the time you come back this afternoon."

Payne nodded, then said, "Speaking of this afternoon, Jim Byrth is headed to Philly, too."

That caused Washington to change his facial expression.

His eyebrows went up as he said: "Jim's always welcome, as I told him. What's the purpose of his visit this time?"

Matt repeated the description of the camp by the lake in northeast Texas and all that was found there.

When he had finished, Jason Washington said, "I've heard about those sulfuric acid baths. But the cartels aren't the first to liquefy their enemies. The head of the Sicilian mob, Filippo Marchese, used lye and called it *Lupara bianca*. White shotgun."

Matt clicked on a file, and the photograph of him in the right bottom corner was replaced with the Cusick ID.

"This is the ID that the sheriff found in the RV trailer."

"Pretty girl," Harris said.

Matt went to click it to close the image but instead managed to open the file next to it. The image of the girl in the blue barrel popped up in its place.

In the upper right window of his screen, Matt watched as Tony Harris's eyes went wide and coffee sloshed from his cup. He slowly said, "Damn!"

"Sorry. Hope everyone's had their breakfast," Payne said, and clicked to make it go away.

"As horrific as that is—and it genuinely is—your priority is the McCain case, Matthew."

"Understood. Trust me, I have Amanda reminding me of that by the minute."

And I'm well aware that the sooner Maggie comes home, the sooner I can come back down here.

The three images of Washington, Harris, and Rapier started to become pixelated again. Then that snow of tiny multicolored dots turned completely black.

All that was left on Matt's screen was his own live image.

"Are you still there, Matthew?" Washington's deep voice came through Payne's laptop speaker. "We lost your picture again."

"And I lost all of yours," Matt said. "Damn it! Why won't this work?"

"It's the ECC's fault, Marshal," Kerry's voice then announced. "It's why, I think, it took so long for you to get patched in, then that other pixelated burp. I really thought I had the bugs out."

"Well, we're finished for now anyway," Harris's voice said.

Matt glanced at the corner of his screen, saw it read MON 8:01 AM, and said, "Okay. If there's nothing else, time for me to go pack up."

"Kerry, log us out," Washington said, from the darkness of his box.

Payne stood, felt the black pillowcase brush his head, then yanked it from the ceiling.

"Yes, sir," Rapier's voice said, then added, "Hey, here's an error message."

Payne looked back at the screen. The images of all three men had returned.

"*Nice* boat, Marshal!" Rapier blurted.

Jason and Tony grinned as Kerry placed his head close to the camera. His eyeball now filled his on-screen box, and he rolled it around, pretending to be looking around the Viking.

Jason chuckled deeply as Tony said, "So you're doing hard time at Club Fed? Looks rough, buddy."

[FOUR]
Suite 2400, Two Yellowrose Place, Uptown Dallas
Monday, November 17, 9:30 A.M. Texas Standard Time

"Hey, Rapp, come on in!" Mike Santos said. "Me and Bobby here were just talking about what a fine time we had getting to know you last night."

The office of the chief executive officer of OneWorld Private Equity Partners was penthouse level, twenty-three floors above the Southwest Chop House and the other street-level businesses.

Bobby Garcia stood looking over Santos's shoulder at the two side-by-side large flat-screen computer monitors on Santos's desk. The desk was an eight-foot-long slab of thick, perfectly polished petrified wood with two wide stainless steel cylinders for legs. Santos followed Garcia out from behind it.

•

"Good morning," Rapp Badde said, forcing a smile, and shook Bobby Garcia's hand, then that of Santos.

Badde glanced around the office. An impressive space, it was expensively decorated. The walls were filled with large photographs, ones that looked like fine art, of buildings and various commercial developments. And there were artist conceptions of future projects. There had to be more than a hundred. The walls of floor-to-ceiling windows looked out over downtown in one direction and out west in the other direction.

"Can we get you something? Coffee?" Santos said. "Maybe something to kick-start your day? A little hair of the dog?"

"Tempting, but no, thank you," Badde said. "That was one helluva nice time last night. Exhausting, though. It was tough getting up this morning, and I slept hard all night."

Well, not exactly all night, Bobby Garcia thought, then noticed Badde absently rubbing his wrists.

"It was a good night," Santos said. "Glad to hear you got rest, too."

"I can get used to that nice scenery last night. What business were those women in? Hospitality?"

Is he serious? Garcia thought.

"Right. The service industry," Santos said. "They come here to train at our hotel across the street—it's sort of a finishing school—then travel from property to property. It keeps them"—he glanced at Garcia knowingly, clearly enjoying himself—"what's the word I'm looking for, Bobby? 'Nimble'?"

Garcia, literally biting his lip, raised his eyebrows, then nodded.

Santos went on: "Now that we're providing the initial hundred million for your little hotel in Philly, and maybe more, I'm sure we'll be able to have them there—say, for the grand opening?"

Garcia, watching Badde nod agreeably, thought: *The sonofabitch really doesn't remember a damn thing.*

Santos and Garcia had spent the previous fifteen minutes reviewing parts of H. Rapp Badde, Jr.'s first night in Dallas.

"Here's the footage we got from the chophouse security cameras," Santos said. "Shows us at the table, having drinks as the girls arrive."

Garcia watched the image on the left flat-screen that showed Santos and Garcia and Badde getting to their feet. Introductions were made, and then the group walked out of the lounge.

The next image picked up their party a moment later stepping out to the outside bar of the chophouse. In a corner of the softly lit area was a stone fire pit, natural-gas fed and flickering with orange flames, that was surrounded by plush couches with oversized cushions and pillows.

As soon as they sat, Badde with a blonde on one side and a brunette on the other, a waitress arrived with a bottle of champagne and three crystal stems and another round of the men's drinks.

"He really was giddy over those girls," Garcia said. "I almost feel bad about all this."

Santos chuckled.

He fast-forwarded the image. The girls fawned over Badde, laughing and touching his hand. After a short time, Badde glanced over his shoulder, looking around the bar area, then stood, put his drink on the table, and with the now empty hand motioned to excuse himself. The brunette grabbed his hand and playfully tugged him back. He grinned broadly, then broke free and went out of camera view.

Bobby Garcia watched himself on the video take a sip of what then was his fifth club soda and lime.

"I should have been the one going to take a piss," he said, and laughed.

The young women emptied the champagne bottle and talked among themselves.

Garcia put his drink beside Badde's. Both glasses looked identical with the flickering orange flames reflecting on them. Garcia then discreetly pulled from his coat pocket a glass vial the size of a cough drop. It contained a double dose—two ten-milligram tablets—of zolpidem dissolved in water. After a long moment, he reached for Badde's drink. He popped the vial's plastic top, emptied the clear liquid into the drink, then stirred it. He then returned the cocktail to the table, tossing the vial into the fire pit. The heat almost immediately caused it to shatter and disappear.

When Badde reappeared five minutes later, Garcia retrieved his club soda as Badde sat back down between the girls.

Badde grabbed his drink, took a healthy swallow, then leaned over and whispered in the brunette's ear. She tilted her head back and laughed. Badde grinned broadly as she touched her champagne stem to his glass.

"He really fell all over himself. And them. Literally. Check out later."

He clicked to another box that was on the right flat-screen. This video showed the interior of a luxuriously furnished condominium. The camera angle was from a high corner of the living room. The blondes and brunette now wore only panties. Badde was trying to get his pants off, but was having difficulty because he still had on his shoes. He was wobbling on his right leg, tugging at his left, and falling toward the brunette as she tried to help him keep his balance.

Santos clicked on the FAST FORWARD button, and the image blurred as more and more clothes came off.

Then no one wore anything.

Santo clicked FAST FORWARD again, blurring the image a bit more.

There next came some enthusiastic kissing and petting. Then Badde paired off with the brunette while the blondes turned to one another. The brunette lay on the leather couch, then reached for a wooden box on the coffee table. She pulled from the box a small packet, emptying its contents on her breast.

Shortly after snorting the cocaine, Badde lost all inhibition. The women were more than compliant to his wishes. Even with the video moving fast, the various acts left little to the imagination.

"I really would rather you not slow that down, Mike. I don't want to see any detail."

Santos clicked on the STOP button, and the screen became a black box.

"Thank you."

"But here's the coup de grâce," Santos said.

Santos clicked a PLAY button that was in another box on the left screen.

"What the hell?" Garcia said, then sighed. "You know, Mike, some might suggest that this is borderline over the edge."

Santos looked up at Garcia. He looked serious.

"It's always good to have insurance, Bobby. Always. Yuri said Badde could be damn difficult, and to be careful with him. But until we met Badde in person, I didn't know if Yuri said that because Yuri can be a pain in the ass. Now, since Yuri is connected to him with Diamond Development, we have something on both of them." He looked back at the screen. "I got the idea for this from pictures I saw on the wall of that gayborhood bar we foreclosed on."

"That's a little comforting, I guess. I seriously was beginning to worry. I don't think I could handle you coming up with this all by yourself. I mean, a *piñata?*"

Badde was lying on his belly on the white comforter of the bed, trussed up with his wrists and pudgy ankles tied above his buttocks with the soft fabric belt of a dressing robe. He was naked except for being wrapped in lengths of bright yellow and blue and green papier-mâché. There was a small sombrero on his head.

"Hey," Santos said, "I bet your sorry half-gringo ass didn't know that the Chinese had their own *piñata* first."

"They didn't call it that."

"I forget what it was called. Probably couldn't pronounce it if I did. Anyway, a version of whatever it was called made its way to Mexico in the 1500s, when the Catholics started making them with seven points for the seven sins. Beating one with a stick till it broke represented man's struggle—good versus evil—and the treats inside were the reward for keeping the faith." He glanced at Garcia, then back at the screen. "He looks pretty festive, don't you think?"

As Badde squirmed on the bed, a short, effeminate Hispanic male wearing a ridiculously small white cowboy hat strode into view. The camera angle was such that only his backside was visible—but it was a great deal of backside, as he wore only a pair of leather chaps with a holstered revolver hanging from each hip. He had a very well-defined and muscled body.

Then he turned and placed his groin in close proximity to what in role-playing would be considered the *piñata's* face.

"Damn! He's hung like a horse, an angry one!"

The camera then captured the "cowboy" removing the sombrero and performing on the *"piñata"* a sexual act that Garcia thought could never be described in polite company.

Garcia shook his head.

"You are one sick sonofabitch, *mi amigo*."

"Thanks to that zolpidem, Bobby, he'll never know that this ever happened—as long as he does what he's supposed to. I haven't decided if I'll get a snipped version of it to Yuri or not. But we'll have the whole thing here for safekeeping."

Garcia studied Badde, who looked severely hungover. He knew that it was from all the alcohol and cocaine—and there had been a lot of it—because the zolpidem left no side effects. Garcia also found it interesting that one of the results of Badde being so badly bent was that he didn't exhibit his usual flashes of arrogance.

Still, no matter how hard he tried, Garcia simply could not look at Badde and shake the vision of him trussed up in the video.

Maybe he's lucky he doesn't remember a thing about it. . . .

"I'm going to run down to my office, Rapp, and get the papers for you to take back to Philly for your people to review and for signature," Garcia said, and moved toward the door. "Sooner we get the paperwork in motion, the sooner we can get preapproval of your project for the EB-5 funding. I'll be right back."

After Garcia went out the door, Badde turned to Santos.

"You know, Mike," he said agreeably, "you could have just overnighted those papers to me. You really shouldn't have gone through all the trouble of bringing me here to Dallas."

Santos grinned.

"It just wouldn't have been the same, Rapp. And it was no trouble at all."

"Well, I am glad you did."

"And I'm glad we did, too."

VI

[ONE]
Cyril E. King International Airport
Saint Thomas, United States Virgin Islands
Monday, November 17, 10:30 A.M.

"Mr. Garvey, nice to see you again. Headed home for the holiday?"
the U.S. Airways desk agent said, her tone genuinely sincere. She was
a pleasant-looking dark-skinned Crucian (one born on Saint Croix)
who was maybe thirty. "I thought you might treat your family, get
them out of Philadelphia by bringing them here to our paradise.
Weather says it's snowing there again."

John Garvey, thirty-six years old, was a fit five-eight. Fair-skinned,
he had a scholarly, angular face with a full head of sandy blonde hair.
He wore starched cuffed khakis, a white collarless shirt under a linen
blazer, and tan loafers with no socks. His business card that was on
his luggage tag identified him as *John A. Garvey, Jr., Associate, D. H.
Rendolok LLC, Historic Restoration & Preservation, Phila., Penna.*

"Nice to see you, too," Garvey said, putting his black fabric suitcase at her feet, then automatically handing over his ID. He then
lied, "Flying here was discussed, but the issue became how much of
the family would get to come. When the wife's side exceeded ten, I
said sorry. Can't afford that."

She made the obligatory look at his driver's license, handed it
back, then noticed that he was sweating.

"Are you well, Mr. Garvey?"

"Just a touch of rock fever, I think," he said, and forced a smile.

Rock fever was the island equivalent of cabin fever—the overwhelming feeling of being stuck in a small place for too long.

"Now, that's just not possible!" she said, smiling. "You've been visiting us how long?"

"Almost six months now. Two weeks every month."

He leaned two white plastic tubes that were four feet in length and six inches in diameter against the counter.

"More blueprints?" she said.

"And architectural renderings. My cross to bear, if you'll pardon the pun."

She smiled. "Oh, I'm sure it is going to be even more beautiful when you're finished."

Garvey—an architect who held degrees in art and in history, as well as a master's in business administration from the University of Pennsylvania's Wharton School of Business—had been hired as chief architect to ensure that the updating of Saints Peter and Paul Cathedral remained historically faithful. Built in the mid-1800s, its ceilings and walls were covered in massive murals that portrayed a dozen scenes from the Old and New Testaments. Saints Peter and Paul—on Kronprindsens Gade in Charlotte Amalie, at the foot of Frenchman Hill, not two hundred yards from the scenic harbor's edge—served as the Virgin Islands seat of the Roman Catholic diocese.

As with all his restorative work, this project had required a great deal of research, which entailed traveling to the Virgin Islands regularly. That of course had triggered the usual expected comments from family and friends about having to quote unquote work in the beautiful Caribbean.

"Another lousy day in paradise, huh, John?"

But that had not been the reality of the situation.

He had, in fact, spent an inordinate amount of time in dark pockets of the buildings, examining construction methods—it originally had been built with stone quarried from the island, but over time new additions employed new methods—testing the load-bearing walls, even doing samplings of mortar to gauge the level of deterioration. Then there were the delicate murals themselves to consider.

By the end of the day, he was simply exhausted and headed to the hotel, which in no time had begun to feel more or less like any other hotel—a bed, a bathroom, a TV, a dusty Bible in a side-table drawer.

Instead of the sunny Caribbean it could just as well have been dreary Camden on the Delaware.

He did try to get out, break up the pattern. And, over time, he had become friendly to varying degrees with the locals. Ones at the church, of course, but also ones frequenting local spots, like the SandBar Grill, which was the next block over from his small hotel.

Two days earlier, as he had left the cathedral for the ten-block walk to his hotel, he heard his name called by a familiar voice.

He turned to see Jack Todd approaching. Captain Jack was one of what the locals called a "continental," someone from the States, visitors either with the means to stay in the islands for a long period or working at seasonal jobs.

A backslapping friendly type, Todd—who Garvey guessed was probably forty but could have been younger; his deeply tanned skin had been severely damaged and aged by the sun—had said that he was from Texas and worked on charter sailboats. How often he sailed, Garvey couldn't say. Captain Jack always seemed to be at the bar, in his usual shorts, T-shirt, and flip-flops, making friends and passing out business cards.

"Hey, John!" he had said, patting him on the back. "Let me buy you a drink."

Captain Jack grabbed two mugs of St. John's Mango Pale Ale draft at the SandBar Grill's bar and carried them to John Garvey. He was sitting at a corner table on the SandBar Grill's patio. It had a view of the big harbor, the seaplane and helicopter ports, and the main airport itself.

"And you leave again tomorrow?" Todd said, making it more a statement than a question.

"That's right. But I'll be back. Like clockwork."

Todd nodded. "Yeah. I know."

What does he mean by that? Garvey thought.

Todd then reached down and produced from the floor a dirty manila envelope. He held it out to him.

"What's this?" Garvey said, putting down his beer mug.

"Open it," Todd said coolly, motioning at it with his hand.

Garvey carefully peeled back its flap. He reached in and removed a short stack of five-by-seven photographs. They were not on slick photo paper. Instead, they had been printed on a standard color printer on regular white paper, two images per page, and the page torn to separate the photos.

"Sorry that the quality of the pictures is so crappy," Todd said. "But you get the idea."

The top one, of John's wife walking with their son in front of Saint Mary's in Philadelphia, initially made him wonder if this had something to do with his work at the cathedral. Then the next photograph was of his wife entering their Victorian house in Northeast Philly. And he quickly flipped to the next, a shot of his son leaving school.

"What the hell is this?" Garvey snapped.

Captain Jack met his eyes.

"They know all about your family. And their schedule. And your schedule."

John Garvey felt the hair on the back of his neck stand up.

"I don't understand . . . and who the hell is 'they'?"

"If it's any consolation, I don't want to work for them, either. But one thing led to another here and—"

John Garvey, starting to stand, interrupted, "I don't know where you got these, but—"

"Sit down, John. There's no way of getting out of this. I've learned that the hard way."

"Get out of what?" Garvey said, staring at Todd.

"Sit."

As Garvey slipped back in his chair, he said, "This can't have anything to do with the church?"

Captain Jack laughed as he looked past Garvey, out to the sea. He took a chug of his beer, then looked back at Garvey.

"Depends on what you worship, my friend. Look. It is very simple. They have a task for you to do. You're a regular business traveler. There's no customs to clear in Philly. You'll zip right through, man. Piece of cake."

"What task?"

"You do this, and nothing will happen to your family."

"What the hell does that mean?" Garvey blurted. "Why are you threatening me?"

Todd's face turned very serious. "Look. You better learn to control your emotions. Not doing so could cause you to screw up, and that would be a very unfortunate thing for you, for your family."

Todd flipped back to the bottom photograph.

Garvey saw that it was of a dark-haired boy about the age of his own blonde-headed son. He was floating facedown along a dirty, rocky riverbank.

"It's terrible when kids have accidents, no? And women, who we know can be careless, clumsy, and unfortunate things happen to them . . ."

Garvey, despite the temperature in the high eighties, suddenly felt cold and clammy.

"What is this . . . this *task?*"

John Garvey looked at his suitcase now sitting on the Toledo scale beside the desk agent's computer terminal. The digital readout showed it weighed forty pounds, then forty-one, then settled on forty-two-five. Fifty pounds, Garvey knew, was the limit that the airline said a bag could weigh. Anything above that and he would have to pay a fee for the excess. He didn't care about the money. He just did not want any extra attention paid to his suitcase—and its hidden contents.

Thank God. I got lucky.

I knew my room scale couldn't be properly calibrated.

He had spent a half hour in his hotel room working with the bathroom scale. He first stood on it, and the round gauge registered his weight as two hundred. He knew he actually weighed one-seventy-five, so he would have to keep the discrepancy in mind. He picked up his suitcase. When he stepped back on the scale, this time holding his suitcase, the scale's circle gauge spun, then slowed and finally stopped on two-eighty. He then stepped off, opened the case, and took out enough slacks and shoes that he hoped would weigh ten pounds. And repeated that process three times before the scale registered two-sixty. He had had to leave behind the extra clothes, in the closet, then called the manager from the airport, saying he'd forgotten them and would get them on his next trip.

Now he looked at the suitcase and could visualize behind the black fabric the two thick bricks that were wrapped in plastic and gray duct tape. Together they weighed right at four and a half pounds.

Two keys. Two thousand grams.

"Four hundred grand on the street," Captain Jack had said.

Cut that once, eight hundred thousand bucks.

And it's never cut just once.

"Don't lose it. I hear people get killed in Philly for a pair of sneakers."

"My favorite is the Last Supper," the desk agent then said.

"Excuse me?"

"The mural of the Last Supper at the cathedral," she said. "It's my favorite."

He nodded as he thought, *That's fitting.*

Jesus' last meal with his disciples before he was killed.

This could very well be my version of it.

The desk agent went on: "I heard that Peter and Paul was built to celebrate the end of slavery. Is that right? That's what Market Square here was, the Caribbean's largest slave auction."

End of slavery? There's been no end! I'm being enslaved now.

Okay. Try to act normal. Answer the damn question.

"That's All Saints you're thinking of. The Cathedral Church of All Saints on Garden Street?"

"Really?"

Act normal . . .

He nodded. "You're certainly not the first. They're pretty much from the same period. Construction started on All Saints about the time Saints Peter and Paul was completed. Back then, when merchant ships docked here to transport the mahogany and sugar products—sugar itself, and the molasses and rum made here from it—the ballast from the cargo holds would be left on the dock to make room. Those huge arched windows in All Saints are lined with those yellow bricks. That was the ship ballast."

And now it's airplanes shipping bricks of coke.

"Fascinating," she said. "God bless you for your talent in preserving that important cathedral."

She handed him his ticket.

"Well, I have you upgraded to first class, our compliments. We appreciate your regular business."

"Thank you. Very nice."

Great. Free booze. I can drink my last supper.

"See you when you return, Mr. Garvey. *Vaya con Dios.*"

As John Garvey stood at the security checkpoint removing his wallet and all things metal from his person, he realized that he'd been wrong about the ridiculous ritual that was the Transportation Security Administration's screening.

It really can get worse than the government-sanctioned and taxpayer-funded public groping.

You can be afraid of being arrested as a drug smuggler.

He cleared security with no problem.

He waited to catch the plastic bin containing his laptop before it came clunking down the rollers of the conveyor and banging to a stop. He glanced back at the unsecured area. A familiar-looking man caused him to do a double take.

Captain Jack, in T-shirt, shorts, and flip-flops, was casually walking with a small crowd toward a sign reading PUBLIC TRANSPORTATION, thumbing a message on a cell phone as he went.

[TWO]
Office of the General Manager
Lucky Stars Casino & Entertainment, Philadelphia
Monday, November 17, 10:30 A.M.

"Damn it! That is *not* what I asked for," Nikoli Antonov snapped. He was on his phone as Dmitri Gurnov entered. "Call me back when you get it right."

He slammed the receiver into its base on his desk, then glared at Gurnov.

"I really hope you have good news for me, Dmitri."

Unlike Gurnov's distinct, hard, old-world Soviet features, the dashing thirty-seven-year-old Antonov looked very Western European. He was of medium build, had dark hair trimmed short, and wore an expensive, nicely cut two-piece suit with a tie-less crisp white dress shirt. While Antonov certainly could speak his native Russian fluently, his early years of attending boarding school in Helsinki had left him with no detectable Russian accent. He generally was softspoken—Gurnov knew that his outburst just now would never have happened in public—an appearance that conveniently masked the fact that Nikoli Antonov could be utterly ruthless.

Behind him, a quad of twenty-inch flat-screens was mounted on the wall. They showed real-time images from closed-circuit cameras around the casino complex, every ten seconds cycling to a different camera view, including one that Gurnov saw was of him just now entering Antonov's office. Gurnov saw himself looking at his cell phone—on which he'd been reading the text message "Mule headed uphill," which Julio had forwarded from the cartel's guy in Saint Thomas—then sliding the phone into his pocket.

There of course were at least ten times that number, and much larger screens, in the casino's security office. But Antonov believed that keeping a finger on the pulse of the complex lessened the chance of surprises. He also knew it did not hurt for those working for him—including his security men, who often were among the first to be offered bribes to look the other way—to know that the boss himself could be watching over their shoulder at any time.

"Well, I don't have any bad news, Nick."

None that I'm going to tell you.

Starting with me having to fix what Ricky screwed up.

And another is you not knowing that my mule just made his flight.

You've never warmed up to my idea of using nonprofessionals to move product.

Antonov grunted. "Good enough, I guess."

The phone on the desk began trilling softly. Antonov's dark eyes darted to it, and when he saw its touchscreen display, he punched the speakerphone button.

"Jorge, my friend!" Antonov said, his tone now cheerful. "Good timing. I have Dmitri with me in my office."

"Hey, Jorge," Gurnov called out.

"Good morning, gentlemen," Jorge Perez said. "How are you?"

"You tell us," Antonov said. "How did it go? I got your message, but Dmitri hasn't heard. You can give us both the details."

"In a word," he said, his self-assured tone bordering on arrogant, "successful."

"Details?" Antonov repeated.

There was a pause, then Perez said, "Well, the bad news is that we won the Poker Run. Worse, we did it with a damn royal flush." He chuckled. "Where do you want your Mustang convertible delivered?"

"Why is that bad news?" Antonov said casually.

"Because everyone was joking that the whole thing had to be rigged, what with a casino's boat winning the hand and all. If I'd thought that was going to happen, I would have played badly on purpose. But you know that I like to win."

"Bad news? I'd say it's exactly the opposite," Antonov said. "The press release will spin it 'Lucky Stars Casino Shows We're All Winners.' Or something like that. And we give the car to charity."

"Now, that's a good idea," Perez said.

Antonov looked to Gurnov, who nodded as expected.

"How did the transfer go?" Antonov went on.

"Surprisingly well. I told you that Miguel Treto was good. He's never let me down, even when it's gotten hairy with the damn Communists messing with him and that cargo ship."

"For example?"

"Like the bastards refusing to accept shipments, just flat out making him haul it back to Miami, or squeezing him for a bribe. He said he had the feeling that they were going to do that this time, especially when they arrived late in the day, after dark. He sweated that big-time, because he knew it would have messed up the rendezvous timing. But Treto's a pro—made it go off without a problem."

"What about the product?" Gurnov put in.

Perez played dumb. "The girls or the—"

"Both," Gurnov snapped.

"It all came through fine. We put the girls on the Citation with Bobby Garcia. He dropped two of them in New Orleans. I talked to him after they landed in Dallas."

"And the other product?"

"Carlos is headed your way with the coke. Twenty keys."

Gurnov had a mental image of Perez's short cousin.

And mine will be here faster, and without having to drive past all those cops sitting on the side of I-95, just waiting for another smuggler to profile.

Then bust the midget—after confiscating the coke.

"What if some cop pulls him over for DWM?" Gurnov said, then glanced at Antonov.

"Driving While Mexican," Gurnov added.

Antonov shook his head.

Perez snapped: "He's an American citizen, you know. He will be fine. He's made the run plenty of times. There's ten keys in each car, and they're running an hour apart."

Antonov was quiet for a moment, then, out of the blue, he said casually, "What about that boatload of Cubans? The ones that crashed the boat ashore?"

What is that about? Gurnov thought, surprised.

Perez was silent for a long moment, then he said, his voice not quite so self-assured, "That went as planned, too, Nick. They were Cubans taking advantage of the wet-foot, dry-foot policy."

"And you weren't taking advantage of our plans? At ten grand a head?"

There was stone silence. Then Perez said, "Yeah, we got paid. But Miguel Treto has done that for me at least twenty, thirty times now. It's why it all went so smoothly with your stuff. A diversion."

"But I didn't know about the plan," Antonov said evenly, as he looked to Gurnov.

Gurnov raised his eyebrows.

Perez said, "I didn't—"

"If you're going to take chances," Antonov said, his voice rising, "you take them on your own."

Perez was silent for a moment.

"Nick, I thought it would be the perfect diversion. And it turned out to be that. Every cop in South Florida showed up when that sheriff boat called for backup to stop them from getting to shore."

Antonov sighed audibly.

"You are not listening again, Jorge. That seems to be a problem with you. Let me be clear: I am not saying that it was a bad idea, Jorge. I am saying that I did not know about it."

Gurnov turned his attention to the quad of monitors on the wall as he thought, *Who was that meant for? Jorge? Or me?*

"I understand, Nick. I thought I was doing the right thing."

"How did our friends do?" Antonov said, ignoring that by changing the subject.

It took Perez a moment to respond. "They said they were very pleased. They said they wanted to go again on the next one."

"Which is?"

"There's another Poker Run in three months."

"Good. If they're happy, then they will make their boss happy."

Dmitri Gurnov could not get Antonov's voice out of his head as he drove the dark blue Audi toward South Philly.

"I am not saying that it was a bad idea, Jorge. I am saying that I did not know about it."

Gurnov glanced at the clock on the dash. The US Airways flight from Saint Thomas was due at Philadelphia International in two hours. He'd have his product an hour after that.

Meantime, he figured, Jorge Perez's pint-sized cousin would probably still be stuck in Fort Lauderdale traffic with ten different cops watching him.

Gurnov stopped at a traffic light, then looked at himself in the rearview mirror. His sunken eyes stared back as he thought for a long moment. He ran his hand over his scruff of beard, then nodded at himself.

Don't be stupid, he thought. *Nick was saying that for my benefit, too. But I'm not about to walk in and drop those coke bricks on his desk.*

"Here. No surprises, Nick, like you said."

And then explain everything?

"I've got my own game going on the side. . . ."

That would be suicide.

I have to figure out something. But first I have to finish Ricky's botched job.

Gurnov double-checked the second of the three addresses that were handwritten on a sheet of paper on the passenger seat. Ricky Ramírez had handed him the sheet at five o'clock that morning, when they loaded four girls into a minivan for the trip to Florida.

The first address, which Gurnov had just driven past in Society Hill, was the burned-out town house where Krystal Gonzalez had been killed. The other two, Ramírez had said, were the houses where the girls had lived when he'd had them recruited.

From the dead girl's go-phone, Gurnov had a name linked to two phone numbers—"Ms Mac 1" and "Ms Mac 2"—both of which when called went to voice mail. And he had the three addresses from Ramírez.

And that was all he had on the woman he was hunting.

I've worked with less . . .

As he tossed the sheet back on the seat, his hand bumped the Sig-Sauer 9mm that was tucked in the right pocket of his leather coat.

[THREE]
Tradewinds Estate
Saint Thomas, United States Virgin Islands
Monday, November 17, 2:30 P.M.

Maggie McCain had gone through the spiral notebooks, then ordered a salad and grilled fish from room service, ate that poolside, and then went through the books again.

She quickly had decided that "meticulous" was not a word that could accurately be used to describe them.

They're sloppy.

They certainly wouldn't pass a high school accounting class, forget a college one.

But there's a lot here—the challenge is making sense of it all.

It wasn't just that the handwriting bordered on illegible. The entries in the books were at times illiterate—words misspelled or written phonetically in a rudimentary "Spanglish"—and structurally undisciplined.

I don't think Ricky would recognize a ruled line, much less a spreadsheet.

But there's no mistaking the numbers. Hundreds of thousands of dollars in drugs alone. They're not selling on street corners. These are retail and wholesale figures.

One of the books tracked the girls, their locations and activity, how much they earned and how much they owed. The other tracked the drugs. It hadn't been difficult to discern which notebook was which. The first clue was the crude doodles of female anatomy and of marijuana leaves, bongs, crack pipes, and other paraphernalia.

And there were lots of phone numbers. Each of the girls' names had one—and Maggie figured they were go-phones given to them, just as Krystal had had hers. And the drug book listed pages of phone numbers. Some with names, some without names, and some names with multiple phone numbers, some of which, apparently the older ones, having been crossed through.

With a few exceptions, most of the area codes were local—a lot of 215 and 267 for the Philadelphia area, and 732 and 856 for New Jersey.

There's got to be a way to use these numbers if I can't get to Ricky through the dive bar.

But that's just going to be a nightmare—worse than hunting a needle in a haystack.

She booted up the laptop and powered on the satellite antenna.

Back online, she launched the program that allowed for video and telephone calls. She clicked on the icon that mimicked a ten-digit keypad on a phone, looked in her computer address book under Krystal's name, and found the number for Players Corner Lounge.

A woman's harsh voice on the recording answered: "Players. Leave a message . . ."

What do I say?

Maggie clicked END CALL.

She looked at the first page of numbers in the notebook that tracked the girls. Then she clicked REDIAL. Then she clicked to hang up again.

Before I do that . . .

She then typed her personal cell phone number and dialed it.

When she heard her own voice recording say, "Hey, it's me. Sorry we missed—" she clicked twice on the keypad's pound sign. That took her past the automated voice-mail recording and to her voice-mail box.

The familiar computer-generated female voice politely but mechanically said, "You have forty new messages. You have ten old messages. Five messages older than seven days have been automatically deleted today."

Forty? No surprise.

Not as bad as the hundred-something e-mails.

But then, there's not a fifty-message limit on e-mails.

She clicked on the keypad's numeral "1" and the female computer voice said, "First message. From Monday, nine P.M. . . ."

Then the voice mail played: "Hi! It's Krystal. Call me back!"

Maggie felt her throat constrict.

She clicked the pound sign, fast-forwarding past that and the older messages.

The female computer voice then announced: "New message from Saturday, ten thirty-one P.M. . . ."

Maggie then listened to her mother's voice, calmly asking Maggie to call when she had a chance.

"Nothing important," her mother said, her voice tired. "Good night."

Well, Mother, that didn't happen.

Maggie deleted the message.

The next message was her mother again, almost two hours later, just after midnight. Her voice now was frantic.

"Maggie! Please answer! Call us! We need to know you're okay!"

It hurt to hear her mother so distressed. She deleted the message.

That bastard Ricky is causing everyone pain. People who've done nothing to deserve it.

She listened to the next one. It was her father, his gravelly voice trying to sound calm.

And that really hurt to hear, too.

She listened to the entire message—felt the moral obligation to do so—then deleted it. And then she did the same with the rest—played them all, ones from family and friends and the police, and deleted them one by one.

The tone of her mother went from the initial frantic to hysterical crying to sheer exhaustion. Maggie thought that if there was any silver lining, it was that some of the messages had been thankfully brief. But toward the end, a few were just one or two words— "Maggie?" "Please call . . ." "Hello?"—almost as if her mother had called the number simply to hear Maggie's voice on the recording.

Listening to them all had been emotionally exhausting. Maggie was glad to finally hear, "You have one new message. From Monday, at twelve-ten A.M. . . ."

"I believe you have something that belongs to me," a man's steely voice said. "Call me at 267-555-9100 and I'm sure we can come to some arrangement that is mutually satisfying."

Maggie shivered at the sound.

That is one cold voice.

And what is that accent? Eastern European?

It's certainly not Hispanic. Not Ricky's.

And "mutually satisfying"?

Like what? What happened to Krystal?

She played the message again, this time writing down the number on a piece of paper. She stared at it for a long time.

It's a Philly area code.

Then she opened a new window on her browser and typed the telephone number in its search field.

The first search result read: "267-555-9100, a KeyCom Mobile Device. Month-to-month service. Never be locked in a long-term cellular contract again!"

Well, only a fool would use a landline number that could be traced.

So, it's a go-phone.

I don't trust myself to call it.

But I can see what happens when I text.

She opened another new browser window, then went to myfreetexts.net and, registering with false information, created a new account that assigned her a new telephone number with an 831 area code.

That page was then replaced with one that was almost a mirror image of the text message screen she had on her cell phone. Almost, because the difference was that both sides of the My Free Texts page had annoying advertisements scrolling from top to bottom.

A small price to pay, I suppose.

She watched the cursor blinking in the field for the recipient's cell phone number. After a long moment, she typed in the phone number.

And then her stomach suddenly knotted.

That could be the killer. Probably is the killer.

Or, if not the killer, then a killer.

She inhaled deeply, then slowly let it out.

I'm okay. He can't get to me here.

And if I'm going to get to him . . .

She hit TAB, putting the cursor in the bubble that represented the message field, and typed:

MAYBE I HAVE YOUR BOOKS. MAYBE I DON'T.

She read that three times, nodded, then added at the end, "Who is this?"

She read it all once, then clicked SEND.

Maybe whoever it is will be stupid enough to tell me.

Or, more likely, lie to me.

She stared at the screen. She picked up the water bottle on the table beside her and sipped.

She then realized that she was shaking slightly.

I'm terrified.

What if I screw this whole thing up?

She drained the water bottle.

Well, I can't sit here forever waiting.

Who knows when they'll reply?

She put her fingers to the keyboard and started to sign out.

Under the bubble that held the message she sent, a new bubble suddenly popped up:

267-555-9100

WHO THE HELL IS THIS?

She immediately yanked her fingers back.

She stared at the reply.

Why do I read anger in that?

And not just any anger.

A fury.

She caught herself typing:

> WHO THE HELL DO YOU THINK?

She stared at that, then immediately tapped the DELETE key over and over.

When the bubble was blank, she turned her head in thought—and realized her impulse had been the right one.

These bastards are killers.

I can't show weakness.

She typed:

> WHO THE HELL DO YOU THINK?
>
> AND WHAT THE HELL DO YOU CONSIDER AN ARRANGEMENT THAT IS MUTUALLY SATISFYING?

It was a long moment before a new bubble popped up:

> 267-555-9100
>
> MY APOLOGY. AREA CODE 831 IS CALIF
>
> I KNOW NO ONE THERE

That's probably a lie.
  She sighed.
  This is all a damn lie. A nightmare.
  What am I doing?
  Another bubble quickly followed:

267-555-9100

WHAT MAY I CALL YOU? MS MAC?

Maggie felt her heart race.
  That's what Krystal called me!
  Don't let your guard down!
  I can hear that Eastern European voice in his sentence structure.
  And then came another bubble:

---

267 555-9100

PLEASE LET'S MEET — ANYWHERE YOU LIKE

I'M SURE WE CAN WORK THIS ALL OUT

With what? Another bullet?
  Slow down, Mag . . .
  She quickly typed:

```
I NEED $200,000 CASH BY TOMORROW.


I'LL BE IN TOUCH.
```

Where did that come from?

She hit SEND, then clicked to shut down the connection with the satellite. Then—unnecessarily, but it made her feel better—she unplugged from the computer the cable that linked to the antenna.

I have to think this through.

She then looked at her hands and realized they were shaking uncontrollably.

With some difficulty, she got the top unscrewed from the bottle of Cruzan gold rum, sloshed some into a glass, and drank it all at once.

[FOUR]
Philadelphia International Airport
Monday, November 17, 2:35 P.M.

John Garvey walked down Concourse A, his nerves on edge despite all the free first-class alcohol he had consumed on the flight.

Once the aircraft had rumbled down the Saint Thomas runway and left the island, he had felt some relief. And the drinks had certainly helped calm, if not numb, him. But now that that period was over, his mind had begun to spin again.

What guarantee do I have these animals will live up to their end of the bargain?

Once I've done this, what's to stop them from coming after me, making me do it again and again? I should've gone right to the cops. But they're watching—and he said that would've been a swift death sentence.

The piece of paper with the telephone number that he was supposed to text after he had his suitcase felt like it might burn a hole in his pocket. As a precaution, in case it did burn a hole or otherwise got lost, back at the hotel he had punched the number into his cell phone.

What if whoever I'm supposed to text doesn't show?

Who am I kidding? I have their drugs.

And they know how to find me. Find us.

John Garvey heard the loud warning buzzer sound over the baggage carousel. Then came the huge metallic clunking of the carousel starting to turn.

The first bag slid down, a black one similar to his. Then another followed it.

They're all black. All the same.

What if someone grabs mine by mistake?

What if mine doesn't show up at all?

Then what?

He tried to look as if he were casually glancing around the baggage claim area. He thought that a couple of people were paying him unusual attention, one a Latino by the exit looking up from his cell phone, but finally told himself he had to be imagining things. He then noticed in the ceiling the black plastic semicircles—ones half the size of a baseball—that he knew concealed security cameras.

Those I'm not imagining.

Three bags later, his suitcase showed up.

Okay. Almost home free . . .

He dragged it from the carousel, then turned it onto its wheels. He forced back his sudden desire to sprint madly for the door.

That bastard Jack was right—I did just zip right on through.

No wonder so many drugs make it here.

He pulled out his telephone, found the 215-555-3582 number, and texted: "PHL."

That was both the airport code and the code that he had the suitcase in hand and awaited direction as to what to do with the coke.

Then, as directed, he went to get a taxicab.

As John Garvey came closer to the exit doors that were already open, he saw parked at the curb a white Chevrolet Tahoe with Drug Enforcement Administration markings. On the window of the back door was: WARNING! DO NOT APPROACH. K-9 INSIDE.

Easy does it. Those guys are always here with their dogs.

You're just noticing it now because you're looking for cops.

John Garvey stopped, then felt a firm hand grip his left bicep.

"Excuse me, sir." It was a man's voice, a deep, authoritative one. "Can I ask you a question?"

Garvey whipped his head around.

When he saw that the man was a uniformed Philadelphia policeman, his heart beat so hard he thought it might burst out of his chest.

"Of course, Officer," Garvey said, and then saw the patch on the sleeve of his blue shirt: PHILADELPHIA POLICE AIRPORT UNIT.

"Is this your suitcase, sir?"

Damn! I grabbed the wrong black one!

He glanced at it and recognized his luggage tag.

Then he blurted: "It's not mine!"

The policeman turned his head to read the luggage tag.

"Then if you're not John A. Garvey, why . . ."

"No, I mean . . . I mean . . ." Garvey started shaking visibly, then quietly said: "The packages . . . they're not mine."

"Yes, sir. Would you mind if we take a look inside your suitcase?"

Twenty minutes later, as John Garvey sat in a battered aluminum chair in a secure room near the baggage claim area, staring at his open suitcase on the steel table, the Philadelphia policeman sauntered in with another uniformed officer on his heels. The second man, wearing a jacket reading DRUG ENFORCEMENT ADMINISTRATION, was stocky and had an inquisitive look on his face. He stopped at the door and said nothing.

Garvey looked at the Philly airport cop.

"Sir, I am advising you that you have the right to remain silent . . ."

Garvey, elbows on his knees, buried his face in his hands.

"He said they'd kill my family."

". . . you have the right to an attorney . . ."

VII

[ONE]

Philadelphia Northeast Airport

Monday, November 17, 2:35 P.M.

Nesfood International's twin-engine Learjet—with Vice President (sales/marketing) Chad Nesbitt, Matt Payne, and Amanda Law aboard—had been descending through a thick layer of gray clouds for nearly ten minutes when it finally broke through the bottom.

Matt looked up from the chess game on his laptop computer. He had been repeatedly toggling back and forth, playing the game, then going to the files on Maggie McCain when he thought of something, then going to the game.

Back and forth—but getting nowhere.

He saw that Chad, in a big reclining seat close to the cockpit bulkhead, was yawning and stretching after waking from a nap. Matt glanced at Amanda, who sat beside him on the leather couch reading a medical journal, then turned and looked out his window.

Visibility was getting somewhat better, but the day had a gray winter gloom to it. Even the fresh snow on the ground, reflecting the cloud cover, looked pallid.

Depressing, he thought.

Which is fitting considering why we're back.

They were coming up the Delaware River, about to overfly the big international airport as they approached Philadelphia. He now could see more of the city than he expected—its sections spreading out in street grids of gray—and his eye automatically started to pick out landmarks.

There were the soaring glass-sheathed skyscrapers of Center City. In their shadow, he saw the statue of Philly's founder atop City Hall—*Billy Penn is probably freezing his bronze balls off*—and then he picked up the distinct shape of the Roundhouse near the Ben Franklin Bridge and, in the distance just beyond that, the Hops Haus high-rise condominiums in Northern Liberties.

Farther up he could make out the rougher areas of Kensington and Frankford, their lines of row houses gap-toothed where dilapidated properties had been torn down. The vacant lots, Matt well knew, were thick with trash and dead weeds under the coat of snow.

And very likely a dead body or two.

This is the polar opposite view of the sunny tropics we saw after taking off in the Keys.

How long is it going to take for us to get back?

He felt Amanda, and the warmth of her body, lean into him.

He turned and kissed her lightly on the forehead.

She smiled as she kept looking out the window at the city.

She's clearly got a lot on her mind.

After a moment he looked back out. He began to make out the long crossed strips of asphalt that were the Northeast Airport's runways.

As the aircraft slowed and the cabin filled with the hum of the hydraulics lowering the landing gear, he said, "We're home."

"I love this city," he heard her say, her tone wistful, "but I think I liked the view earlier better."

Matt nodded. "I know exactly what you mean."

A minute later she said, "I realize this may sound terribly rhetorical, but what if 'on the run' means she's really on the run?"

While they had been driving to Key West International that morning, with Chad behind the wheel of his rental SUV, Matt received a telephone call from Will McCain. He announced that Maggie had just sent a new e-mail, and he wanted Matt's address so he could forward it.

Minutes later, after reading the e-mail on his cell phone, Matt showed it to Amanda:

```
From:    William McCain <mccain.w@mccain.inc.com>
Date:    17NOV  0859
To:      <w.earp.45@pa.blueline.net>
Subject: FWD: I'm fine!!!


Begin forwarded message:


From:    Maggie <magpie417@libertymail.com>
Date:    17NOV  0832
To:      Mother, Dad, Emma
Subject: I'm fine!!!


Hi!! I'm in a good place but on the run. More
shortly. Promise! Love you!! Mag
```

"You know her better than I do," Matt said. "What do you make of it?"

Amanda, handing back the phone, sighed heavily.

"I have no earthly idea," she said. "Everything and nothing? That's her upbeat personality. And her wanting to be in control. She gets that from her father. Being orderly and in control. But if she's in a good place . . ."

"I don't get it either," Matt said. "But I can see the control thing. And see it being a problem."

"What did Maggie say?" Chad said, then added, "If I'm allowed to ask."

"Hell yes you're allowed to ask," Payne immediately replied. "We need to find her. Or at least find out what's going on with her."

Payne read the e-mail aloud.

"On the surface," Chad said, "I'd say it sounds promising."

"Maybe," Matt said, gazing out his window. They were driving down a narrow strip of island, the Overseas Highway down to just two lanes, and practically surrounded by water. "But like all that out there, there's always something going on beneath the surface. Sometimes good, sometimes not. What could be the reason, besides control, that she won't allow anyone to communicate with her?"

Is she doing it because she can't—someone's not letting her—or because she thinks she shouldn't?

After a moment, he thought, *Hell, if you don't try, you don't get . . .*

He turned to his cell phone and, after hitting a couple of keys, typed out and sent:

From: <w.earp.45@pa.blueline.net>

Date: 17NOV   0910

To: Maggie <magpie417@libertymail.com>

CC: SGT M.M. Payne <payne.m@ppd.philadelphia.gov>

Subject: Your safety

Maggie . . .

This is Matt Payne.

It is critical that you and I communicate.

As you should know, everyone is looking for you.

I've been put on the job to ensure that you
genuinely are safe. And, with the full force of the
police department, to catch whoever is behind the
attacks.

We will catch them. But right now I need to
establish your safety before this escalates into
something worse than it already is.

I can help you. I can protect you.

But I cannot do it without communication. And
an e-mail like you sent your parents isn't
enough.

Call me. And if you feel you can't call, please
send real-time proof of how you are. Text or e-mail
a photograph of yourself with today's newspaper
or a TV or Internet newscast — something that
indicates you are okay right now.

Please, Maggie, take these first steps so we can

```
get your life back to normal. And give your family
some peace of mind.

                                      M. M. Payne
                          Sergeant, Homicide Unit
                    Philadelphia Police Department
                          215-555-1010—office
                          267-555-4898—cell phone
```

"Appealing to her sense of order might get her to respond," Matt said, showing it to Amanda. "It's likely a long shot. But sometimes they pay off."

The aircraft banked, then lined up with the runway.

Matt discovered he'd left his telephone turned on for the entire flight when it suddenly vibrated at least five times in a row. When he looked at it, still vibrating, there were four new text messages and three new voice-mail messages stacked up. None were from Maggie McCain, and when he checked his e-mail, she had not replied there, either.

There was an e-mail from Kerry Rapier. He reported that the e-mail Maggie McCain had sent to her family that morning was tracked back to an Internet Protocol address of a computer server in India.

India! he thought. *That's nine, ten thousand miles?*

That's more than on the run—that's impossible.

Kerry added that the server was a portal that had relayed the e-mail, effectively masking the originating address. No one believed it was credible that Maggie was there.

Payne then read a text message from the yacht broker in the Keys that said he had the Viking and Matt's Porsche secured as they had discussed.

Matt replied: "Keep them both fueled—I'm back ASAP."

Who am I kidding? I'm stuck here.

I'm going to have to pay a car hauler company to ship the 911 up.

As he hit SEND the aircraft touched down with a chirp of tires.

Chad leaned over and pointed out Matt's window as the Lear turned off the taxiway. Matt, who was listening to his voice-mail messages, looked. He saw that they were approaching a pair of airplanes being serviced by ground crew at the fixed-base operator. The closest was a slick white jet with a paint scheme that featured a pair of bright red gambling dice on its tail fin. The aircraft stood out, shining in the gray gloom.

"There's the casino's Citation that was in Key West," Chad said.

They then saw a black man in a dark suit and black bow tie appear in the open doorway. He quickly pulled on a dark overcoat as he looked around the tarmac, then found a black Range Rover waiting nearby. He carried a pink-accented black suitcase down the stair steps and, somewhat strutting, tugged the luggage toward the luxury SUV. He looked visibly annoyed at having to walk around piles of gray snow slush.

"Well, that's not Nick Antonov," Payne said, deleting a voice-mail message, then hanging up his phone.

"That looks like Badde," Chad said.

Matt looked again. "You're right. It is the distinguished councilman."

What is that bastard up to?

He looked at Chad. "Did you see him in Key West?"

Chad shook his head.

Matt held his cell phone up to the window and took a photograph of the aircraft. As he did, an attractive young cocoa-skinned woman hopped out from the driver's seat of the SUV. Badde gave her a quick hug and pecked her cheek as she barely slowed before going around and getting in the front passenger seat.

"And there's his lovely paramour," Payne said.

Amanda automatically looked out the window, said, "You're bad," and then unbuckled her seat belt and began stuffing the journal into her bag.

After a minute, Payne said, "You know, even if you didn't see him there, you would have heard about it. He likes to make his presence known."

"You're right about that, Matt. I'm glad he didn't find me."

"Well, when in doubt, go to the guru."

"What?" Chad said, then watched Matt hit a speed dial key on his phone.

"Hey, Marshal," Kerry Rapier answered on the second ring. "You home yet?"

"Just landed. Quick question, Kerry. What's the best website to track aircraft?"

"Depends. What's the tail number?"

Matt looked out the window. "N6556TR."

"Hold one."

After a moment, Kerry said, "Yeah, this guy's tried to block it."

"Block what?"

"Block the ability to track the aircraft. Bigwig corporate types do it to protect themselves, or so they say. I like to first try the general websites, see if someone's trying to hide."

"You're a bottomless well of info. How do you know all this stuff?"

"I worked for a while with our Aviation Unit at Northeast Airport. Those chopper pilots are full of tricks."

"You said 'tried to block.'"

"Yeah. Hold another sec. I have access to the FAA's stuff. . . . Okay, here it is. The log shows it's a Cessna Citation Ten twin-turbofan that just landed fifteen minutes ago on runway twenty-four at PNE. And, bingo, here's why it was blocked. It's registered to Lucky Stars LLP here in Philly."

"Right," Payne said. "We knew it was the casino's."

"So, what else do you want to know? I can tell you pretty much everything short of the stewardess's bra size. Sorry. I believe the politically correct term is cabin crew's bra size."

Payne chuckled. "Where did the flight originate? Key West?"

"Nope. Dallas. Went wheels-up at Dallas Love Field at ten-fifteen local time. You want that in Zulu time?"

"Dallas?" Payne repeated, looking at Chad, who shrugged.

"Flight duration was right at three hours. Fourteen hundred seventy statute miles, most of the time at four hundred thirty-one knots and forty thousand feet."

"When did it get to Dallas?"

"Hang on . . . okay, looks like last night. Landed twenty-fifty hundred hours local. Route was Key West to New Orleans Lakefront, then on to Dallas. Before that, it left PNE Friday morning for Key West."

Matt looked at Chad. "You landed at Key West last Friday morning."

Chad nodded as the Lear came to a stop and its engines began winding down.

"Okay, Kerry," Payne said. "I'm not sure what I learned. But thanks. See you in a bit. I'm begging a ride to the Roundhouse from my buddy."

"The party is going on here in the war room."

"Got it."

Payne ended the call, then said to Chad, "You're a corporate big-wig type. Do you block your tail number?"

"We don't need to. We're not a publicly traded company with everyone second-guessing our every business decision, including how we use our planes. Although I have to admit I agree with the activist shareholders who want true transparency from the hypocritical politicians screaming about carbon footprints—and sticking it to me to pay what essentially is a luxury tax on a business tool—while they're secretly jetting around in corporate aircraft."

Payne grunted as he looked at the casino's jet.

"Transparency and politicians? Dream on, buddy."

[TWO]
Locust Near Fifty-fifth Street, West Philadelphia
Monday, November 17, 2:47 P.M.

Dmitri Gurnov had slipped back behind the wheel of the Audi, which was parked a block down the street from the address that Ricky had said was the place called the Sanctuary.

A three-story brick-faced building, the facility looked from the outside like a small apartment complex with an interior central court-yard. It was much bigger—maybe three times the size—than the two row houses on Girard Park that made up Mary's House.

Like Mary's House, the Sanctuary had no signage that said what the facility was. It did have one reading RESIDENTS ONLY. NO TRES-PASSING. SMILE! YOU'RE ON CAMERA! And, also like Mary's Place, the intercom buzzer was answered by a woman well practiced at not answering questions, particularly those of strangers.

Neither woman had admitted to knowing a Ms. Mac or a Krystal Gonzalez.

And when he tried pressuring the woman at Mary's House, saying he knew that Ms. Mac worked there, the woman sternly but calmly said that he had exactly ten seconds to leave the property or she would call the police and have him arrested for trespassing. And she began counting, *Ten, nine . . .*

He'd used the first five of those seconds to quickly apologize if he in any way had offended her—then headed for his car parked around the corner.

Sitting in the Audi now, he watched people coming and going from the Sanctuary building. They mostly were teenagers, both male and female, and the occasional adult with a child in tow. To enter the locked door, he saw that they used some sort of electronic card key.

Getting inside the facility would pose Gurnov no challenge whatever—the teens, for example, were standing there and talking while holding the door wide open with no care in the world—but gaining entry would serve no purpose other than drawing the wrong kind of attention.

What he needed was information.

When he had asked Ricky if there were any other girls recruited from these two facilities, he'd said only the two who were gone.

"What do you mean 'gone'? They're working in Florida or Texas?"

"They were."

"And now?"

"Now they're gone. For good."

I should check on him.

Gurnov's go-phone vibrated. He looked at its small screen. It showed a text message from Julio:

215-555-3582

MULE AT BAG CLAIM

Finally! Good news!

Gurnov, waiting for an update, went back to watching the activity at the Sanctuary.

Ten minutes later, Gurnov's primary cell phone rang.

He looked at it and answered in Russian: "Everything okay, Nick?"

"I've been thinking. I need you to handle the product."

Product?

"Okay. What is going on?"

Gurnov's go-phone vibrated. He read Julio's update:

215-555-3582

MULE JUST LOST LOAD

Gurnov blurted, "Shit!"

"What happened?" Nick said, still in Russian.

"Nothing. Just realized I lost something."

He texted back:

```
LOST??? HOW WAS IT LOST?? ARE YOU SURE?
```

It was a moment before Nick said, "Jorge Perez is up to something."

"What do you mean?"

"I keep replaying what was said during the call this morning."

Me, too, Nick.

"And what, Nick?"

"He's up to something. I smell it. If I caught him smuggling those Cubans, who knows what else he is up to. That could have blown everything, the girls and the coke."

"No argument."

"Good. That is why I need you to arrange to meet Perez's cousin and secure the product."

Jorge said Carlos left this morning, so he will not get here until to-morrow morning. At the very earliest.

"Not a problem. I will handle it."

Gurnov's go-phone vibrated again, adding a new text:

```
215-555-3582


DEA HERE . . . DOG MUST HAVE SNIFFED IT OUT


DUDE LOOKS BAD
```

This time Gurnov stopped himself from saying anything.

But he thought: *Bad? Of course!*

As one should when he realizes he has just screwed up and got his beautiful young wife and son killed!

Damn it!

"Dmitri, are you there?"

"Sorry. I was distracted."

"You must have lost something big."

If only you knew. Which I cannot let happen.

"You have Perez's number, yes?"

I actually have his and Carlos's.

"I do."

"Call me, Dmitri. Let me know how it goes. And find whatever it is that you lost—you need your head straight."

"Of course."

He hung up and looked out the windshield, thinking.

Then his go-phone vibrated.

Now what the hell is Julio going to tell me?

He looked.

Who . . . ? he thought, as he read:

```
831-555-6235


MAYBE I HAVE YOUR BOOKS. MAYBE I DON'T.


WHO IS THIS?
```

Dmitri Gurnov felt his anger flare. It bordered on fury.

Do not dare to play games with me.
You are dead!

Five minutes later, after firing off a string of messages, he got what would be the last one from the woman. Two minutes after that, beyond furious, he was still looking at it:

```
831-555-6235


I NEED $200,000 CASH BY TOMORROW.


I'LL BE IN TOUCH.
```

This dollar amount, it is not random.
She knows. She does have the books.
I should kill Ricky.
But first this woman.

He wrote:

```
IT WILL TAKE A LITTLE TIME TO GET THAT MUCH IN
CASH.


BUT YOU SHOULD HAVE WHAT YOU WISH BY TOMORROW.


IF YOU WOULD MEET ME WITH PROOF THAT YOU HAVE WHAT
IS MINE?
```

A PAGE WOULD SUFFICE.

AND OF COURSE IT SHOULD BE A PUBLIC PLACE OF YOUR
CHOOSING.

He read it over.

Not all a lie.

Cash will be short now that I have to pay for the coke that was lost.

And she can pick any place she wants to die.

Dmitri Gurnov hit SEND, then threw the go-phone onto the passenger seat.

He yanked the transmission into drive and sped toward Chestnut Street, trying to decide if it was the fastest route to the Fishtown dive bar.

[THREE]
The Roundhouse
Eighth and Race Streets, Philadelphia
Monday, November 17, 3:15 P.M.

Matt Payne approached the heavy wooden door of the Executive Command Center on the top floor of police headquarters. He could hear the low hum of activity inside.

When he pulled the door open, it didn't surprise him to find maybe twenty men and women, both sworn officers and civilian staff, in the brightly lit room. Most were seated at the T-shaped conference tables, busily working at the rows of laptop computers and multiline telephones. On the ten-foot-tall wall before them, the three banks of sixty-inch flat-screen monitors, twenty-seven total, were all glowing, their screens reflecting on the glass-topped conference tables.

Payne felt some people glancing at him as he entered. He exchanged nods with those who made eye contact with him—including Kerry Rapier, seated across the room at the ECC's control bank, who greeted him by raising one of Matt's coffee mugs and mouthing *Marshal*—then they turned back to their computers and phones.

Being called the Wyatt Earp of the Main Line cut both ways. While Matt had widespread support—beginning with Mayor Carlucci—he was acutely aware that not everyone thought he should be a cop. There were more than a few who felt his privileged upbringing and high connections gave him, put very politely, an unfair advantage. And his reputation for headline-grabbing O.K. Corral shoot-outs that left a long trail of dead bad guys only poured fuel on what was their fiery rhetoric.

Matt knew that no matter what he did, some opinions would never change. He didn't dwell on his detractors, but he also made sure he didn't forget that they were there—and would love nothing better than to see him fail.

Preferably in a very public way.

I don't give a damn what they think about me.

But failure for me would mean failure for Maggie and the others.

He glanced around.

So far as I know no one in here has knives out for me, he thought, turning to the big wall.

He scanned the banks of monitors. There were four prominent

images of females, each with her name in white letters on a red bar across the top. The one he recognized immediately was that of Maggie McCain. It was a very attractive shot of her, fashionably dressed for a children's charity fund-raiser, standing on the wide steps in front of the Philadelphia Museum of Art.

From their files that Kerry Rapier had e-mailed him that morning, Payne also recognized the others. The name bars above them identified them as Krystal Gonzalez, Emily Quan, and Jocelyn Spencer. Each had a box at the bottom that listed her height, weight, date of birth, last known address, aliases (all had "none"), and police file number.

The Gonzalez girl's photograph was a self-portrait. It came from her Mary's House file and showed her, at age seventeen, standing in front of a bathroom mirror holding a small digital camera. She wore snug shorts, a very tight New York Yankees three-quarter-sleeve shirt, and she was flashing a radiant smile.

The image of the twenty-six-year-old Quan was of her sitting at an office desk, her straight black hair framing her thin ivory face and doe eyes and falling to the black cardigan sweater she wore over a white T-shirt.

The tall, somber-faced Spencer, who was twenty-seven, had been photographed on a city neighborhood sidewalk. She wore blue jeans and a red Temple University sweatshirt. A gold sequined purse, hanging from her shoulder by a thin chain of gold links, glinted in the sunlight.

The other monitors displayed a wide variety of information from the files that were being updated constantly—Matt saw the forensics report on the Molotov cocktail stating that the fingerprint analysis ultimately had failed—to crime-scene photographs of Maggie Mc-

Cain's burned home, to exterior shots of Mary's House and the West Philadelphia Sanctuary, and more.

Payne felt a massive hand on his shoulder, then behind him Lieutenant Jason Washington's deep voice said, "Glad you made it back safely, Matthew."

Payne turned and held out his right hand.

"Thanks, Jason." He nodded toward the high wall of monitors. "So we're working all four cases as one."

"With the CPS thread, it's clear that the disappearances are connected. They have to be. We just haven't yet turned over the rock beneath the rock that has the link from them to the miscreant."

"Or miscreants plural?"

Washington nodded. "My instinct tells me that solving one will lead to solving them all. Worst case: If I'm wrong, at least we've solved one. Which is more than has been accomplished thus far."

Matt looked back at the banks of monitors.

"Let's hope we find the others alive," he said.

"Did you see the e-mail from this morning that Maggie sent her family?" Washington said.

"The one by way of India? Yeah, I did. And, taking a shot in the dark, I sent her one saying she has to communicate with us. At least send some proof of life."

Washington nodded. "And?"

"And so far nothing but absolute silence."

"Well, it certainly was not a wasted effort. You know what Franklin said, 'One catches more fish with more hooks in the water.' Or perhaps it was my father who said that."

Payne chuckled, then said, "I see the fingerprints failed. Anything else come up?"

"A couple items of note," Washington said. "One, Mickey O'Hara was the first in the media to figure out it was Maggie's house that had been hit."

"He told me last night. The connection goes back to when she contacted him about his series of articles that triggered reforms in Child Protective Services. Mick likes Maggie. He wants to help."

"I know. After you called and talked to Tony, I talked with Mickey about that. Because he likes Maggie, and also has a deep appreciation for what she does at Mary's House, I got him to agree to embargo her name." He paused, then added, "That all changed when Maggie's father called today and said he wants his daughter's face in every newspaper and on every newscast. Said if we didn't make the call, he would. Carlucci failed to dissuade him. So, for giving us a little time by not releasing Maggie's name, I gave Mickey the murdered girl's name and the promise of another scoop. He just broke the story on Maggie and the girl."

Washington stepped over to an unattended laptop, opened it, and pulled up CrimeFreePhilly.com.

The website, which O'Hara had developed with the backing of communications giant KeyCom, was what he described as "a clearinghouse of all things related to reducing crime in the city." It aggregated articles and more—everything from lists of the Most Wanted to sending out crime news alerts—making it easier for the local citizenry to stay informed and involved. With Crime-FreeLA and CrimeFreeNYC in development, O'Hara, ever the enterprising journalist, also had recently launched PhillyNewsNow.com, which covered not just cops and criminals but all news in the city.

Washington pointed at the computer screen. "It's now the lead article."

Matt, reading over his shoulder, saw that CrimeFreePhilly had picked up Mickey's story from the new website:

BREAKING NEWS FROM PHILLY NEWS NOW

Update: Society Hill Home Invasion

By Michael J. O'Hara

A Philadelphia Police Department source has confirmed that the Society Hill townhome invaded last Saturday night and set on fire is the residence of Margaret McCain, the twenty-five-year-old scion of one of Philadelphia's founding families.

The police source also confirmed that a nineteen-year-old, Krystal Angel Gonzalez, had been killed in the kitchen. She was the only person found in the burning home. The cause of her death was a gunshot to the head.

The police, who do not consider Ms. McCain a person of interest, are asking anyone with information on the crime to call 215-686-TIPS (8477) or send a text message to PPDTIP (773847).

Click here for the original news report. And check back for further updates on this developing story.

Payne, looking from the screen to Washington, then noticed a familiar face in a corner of the room. The tall, muscular thirty-one-year-old was at the far end of a T-shaped conference table and talking on one of the multiline telephones.

Washington followed his eyes.

"That was the other item of note," Washington said. "We have a visitor."

Jim Byrth wore a navy blazer, white dress shirt, and dark necktie. Upside down on the seat of the chair on the other side of him was his white Stetson.

Matt knew that, under the blazer, Jim wore a silver badge, a star within a circle engraved with TEXAS RANGERS, pinned just above his shirt pocket.

"He asked if I minded him having a look at what we were doing," Washington said.

Payne nodded appreciatively.

"I have to admit that I hoped that would happen. He's one helluva cop. And with murders up and budgets slashed, we can't afford to turn down free help."

Byrth looked their way, noticed Payne was with Washington, and nodded. He stood while still on his call, then hung up and headed their way.

Matt turned as Jim approached. More than a few sets of eyes followed the two men as they shook hands and then patted each other on the back.

"Nice tan, Marshal."

"Not nice enough. But I'm here now. Good to see you, Jim." He glanced at Washington, and added, "I hear you're earning your keep."

Byrth shook his head as he looked at the big wall of monitors. "I don't think so. There is a lot of solid information." He looked back to Matt. "But I'm just a simple country boy. I'm not coming up with what to make of it."

"Welcome to the club, country boy," Payne said, then turned to Washington.

"What else are you going to give Mickey?" Matt said. "That other scoop?"

"The names of Emily Quan and Jocelyn Spencer," Washington said.

Payne considered that, then said, "You don't think it will trigger serial killer headlines? Mickey won't sensationalize it, but others will jump to conclusions."

"All we can do is stress that the women are missing, not dead. And then Mickey, and the others, can run with 'Police need your help in locating . . .' "

Payne nodded.

"And giving him the names would be a good time to pick his brains on CPS," Washington said. "He really knows it well, the good and the bad."

"Liberties?" Payne asked, but it was more a statement.

Jason was nodding. Liberties Bar was the official watering hole of the Homicide Unit.

"I'll buy," Byrth said.

"I was expecting you to," Matt said. "The best drinks are ones that someone else pays for."

Byrth chuckled.

"I may even let you buy dinner," Matt added.

"And maybe afterward we can swing by that flophouse?"

Payne looked to Washington for his input. He had not forgotten that when Jason had seen the image of the girl in the blue drum of sulfuric acid in that morning's videoconference call, he had said it was horrific but that Matt's priority was the McCain case.

Washington hadn't forgotten either.

"Since Jim is devoting time to working these cases," Jason said, "I believe it's fair that you spend time on his. I have confidence in your ability to simultaneously chew gum and walk."

Payne nodded as he pulled out his cell phone and sent a text message to O'Hara: "Liberties at 4."

"Thank you, Jason," Byrth said.

Payne's phone vibrated. He looked and saw O'Hara's reply.

"Mickey says he'll be there in thirty."

"I'll try to catch up with you," Washington said, checking his watch. "Denny has requested my presence. The mayor is dealing with Commissioner Gallagher."

Payne looked at Byrth. "When Gallagher—the Commish—retired, Carlucci took the job. Like Hizzoner, the Commish is a cop's cop."

"He is a very good man," Washington said.

Byrth nodded.

"So, what's Gallagher's problem?" Payne said.

"Does the name John Garvey ring a bell?"

Payne shook his head. "Should it?"

"And here I thought you knew everyone. Garvey was arrested this afternoon at PHL and just brought in. They put him in an interview room downstairs. Denny wants me to look in with them as he's being questioned."

"What's he charged with?"

"Drug smuggling."

"John Garvey?" Payne said, clearly searching his memory.

"John Garvey," Washington confirmed. "He's in his mid-thirties. An architect-slash-historian. His specialty is restoration of historic buildings. He travels the world doing it. He looks like a well-dressed professor, a bookish type who would release a bug outside before squashing it in the house. I met him when my better half had me attend a museum function. I learned then that he's married to the daughter of his boss, Harvey Rendolok."

"A-ha!" Payne said. "Harvey, I know. Damn decent guy. Long-time member of the Union League. And his wife is running for judge. Needless to say, they're big supporters of the military and police."

"Right. And Harvey's father-in-law is?"

Payne's eyebrows went up as the connection was made.

"The Commish . . ." he said slowly, and then was silent for a moment. "My God! And now the Commish's grandson-in-law, or whatever the hell that would make him, has been arrested for smuggling drugs?"

"I was told that for the last six months he's been working on the renovation of Saints Peter and Paul Cathedral."

Payne pointed. "The one down Race, over by Logan Circle? What's it called? Cathedral Basilica of Saints Peter and Paul?"

"There happens to be more than one in the world, Matthew," Washington said dryly. "And this particular one happens to be in the Virgin Islands. On Saint Thomas."

Payne's face brightened.

"He's been working in the Caribbean for six months? Now, that's something I could get used to."

"Not a solid six months. He was going down for two weeks at a time."

"Still beats being stuck in this miserable winter weather."

"And he got caught smuggling what?" Byrth said.

"Two one-kilogram bricks of cocaine to PHL."

"No offense," Byrth said, "but grabbing two keys is a slow morning on the Texas border. The Rangers alone average that. The Customs and Border Patrol guys get even more."

"I understood a very slow morning," Washington said. "And that proves the point that it's cause and effect."

"Meaning?" Payne said.

Washington gestured at Byrth. "While our friends along the Mexican border may not be stopping all the trafficking, they are shutting down a lot. The pressure is forcing the cartels to develop old and new routes. There has been a sharp rise in cocaine moving from Colombia and Venezuela through the Caribbean to the States. That's why direct flights coming here from the islands and South Florida are getting much heavier scrutiny."

"Too bad they didn't let him make the delivery," Payne said, "follow the package farther up the chain."

"From what I was told, they were not certain that he had the drugs. And he certainly did not have the characteristics of a courier. Following him could have turned into a wild-goose chase. The best they could do was ask for permission to search. And he instantly owned up that he had the drugs."

Washington suddenly produced his cell phone from his jacket pocket.

He looked at it, then said: "We can discuss further at Liberties. I have been summoned downstairs."

When Washington had gone out the door of the ECC, Payne turned to Byrth.

"Okay, we grab dinner and some liquid encouragement with Mickey at Liberties before heading over to the flophouse. That should put us there right about the time the crackheads come home to roost."

"Perfect."

"Do you have a room?"

"Not yet."

"You could use my apartment if it wasn't a mess of half-packed moving boxes. Hang on." He searched his address book, found the number he wanted. After a moment, he said into the phone, "Hello, this is Matt Payne. I have a guest I'd like to get a room for—" He listened for a moment, then said, "You are? Very well. Please call me if that changes. Thank you."

He raised his eyebrows as he looked at Byrth.

"What?" Byrth said.

"Plan B, as in Byrth," Payne then said, holding up his left index finger as his right thumb hit a speed-dial key on his phone.

He recognized the slight Polish accent when his call was answered on the first ring.

"David, it's Matt Payne. How are you fixed for an overflow room tonight?" He paused to listen. "Great. Save it for me for the next week, starting tonight. I'll get the key around nine."

He hung up and looked at Byrth.

"What was that about?" Jim said.

"I called the Union League, where you stayed last time?"

Byrth nodded.

"They're sold out. Then, I don't know why I didn't think of it first, I called the Hops Haus. They maintain a couple of one-bedroom condos that they rent out like hotel rooms. If you don't have room for a guest in your condo, you can put them up downstairs in a place that's as nice as any five-star but at a quarter the price."

"Thanks. But a week? My blood is too thin for this cold weather, and I'm accustomed to closing cases faster than that."

"However long you like. Now, I need to find us a car."

"I've got a rental," Byrth said, pulling out a key. "You want to drive? It's your town."

"You do remember what happened to the last two cars I had."

Byrth met his eyes, then stuffed the key back in his pocket.

"On second thought, you can navigate."

VIII

[ONE]
Kensington, Philadelphia
Monday, November 17, 3:21 P.M.

Driving back into Philadelphia, Ricky Ramírez knew he was on extremely shaky ground with Dmitri Gurnov.

Gurnov was the angriest he had ever been with him after he allowed Krystal Gonzalez to get her hands on the ledgers and then screwed up the chance to get them back. He shook his head, remembering what Dmitri had said.

"There's gonna be hell to pay for this. Mr. Antonov does not like surprises."

And now, driving back from Atlantic City when Gurnov thought Ramírez was headed to Miami would probably put him over the top.

But not if I get this woman, get the books.

Everything, it will be good again.

Especially since he called and said he hadn't found her at none of those places.

Héctor, he will know what to do.

Ricky was on his third NRG! drink in as many hours, sucking down the small cans of caffeine and sugar water to battle his hangover and exhaustion. It was starting to make him even more anxious.

It had been a miserable trip to the Jersey Shore. The drive had begun early that morning, after he had loaded into the Mazda minivan four girls who had spent the last week working out of the Players Corner Lounge. It was snowing, and the road conditions were poor, making rush hour traffic worse than usual on the way out.

It had taken more than two hours to reach Atlantic City. At Tiki Bob's Surf Shack—which was eight blocks inland from the Lucky Stars Casino on the boardwalk and set up similar to Players Corner Lounge, with strippers downstairs and two floors of beds above—the exchange of the four in the minivan for the three girls who had worked the week at Tiki Bob's had taken far longer than Ricky would have preferred.

Then, on the way back on the Atlantic City Expressway, just past the exit for Egg Harbor, New Jersey, a bus had been in the middle of at least a ten-car pileup.

Worse, he had been stuck listening to the girls whine.

"I still don't get why we aren't hitting Florida next, Ricky," Janice, a twenty-year-old pasty-skinned brunette, had said from the backseat.

His chunky, pockmarked face filled the rearview mirror as he met her eyes.

"I told you it is now next week!" he snapped. "I had something come up!"

"But it's, like, warm there," Janice went on. "And I'm so, like, sick of this snow."

"And it will still be warm there next week," he said impatiently.

"I'm tired of being cold, too, Ricky," Shanika, a nineteen-year-old who had pale, freckled skin and her hair dyed ruby red, chimed in.

Jasmine, the bleached blonde in her mid-twenties sitting beside him, joined in, "Why are we missin'—"

"Will you all just fuckin' shut up?" Ramírez said.

Jasmine turned toward him. "But—"

He raised his right hand to backslap her, then realized they were in heavy stop-and-go traffic and quickly lowered it.

"Shut up!" he said. "Now!"

The girls finally got the message and, after leaning their heads against the windows, slept the rest of the trip to Fishtown.

It had taken more than three hours to cover the sixty miles. He did not want to think how long driving south would have taken.

And now I got to change the ads on that escort website. Take the ones off the Miami pages, put them up on the Philly ones.

Then change it all back next week?

Maybe just change the dates on the Miami ones, and leave them up? Damn! Keepin' these putas *moving around is too much work!*

At Players Corner Lounge, it had taken the better part of an hour to get the girls, sleepy and dragging their feet, out of the minivan and settled in the rooms above the dive bar. Then Ramírez hopped back in the minivan and headed up Frankford Avenue.

Near the circular building that was Horatio B. Hackett Elementary School, he turned onto Trenton Avenue and followed it three blocks, looking in his mirror for anyone following him, as Dmitri had taught him. He made a right turn. At the second intersection he made a left onto Tulip Street, and again checked the mirror as he drove. After three blocks he made a right onto Sergeant, found the first open spot along the curb, and parked.

Ramírez got out and pulled his coat closed against the cold. The icy breeze carried with it a sharp industrial smell. The metallic burning odor—which he guessed came from the auto salvage yard just across Lehigh Avenue, or maybe from the old distillery down the street—irritated his nostrils.

A couple hits of that blackberry brandy they make would be good to cut this damn cold, he thought, then rubbed his nose. *And this smell.*

He turned back a block—crossing the street with the flophouse that he realized he had not visited in a couple of months—then quickly went over two more blocks. As he walked, he hit some slippery spots on the sidewalk, recovered before actually falling, and wished he could have parked closer. But Dmitri had said to always park at least three blocks away from the grow house and approach it on foot so that he would not draw any extra attention to it. The worst thing he could do was park right out front. Cars coming and going wasn't good, Dmitri said.

Almost to the next intersection, he saw across the street three men in their thirties sitting on the stoop of a boarded-up row house. They were all brown-skinned and gaunt and looked like they hadn't had a bath in a long time. The tallest one, with a scraggly beard and hair matted in dreadlocks under a dirty, multicolored knitted cap, had to his lips what at first glance appeared to be a cigarette. But then Ramírez recognized it, and caught in the air the unmistakable pungent smell of marijuana.

The three, who Ramírez decided had to be from one of the nearby flophouses, did not pay him any attention as he passed.

That was not the case with the pair he encountered next.

On the opposite corner, Ramírez came up on two Hispanic teenagers—they looked maybe sixteen and were probably Puerto Rican—with a battered gray Yamaha FZ1 motorcycle on its stand between them. They wore bulky dark coats, their hands stuffed in the deep pockets, and had black stocking caps pulled down low on their heads. They talked to each other as their eyes darted between the three brown-skinned men sharing the joint and the approaching Ramírez.

The teenagers didn't recognize Ramírez, nor he them. But he knew what they were.

Some of Héctor's halcónes.

And he knew that the "hawks" had more than their hands in their coat pockets. Lookouts always carried a disposable cell phone, of course, and often a pistol.

Ramírez turned the corner, and midway down the street he crossed over. He went up to the door of the last of the five rough-looking row houses on the block. The first two houses, tagged with graffiti, had realtor signs nailed to their doors that read FOR SALE—BANK FORECLOSURE. There was chain-link fencing, eight feet high, vine-covered and topped with coils of razor wire, blocking off the side and rear yards.

Just as Ramírez knocked twice on the door, wondering if there was an eyeball on the other side of the dirty peephole, he heard dead bolt locks turning.

The door swung inward. The row house interior was dark, but just beyond the door—and behind a wall of thick, clear plastic sheeting that hung from ceiling to floor—Ramírez could make out two human forms standing midway in the room. They were aiming the Kalashnikovs he'd brought at him.

"Get inside, Ricky!" the one on the left gently urged in Spanish, lowering the AK-47 he'd converted to fully automatic.

Ricky, recognizing Héctor Ramírez's voice, went through the door. It was immediately closed behind him and the dead bolts thrown. An overhead lightbulb came on, and Ricky saw the short Hispanic male who had locked the door and hit the switch. He now was pulling the sheeting from the wall. He gestured for Ricky to go through.

There was another motorcycle, a big Kawasaki, by the door. Duct tape held more of the clear plastic sheeting over the windows, sealing them. Ricky crossed the big front room of the house. It was mostly empty except for a ratty sofa, a wooden box that served as a coffee table, and a big flat-screen TV mounted on a wall.

"*Hola, mi amigo,*" Héctor said, his tone friendly.

Just hearing that caused Ricky to start feeling a little better. They had developed a strong relationship—*maybe 'cause of our Latin thing, and being from the islands*—one far better than what Ricky and Dmitri had. Héctor's calm demeanor helped ground him, balancing out Ricky's quick temper and his tendency to be reckless.

Héctor was a swarthy forty-year-old whose hardscrabble life had included spending his early thirties in a Cuban jail. After growing up on a tobacco farm in central Cuba, he had made his way to Havana. He worked various jobs in the restaurants and bars, then wound up running hookers to the tourists out of a Havana apartment building. And got busted. He discovered that his primary crime against the socialist motherland wasn't pimping—which, unlike the prostitution, was illegal—it was his failure to pay off the correct *policía* with U.S. dollars or free *putas* or both.

In jail he had heard about the smugglers who, for a fee that he could work off, would get him to Florida. When released, he had wasted no time seeking them out. Once in the States, and owing ten grand for his passage aboard the fast boat, he had his horticulture skills put to the test. The smugglers were Cuban exiles and had grow houses near Miami. Héctor found cultivating marijuana indoors much easier than hoeing rows of tobacco under the Cuban sun. He also found himself almost back behind bars—someone had tipped off the house to the DEA. His handlers sent him to Philadelphia, subtracting a little from his bill for transporting a kilogram each of black tar heroin and cocaine.

Ricky Ramírez, after getting a call from Dmitri Gurnov, had taken delivery. When he heard Héctor's story—and Héctor convinced him that running a grow house would be easy money—Ricky set him up in the rented row houses in Kensington. Ricky had lied to Dmitri that that money—which had included what he advanced Héctor to satisfy his debt in Little Havana—was a loan. It really was Ricky using Dmitri's money. Héctor now worked for him.

Ricky knew he'd luckily gotten away with all that. So far.

"I'm glad that you are here, Jefe," Héctor said, patting Ricky on the back. "It's been months. I have something to show you."

Ricky motioned in the direction of the teenagers outside.

"Your *halcónes* look about ready to shoot someone," he said.

Héctor laughed. "They all want to think they're *sicarios*. But those two, Tito and Juan, they are only couriers. One drives and the other rides to deliver the pot."

"Courier, assassin," Ricky said, "only difference is a shooting."

Héctor laughed again.

"Yes, I guess that is true, Ricky. Now come with me. . . ."

[TWO]
Liberties Bar
502 N. Second Street, Philadelphia
Monday, November 17, 4:45 P.M.

"Teenaged kids in foster care are ripe for the picking by pimps," Mickey O'Hara said, sliding the files on the two missing West Philadelphia Sanctuary case workers that Matt Payne had given him back in the envelope. He then put that in his laptop case at his feet. "It is tragically simple."

Payne and Jim Byrth, having arrived at Liberties first, were seated at the far end of the enormous dark oak Victorian bar that ran along most of the wall. They had a view of the entire room, including the front window—through which could be seen the back of the bar's five-foot-tall replica of the Statue of Liberty—and the front door. O'Hara, his back to it all, stood near them at the corner, leaning with his forearms against the bar as he nursed a Guinness Black Lager. Matt had before him a half-finished eighteen-year-old Macallan single malt whisky, slightly cut with water and two ice cubes. Jim sipped at a Jack Black on the rocks. They picked at two overflowing baskets of hand-cut onion rings and fries.

The narrow brick-faced three-story Liberties was at the end of a hundred-year-old building that went the entire block. A half circle of canvas awning with an inviting Lady Liberty painted on it overhung its front door.

The heavy wooden interior was rich in character, warm and intimate, what came from decades of crowds drinking, eating, laughing, living. The crowd was light now—only one other man at the bar, close to the window and talking with the bartender, and two couples, one at a table in the middle of the room and another in one of the wooden booths lining the opposite wall—but it would quickly build as people stopped in on their way home from work.

O'Hara went on: "Like all kids, the ones in foster care are hungry for love and attention. Arguably more so. Their fathers and mothers who should have provided that instead failed them miserably—often because their parents had failed them, too. It's a vicious cycle."

He paused and took a sip of beer. Then he chewed on an onion ring as he gathered his thoughts.

"Okay," he went on, "so here's the fairy-tale version. Let's give our foster child a name. Call her, oh, say, Joyce. She's fourteen. Her parents die in a car wreck, leaving her an orphan with no other family. The courts take custody, put her in the care of CPS. She's matched with a foster family, who raise Joyce as their own. She graduates high school, then at eighteen exits CPS and maybe goes to community college down Spring Garden Street here, or to a beautician's school, or just gets married. And Joyce lives happily ever after."

"And we all know that's not what happens . . ." Matt said.

Jim grunted, nodding as he sipped his bourbon.

Mickey looked between them.

"And we know that's not what happens," Mickey parroted. "The cruel reality of what happens is that Joyce is fourteen going on twenty-four. She has a father she's never known. Her mother, who might have two or three baby daddies, is bipolar, a crackhead, a hooker, dead. Pick one, or more. The courts send Joyce to CPS. But there are no available foster homes, so Joyce winds up, if lucky, at a place like Mary's House, run by someone like Maggie. Or at a larger facility that has, shall we say, less considerate caretakers. Now, one of two things can happen. One, Joyce remains there in the group home due to the lack of an available foster family. Or two, she gets placed in a foster home, where she learns that the foster parents may mean well but really are not a helluva lot better than the caretakers in the large group home. Many foster parents do not supervise the kids. Cannot, because they're working to keep food on the table and a roof over their heads."

"There's the subsidy check," Payne said.

O'Hara nodded. "There is that. But try covering your monthly nut with three hundred bucks from CPS, maybe another three hundred in food stamps."

Payne shook his head. "That's not even seven grand a year."

"If that much," Mickey said. "Further, a lot of foster families, sad to say, are not going to win Parent of the Year by, for example, slapping around Joyce for not cleaning house quietly enough while they're on their fat asses watching the Eagles lose. And if there are other kids in the house, and there usually are, either other foster kids or biological ones, they take advantage of the new kid on the block, including abusing Joyce physically and/or sexually." He paused, then raised an eyebrow. "Maggie phrased it, 'Think Cinderella but a triple-X-rated version.'"

"Kids can be incredibly cruel," Jim said matter-of-factly.

"And so much for any chance of Joyce's fairy-tale ending," Payne said bitterly, then shook his head. He took a healthy swallow of scotch.

"So," Mickey went on, "Joyce, enduring a living hell, has limited options. She can go back to step one, the group home, and hope for a better foster family to come along and take a chance on her. Or she can run away. Let's say Joyce is sixteen now. What is she going to do to survive? How does she provide basic food and shelter? And safety?"

He looked between Jim and Matt.

"So, she goes back to square one," Matt said.

"And reserves the runaway option," Jim added.

"Joyce is still essentially a child and operating in survival mode, doing the best she can with what little she has learned the hard way. Keep in mind that she has never had any good adult role models." Mickey sipped his beer for a moment, then went on: "Okay, so she's back in the group home. She's frustrated to the point that she's contemplating the runaway option when one of the staff—say, someone in the kitchen who's been watching her—approaches Joyce and says, 'You're a beautiful girl. I know how you can make a lot of money. I can hook you up with this guy. . . .' And Joyce hears all about the other girls who at her age went to work waiting tables or as a hostess and earned enough money to get out on their own."

"Bingo," Matt said. "Just what Joyce wants to hear. She's sold."

Jim grunted again. "Literally. Sold out."

"For a lousy hundred-buck kickback," O'Hara said, nodding. "You've got kitchen staff making maybe eight bucks an hour. At forty hours, that's three-twenty a week—sixteen grand a year—before taxes, et cetera."

"And the social workers don't make a helluva lot more," Payne put in, grabbing an onion ring.

O'Hara, still nodding, said, "At this level they average about forty grand, give or take. To get that, they have to have a good degree, which means they're strapped with college student loans to repay. A couple hundred bucks coming in tax-free is golden. Better than manna from the heavens! They justify it by saying what they're doing is a matching service. They're just getting the girls a job, an opportunity. If the girl decides to go and dabble in something on the side, that's the girl's decision. So, one girl goes out the door, and new ones come in."

Payne was shaking his head. "I was about to say it's disgusting that people in a position of power over kids would take advantage of them. But then I had the mental flash of those high school teachers banging their students."

"Obviously not everyone's dirty," O'Hara said. "But that certainly doesn't ease the pain caused by those who are."

He waved for the bartender to bring them another round.

"Meanwhile," O'Hara went on, "Joyce meets the guy, who then says he has no openings for waitresses. He tells her he's got something higher paying but he's not sure she can do the job—which of course only makes her want it more. Then he quote unquote reluctantly agrees to give Joyce a chance, saying he'll personally show her the ropes. He says it's a massage business. Really just body rubs. He tells her that he will bring in the customers, she massages them for a half hour, then they split the hundred bucks.

"Suddenly she sees that the guy is giving her the attention she's been craving. He lays on the affection and the material things to make Joyce feel special. Then he feeds her drugs, her inhibitions go down, and next thing she knows it's no longer massages. She's being paid for sex. And he's keeping all the money. And she's trapped."

"Did Maggie say she'd seen this happen?" Payne said.

"Last time we spoke, I guess maybe six months or so ago, she said she'd heard about it from the girls and other case workers. Nothing concrete that she could take to the cops. And she said absolutely nothing at Mary's House."

"Well," Payne said, "that would be an expected answer. But clearly Maggie would never do it. Moncy is not an issue. Not to mention sex trafficking a minor carries a sentence of ten years minimum. But what about the other women, Emily Quan and Jocelyn Spencer?"

O'Hara shrugged. "Who can say? I don't think so. But it cannot be automatically dismissed."

Payne, looking at O'Hara, then looked beyond him to the front door. "Here comes Jason. And he doesn't look happy."

[THREE]
Little Bight Bay
Saint John, United States Virgin Islands
Monday, November 17, 4:50 P.M.

Maggie McCain, holding the fifty-foot-long white-hulled catamaran on a fast course, looked up from under her navy cap and smiled. The sails were finely tuned to the point that the big cat hummed with the steady stiff wind. It felt alive, knifing with a smooth rhythm through the waves. And that had made Maggie feel more alive. And given her time to think.

It had taken Maggie a half hour to reach the north shore of Saint John, the next island over from Saint Thomas. Farther east, she could make out Sage Mountain rising on the horizon at Tortola—where not even a mile of water separated the British Virgin Islands from the USVI.

Maggie, the wind whipping her ponytail, scanned the Saint John shoreline looking for her landmark. The lush green hills rose steeply above the enormous volcanic boulders and the strips of white sand beach.

She loved the seclusion of Little Bight and the fact that few could find it. The mouth of the small bay was barely twice as wide as the catamaran's beam of twenty-five feet. It was tucked in behind a mass of boulders that formed a crescent at the foot of a tall hill, making the entrance all but invisible.

After a moment, among a line of brown boulders, she found the landmark—an enormous rock softly etched by wind and water that to her eye resembled one of Picasso's contorted human faces.

She spun the big stainless steel wheel, putting Pablo's big-eyed boulder dead ahead. Then, coming up on the gap to the bay, she uncleated the mainsheet, letting the air spill out. She dropped the mainsail. Minutes later, sailing on just the jib, the big boat smoothly slipped behind the crescent of boulders and into the protected bay.

What a difference being on the water makes.

I am back in control.

An hour earlier, Maggie had felt completely overwhelmed. Shaking out of control, she had taken the heavy shot of Cruzan rum to calm her—and then immediately knew that she could not keep drinking. She needed to clear her mind, and to think.

She had looked out at the sea and seen the small white triangles that were the sails of boats moving between the islands. She then immediately hopped up and grabbed her gear.

She went through the gap in the thick wall of sea grape trees Beatrix had told her about and found the stone path that cut back and forth down the hill to the beach and marina.

The dockmaster turned out to be in his thirties, a very tanned bald-headed man named Captain Jesse, who was the epitome of efficiency. Just as Beatrix had said, he had had the boat ready to go and insisted on a thorough walk-through, even after Maggie's announcement that she had sailed the very small model catamaran a few times.

"As you know," Captain Jesse said, "no two boats are the same."

The layout of the boat was basically similar to all other catamarans—the main cabin, with the galley and large living area, was between the two big hulls. Steps on either side of the main cabin led down to the four staterooms in the hulls, two queen-sized beds forward and two aft, which were separated by their lavatories.

Back up on the deck, the dockmaster had shown her that the electronics—from the VHF radio to the GPS to the wind-speed and water-depth gauges—all were in working order. He then pointed out the location of everything else she might need—the three anchors to the life jackets, emergency flares, first-aid kit—as well as the array of black panels affixed to the topside of the main cabin.

"Not all our boats have those," Captain Jesse said. "They're the solar cells that charge the batteries. Don't want to step on them."

He had shown her that the fuel and freshwater tanks were topped off, and that the galley was freshly provisioned. There was food enough to last a week, if Maggie stretched it, as well as nice wines—including two bottles of champagne—and beers.

"And," he'd said, "enough of our ubiquitous rum to throw a wicked party."

She smiled. "My friends I'm about to pick up will be excited to hear that."

He leaned forward and quietly added, "And if there's anything else they might need, I can handle that, too."

Else? What else?

Oh . . . that.

"It's quality. Only the best. There is a lot of bad stuff sold here."

Careful. Don't come off as a prude. . . .

"That's always good to know."

He handed her a card. "My cell is on here."

"Thank you," she said, then shook the dockmaster's hand, discreetly slipping him a folded hundred-dollar bill.

"Just let me know," he said, hopping onto the dock.

As he began untying lines, she pushed the starter button on the small outboard diesel engine. A couple of minutes later, all lines free, she eased the boat out of the slip.

At anchor in Little Bight Bay, the big catamaran floating in water so clear and still it looked to be suspended in air, Maggie pulled out the laptop and the satellite antenna and powered them up.

The window for her e-mail was up, so she clicked to update the list that was her in-box. There were a dozen new e-mails, including one from Matt Payne, and that made her curious.

The voice mail Amanda left me said she was in the Keys with Matt when she heard about the attack from Chad.

She clicked on Payne's e-mail, nodding thoughtfully as she read it. When she had finished, she realized she had begun to tear up.

If Matt has that e-mail I sent, then my father is behind this.

But Amanda has to have something to do with it, too.

I know the last thing she wants is Matt doing police work. Especially chasing another murderer.

She's carrying his baby . . .

She had to give her blessing for him to help me.

Maggie sighed, then quickly opened another browser window and typed in PhillyNewsNow.com.

"Well, so there you go," she said aloud, after reading the lead story's headline: "Update: Society Hill Home Invasion." *Tailor-made real-time proof.*

She reached into her canvas sail bag, pulled out a small digital camera, then, holding her head beside the laptop screen while holding the screen at such an angle that there would be only blue sky in the background, she forced a smile and snapped a series of photographs. Using the camera's wireless function, she sent the images to her laptop. And, after picking the one that clearly showed the headline, she went back to her e-mail window, clicked on REPLY, attached the photograph, and wrote:

```
From:    Maggie <magpie417@libertymail.com>
Date:    17NOV 0510
To:      <w.earp.45@pa.blueline.net>
CC:      SGT M.M. Payne <payne.m@ppd.philadelphia.gov>
Subject: RE: Your safety
Attachment: 1
```

Dear Matt,

Thank you for writing. It is difficult to express how much I deeply appreciate your concern.

I hope the attached photograph is what you need to know that I am genuinely safe.

With all due respect, and with admiration for your proven skills as a police officer, considering the circumstances I could not be in a safer place.

Please know that while this is an arduous situation, one that I do wish were resolved, I feel there are a few things that I have to do before, as you put it, life is back to normal.

I sincerely hope to see you and Amanda soon.

Fondly,

Maggie

She read it over, nodded, then sent it.

Then she thought: *Why should my family get it secondhand?*

And she then forwarded it to her parents and to her cousin Emma.

She then went to the My Free Texts page, punched in the California telephone number it had assigned to her, then her password.

The conversation string of text message bubbles was still there, along with a new bubble. She read it.

He wants me to bring him a page from the book as proof?

How stupid does he think I am?

"A place of my choosing"?

How absolutely magnanimous of him.

She read the message again.

I need to give him something, though.

She took the camera inside the cabin. She pulled from her backpack the notebook that was the ledger on the girls. She turned to a page that had a list of the girls' names and the cities where they were working. At the top of the page there also was a crude doodle of a woman's crotch.

She took a couple of photographs of that page, then repeated the process of sending it to her laptop.

Sliding the notebook inside the backpack, she had to work it around the thick brass-zippered bank pouch. And then she had an idea.

She pulled the pouch and the plastic bag that was imprinted in gold with Lucky Stars Casino & Entertainment from the backpack. Then she removed a handful of the hundred-dollar poker chips that were in the bag and fanned a wad of the hundred-dollar bills from the pouch. She took shots of the chips on top of the cash and bank pouch.

At My Free Texts, she attached one of the images of the ledger page to her reply and wrote:

HERE IS YOUR PROOF. NOW GET ME MY MONEY. I WILL
TELL YOU LATER WHERE THE PUBLIC TRANSFER WILL TAKE
PLACE.

She sent it, and a minute later was about to sign out when a new bubble popped up:

```
267-555-9100


THANK YOU VERY MUCH.


BUT I AM AFRAID THAT I DO REQUIRE PHYSICAL PROOF.
PLEASE.


THIS IS A GREAT DEAL OF MONEY INVOLVED.
```

We are not meeting, she thought, *even if it were physically possible. Not now. Not ever.*

Maggie, after attaching an image of the poker chips and cash, fired back:

```
PROOF? THIS IS ALL THE DAMN PROOF YOU NEED.


GET ME THE $200,000 AND YOU GET THE ACTUAL BOOKS.
```

[FOUR]
Kensington, Philadelphia
Monday, November 17, 3:30 P.M.

Ricky followed Héctor out the back door of the row house. As they walked toward a gate—the same razor-wire-topped chain-link fencing that surrounded the three backyards also separated them—he noticed that there was another heavy smell in the air, a different one, not quite as metallic as earlier.

On the other side of the gate, Ricky saw the large-gauge electric power cables, more or less concealed, running to the center row house from the PECO meters of the houses on both sides of it. He followed Héctor past the enormous air-conditioning unit, a new one that had been spray-painted in clouds of black and gray so it would not stand out, then onto the small wooden back porch.

The industrial smell was getting stronger. Ricky turned toward it and saw where it was coming from. A sheet-metal hood, bowl-shaped and also spray-painted with gray-black clouds, was mounted outside a rectangular hole at the foot of the back wall. It covered what had been a small window to the basement. Ricky visualized the four-inch-diameter vent tube behind it. The tube went down to the heavy steel lid that was cinched tight to the top of a 110-gallon drum, a ring of flames from a gas burner flickering under it.

Héctor, approaching the back door, saw him looking at the vent.

"Another day and then that's done." He shrugged. "Bigger ones take a little longer than usual."

Héctor slipped a key in the door's dead bolt, turned the knob, and swung it open. When they stepped inside, Ricky saw that there was another curtain of floor-to-ceiling clear plastic. Immediately beyond it, at the top of the stairs that led down to the basement, there were two cardboard boxes, their sides labeled "Technical Grade Sodium Hydroxide Lye Beads." One bulged with women's clothes. The other, half full, contained shoes and purses.

"All that," Héctor said, "is to get incinerated."

Ricky nodded.

Héctor pulled the plastic curtain aside, and they entered.

Héctor grinned and made a sweeping gesture toward what was

the main floor of the house. It held a giant tent made of the plastic sheeting—inside which was a small forest, two long rows of bushy green plants six feet tall—and what looked, at least by comparison to the old house, like a space-age array of hoses and wires and tubes supporting the tent.

"My controlled growing environment," Héctor said, waving Ricky inside the tent. "This is much better than what I started with in Miami. And soon we start another one in the first house."

Héctor had stripped the interior shell of the house bare. Then a framework of two-by-four studs had been added, and between the studs thick fiberglass insulation installed.

The entire room was then outlined in the tent of heavy plastic sheeting. Industrial-sized sheet-metal vents brought in the air-conditioning while other sheet-metal boxes drew the air out of the tent, sending it to activated carbon charcoal filters that removed odors and contaminates, then routed the scrubbed air back to the air conditioner. The complete volume of air in the tent was refreshed once an hour. The recirculated air was augmented with carbon dioxide created by burning natural gas in what once had been the kitchen and in the basement.

The forty plants were in two neat rows of twenty. They grew in plastic pots that sat on wooden racks built two feet high, allowing warm air to circulate around the roots. A web of black irrigation lines, on an automated pump system, regularly fed the plants a solution of nutrients from a sterilized stainless steel reservoir that resembled an oversized hot water heater.

Hanging a few feet from the ceiling were two rows of fluorescent light fixtures, each with ten one-thousand-watt lamps. The ropes passed through pulleys mounted to the ceiling, allowing the lights to be raised as the plants grew. Wall-mounted fans, above and below the height of the lights, circulated the air, as did big box fans, some set up to push air through the thick plant leaves while others pulled the air.

While it had been chilly outside the tent, the air now felt very warm and, with the high humidity, almost steamy.

And there was the strong, distinct smell of marijuana.

Ricky remembered what Héctor had told him when he first started the project. It sounded like another language.

"When the plant terpenoids evaporate, there is produced a chemical. It has an odor that is organic and heady. It smells the same as pot when it burns. If that gets to the outside, word would spread and we will have a rip-off. Or what happened to me in Miami—the cops come. So I will create a sealed space."

"These plants are healthier than our first ones," Héctor now said. "With more air flow, their stalks grow bigger. And with bigger stalks, the nutrients can travel better. And with more nutrients, the yield is bigger and better."

Héctor showed him the bank of monitors.

"This is the perfect growing environment," he said proudly.

Ricky saw that the readouts showed:

TEMPERATURE: 78 DEGREES F

HUMIDITY: 50 PERCENT

CO_2 (PARTS PER MILLION): 1,500

"And see these leaves?" Héctor went on. "No webs of mites, no bugs, no nothing but perfect formation."

Ricky nodded. "How did you get rid of them?"

"Same as we kill all pests, whether they have two legs or eight. We turn up the gas burners and create more carbon dioxide—the see-oh-two." He pointed to the monitor. "If we crank that up to ten thousand parts per million for an hour or two, spider mites and everything else is wiped out."

Héctor pulled from his pocket a jeweler's loupe and handed it to Ricky.

"Check the color inside the heads of the trichomes. Almost perfect. This crop is about ready to harvest."

Ricky nodded, made a cursory look with the magnifying glass, then handed back the loupe.

He looked him in the eyes.

"It is good, Héctor. Really good. But I came for something else. I need your help again."

Ricky glanced at the cardboard boxes labeled "Technical Grade Sodium Hydroxide Lye Beads."

"Another?" Héctor Ramírez said. "Just say who and when."

Ricky Ramírez looked back at him and began: "When is right now. Who is not as simple. That is why I need your help. That woman Krystal ran to? She is . . ."

Five minutes later, Ricky finished, ". . . and we don't know how to find her to get the books."

Héctor began to laugh.

"What?" Ricky snapped, thinking he was being mocked.

"No, Ricky. But this also is simple. You have already called it."

"Called what?"

"The *halcónes*. You said they want to be assassins. Then we can make them assassins."

Ricky thought about that for a moment.

"How can they shoot this woman if we don't know where she is?"

Héctor shook his head.

"You know where she works . . ." he began.

"But she might be there. She might not. There is no time to wait."

"So you repeat what happened with that Krystal. You do not wait. You draw the woman out with bait. Use the girls from the home. Kill one or two to make a point. Then leave a message: 'Another dies every day until you bring my things.'"

Ricky thought about that, then nodded. "Or every hour. That could—"

He jerked his head at the distinct sound of gunshots coming from down the street, then exchanged glances with Héctor.

Wordlessly, both men hurried toward the rear door.

As Ricky followed Héctor back through the first row house, with Héctor again holding his Kalashnikov, he saw the short Hispanic was leading the lookouts in through the front door.

"What happened, Jaime?" Héctor demanded.

"Tell him," the short Hispanic said to the teenaged lookouts.

Héctor looked at the heavier of the two.

"Tito?"

Ricky saw that Tito was grinning.

"That scrawny-ass Jamaican bastard came up to Juan demanding weed," Tito then said. "I told him to get him and his stinky ass homies off our street. Then he took a swing at me—and missed 'cause he's fucked up and all—and then the other two started coming across the street at us, and Juan pulled his nine out."

"That didn't stop the fuckers," Juan picked up, holding his right arm straight out, his palm parallel to the floor with his finger and thumb mimicking a pistol. "So I squeezed off a pop at 'em."

Héctor exchanged a look with Ricky.

Told you, Ricky thought.

"One?" Héctor challenged. "We heard more."

Juan shrugged. "Maybe three, four. That got 'em turned around."

Chubby Tito started laughing.

"What?" Héctor snapped.

"You shoulda seen that Jamaican dude then. I never thought he could get that scrawny ass runnin' that fast!"

Juan said, "Sure did. Ran right past the others. Left 'em."

"Did they see you come here?" Héctor said.

"Never looked back," Juan said.

"Assholes and elbows, that's all we saw," Tito added.

Héctor looked between them, then turned to Jaime.

"Go get the motorcycle. Take it around back." He pointed at the Kawasaki motorcycle by the door. "Then take that one out back. And call in more lookouts."

Jaime nodded and started for the door.

"You two," Héctor said to the teenagers. "Come with me."

[FIVE]

Forty minutes later, Tito and Juan, in different winter coats than earlier and now wearing helmets, sat on the idling Kawasaki in South Philly. They waited on the sidewalk that edged Girard Park, Juan with his gloved hands on the handlebar grips, chubby Tito on the higher seat behind him, holding a small cardboard box with UNCLE OOGIE'S PIZZERIA printed on the lid.

Tito was getting parts of his face, helmet, and gloves greasy while more or less successfully stuffing a steaming slice of Italian sausage and peppers in his mouth.

They had been there not quite five minutes, looking at the well-kept duplexes lining the opposite side of the street, when Juan nodded in the direction of an overweight girl walking down the sidewalk. She was maybe fourteen or fifteen.

"Think she's one?" Juan said.

"Shit," Tito mumbled, trying to finish the chewy slice.

She approached the duplex with the address that Héctor had written on the outside of the folded notepaper. Juan had it in his coat pocket.

"She is," Juan said. "Get ready."

"Shit," Tito said again, then swallowed hard.

He reached in his coat pocket and pulled out the folded paper. He tossed it in the pizza box, then with some effort got the lid finally closed with the flaps tucked in.

The overweight girl took a shortcut across the front yard of the duplex.

"Here we go," Juan said, quickly checking for traffic, then revving the engine with a twist of the right grip and dumping the clutch.

Tito quickly squeezed his knees and thighs against the seat as the big bike jerked into motion. He switched the pizza box to his left hand and put his right on the nine-millimeter semiautomatic in his coat pocket.

The motorcycle roared across the street, then bumped up onto the opposite sidewalk.

They closed fast on the girl. About the time she heard them approaching and started to turn her head back, Tito threw the pizza box onto the walkway ahead of her. He pulled out the pistol and tried to aim as Juan almost ran over her with the front tire.

Tito began squeezing the trigger repeatedly, the pistol bucking as the plastic grips slipped in the greasy glove.

The overweight girl went down.

Tito slapped Juan on the back.

"Got her!" he said, looking over his shoulder. "Go! Go!"

Juan saw the door of the duplex open. A heavyset dark-skinned adult woman came out, then screamed as she ran down the steps to the girl lying facedown in the snow.

IX

[ONE]
Little Bight Bay
Saint John, United States Virgin Islands
Monday, November 17, 5:04 P.M.

Maggie McCain looked out the mouth of the bay and saw on the big water the crisscrossing sailboats, ones she knew were headed to find a mooring buoy or marina to tie up for the night. She was glad to be anchored in her protected cove, with the option of staying there the night or making the run back to the resort after dusk. Her boat, her choice.

As was her ritual, she had uncorked one of the bottles of nice merlot and poured her traditional sunset glass of wine. She had done it countless times in more anchorages than she could recall, and while the wine and the scenery were as sublime as ever, it now felt somewhat mechanical.

She had sipped at the wine, hoping it might loosen the knot that had formed in her stomach after she had gone back to read Philly News Now. She wondered if she should have asked Matt Payne if her not being considered a "person of interest" meant anything more than the obvious. And then there was the update to the article that mentioned the missing case workers from the Sanctuary.

She had closed down that window and gone to the text message page, read over the exchanges, then, shaking her head, signed out of it.

She was about to do the same with her e-mail account when a new e-mail appeared in her queue. Like the majority of the recent— and unread—e-mails sent to her in-box, this one was color-coded in bright red, indicating the sender had assigned it Highest Priority.

It was another message from one of her assistants at Mary's House.

Maggie was about to ignore it, too, but then read the subject line—and her heart skipped a beat.

Attempted murder?

She clicked on it and read:

```
From:  Charlotte Davies <c.d@maryshouse.org>

Date:  17NOV   0501

To:    Maggie McCain work <m.mcm@maryshouse.org>

CC:    Maggie McCain home <magpie417@libertymail.com>

Subject: PLEASE REPLY!!! Attempted Murder at Work

Attachment:  1
```

Dear Maggie,

I pray to God that you are safe and that you get this e-mail fast.

Someone just tried to kill Chantal as she walked up to the home!

I saw them — two teen boys on a motorcycle. The one on the back had a pistol. I heard the shots, looked out, and saw Chantal fall face-first to the ground.

She is alive! Somehow all those bullets missed. But the next girl may not be that lucky.

PLEASE READ THE ATTACHED NOTE NOW!

If whoever it is carries out this threat to kill another girl, THERE ARE ONLY 45 MINUTES LEFT in the next hour!

The police are here. So they say the next one won't be here.

We have text-messaged all our residents who are not on the premises that there is an emergency and to call in. Six have yet to do so. We are following up with calls.

Maggie, I don't know if you'll get this — I have been calling and e-mailing since Krystal was killed in your home — but I don't know how else to try to reach you.

> I will do anything you want me to. I just don't
> know what else to do.
>
> > In the Service of the Lord
> > and His Children,
> > Charlotte

Maggie clicked on the attached file. It was a photograph of a handwritten note in a pizza box. The lined page that had been torn from a spiral notebook—not unlike the ledgers she had—was on top of a half-eaten pizza.

And then she gasped.

While the paper had soaked up grease from the pizza, causing the ink to run and blur a few words, the message was clear:

> The blood of this girl is on your hands
> Just like those two women and Krystal
> One of your girls dies EVERY HOUR until I hear from you
> And I get back what Krystal took
> Call me now! 215-555-3452

This is not the same person as the man I've been texting. We have already basically reached an agreement.

So, it's Ricky, then? It's not the same handwriting that's in the ledgers.

But who else but Ricky would know about the connection between Mary's House and Krystal and "what Krystal took"?

And he killed her. After raping and badly beating her.

She saw the clock in the top right corner of her screen. It had just ticked off another minute. It showed: MON 5:09 PM.

She glanced back at Charlotte's e-mail. The time stamp showed it had been sent a minute after five. And Charlotte had said in it that only forty-five minutes were left.

Oh my God!

So he could kill another girl after five forty-five.

And she said six girls are unaccounted for?

She hit REPLY:

From: Maggie McCain home <magpie417@libertymail.com>

Date: 17NOV 0511

To: Charlotte Davies <c.d@maryshouse.org>

Subject: RE: Attempted Murder at work

Charlotte:

Got it. I'm heartbroken over the news, and soooo
very sorry.

   Please tell Chantal that I'm praying for her and
everyone else there.

   This is all so crazy. I'll be back in touch ASAP.

   First, however, know that I AM RIGHT NOW con-
tacting him so that he does not try anything else.

                                          Maggie

She sent that. Then she launched the video and telephone call program and clicked on the icon that mimicked the ten-digit keypad, entering the telephone number from the image of the greasy note and clicking CALL.

It rang and rang, then finally went to voice mail.

"Yo, talk to me," the arrogant male's recorded voice answered. He sounded Puerto Rican.

It gave Maggie goose bumps.

That has to be Ricky!

She clicked on the END CALL button.

"Why the hell didn't he answer?" she said aloud. "Is he already running down another girl?"

She quickly went back to the text messaging window, signed back in, then clicked the icon that created a new text message. She typed in Ricky's number—too fast, and had to correct it twice—then tabbed to the new bubble:

```
OKAY, RICKY. I GOT YOUR MESSAGE.


I JUST CALLED. WHY THE HELL DIDN'T YOU ANSWER?


I HAVE WHAT YOU WANT. PROOF IS ATTACHED.


NOW WHAT DO WE DO?
```

What else do I say?

The clock on her screen ticked off another minute. It read: 5:13.

She quickly attached the same image of the page with the girls' names she had sent earlier and clicked SEND.

She looked back at the clock.

Half an hour.

Now what?

She stared at the screen, and two minutes later a new bubble appeared:

215-555-3452

BITCH . . . MY PHONE DID NOT RING. AND YOU DIDN'T
LEAVE MESSAGE.

BUT NOW WE TALK.

I SEND A COURIER FOR MY BOOKS AND MONEY.

He did not deny being Ricky, she thought, then sent:

HOW CAN I TRUST YOU, RICKY?

I AM NOT GIVING THEM TO ANYONE BUT YOU.

He took a long moment before replying:

215-555-3452

OK. THEN WHERE?

Now what?
I have to stall him.

```
I NEED A DAY.
```

And tomorrow I will need another day.
I have what he wants. He can wait.
Then her stomach really knotted up as she read:

```
215-555-3452


NO! NOW. OR BLOOD OF ANOTHER GIRL IS YOUR FAULT.
```

You bastard! Enough with the threats!
She exhaled audibly.
But they're not idle threats . . .
I need time to figure this out.
He's got to learn not to fuck with a McCain.

```
LISTEN, RICKY. STOP WITH THE DAMN THREATS.


YOU CREATED THIS MESS. I AM TRYING TO
FIX IT.
```

TRUST ME, YOU MORE THAN HAVE MY ATTENTION.

YOU WILL GET THE BOOKS. BUT I DECIDE HOW — NOT YOU!

She sent it. Five minutes passed before he replied:

215-555-3452

TWO HOURS.

Good. I got to him, at least in some small way.
Maggie looked at the laptop's clock: 5:30.
But now what? Two hours to do what?
She stared out at the ocean. The sun had almost set. It was casting out the bold, dramatic rays of golden light that always made her feel at peace.
Gazing at it all now, she just felt numb.
A minute later another text message bubble popped up:

267-555-9100

IT TOOK A LOT OF WORK BUT I HAVE YOUR MONEY.

Maggie looked at it for a long moment.

What is it about these books that is worth so much? That these two will kill?

And why can't they just kill each other?

Then—problem solved.

"Is that possible?" she said aloud.

She shook her head, then turned and watched the sunlight slip away.

[TWO]
Players Corner Lounge
Front and Master Streets, Philadelphia
Monday, November 17, 5:15 P.M.

Dmitri Gurnov was back down on his knees, looking again inside the door of the old steel safe. It was three feet tall, about that wide, and bolted to the concrete floor in the corner of the small, dirty office. He had to use his cell phone as a makeshift flashlight because the dim light from the bare bulb hanging from the power cord overhead was worthless.

He first had gone in the safe to make sure that there was enough cash before he sent the message to the woman saying that he had the money she demanded. It wasn't the entire two hundred grand—more like fifty grand—but he never intended on delivering it all. He was getting just enough, if it came to that point, to look to her like he had the full amount.

She won't know because she will be dead.

And this problem will go away for good.

Then I have to deal with Carlos Perez. And eventually Ricky.

Gurnov's go-phone had then vibrated. Its small screen showed a message from Julio:

```
215-555-3582


CAPT J WANTS TO KNOW IF MULE DELIVERED


WHAT DO I TELL HIM?
```

And I have to pay for that damn lost coke!
He texted back:

```
NOTHING! COME TO BAR. WE NEED TO TALK.
```

It was more or less quiet in the office, the only sound the heavy bass beat thumping through the walls from the lounge's sound system. The bar crowd was already building.

On the floor near Gurnov were four clear plastic 750-milliliter bottles—the labels had "Viktor Vodka" in large red Cyrillic-like lettering, suggesting it was genuine imported Russian, but the very small print on the back stated it was made in a Kensington distillery—that he had tossed from a cardboard box imprinted with the same cheap vodka's typeface.

Gurnov had put a five-gallon brown garbage bag inside the box, and into that he was carefully stacking the cash he was taking from the safe.

Some of the money was in crisp, large-denomination bills and neatly banded in Federal Reserve Bank inch-wide currency straps. The color-coded kraft paper bands that wrapped around the fifty-dollar bills were printed with brown stripes and "$5,000"; the bands printed with mustard yellow stripes and "$10,000" held one-hundred-dollar bills that appeared to be new.

The majority of the money, however, was in tall stacks of rumpled ten- and twenty-dollar bills. These were bound by thick red rubber bands, under which were yellow sticky-back notes with a hand-scrawled "$2k."

After closing the garbage bag, he looked back in the safe. There were three spiral notebook ledgers, and he wondered why Ricky Ramírez had not taken at least one with him to Atlantic City and Florida.

On top of the ledgers was an unmarked brown paperboard box. A clear plastic box with a label bearing a CVS Pharmacy logotype was near it. The label read "Insulin Syringes—25 count," and the plastic box held maybe twenty. He tossed the syringes into the vodka box, then opened the unmarked brown box. In it were four glass vials, each about the size of a roll of dimes and labeled "Succinylcholine." He removed one.

I could just shoot her. But Nick said the muscle relaxant leaves no trace.

He was right how fast it took out the holdouts.

Half a needle and their heart stopped in minutes.

When Nick Antonov had given Gurnov the assignment two weeks earlier, he had told him only a little about who it was that Gurnov was to inject—and even less as to why. Antonov had simply announced that they were troublemakers, ones who had been evicted from—but refused to leave—the last few row houses that stood in a large section of Northern Liberties. Antonov added that they were holding up a Diamond Development project and had to go. And that was it.

Gurnov had figured out the rest, a lot of it from information Antonov had shared piecemeal over time. The most important part being: Yuri Tikhonov.

Gurnov knew that the forty-eight-year-old businessman had not become a billionaire by being a nice guy. He had served in the SVR as an intelligence officer with men who also went on to become wealthy beyond belief—as well as the highest officials in the Kremlin.

"Including the president and prime minister," Antonov had said, his tone boastful. "That is why the drug cartels fear Yuri, even as they invest in his projects."

Gurnov did not know if that last part was in fact true. He saw the Colombians and Mexicans as irrational and fearless—savages mad with power and money. But it did not matter what he thought. He was a foot soldier who had been sent to solve a problem. And, more or less effortlessly, he had.

But the information he had pieced together he thought could one day be beneficial.

What he learned was that Yuri Tikhonov was heavily invested in a Philadelphia company called Diamond Development—*As are maybe the drug cartels,* he thought, *but who is to know?*—and that Diamond was behind the Lucky Stars Casino on eighty acres of prime riverfront and the giant new coliseum to be built in Northern Liberties. And that those were part of a city program called PEGI.

Gurnov figured there probably were other Diamond projects, as PEGI was under the City of Philadelphia's Housing and Urban Development. Its chairman, a councilman named Badde, was pushing the master plan of rebuilding the area—including the riverfront casinos, the high-end mix of luxury condominiums and restaurants, theaters and upscale retailers. And of course what would be the area's iconic anchor: the entertainment complex with sixty thousand seats under a retractable roof.

PEGI, using Title 26 Eminent Domain, had seized the necessary properties. As that was happening, the troublemakers went all over Northern Liberties and Fishtown plastering handbills. They were home-printed with a crude image of a black politician wearing a tiny black bow tie and "Councilman Rapp Badde WANTED for Crimes Against the Poor & Disadvantaged of Philly! Last Seen Stealing Homes & Tearing Down Neighborhoods! Help Stop Him, Or Yours Is Next!"

Then the troublemakers, ignoring the eviction notices, stood their ground. It brought Turco Demolition & Excavation—which had been tearing down all but those few remaining properties and scraping the multi-block area back to bare dirt—to a halt.

Yuri Tikhonov had not been pleased—neither with the delay nor with Badde's inability to deal with it.

Thus, early on the first day of November, Gurnov found himself knocking on the door of each holdout. He had offered his hand as he introduced himself as one supporting their cause—and when they shook it, he jabbed the needle of the syringe that was in his left hand into their forearm. After injecting the muscle relaxer, he removed the needle, pushed them back in the house, and closed the door.

Shortly thereafter, the demolition crew had gotten a call from someone saying they were with HUD: "You're good to go." The bright yellow nine-ton bulldozers and the red-and-white Link-Belt crane swinging a two-ton forged steel wrecking ball went back to work. Almost immediately, the massive steel wrecking ball broke through one of the row houses—and came out with one of the dead

troublemakers snagged on it. Police then discovered the bodies of the
other holdouts.

It had been messy, and caused another day's delay in the demolition, but the troublemakers were gone, the news media calling their
cause of death a mystery.

And, knowing all this, Gurnov had what he considered a hole
card to play if ever he fell out of Antonov's graces.

Gurnov removed one of the glass vials labeled "Succinylcholine"
from the brown paperboard box and put it in with the syringes in the
plastic box. He placed the paperboard box of vials back in the safe
and closed and locked it. Then he stood and carried the vodka box
containing the cash and succinylcholine and needles to the battered
wooden desk, his foot finding a plastic bottle of vodka as he went.

There the light of the overhead bulb was better. But he had to
make room on the messy desktop. In the process he knocked some
forms to the floor. Then he saw that the small box of used cell phones
was still there—and next to it Ricky's black laptop computer and
small digital camera he'd used for posting the online ads for the girls.

I wonder why he did not take them to Florida?

Did he forget?

I could call him again, but it is too late.

He will have to figure out what to do when he is there.

The light from the bulb flickered, and when he looked up, he saw
it swaying slightly. He then heard, in addition to the heavy driving
beat from the sound system, the headboard banging in a bedroom
above the office.

If that is Ricky's new one, it is only a matter of time before she causes
some problem.

I need out of this business.

His cell phone rang. The caller ID announced that it was Antonov.

"Everything okay, Nick?" he answered in Russian.

"Did you get in touch with Carlos?"

"Yes," Gurnov lied. "It is all set."

"When and where?"

Gurnov sighed audibly.

"You have a problem with me asking about an important shipment?"

"No, Nick. But are you going to micromanage this? Or can I do my damn job?"

"You have any more of the muscle relaxer?"

Gurnov almost dropped his phone. *What?*

"Why, Nick?"

"Yes or no?"

"I'll have to check the safe. But it should be there."

"Get it. I will let you know if it will be necessary."

"Carlos?"

Antonov ignored the question and said, "Call me when you know how much there is."

Gurnov, shaking his head in wonder, looked at his cell phone as the screen went dark.

Then it suddenly lit back up with a text message box:

```
831-555-6235


HAVE THE CASH READY BY 10 TONIGHT.


I WILL TELL YOU WHERE TO MEET IN CENTER CITY.
```

Center City?

He looked at the cardboard vodka box.

He texted back: "Okay."

[THREE]
Penthouse Suite 2400
Two Yellowrose Place, Uptown Dallas
Monday, November 17, 4:45 P.M. Texas Standard Time

The chief executive officer of OneWorld Private Equity Partners was leaning back in his black leather chair, the heels of his crocodile-skin Western boots resting on the massive stone desktop and his fingers laced behind his head. Mike Santos was watching an intense Bobby Garcia pace in front of the desk. They were alone in the cavernous office, listening to Nick Antonov's voice over the speaker of the desktop telephone.

Antonov, in Philly, in his casino office, was saying: "But did Palumbo know Jorge Perez had any connection with the Cubans wrecking that boat and drawing so many police? Because if he did, I think that that would be the first thing a chief of staff would tell his senator."

Garcia had a mental image of the portly forty-year-old Charles A. Palumbo, Esquire, and his senatorial office colleague, Anthony N. Navarra, forty-six—both wearing khaki shorts, baggy Cuban shirts, and foolish grins—almost staggering off the casino's big boat onto the dock at Lost Key Resort.

"No, he didn't," Garcia said evenly. "And I don't think that he— for that matter, neither Chuck nor Tony—really gave a damn it even happened. Keep in mind that they spent the day drinking during the

Poker Run. They were too interested in Tatiani and the girls from
Kiev. I know they didn't see it happen."

"You can be sure?"

"Yeah. Jorge already had the go-fast tied up at the marina. But it's
a moot point. When the Cubans crashed on that island, word spread
quick over the radios and phones and around the bars. There was a
shitload of bitching about immigration reform, and I bet they took
that back to their boss."

Antonov considered that, then said, "If such is the case, good then.
I will tell Yuri. And keep a closer eye on Perez. Yuri was concerned,
especially because of the recent troubles with Diamond Development.
He does not tolerate such distractions. Let us say there is not complete
confidence in a certain member of the majority partnership."

"Why didn't Yuri call us and ask about this?" Santos said.

"He is dealing with the new casino in Macau and asked that I
handle this."

Garcia thought that Antonov had replied quickly—too quickly. It
sounded like a prepared answer.

Garcia looked to Santos, who mouthed *Bullshit!*, then said evenly,
"Nick, we don't anticipate there being any problems with any development deal with our good friend the councilman-at-large, if that is
what you're referring to."

Antonov was quiet a moment.

"I am to assume you have additional photographs?"

Ten minutes earlier, Santos and Garcia had shared a slideshow over a
video stream between their computers.

"Where were these taken?" Antonov had said, watching images of
Palumbo and Navarra that were being played from Garcia's laptop.

The slideshow started with shots of the two pasty middle-aged men sitting at a seaside tiki bar. It then showed them, first Palumbo and then Navarra separately, with young women in large luxury hotel rooms that had views overlooking the bar and the ocean.

"At Queens Club," Santos said, "the Yellowrose property on Grand Cayman. Cavorting with quote British Overseas Territory citizens unquote. I hear it said that sex tourism is a rising industry."

"What do they call that? A 'constituent fact-finding trip'?" Antonov said, either ignoring or missing his witticism.

"Simply a fact-finding trip," Garcia said. "Their constituents would be in their home state."

"Right," Antonov said sharply, clearly annoyed at the correction.

"This shot showing Palumbo's so-called manhood," Santos said lightly, "would seem to give new meaning to the title 'chief of staff'—or at least call into question his right to use it."

The image changed to one of Navarra with two women.

Garcia chuckled. "Maybe they should change both of their titles to simply 'foreign affairs adviser.' "

"This was an official trip?" Antonov said, his tone humorless.

"Absolutely," Garcia said.

"Who paid?"

"Who else? OneWorld did."

"And this is legal?"

"Excuse me?" Garcia said, mock-indignant. "As corporate counsel of OneWorld, Mr. Antonov, sir, I can assure you that absolutely every act of this company is conducted to the letter of the law."

There was a moment's silence.

"Nick, for your edification," Garcia then said, "I'll recite from memory from the 'United States Senate Ethics Manual'—said title being, I might add as a sidebar, a classic oxymoron. In chapter four, I believe on page one-twelve, it states quote For expenses other than those enumerated in Section 311(d) as amended by the Act . . . yada, yada, yada . . . if an expense is deemed by a Senator to be related to official duties then the expense may be paid with either (or a mixture of) Senate funds, the Senator's personal funds, or—"

"Can you get to it?" Antonov interrupted.

"I'm getting there, Nick," Garcia shot back. "Sounds like you're not having a good day."

Garcia had exchanged a glance with Santos, who smiled and nodded, appreciating that Garcia was sending Antonov the less than subtle message that he wasn't easily pushed around.

"Patience is a virtue," Garcia went on, in a lighter tone. "You should write that down. I was just getting to 'it' here: Quote paid with the Senator's personal funds, or in the case of 'fact finding,' funds provided by a third party otherwise consistent with applicable requirements governing such activities. Unquote. OneWorld would be that third party."

"And the purpose of this fact-finding trip was for what?"

"The Cayman Islands have no casinos, as I'm sure you know, being in the business," Santos said. "No gambling, outside the financial industry, that is. Ironic, no, what with all that investment money flowing through there? I envision building a Caymans' version of GoldenEye. But bigger and of course with gaming."

"What is this GoldenEye?"

"It's in Jamaica, which has the closest casinos, a dozen of them. But Kingston's a forty-five-minute flight."

"And GoldenEye is . . . ?"

"The resort that used to be James Bond's home. Or at least where

Ian Fleming wrote double-oh-seven spy novels, including *GoldenEye*. Considering your boss's background, I really thought you would have known all about that." He paused, and when it was clear Antonov was not going to respond, he went on: "Okay, so the senator sent his two top advisers—or perhaps it was Palumbo who had the senator send him and Tony—to George Town to open a dialogue on gaming with His Excellency the governor. I understand a follow-up with the senator has been scheduled there."

Santos grunted as the slideshow continued.

"And the other purpose, I suppose," he said, "being to determine if Palumbo can maintain his tiny hard-on longer with one, two, or three partners. . . ."

"Or maybe one underage?" Antonov said.

"Nick," Santos then said evenly, "it's not if she is or isn't. It's the appearance thereof."

Garcia chuckled.

"What?" Antonov snapped.

"Hell, even Palumbo said it this weekend," Garcia explained. "He was feeling no-pain drunk at the time."

"And what did he say, Bobby?" Antonov pressed.

"Navarra, on his pious high horse, was babbling on about all the good they do in Washington 'for the people.' Then Palumbo said, 'But, you know, as an individual you can do millions of things right. Mess up once, that's what you're remembered for.'"

"Fact is," Santos said, "a married forty-year-old snorting a small mountain of coke off the ass of a seventeen-year-old Russian hooker ain't exactly 'messing up once.'"

Garcia, shutting down the slideshow, added: "Particularly when he's caught with different girls in different locations. . . ."

"Nick, I'm not sure what additional photographs you might be inferring," Bobby Garcia said, unconvincingly. "I'm just saying that we don't anticipate any problems with any development deals."

Antonov grunted. "Well, no problems is good to hear, Mike. But being a politician, Badde talks much more than he accomplishes. He is, to use that quaint American phrase, only a big fish in a small puddle."

Garcia and Santos exchanged grins, knowing it was not worth it for either of them to say, "Small pond."

"Unfortunately," Antonov went on, "I had to send my man to take care of what he should have handled. There were obstacles, human ones, holding up the project. Badde proved either unwilling or unable to deal with it. Which suggested to Yuri that, to use another American phrase, Badde plays out of his league. And that is dangerous."

"Okay," Santos said. "So we'll keep an eye on that, on him."

"Speaking of a bigger fish in a bigger puddle," Garcia said, seeing Santos smirk at that and shake his head, "when you report back to Yuri, tell him we need the senator to have a word with someone at DHS."

"U.S. Citizenship and Immigration Services, Nick," Santos put in helpfully, "is under the Department of Homeland Security. Pressure from the top down works best."

"I am well aware," Antonov said, not pleasantly, "having suffered my own time dealing with them." He paused, then added, "Perez told me that Palumbo and Navarra enjoyed themselves this weekend."

"Clearly," Garcia said, "and I reminded them this weekend to talk to their boss about CIS greasing the skids on getting our visas approved. Maybe suggest that CIS not sweat every detail on certain applications. Palumbo said it already had been done, that he'd personally set up the call with him and the DHS undersecretary who handles CIS. But we're just not seeing anything change."

"The delay at CIS is our biggest bottleneck, Nick," Santos added. "My investors are sitting on a lot of cash that must move. They are anxious. But without their first investment in the EB-5 visa being approved—they want those green cards for their families—they will not dump another dime in."

Antonov grunted. "Perhaps there would be more response if certain photographs found their way to Mrs. Palumbo. . . ."

"Now, that's just damn devious, Nick," Garcia said with a chuckle. "As we say here in Texas, 'Cold as an ex-wife's heart.'"

[FOUR]
Liberties Bar
502 N. Second Street, Philadelphia
Monday, November 17, 4:45 P.M.

A grim-faced Jason Washington crossed the room to where Matt Payne, Jim Byrth, and Mickey O'Hara were at the bar.

"Gentlemen," he said evenly, his deep tone sounding flat and tired.

Washington patted O'Hara on the back.

"I trust you're doing well, Michael?"

O'Hara nodded. "Well enough, considering. Thanks. And thank you for having Matt fill me in on the other case workers. I updated the story with their names."

Washington's eyes went to Payne, then Byrth, then back to O'Hara.

"I'm afraid I don't know what you're talking about, Mr. O'Hara," Washington said.

"Of course not, Lieutenant," O'Hara said, nodding.

"But you're welcome," Washington added. He then said, "Hope I didn't keep you waiting. I had to get a ride from Highway Patrol. The Crown Vic I was given to drive while they repaired the one they gave me last week has also died. I suggested that they start using bigger Band-Aids."

"I don't even have a car," Payne said.

"Unlike my unfortunate circumstance, Matthew, that is not because the city has slashed our budgets."

"It's because," O'Hara put in, raising his drink toward him, "you keep totaling them, Marshal Earp."

The bartender, a great big guy, came up and slid a cocktail napkin onto the bar before Washington.

"What can I get you, Jason?"

Washington looked at the others' drinks, then announced, "I need something strong, Craig. How about a Jameson twelve-year-old martini, please."

"You got it," the bartender said, then reached down, produced a battered stainless steel shaker, and walked down the bar.

Washington turned to the others and said, "Well, the good news is you won't have to worry about Carlucci looking over your shoulder. He and Denny are busy dealing with Commissioner Gallagher. The bad news is the same as the good news."

In the background came the sound of ice cubes rattling as the bartender vigorously worked the cocktail shaker.

"What happened with the interview?" Payne said.

"It was not good, Matthew."

The bartender returned and placed a martini glass on the napkin, then with a grand flourish poured the golden Irish whisky.

"Thank you," Washington said to him, then picked up the glass and held it up as he intoned, *"Fiat justitia ruat caelum."*

As Payne raised his glass, he thought, *"Let justice be done though the heavens fall"*?

What triggered that?

They all touched glasses.

Payne, after taking a sip of his single malt, said, "I assume that is in reference to Garvey?"

"At the moment especially him," Washington said. He then looked at O'Hara and added, "Off the record for now, Mickey?"

"Of course," O'Hara said. "Who is Garvey?"

Washington glanced around the immediate area. No other customer was in earshot. Craig the bartender had gone down to the opposite end of the bar and, using a white dish towel, was pulling glasses from the washer, methodically polishing them, then putting them on the bar shelves behind him.

"Garvey is married to Commissioner Gallagher's granddaugher," Washington said.

"Okay. And?" O'Hara said, as Washington took another sip of martini.

"And," Payne put in, "he just got busted this afternoon smuggling two keys of coke at PHL."

O'Hara's bushy red eyebrows went up.

Washington, nodding, picked it back up. "They were doing a routine sweep of bags coming off the plane from Saint Thomas, where Garvey had been on business." He glanced at Byrth and added, "Because the Texas Rangers are doing such an effective job at our border with Mexico, there is a surge of drugs coming up via the Caribbean."

"Newsflash," O'Hara said. "There's a history of that with Phillyricans."

Byrth looked at him. "Is that like a Texican?"

"Yeah, Philadelphia has a Hispanic population of about a quarter-million," O'Hara explained, "seventy percent of which are Puerto Rican—Phillyricans. It's second only to New York City's number of Nuyoricans. That generates a lot of traffic between here and San Juan."

Byrth, nodding, said, "And trafficking."

"And," Payne put in, "now apparently it's the same with the USVI."

"So that's what happened with this Garvey?" O'Hara said.

Washington went on: "As the bags were put one by one from the cart onto the conveyor belt, a chocolate Lab alerted on his suitcase. One of our blue shirts stopped him as he started to leave the building with it. Garvey's wife—Commissioner Gallagher's daughter's daughter—had gone to surprise him by picking him up. She witnessed him being escorted to a secure area near baggage claim."

"Guess who surprised whom," O'Hara said, shook his head, then added, "Another family ruined by being greedy. That's a lot of money."

"And that's the problem," Washington said. "It wasn't about Garvey's greed or needing money. That's what came out in the interview. He admitted to the coke being in the bag. He said that he was transporting the drugs under duress."

" 'So said the kid caught with his hand in the cookie jar,' " Payne said.

"In most any other case I would agree with you, Matthew."

"But?"

"Garvey said he was told that if he refused, the cartel would kill his family," Washington said. "Now, it is possible that he was made to think the cartel is involved. The resulting fear would be the same. He is, after all, Commissioner Gallagher's granddaughter's husband, and not cut from the same cloth. And if one is naïve—such as someone like Garvey, who does not have a record, not so much as a speeding ticket—one can be made to believe something they otherwise would not." He paused to let that sink in, then added: "Particularly when one is shown photographs of the wife and young son—and, to make the point, the photograph of a boy's body floating in a river."

"Jesus!" Payne blurted, and suddenly thought of Amanda and her being with child. "Talk about a motivator."

"How did he say they got to him?" Byrth said.

"A guy who became friendly with him at a local tavern," Washington said. "Garvey said the guy claims to be an itinerant charter sailboat captain, and befriended him not long after he started going there six months ago. Looking back, Garvey now can see how he was duped, the guy seemingly making small talk over weeks while slowly mining him for information. It would appear that that information was sent to a connection here, who then shadowed the family and photographed them."

"When did he get the threat about his family?" Payne said.

"Saturday. He was winding up work, ready to come home. The guy 'happened' to run into him and insisted on buying him a going-away beer. Then he handed him an envelope with recent photographs of the wife and son at home, at school, even at church. The guy made it clear that the cartel would kill the family if Garvey did not do as told. He claimed that he also was forced under the cartel's control, but that might well be a ruse to make the cartel angle sound credible."

Washington took a large sip of his Irish whisky martini, then added, "Everything in his statement is of course being investigated. But I have interviewed my share of professional liars, the extraordinary con artists, and Garvey is not one. He was telling the truth. It was quite difficult to watch, and then he completely broke down."

Everyone was quiet for a long moment.

The Texas Ranger broke the silence.

"The poor bastard is fucked," Byrth said matter-of-factly.

"That would seem to be today's vast understatement," Payne said.

"There is as we speak," Washington said, "an involved discussion with the District Attorney's Office."

"I'd suggest that the DA is the least of this Garvey's worries with a cartel involved," Byrth said. "I'd take my chances on jail. Because, unless one of those miracles from the ceiling of that cathedral occurs, the cartel is going to make good on whacking him. They do not like losing product."

"He does fear the worst now," Washington said. "Commissioner Gallagher just moved his grandddaughter and great-grandson to his home, where there now is a squad car detailed round the clock."

"It is absolutely repulsive how little they value human life," O'Hara said. "It's incomprehensible. To kill them over a lousy two keys? Compared to all the tons they move?"

"You would think so, Mickey," Byrth said. "As I told Matt and Jason, snagging two keys is a slow day on the border. It's usually one helluva lot larger. The record is six thousand kilos. One day, one bust. Wholesale, that's three hundred grand."

"I can only imagine their reaction to losing that much," O'Hara said.

"That's when they really start cutting off heads and stacking the bodies like cordwood," Byrth said. "It's not lost on those running the drugs. They are coached to do anything—and will do absolutely anything—necessary not to lose a load." He grunted, then said, "Splash."

"Splash?" Payne said.

"Yeah. We're constantly surveilling the Rio Grande, hunting the mules before they cross. It's not a helluva lot different than hunting deer—you know their patterns and there's so damn many of them— except the cartel bastards shoot back. Since we know where they're liable to cross, or we get a tip from an informant, we generally can find them in the staging process. Sometimes the tip is disinformation to draw us to a certain crossing point, then they make a big deal about loading the boats, and at the last minute act spooked and turn around. It's all a diversion. The big run is taking place up- or down-stream. During one this summer, I was up in our helo with a Bush-master, flying as the shooter—"

"Our Aviation Unit shooters like to say High Altitude Sniper In-tervention," Payne said.

"Same thing," Byrth said, nodding, "but we also wind up doing a lot of treetop flying. Anyway, we had Rangers in the brush of the riverbank watching the bad guys on the Mexico side—maybe a hun-dred yards away—loading bundles of keys aboard a couple of twelve-foot inflatables with outboards. We cannot do anything until they're on our side, so we let them transfer the bundles to the waiting pickup or van, then either bust the load just down the road or follow it to the delivery. This time we were told to take them sooner rather than later."

He took a sip of his bourbon, then went on: "Once the pickup was loaded, it took the dirt road to the highway. We were up in the bird and caught up to the pickup just as an unmarked DPS unit moved into place ahead of the truck and a marked DPS Tahoe pulled in behind and lit him up. The minute the pickup driver saw the lights, he pulled a hard left, cutting across the grass median, then started hauling ass back in the other direction.

"We were pacing him with the helo. I was in the open door with my Bushmaster and could see his every move. He knew he was close to getting caught—he frantically kept glancing up at us and in his mirrors—while yelling into his two-way radio and cutting in and out of traffic. He caused two wrecks before making it back to the dirt road leading to the river. Now that he was away from the populated areas, I got the go-ahead to take out his tires. The Bushmaster's chambered in that heavy 6.8mm SPC. I popped the left tires with a couple three-round bursts, but he just kept running. Ahead we could see the river and the two inflatables waiting just their side of the middle."

"They were going to come back and unload the truck?" Payne said.

Byrth shook his head. "They wouldn't need to. The pickup raced to a part of the riverbank that was five feet above the water—and sped up, launching into the air."

"Splash," O'Hara said, shaking his head.

"Splash," Byrth confirmed.

"And then it sank?" Payne said.

"After a few minutes. Meantime the inflatables moved in, the mule climbed out of the truck window, bloodied but okay, and they loaded him aboard. Then, as the pickup sank, the bundles started floating, and they grabbed them and motored back to grand ol' Meh-hee-ko."

"To wait and try again," Payne said.

"And again and again. We have to hire a giant wrecker to come and recover all the vehicles. There's no end to it."

"Remarkable," O'Hara said, then after a moment added, "Which just inspired me."

He reached down to his feet and brought up his briefcase. He pulled out a small laptop and put it on the bar. After opening it, his fingers flew across the keyboard.

A couple of minutes later, he held out the computer to Washington.

"I am honoring our agreement that it's off the record, Jason," Mickey said. "But when you say that changes, this might help."

Jason's eyes went to the screen:

```
HOT HOT HOT - Proofread for typos only then
IMMEDIATELY POST to website!!! -O'Hara


Breaking News . . . Posted [[ insert time stamp ]]


Dog Stops Mule


Bust by Airport Police Nets a Million Dollars in
Cocaine Hidden in Drug-Runner's Luggage


A Philadelphia man returning today from a business
trip in the Caribbean was arrested at Philadelphia
International Airport after two kilograms of
cocaine were found hidden in his luggage. The
```

flight originated in Saint Thomas in the U.S. Virgin Islands.

Calling the bust unsurprising, a police spokesman explained that baggage is constantly monitored at multiple levels for various types of contraband, from explosives to illegal drugs.

In this instance, the detection device was the nose of Molly, a two-year-old chocolate brown Labrador retriever. On a routine check of bags, Molly alerted on the suitcase containing the bricks of 100 percent pure cocaine powder estimated to have a street value of around one million dollars.

"In the last year Molly has sniffed out more than a thousand keys of marijuana, cocaine, and heroin. She has never had a false-positive," the police spokesman said, referring to when a dog mistakenly indicates a suitcase as carrying illegal drugs or other contraband.

"The mule trying to smuggle the cocaine didn't have a chance with this dog on the job," the police spokesman added.

Police have not released the name of the man arrested. He now faces felony charges for

```
possession with intent to distribute, which carries
a mandatory four-year sentence.


More details to come.


—Michael J. O'Hara
```

Washington looked back at O'Hara.

"Good idea, Mickey. Do it, please."

"What?" Payne said.

O'Hara turned the computer so Payne and Byrth could read it.

"It's worth the chance," Byrth then said. "Getting it in the news could help get Garvey off the hook with the bad guys. Whoever they are."

"Then he's back to dealing with going to jail," Payne said. "I wonder how many innocent mules wind up serving time."

"Or get whacked," Washington put in.

[FIVE]

Matt's cell phone rang as Mickey, having quickly sent the drug bust article to be posted, was putting up his laptop computer.

When Matt saw the caller ID, he said, "Perfect," then answered the phone with, "Hold that thought, Kerry. I need you to drop everything and punch up Philly News Now. Go to Breaking News, then 'leak' to every other news outlet in town the article on the drug bust that Mickey just posted there. Anyone asks why he got the scoop, blame me. Say I called them but their number was busy."

"Matt—"

"Got it?"

"Got it, Matt. But—"

"But what, damn it?"

"We just got a couple units responding to a nine-one-one shots-fired call, on the scene at Mary's House. Came in hours after Special Operations pulled their unmarked. Tony Harris is en route."

"What scene? A homicide?"

Matt saw that that question caused eyes to turn to him.

"Almost. Two guys on a motorcycle shot up the place pretty good trying to take out one of the girl residents. Left a trail of nine-millimeter casings."

"Anyone hurt?"

"Not this time," Kerry said.

"What does that mean?"

"The shooters left a message—here, I'll read it."

After Kerry finished, Matt said, "What the hell? I'm guessing no word from Maggie?"

Eyes turned to him again.

"No. And there's only thirty minutes until the hour is up. They have six girls unaccounted for. And the woman who is Maggie's assistant, and witnessed the shooters on the motorcycle, sent an e-mail to Maggie and called her cell phone. It's all she knows to do."

Matt pulled the pen from his pocket, then stole Washington's cocktail napkin. "Give me that phone number again."

Kerry did, and added, "We are running it down. But dollars to doughnuts it comes up a go-phone dead end."

Matt stared at the number. "Kerry, get word out right now that nobody calls or otherwise communicates with the number without my permission or Lieutenant Washington's. Give whoever is in charge of the scene my number and instructions to call. And shoot me a copy of that note, please."

"Done, Marshal. Last one first."

Matt felt his phone vibrate.

The guy is good.

"And don't forget to feed the drug bust article to the media, Kerry. Keep me posted."

Matt broke off the call and went to pull up the image of the note left at Mary's House. He found Rapier's e-mail at the top of his in-box, right above an e-mail from Will McCain that was a forwarded e-mail of the one below it—Maggie's reply to Matt.

"Shit!" he blurted. "How did I miss this?"

"What, Matthew?"

"Maggie answered my e-mail," he said, as he opened her reply.

Matt saw that it had been sent almost a half hour earlier. He scanned through it, made a face as he shook his head in frustration, then opened the image she had attached.

"Huh," he said. "Well, she appears to be okay. But she really is starting to piss me off with this control issue of hers."

He forwarded it to Amanda—*Maybe it will ease her mind,* he thought—then he went to Kerry's e-mail and opened the image of the greasy handwritten note.

He handed Jason the phone and said, "You were right. Again. They are connected. Looks like Maggie may be the last witness. But witness to what? To what was stolen? At least we have some idea as to motive." He took a sip of his drink, lost in thought, then said, "But it doesn't track that the same person who would professionally take out the Gonzalez girl with .22 rounds behind the ear would attempt pulling off a third-world assassination stunt with a motorcycle and a spray and pray of nine-millimeter."

"And do not forget the note in the pizza box," Washington said dryly, nodding as he looked at it all.

Then he passed Matt's phone to Byrth, who then gave it to O'Hara.

"Congratulations, Michael," Jason said, gesturing at the image that Maggie McCain sent as her proof of life. "You're now part of the story the breaking details of which you have to sit on."

O'Hara nodded thoughtfully as he handed the phone back to Payne.

Washington then said: "We need details back on both Mary's House and the West Philadelphia Sanctuary."

At the thought of another attack, Matt felt his temper flaring, and forced it back.

"That Sanctuary has at least twice as many residents as Mary's," he said, his tone frustrated. "It is going to be a helluva lot harder to secure—if we can find enough blue shirts available for however long it will take."

He then rapidly replied to Maggie's e-mail: "I have seen the note about blood on your hands. Who is this guy? He will kill again. You may be safe now, but that can change. And your girls *are* at grave risk. I need your help, Maggie. Call my cell phone now."

He hit SEND and then looked at Washington.

"I just told Maggie we have the note and to call me." He picked up the cocktail napkin. "This number really is our only good lead now. But if we contact it, we could make things worse for her."

"Agreed, Matthew," he said, watching him shred the napkin, the pieces floating to the bar. "Stating the obvious, this is a desperate act on the miscreant's part to get to her. And he has the advantage of using violence to draw her out."

Payne glanced at his wristwatch.

"While we know he is capable of it," Matt said, "we don't know if he will act on his threat after this first hour, or the second, or whenever. We also don't know if Maggie is even aware of the note, of its threat. And if she is, if she has called the number."

He then met Washington's eyes. "What am I missing, Jason?"

Washington raised his eyebrows.

"The rules have changed, Matthew."

"How do you mean?"

"Maggie, with her need for control, created an impasse for everyone looking for her. What she did not—perhaps being in fear for her life *could* not—anticipate was that her stall tactic would force the miscreant to act again."

"Which, as Matt notes, could happen in a minute, a day, a week," Byrth said.

Matt looked at him, then Mickey, then Jason.

Then he checked his e-mail.

"No reply from Maggie. Fuck it. I'm calling the number."

X

[ONE]
Kensington, Philadelphia
Monday, November 17, 5:13 P.M.

Ricky Ramírez, draining his bottle of Yuengling lager, watched as Héctor Ramírez reached into the rusty refrigerator and pulled out two more beers. Ricky threw his empty bottle across the bare kitchen. It smacked the far wall, leaving a wet mark on the peeling tan paint, then landed in a cardboard box in the corner that served as a trashcan.

"That ain't bad stuff," Ricky said, "but we need something better. Something stronger, like some good dark rum. Or . . ."

He looked past Héctor at the warped kitchen counter. The dark green Formica had separated from the wooden backing. On the counter, next to the rust-stained porcelain sink, were two zip-top plastic bags packed with dried marijuana buds. A squat ceramic pipe, its bowl crusted with dark resin residue, sat between them.

Ricky stepped over and opened a bag. He dug into it with his fingers, pinching off a thumbnail-sized piece of the gold-veined green leaf. He tamped that in the bowl of the pipe, then lit it, inhaling deeply.

Héctor popped the cap off one of the Yuenglings, then handed the bottle to him. Ricky heard his go-phone make a *ping*.

Still holding his breath, he put the beer on the counter, handed the pipe to Héctor, then pulled the phone from his pocket.

He read the text message—and suddenly exhaled, the smoke billowing out.

Staring at the phone screen, he slowly rubbed his fingertips across his chunky pockmarked face.

Héctor was right!

Wide-eyed, he held out the phone to show Héctor the message.

"It fucking worked, man! It's her."

He picked up his beer and took a big swallow.

"And you had a doubt, *mi amigo*?" Héctor said, smiling, and tapped the neck of his beer bottle against Ricky's.

Ricky grinned back and shrugged. Then he suddenly felt even more light-headed, the buzz from the marijuana now rising far above that from the beer.

And that hydro is really good shit.

This is all coming together!

Especially with getting Dmitri off my back.

Ricky read the next text, then fired back a reply.

There was the sound of a motorcycle pulling into the backyard. They briefly turned to it.

"And here come your *sicarios*. They made it happen," Héctor said.

"Should we reward them?" Ricky said.

"I will think of something. Not too much too soon. Or they begin believing they really are assassins."

Ricky's phone then began ringing. He didn't recognize the number and pushed the key to send it directly in voice mail.

A moment later—*ping*—his phone suddenly lit up with another text message box, this one from the number that had just called:

```
215-555-4525


I HAVE YOUR NOTE.


AND I HAVE WHAT YOU WANT.


NO MORE KILLINGS.
```

What the hell? Who is this?
How can this person have the books?
Or . . . was she shitting me?
"What?" Héctor said, putting the pipe to his lips.
Ricky held the phone back up to show him.
After a moment Héctor nodded thoughtfully. He exhaled.
"You believe that first one is the woman?" he then said.
Ricky nodded. "And I gave her two hours."
"So ignore this one. For now. First work the woman." He thought for a moment, then said, "We will give her more incentive. Where's your car?"
"Not far. Blocks. Why?"
The back door began opening.
Héctor reached back into the refrigerator. He came out with two more beers.
Tito and Juan sauntered inside. They acted more cocky than usual.
"You did good," Héctor said, handing them the bottles.
Héctor grabbed his Kalashnikov and looked at Ricky.
"You and I go," he said, then added to Tito and Juan, "When you

finish those, go out and keep watch till Jaime gets back with more *halcónes*."

Ricky started to follow Héctor, then turned back and grabbed one of the bags and the pipe from the counter. He tossed the other bag to Tito.

"A little bonus for you two," Ricky said, smiling.

[TWO]
New Hope House
Hazzard Street, Philadelphia
Monday, November 17, 6:01 P.M.

"Next block make a right," Matt Payne said, as Jim Byrth drove the rental Ford SUV through Kensington. When they had made the turn, it was not difficult, even in the shadows, to make out the flop-house and the small crowd outside it midway down the snow-crusted street.

Byrth saw Payne looking at his cell phone, which he had put in the right cup holder of the console.

After going into the phone's mobile multi-line application and activating a new number—giving him a third line, in addition to his personal and office ones—Payne had used it to call the number on the grease-stained note, then to send it a text massage.

"Like Jason said, Matt, it was worth the chance. There could be any number of reasons why there's been no reply yet."

Payne shook his head. "It just makes me wonder what—if any—dominoes it started toppling. My call going right into voice mail and then no reply to the text could mean the phone is out of range or dead or . . ."

"Or it could mean nothing. Maybe it's just because the badass— 'Yo, talk to me'—didn't recognize the number and didn't want to answer. At some point he will get the text."

"Meaning no news is good news. . . . You're probably right. But something needs to break with this." He looked up ahead. "What makes me think our luck here will be just as crappy?"

New Hope was in a two-story row house that had seen some really bad days—not unlike the neighboring properties that were in even worse shape—and certainly far better ones in its hundred years. Its brick exterior looked as if it had been painted in the last year or so. Faint graffiti was still visible through the whitewash, and there was new graffiti tagging the sign that read "New hope—for a new life." Industrial steel roll-up doors, painted canary yellow, covered the two first-floor windows and the front door. The ones over the windows were rolled up, and the tall one over the door was halfway open, and moving upward.

"Well, look at that," Payne then said, "at least we're just in time for high tea."

Byrth pulled to the curb across the street from the flophouse. As he put the SUV in park and turned off the engine, they took in the scene.

Ten women, standing close together on the snow-packed sidewalk, formed a crooked single-file line that began at the door of the house. They appeared to range in age from their late teens to maybe early forties. Some were smoking, some talking—all of them clearly bitter cold despite wearing multiple layers of ill-fitting thrift shop clothing.

A ragged group of a half dozen men—mostly brown-skinned and gaunt, with sullen looks—milled near the end of the line.

A few of them glanced at the dirty SUV. They quickly lost interest. They were focused on the opening door, obviously more concerned with getting inside, out of the cold.

"First come, first served?" Byrth said.

"Yeah, some places will give women priority. But if they don't get here early, and before they later lock the door, they're going to have to find another place, even if they've paid for the month. Demand for an empty bed far outstrips supply."

"Like that guy?" Byrth said.

Just up the street a gray-haired man, his clothes filthy, was curled up on the stoop of a row house. He clutched a brown liquor bottle to his chest. On the front door above the uneven hand-painted lettering that read "House of Lord Fellowship" there was a simple golden crucifix.

"A church across the street from a flophouse?" Byrth then said. "The Lord works in mysterious ways."

"Amen to that, Brother Byrth," Payne said. He pointed over his shoulder, adding, "And there's a middle school two blocks thataway. Think any of these pillars of the community ever stagger past the playground? Is it any wonder the kids growing up here think that crackheads, drunks, and hookers are the norm of society?"

Matt pushed back the tail of his coat and pulled his .45 off his right hip.

Like Byrth, he was sitting on his seat belt, its tang inserted in the buckle behind him. The practice of securing the belts in such a way—which of course violated Section 4581 of the Pennsylvania Vehicle Code requiring the wearing of passive restraints, and accordingly was "officially" prohibited by the department—not only stopped the damn seat sensor from incessantly sounding its annoying *ding-ding-ding* warning. It more importantly also allowed them faster access to their pistols and to exiting the vehicle.

With a shooter fast approaching, being "safely" strapped to a seat could turn a vehicle into a coffin.

Payne, aiming at the floorboard, thumbed the hammer back, then flipped up the lever to lock it, then slipped the pistol back behind his waistband.

Looking out the windshield and studying the crowd, Matt said, "You ever hear that a pistol is like a parachute?"

Byrth grinned. "Tell me. How?"

"When you need one, and you don't have one, you'll never have the need for one again."

Byrth chuckled.

"Pabody," he said, "the sheriff who found this Cusick girl's ID in that trailer in the woods? He served in Special Forces and had his share of jumps—he'll appreciate that one." He looked at the group of men. The tallest one—who wore a multicolored knit cap and had thick dreadlocks and a scraggly beard—was jabbing his finger in another man's face. "It's like having to deal with the pissed-off Rastafarian there. Pabody's always saying, 'We're trying to win hearts and minds, but we're willing to splatter 'em if necessary.'"

At the end of the line were two Latinas who looked about thirty but could have been younger. One had on an oversized faded blue sweatshirt, the hood covering her head. The heavier one wore a patched black knee-length woolen coat. They were passing a stub of a joint between them. After a moment, the heavier of the two took the last toke, a very short one, and tossed the sliver of glowing paper to the ground, crushing it into the snow with the toe of her once white sneaker.

The Jamaican walked over and said something to the girl in the sweatshirt. She impatiently waved him off and turned her back to him. He had the last word, an angry one, then went back to the other men.

Byrth glanced at Payne.

"Call me a skeptic," he said, "but I'm guessing neither girl—or any of them, for that matter—is going to be rushing across the street to confess their sins of the day. . . ."

Payne grunted. "If you mean the pot, the times they are a-changin', as someone once said. They know nothing's going to happen. These days the SOP for that would be to charge them with personal possession. Less than thirty grams. That would get them a night in jail, and they'd just pay the fine."

"That's what happened with the Cusick girl?"

"Yeah. Twice, as I recall. But she skipped the option of being sent to SAM—Small Amount of Marijuana program. It's another couple hundred bucks to take a one-day drug class, and then the charge is expunged from the record."

"All but decriminalized."

"All but. In these austere times, the powers—particularly the DA, who's pretty outspoken about it—have decided that spending thousands to prosecute someone with twenty bucks of weed isn't exactly efficient. They say it's a money-saver. Frees up courts for bigger cases. Keeps cops on the street, not filling out paperwork or waiting to testify in court and collecting overtime."

"A couple hundred? These people don't look like they have a couple bucks."

"No argument." He slipped his phone into his pocket and grabbed the door handle. "Come on. Let's see what they have to say. If anything."

Byrth cocked and locked the .45 from his hip holster, then pulled his Stetson from the backseat.

As they crossed the street, Payne wasn't surprised that now all eyes were on them.

"Damn, this cold is miserable!" Byrth muttered.

Like Payne, he had left his coat unzipped. Suffering the wicked weather—like not wearing a seat belt in the event of a wreck—was the trade-off for faster access to their weapons.

Toward the front of the line, they walked past a pale-skinned girl with dark hair. She looked maybe eighteen and, though it took a little imagination to see it, had a pretty face. Across her white cheeks was a disturbing pinkish brown web of scarring that looked not quite healed. The lines cut from near her temples to her chin, and from ears to nose. She lowered her head and turned away.

After they passed, Payne looked at Byrth and answered the unasked question: "That's called a 'buck-fitty.' She pissed off someone, probably by saying no to some gangbanger's girlfriend who was trying to recruit her as fresh meat for her gangbanger buddies. Or maybe to pimp her out. Probably both."

"She dissed them?" Byrth asked, but it was more a statement.

Payne nodded. "And to make the point you don't disrespect the gang, they disfigured her. Held her down so the dissed gangbanger's girlfriend could carve her up with a box cutter razor blade. Buck-fitty is a hundred fifty, the number of stitches they hope it will take to close the wounds."

Byrth exhaled audibly. "I've heard of that happening in Houston's Third Ward and in south Dallas, just not called that. Barbaric beyond belief . . ."

Payne and Byrth reached the two young women bringing up the end of the line. They reeked of marijuana. Expressionless, they looked numb from the cold, if not the pot, and seemed slow to focus when Payne held out his badge. He saw that under the blue hoodie the woman had a black eye, one that was almost faded.

"Evening, ladies," he said. "I'm Sergeant Payne. Need to ask you a couple quick questions."

They did not answer and made no eye contact.

No surprise, Payne thought. *No one talks to cops.*

But we have to go through the motions . . .

Byrth already had his cell phone out and was holding it up, showing them Elizabeth Cusick's photograph on the Department of Transportation ID.

"Do you know this girl?" Byrth said, then added in Spanish, *"¿Conoces a Elizabeth?"*

They both glanced at it, then at each other, then shrugged and slowly shook their heads.

"How long have you been coming here?" Payne pursued.

They shrugged again. Then the line moved forward. They wordlessly turned and quickly shuffled across the snow to close the gap.

Payne looked at Byrth, and nodded toward the door.

"Let's just work the line. We know where they're going if we need them."

Ten minutes later, they had reached the door. Not a single person acknowledged knowing the girl in the ID photograph.

"Let's see how much worse our luck can get in here," Payne said, and stepped through the doorway.

The house was warm but had a stale, musty odor.

Just inside the door, a folding table was set up, behind which an obese black woman sat in a folding chair. Her weight stressed the flimsy chair to the point it leaned left. She had her head down and was writing on a yellow legal pad. When she looked up she immediately looked right past Payne, then farther up, at the Hat. The white of her eyes grew impossibly large. Then she tried to recover from the initial surprise.

"What you two want?" she blurted, finally finding her voice as her big eyes darted between them.

"I'm guessing you're in charge?" Payne said.

"Guess all you want. Who's asking?"

Matt showed her his badge.

"No offense," she then said, "but you don't look like you walk no beat. Never can trust who's who coming round here."

"I'm with the Homicide Unit," Payne said, as he saw Byrth surveying the area.

The dirty living room, with a flight of stairs along the left wall leading to the upstairs bedrooms and baths, had a wooden floor worn bare. A mismatched pair of sagging threadbare sofas faced each other in the middle. A dozen plastic stackable chairs were scattered around a low table that held an old television with an antenna of aluminum-foil-wrapped rabbit ears and a picture that flickered between color and black and white. On the right wall, beyond one of the sofas, a dusty hand-printed poster with faded lettering read: NO SMOKING, NO DRINKING, NO DRUGGING, NO DAM EXCUSE!

"Someone dead?" the woman said, her tone matter-of-fact.

"From the looks of it . . ." Byrth muttered, looking toward the back of the room.

The woman's eyes went to him, and not pleasantly.

Payne forced back a grin.

"We're looking into that," Payne said, "and need to ask some questions."

She glanced over her shoulder toward the open doorway at the back wall.

"Eldridge!" she called out.

A moment later a muscular black male stood backlit in the doorway that obviously led to the kitchen. Eldridge wore a stained chef's apron. With a practiced rhythm he was working a large carving knife up and down a foot-long sharpening rod. He had very short gray hair and looked to be in his forties. His bulging biceps stretched the sleeves of his black T-shirt.

The enormous black woman looked at Payne.

"He the man. Talk to him."

[THREE]
Little Bight Bay
Saint John, United States Virgin Islands
Monday, November 17, 7:10 P.M.

After shutting down the Internet connection and finishing her traditional sunset glass of wine, Maggie had gone inside the cabin and thrown the lighting breakers on the electrical panel. Then, back on the well-lit deck, trying to figure out what she could possibly do next, she busied herself going around the boat methodically making sure everything was as it should be.

She neatly coiled all the lines on the deck—from the mainsail and jib halyards and sheets down to the last docking line—and then recoiled ones that she thought didn't look exactly right. She went forward to where the anchor line was cleated, untied it, tugged hard on the line to ensure the hook was still secure in the bay bottom, then re-cleated the line, snugging each wrap before finally tightly cinching the line. Then she neatly coiled the remaining line.

And then she went around the boat a second time.

And then, frustrated, she leaned against the aluminum mast, sighing as she looked out.

Now what? I can't keep spinning my wheels.

Ricky said two hours. And that was at five-thirty.

So—after what, the next twenty minutes?—he carries out his threat?

Who gets to die now?

Under the thin crescent of moon she watched the navigation lights of sailboats slowly moving in the distance. A blanket of twinkling stars reflected everywhere. Waves crashed just outside the mouth of the bay.

I'm just so damn far away.

She went back inside the cabin and poured another glass of wine.

She saw the notebooks on the table, next to the casino bag with the poker chips and stack of cash she had photographed.

This is absolutely insane.

It's impossible to physically get those books back.

And even if by some miracle I did give them to those bastards, there is no question that they would kill me. Either right there on the spot, or eventually . . .

She rocked the wineglass stem, slowly spinning the merlot around the glass as she thought, then took a big swallow.

But . . .

She quickly went to her computer and got back online.

Signing in to the text messaging website, she found the conversation with the one she considered the Eastern European.

She rapidly typed in the new bubble:

> MEET AT LUCKY STARS CASINO AT 10 TONIGHT.

She then quickly clicked SEND—and stared at the screen.

The clock in the upper corner showed: 7:14.

Come on, c'mon . . .

It took three minutes for him to reply:

> 267-555-9100
>
> CASINO IS NOT SATISFACTORY.

I wonder why? Too many people?

Too bad. Then all the more reason to do it there.

My rules . . .

She sent:

> I GET TO SELECT THE PLACE. AND THE CASINO IS QUITE
> SATISFACTORY.
>
> BUT NOT INSIDE.
>
> ON THE BOARDWALK ALONG THE RIVER IS A PIER. WHERE
> THE CASINO HAS A TOUR BOAT.

She waited, sipping her wine, her eyes darting to the clock as the minutes ticked off: 7:16 . . . 7:17.

Why the hell no reply?

I don't have much time . . .

She then typed:

OKAY. THE NOTEBOOKS WILL BE IN THE CASINO BAG
THAT WAS IN THE PHOTO I SENT YOU EARLIER. I WILL
TIE ON ITS HANDLE ONE OF THOSE SMALL PLASTIC
BAGS FROM THE DOG PARK THAT'S THERE AT THE
BOARDWALK.

YOU WILL GET AN EXACT SAME BAG FROM THE CASINO,
PUT THE CASH IN IT, AND TIE ONE OF THOSE PET BAGS
TO ITS HANDLE.

AT 10 P.M. YOU WILL WALK TO THE END OF THE
CASINO'S PIER, DROP THE BAG IN THE TRASHCAN
BESIDE THE LAST IRON BENCH THERE, THEN LIGHT A
CIGARETTE. YOU WILL THEN LEAVE THE BOARDWALK
AND CIRCLE THE PARKING LOT, FINISHING YOUR
CIGARETTE.

EXACTLY 20 MINUTES LATER YOU WILL REALIZE YOU
ACCIDENTALLY LEFT SOMETHING IN THE BAG AND RETURN
TO RETRIEVE IT.

> IF I FIND THAT ALL THE MONEY YOU PROMISED IS IN
> THE BAG THAT YOU LEAVE, YOU WILL FIND THE
> NOTEBOOKS IN THE BAG THAT I LEAVE.
>
> I WILL BE WATCHING. WHAT WILL YOU BE WEARING?

She read that over once—*Not that I could possibly count two hundred thousand dollars in the freezing dark*—then sent it.

Five minutes later she nervously upended her wineglass, then fired off:

> WELL?? THESE ARE MY RULES. DO YOU WANT THE BOOKS
> OR NOT?

The clock now read: 7:23.

Then a bubble popped up:

> 267-555-9100
>
> I WEAR BLACK PANTS AND A BLACK LEATHER JACKET.
> ALSO WILL HAVE A GRAY WOOL FEDORA WITH SMALL
> FEATHER IN HATBAND.
>
> BUT I WARN YOU — DO NOT WASTE MY TIME.

Maggie felt her heart trying to burst through her chest.

Okay, now, Ricky . . .

She went to that conversation thread, then looked at the clock. It turned to 7:25.

Her hands shaking, she quickly typed:

```
BE AT LUCKY STARS CASINO BOARDWALK TONIGHT.


THE NOTEBOOKS WILL BE IN THE CASINO BAG THAT

WAS IN THE PHOTO I SENT YOU EARLIER. YOU WILL

GET FROM THE CASINO ONE OF THE EXACT SAME BAGS.

THERE IS A DOG PARK BY THE BOARDWALK. TAKE ONE

OF THE BLACK PLASTIC BAGGIES FROM IT AND TIE IT

TO THE CASINO BAG HANDLE SO MY MAN WILL

RECOGNIZE YOU.


THEN AT 10:15 BE WAITING ON THE BOARDWALK FOR THE

EXCHANGE TO TAKE PLACE.


MY MAN WILL WEAR BLACK PANTS AND JACKET

AND A GRAY FEDORA THAT HAS A FEATHER IN THE

HATBAND.
```

She reread it and clicked SEND.

Five minutes later, a bubble popped up:

```
215-555-3452


WHO IS THIS MAN? THIS IS BULLSHIT!


I GAVE YOU TWO HOURS!
```

She looked at that for a long moment, took a deep breath, and then sent:

```
CALM DOWN, RICKY. JUST BE THERE. 10:15.
```

The next minute felt like it lasted forever. Then came the reply:

```
215-555-3452


THIS IS THE LAST CHANCE!


DO NOT SCREW UP. YOU OR YOUR MAN.


OR HER BLOOD IS ON YOUR HANDS.
```

Her?
Almost immediately another message bubble popped up.
Maggie gasped.

The message had no words, only an image.

It was a close-up photograph of the face of a very young brown-skinned girl, maybe ten or eleven, her head turned at a sharp angle. A strip of silver duct tape covered her mouth. Her big dark eyes were looking as far left as they could possibly turn—toward her temple, where the muzzle of a big black pistol was pressed.

Oh my God . . .

Maggie's mind flooded with thoughts.

The first, which caused Maggie to begin tearing up herself as she stared at the young girl's tearing eyes, was: *That is the look of total terror.*

The next was: *I can't tell who that is. It could be Janine. But does it matter who it is?*

Then: *What have I done? This is crazy. Completely out of control.*

And finally: *I give up. Now there's only one option. . . .*

[FOUR]
New Hope House
Hazzard Street, Philadelphia
Monday, November 17, 6:22 P.M.

After Payne and Byrth made their introductions, Byrth showed Eldridge his phone with the photograph from the Department of Transportation ID.

"Elizabeth Cusick," Byrth said, "age twenty, five-one, one-ten, blonde, blue eyes. The address on this ID is this address."

"Beth?" Eldridge said, nodding. "Sure. She was here maybe two months ago. And most girls use this address, especially when they apply for SNAP?"

Payne nodded and said, mostly for Byrth's benefit, "Supplemental Nutrition Assistance Program. Food stamps."

"Right," Eldridge said. "She came with a friend, nice-looking girl afraid of her own shadow. Hardly ever talked, this girlfriend. Beth did most of the talking. But when she did, it was with an accent. I'm guessing Russian?"

Payne and Byrth exchanged glances.

Byrth then said, "How long were they at your flophouse—"

"'Transitional housing,'" he interrupted. "We prefer that. Lots of folks winding up here first got referred to other homes right out of jail. To get in those, though, they got to be clean. Which sometimes the jail time does for them. But when they sometimes slip—and *most* times they slip—they're thrown out. Tragic cycle, sad to say. That's how come we tell them to be clean, just don't demand it. We're hoping they can ease off the addiction."

"Does that work?" Byrth asked, his tone skeptical.

"Sometimes. It ain't easy. Ever. Believe me, I know. I've been fighting my own monkey on my back longer than I care to say."

"What about this Cusick girl?" Byrth said.

He shrugged. "A runaway at some point is what I'm thinking. She never said outright. But some signs were pretty clear. She was hiding from a pimp. Both girls were. Some figure it out faster than others."

"Figure out . . . ?" Payne said.

"That they ain't gonna last long. Pimp makes them charge fifty bucks for fifteen minutes of screwing, thirty bucks for a blow job. Twenty, thirty tricks a day. Day after day. And then maybe split that money with the pimp, or he takes it all? Bastard who beats them, maybe sells them to another pimp, and worse?" Eldridge looked between them, then added, "You're cops. You know they wind up dead all the time."

"Wish I could say that's the first I've heard of that," Payne said, nodding.

Byrth said, "So, any idea what happened to Beth and her friend?"

"Only that it was same as most. One day here, next never heard from them again. Till you guys showed up."

"They leave anything behind?"

Eldridge cocked his head. "You kidding me? Place like this?"

"I have to ask. You never know. And we need something we could run for fingerprints—a hairbrush, toothbrush, razor—or DNA off, say, a pair of used panties."

Eldridge shrugged. "It's been two months. If it ain't nailed down, it's stolen in minutes. Even clothes, old underwear, too. Still, we're better here than a lot. We take in only twenty, four to a room, each paying three hundred a month. Some places it's forty or more packed in. Plus we feed them and preach the . . ."

His voice trailed off as he looked past them toward the front door.

"Don't be coming in here causing no trouble!" the big woman at the table then called out.

Byrth and Payne looked. It was the Jamaican, the big guy with the dreadlocks, at the front door. He towered over the crowd and was pacing, pointing his finger at the Latina with the black eye and blue hoodie.

"What's Bob Marley's problem?" Payne said.

"Name's Marcus," Eldridge said. "Says some punks shot at him this afternoon. He's been on edge ever since. Usually really mellow, especially when he's high."

Byrth, pushing back his jacket and moving his right hand near his hip, said, "Well, mellow or not, that bastard's a few sandwiches short of a picnic."

"I told you I want another spliff, bitch!" Marcus then demanded, his deep Caribbean accent booming through the room.

"And I told you fuck off, I ain't got none!" the Latina snapped back.

In the next instant, Marcus had pulled a knife from his pants pocket and was swinging it wildly.

A moment later he heard two men shout:

"Drop it!"

"Drop the damn knife now!"

When Marcus looked toward the back of the room he saw that the man with the big hat and his partner had pistols drawn—and that they were aiming if not directly at Marcus's head then just above his multicolored knit cap.

They stepped toward him.

Marcus started to run, then stopped and grabbed the Latina, putting the knife point to her throat. Marcus quickly moved backward with her toward the front door—then let her loose and bolted outside.

"Great," Payne said, pointing his pistol at the ceiling as he and Byrth started moving faster. "I was tempted to just let the sonofabitch run before he stuck the knife on her."

Matt Payne, keeping the muzzle of his .45 up, flew through the doorway—then slipped when he hit the snow-packed sidewalk. He managed to recover just as Jim Byrth leapt over the slippery spot, landing in the street. They exchanged glances, then took off.

They saw, half a block ahead, Marcus moving quickly. He had his head back, knees flying high, arms pumping.

"Stop! Police!" Payne yelled.

Marcus then made a sliding right turn at the corner.

Approaching the next block, Payne saw that he and Byrth were slowly closing the gap. Payne then saw Marcus look back, then cut across the street. Then he saw at the far corner two human shapes standing beside a dumpster. Marcus, looking back again, ran right toward them.

One of the pair pulled something from his coat pocket. As it was raised, it glinted.

"Sonofabitch! Gun!" Payne said, and quickly crouched, motioning for Byrth to get down.

The *pop-pop-pop* of gunfire immediately followed, the muzzle flash reflecting on the icy street. The big Jamaican tried to change direction but lost his footing. He went down, striking the base of a metal utility pole headfirst.

Payne was trying to get a good aim on the shooter when there was another series of three shots. And then the firing stopped and there was a *clunk* as the gun hit the concrete.

The shooter and his partner bolted toward an empty lot beyond the dumpster.

Payne was about to kneel beside the Jamaican when Byrth called, "I've got him. Don't let those other fuckers get away!"

Byrth, sliding to a stop at the Jamaican, pulled handcuffs from his coat pocket. He smoothly slapped a cuff on the man's big right wrist, then pulled him in place so that he was hugging the metal pole and clipped his left wrist.

Then Byrth took off after Payne.

"Over here!" Payne called in a loud whisper from the shadows at the back corner of a line of row houses. He was breathing heavily, the cold air feeling like ice picks to his lungs.

When Byrth came up, Payne said, "They're in here. They tried wrapping the cable back but didn't get it locked."

Payne pointed to a gate in the chain-link fence topped with razor wire. Hanging from the gate was the loose end of heavy-gauge steel cable that had been threaded around a metal post.

In a crouch, his pistol close in at chest level, Payne slowly swung the gate open. He cleared the immediate area, then entered the backyard, signaling with his left hand for Byrth to follow.

Suddenly, the cold air carried a chemical-like stench. It burned his nostrils.

What the hell is that? he wondered, and had to clear his throat.

He heard Byrth grunt, then cough involuntarily.

They moved quickly toward what was the back porch of the completely darkened house, snow crunching with each step. Once across the backyard, they came to another gate. It was wide open. They cleared it and went through.

Then from the far side of the next yard came the clanking sound of another chain-link gate opening, then the fast crunching of feet running on snow and the whine of an engine starter engaging. A big motorcycle rumbled to life—and almost instantly roared off.

"Damn it!" Payne said.

After a moment he felt a nudge on his right shoulder and he saw Byrth pointing at the back door. The porch light was on.

They could see that the door had a piece of torn fabric from an overcoat, and what looked like its insulating filler, caught in the jamb right above the dead bolt.

And that the door was cracked open.

XI

[ONE]
Office of the General Manager
Lucky Stars Casino & Entertainment
North Beach Street, Philadelphia
Monday, November 17, 8:53 P.M.

Nikoli Antonov, his palms together and index fingertips touching his lips, was deep in thought as he looked at the plain brown paperboard box. It was on the far side of his desk, where Dmitri Gurnov, who had just left, had placed it ten minutes earlier.

Antonov was trying to figure out why Gurnov had been acting oddly.

Why is he so nervous?

He said he was distracted with the plans to get the keys from Carlos. But I do not believe that.

It is something else. He is not thinking clearly. Evidence of that is that I told him to call me about this box of muscle relaxer.

Instead, he chose to bring it here, to the casino! Careless!

I told him over and over there can be absolutely nothing associated with those killings and the casino or Diamond Development.

And this drug could most certainly be a "direct connection," as Bobby and Mike said.

I do not like either of them. But that is different from having a professional respect for them. . . .

"Let's be clear on this, Nick," Bobby Garcia's voice had come over Antonov's speakerphone, his tone impatient. "This is not our first rodeo. We know what we're doing." He paused, then added, "Apropos of nothing whatever, per federal law, there has to be proof of a gift being given to a politician that actually caused him to act in some official fashion—and that proof has to be a direct connection."

Antonov was quiet a moment, then said: "An example?"

"Okay," Mike Santos had said, his tone equally impatient. "For example: Giving said senator regular use of your Citation results in him having included in another law—one wholly different, say, on immigration reform—a line item that provides a tax exemption for any corporation that engages in the gaming industry *and* said corporation is run by a blonde-haired former Russian national whose suit size is forty-two long."

Antonov grunted.

"Short of that, Nick," Garcia said, "federal prosecutors know they are pissing up a rope at any chance of conviction."

"That's the beauty of being a politician, a 'lawmaker,' " Santos added. "You get to write your own damn laws."

"And what about his chief of staff?"

Garcia laughed. "Are you kidding me?"

"What do you mean? This is no joke."

"You know, I learned way back in boarding school that Lenin had a name for people like that. I'm surprised you don't know it."

"Which is?" Antonov said, ignoring the shot.

"*Tontos útiles,*'" Garcia said.

"That's Spanish, not Russian."

"Well, I learned it in Spanish first. The translation to English is the same: 'Useful idiots.'"

"And when they are no longer useful, we replace them," Santos said. "Shall we paint you a picture?"

"No," Antonov said, after a long moment. "No picture necessary."

And the manner in which Dmitri placed that box on my desk, Antonov now thought, tapping his fingertips anxiously. *It was suggestive. As if it was somehow a power thing.*

Antonov turned and watched the images cycling on the quad of monitors on his wall. A surveillance camera captured Gurnov carrying a casino bag out through the revolving doors.

Dmitri is more and more a liability. He must be replaced. Perez, too.

His desk phone began to trill softly, and when Antonov glanced at the phone's touchscreen display, he snorted and shook his head.

How does he always know?

He cleared his throat, then smoothly picked up the receiver.

"Ah, Yuri," he answered in Russian. "How are you? . . . What—? . . . No, no. Everything is perfect. And I'm very glad you called. I was just about to call and update you on the dealings with our good friend the senator. . . ."

[TWO]
Kensington, Philadelphia
Monday, November 17, 9:08 P.M.

"And I thought that room full of pot plants was surreal," Matt Payne said, shaking his head. "This is beyond surreal. It's . . ."

"Evil," Jim Byrth said, finishing the thought.

After searching the upper floors and finding no one in the house, they now stood in the basement.

The largest object in the room was the most disturbing one—an orange 110-gallon drum near the back wall. It had a natural gas line fueling the fire box beneath it and a tin vent tube leading from its metal lid up to the ceiling. And metal ductwork ran to a hole in what was the main room of the first floor.

Coming from the drum was the same stench, though somewhat fainter, that had burned their nostrils and throats as they had approached the back door.

Byrth gestured at the long wall where "El Pozolero" had been spray-painted in highly stylized graffiti-like four-feet-high lettering.

"The sick bastard takes a perverse pride in being called the Stew Maker," he said. "Like it's something to boast about. Incredible."

In the middle of the room was a heavy cast-iron incinerator the size of an office desk. It also had a natural gas line feeding it, a vent tube, and metal ductwork that ran to the first floor. A digital gauge on its ductwork read CAUTION! CO_2.

Beside the incinerator, on the raw concrete floor, were two cardboard boxes, each labeled "Technical Grade Sodium Hydroxide Lye Beads." One was empty.

"This is getting worse by the second," Matt Payne said ten minutes later, kneeling by the cardboard box. It was half full of women's clothing, and he was using the tip of his pen to carefully look through it.

He had just put back a leather string necklace with an Eleguá medallion threaded on it—the clay disc of a child's face that was the Santería god of destiny—and uncovered an unusual purse.

Some damn destiny, he thought.

He looked at the purse for a long time, dug some more, then looked back at the purse. He pulled out his cell phone and went to the folder he had made with the files Kerry Rapier had sent him in the Keys. He opened one and clicked through the images.

"How can it get worse?" Byrth said.

"Here. Look at this photograph of the Spencer girl."

Byrth saw that it showed the tall twenty-seven-year-old in jeans and a Temple University sweatshirt and carrying a gold sequined purse that was glinting in the sunlight.

"Okay, the same photo from her file," he said. Then he turned to look in the box. "Jesus Christ . . ."

Payne met his eyes. "I didn't find a Temple sweatshirt in any box, and I'm sure there's more than one purse like this in Philly, but . . ."

Byrth nodded. "There will be plenty of DNA in that purse to see if it's a match," he said.

Payne pulled out his phone and hit a speed-dial number. "Mickey, drop whatever you're doing. I'm about to call in this scene. You're not going to believe this. . . ."

After he gave O'Hara the address and broke off the call, he saw Byrth watching him.

"What's the worst that would happen, Jim? They'd fire me,

thus denying me sublime moments such as this?" he said, gesturing around the basement. Then he looked back at Byrth. "Remember what Eisenhower said at that Nazi death camp at the end of World War Two, when he was supreme commander of Allied forces?"

Byrth nodded. "Indeed I do. 'Get it all on record now—get the films, the witnesses—because somewhere down the road of history some bastard will get up and say that this never happened.' To this day those images are hard to look at."

"And," Payne said, "no one would believe that this is happening now. That, however, is about to change."

Payne hit another speed-dial key and after a moment said, "Kerry, are you picking up my location from this phone?" He paused to listen, then said, "Right. That's it. We were at the Hazzard address. I need you to send a Crime Scene unit here. I'll call you back." He broke off the call and speed-dialed another. "Dr. Mitchell, Matt Payne. You too busy to break away . . . ?"

"We're talking with Philadelphia's chief medical examiner, Dr. Howard Mitchell," Mickey O'Hara said, panning the broadcast-quality high-definition digital video camera around the basement of the row house, the lens tracking across the wall with the elaborate four-foot-tall "El Pozolero" graffiti.

. He stopped when he had in view the balding, rumpled doctor in the well-worn two-piece suit. The medical examiner stood to the right of the giant orange drum, which towered over him.

"Dr. Mitchell," O'Hara said, holding a microphone in front of him, "you were calling this process alkaline hydrolysis?"

"That's correct," Mitchell began, then stopped as he furrowed his brow. "This is not for public broadcast or any other publication, correct?"

"Not for broadcast, Dr. Mitchell," Matt Payne confirmed. He was standing behind O'Hara. "Just for documentation purposes."

Mitchell, looking beyond the camera, nodded and said, "Okay, Matt, I take you at your word. I damn sure don't want to see myself in those fifteen-minute TV news loops, over and over discussing such an indelicate topic. And that's what would happen, because I'm too old to try to be politically correct."

He then looked back into the lens and went on: "The university's medical school has what is called the Tomb—a large stainless steel cylinder that is about the size, not surprisingly when you consider it, of a human coffin. When bodies are signed over by the families of the deceased and these bodies meet the needs of the medical school, they're used for teaching gross anatomy, et cetera. Afterward the carved-up cadavers are taken to the Tomb."

"And how does the Tomb work?" O'Hara said.

"The cadaver is placed in a lye solution in the cylinder, which then is sealed and heated to three hundred degrees Fahrenheit under a pressure of sixty pounds per square inch. In about three hours the alkaline hydrolysis turns the cadaver into a liquid that's about the color and thickness of motor engine oil. It is an inexpensive and efficient process."

"But is it safe?"

"Of course. Completely. Safer, in fact, than the embalming fluids that get washed down drains. There is only a bit of bone shadow left over."

"Bone shadow is what?"

"Calcium phosphate. It's what makes up most of our bone and

teeth mass. This can then simply be ground to a harmless fine powder and disposed of."

Dr. Mitchell motioned with his hand at the enormous drum.

"And this is essentially the same process—the use of lye and heat. Clearly, the drum here is much more crude than the pressurized Tomb. And considerably less efficient. But lye is cheap and readily available for soap making, biodiesel manufacture, and many other general uses. Any farm supply house in Amish country will sell it to you, or you can order it on the Internet. I would estimate that two hundred dollars' worth could easily cook four or five bodies. Just add water. And boil."

After O'Hara recorded Dr. Mitchell releasing the row house to the Crime Scene Unit—video that the medical examiner said O'Hara did have permission to use on Philly News Now—he followed Mitchell out the door.

Jim Byrth now watched the Crime Scene blue shirts photographing the large room with its clear plastic tent and small forest of ready-to-harvest marijuana plants. He had his handcuffs in his right hand, having gone back and retrieved them from the Jamaican after confiscating his knife and throwing it in the nearby dumpster. Byrth and Payne had agreed they had more pressing problems and that the stoner had had enough justice served for one day.

"That Rastafarian would've pissed his pants over this hydro," Byrth now said. "It's maybe four, five times as potent as average Mexican pot. Which is why it goes for a premium. A pound of average weed runs around four hundred bucks. That puts hydroponic at four grand, at least."

"This room is worth a fortune."

"Was . . ."

After a long moment, Payne said, "Have you ever seen an operation like this, Jim?"

Byrth turned to him.

"Well," he said, "I have seen acre after acre of pot fields. And I have seen grow houses in everything from Houston condos to suburban Fort Worth ranch homes. And, I'm sorry to say, to my grave I will take the memory of seeing the horror in the barrels of Pozole. But all this?" He slowly shook his head. "I have never seen anything close to this place. And pray I never do again."

Byrth felt his phone vibrate. He pulled it from his pocket and read the text message:

GLENN PABODY

JUST GOT WORD THAT THEY FOUND IN THAT RV TRAILER A BUNCH MORE IDS AND THOSE STRIP CLUB BUSINESS CARDS.

FIFTEEN IDS WERE MEXICO NATIONAL ONES, ALL BUT TWO OF THEM GIRLS IN THEIR EARLY 20S.

THE STRIPPER CARDS WERE FROM THE HACIENDA BUT ALSO FROM CLUBS IN HOUSTON AND, HERE'S WHAT YOU'RE GONNA WANT TO HEAR, FOR A PLACE CALLED PLAYERS CORNER LOUNGE.

Byrth looked at the message for a long moment and thought, *And how many more girls were killed and then put in those barrels of acid?*

That bastard probably called himself "El Pozolero," too.
He shook his head as he replied:

```
THANKS, GLENN.


I'LL SEND YOU SHOTS OF WHAT WE JUST FOUND IN
PHILLY. AND CATCH YOU UP ON WHAT WE LEARNED ABOUT
THE FIRST GIRL'S ID YOU FOUND.


SO, WHAT PART OF HOUSTON IS PLAYERS IN?
```

A moment later Byrth read:

```
GLENN PABODY


NOT HOUSTON, JIM. IT'S GOT A PHILLY ADDRESS. I'LL
SEND A PHOTO WHEN I CAN.
```

As Byrth typed the bar's name into an Internet search on his phone, he said, "You ever hear of a strip club called Players Corner Lounge, Marshal?"

"Sounds just like my kind of place. Sorry. Never heard of it."

"Apparently it's at Front and Master."

"That's Fishtown. Not far. What's the significance?"

"Sheriff Pabody just said they found more of those stripper cards in the trailer, and this Players place was one of them."

Payne checked his phone. There was no message—not from Maggie, not from anyone.

"It's more or less on the way home. Should be hopping at this hour. Crime Scene's got this place. Let's get the hell out of here."

[THREE]

With the exception of Payne issuing the most basic of directions as Byrth drove—"Two blocks hang a right," then "Left here," then "Straight a couple miles"—they were quiet, lost in their thoughts. To break the silence, Byrth turned on the radio, its volume low but clear. The station was broadcasting the national news.

Payne listened for a moment, then his mind flashed back to the macabre image it had created—thanks to Dr. Mitchell's vivid alkaline hydrolysis description—of the case workers being boiled down.

They basically turned into a vat of Valvoline 10-W-40 . . . Jesus!

There's no way Maggie could've known about that hell and not said something to someone.

With the girl's murder and the firebombing of her home, I damn sure can't blame her for wanting to control everything.

But this?

How do I begin explaining this to her parents?

And Amanda? I don't want to lie to her, but until we catch these bastards I'm going to have to come up with some cover story she won't see right through. . . .

From the radio speakers, the familiar grating voice of the secretary of the Department of Homeland Security filled the vehicle. It was a news report from Capitol Hill, and Payne heard the DHS head declare in a politician's dispassionate monotone, *"Our borders, sir, are more secure than ever."*

"Bullshit!" Jim Byrth blurted, practically spitting it out.

Payne glanced over and said dryly, "You really should learn to speak your mind, Jim. Holding things inside is not healthy."

Byrth grunted. "I just get tired of the damn political lies. You know how long the border with Mexico runs, from the Pacific to the Gulf?"

"A couple thousand miles?"

"Right. The reality is there's no way that's secure—and certainly not 'more secure than ever.' At the San Ysidro entry plaza, the border checkpoint just across from Tijuana, eight million pedestrians cross into the U.S. every year. Another twenty million come in cars. That's just one border checkpoint. Texas's busiest, Laredo, has a daily average of five thousand trucks coming in from Nuevo Laredo, which happens to be the main smuggling route of the Gulf Cartel. We don't know how much contraband gets through our checkpoints—only what we catch—therefore it's impossible to quantify how much crosses at uncontrolled points. Which is why it's disingenuous at best to declare the border secure."

A couple of minutes later the United States attorney general's voice could be heard over the speakers: *". . . these financial institutions, Senator, have become so enormous that we can only fine them, because we have found that if we in fact brought criminal charges there would be a negative impact on the United States economy, and, to coin a phrase, as goes the U.S. economy so goes the world economy . . ."*

"You been following this?" Payne said, pointing at the radio. "Banks caught methodically violating laundering laws? Then fined only a couple billion dollars after moving tens of billions in cartel money?"

Byrth nodded. "Congress should have never done away with the Glass-Steagall Act. Banks in bed with investment brokerages? Banks used to be just banks, and could only operate intrastate. Now we have an alphabet soup of corporate finance giants, some headquartered here, some in other countries, with branches around the world."

"And laundering money."

"Laundering money and who the hell knows what else," Byrth said, reaching over and punching the dash button that turned off the radio.

"And that makes me think of that poor bastard Garvey," Byrth then said. "What kind of world is it when a guy just doing his job gets busted as a mule moving two lousy keys while worrying that the cartel will kill his family? Meantime, these big boys in their ivory towers, willingly moving cartel money and counting their profits, get a Get Out of Jail Free Card from no less than the AG himself."

"They're calling that 'too big to fail, too big to jail.' Apparently Garvey's mistake was he didn't move enough volume."

Byrth shook his head. "I fear we are slowly selling our collective soul to the highest bidder."

"I fear you're right," Payne said, then added, "Master is next street after the light."

Maybe that's what I need to do to get a response from that bastard—raise the bid.

Payne looked back at his phone and reread the first message he had sent to the number on the grease-stained note. He started typing:

```
YOU HAVE ONE HOUR TO REPLY TO THE FOLLOWING
OFFER . . .
```

Then his phone began vibrating, the screen showing the call was to his personal phone number. The caller ID read: UNKNOWN.

He sighed, then switched over to that number and answered it.

"Yeah?" he snapped, unintentionally.

"Matt?" a female voice said, clearly distressed.

"What?" he said impatiently. Then, slowly, added, "Wait . . . *Maggie?*"

"Look, I'm sorry. I need help. Fast. In twenty minutes . . ."

[FOUR]

Lucky Stars Casino & Entertainment
North Beach Street, Philadelphia
Monday, November 17, 9:55 P.M.

Dmitri Gurnov walked out of the revolving doors of the casino carrying one of the big black bags. He glanced up, saw the security camera, then looked forward, snugging his fedora lower.

What are the odds Antonov is watching . . . ?

Gurnov followed a crushed-rock path that wound through the snow-covered park-like area and out to the boardwalk. A stiff wind was coming down the Delaware River. The cold cut to his bones.

As he walked his eyes scanned the area. He did not notice another soul anywhere.

He approached the dog park. It had artificial turf, a series of wooden ramps for exercise, and an oversized red plastic fire hydrant in its center. It was surrounded by a four-foot-high fence, in each corner of which was a pole that held a plastic bag dispenser and, below that, a trash receptacle.

He walked toward the closest pole, took one of the small bags—*I cannot believe I'm doing this*—and tied it to the handle. Then, turning up the collar of his coat, he walked to the boardwalk and out on the short pier.

It, not at all surprisingly, also was deserted.

And colder, if that's possible.

He passed a series of iron benches, then came to the end of the pier. There, next to the last bench, he saw the heavy metal trashcan. It was square, with a horizontal slit on each side just below its flat top.

A gust of wind blew, and he stepped quickly to the can.

He tried stuffing the bag into one of the horizontal slits. It would not fit.

Damn it!

His hands bare, he moved around the stacks of cash, then folded the bag over and tried shoving it in the slit. It still did not fit.

He looked at it for a long moment, considered throwing the cash bundles in loose, then decided against that. Then he grabbed the slit—the cold metal almost burning his bare skin—and with some effort pulled up the heavy lid, tilting it. He shoved the bag in through the gap, then dropped the lid back in place with a loud *clang*.

What if she cannot get that out . . . and if she does, then I have to dig out the bag she puts in?

Damn this!

The wind gusted again.

He turned his back to it, crouched, and tried to light a cigarette. It took three tries, but he finally had it going. He stuffed his hands in his jacket pockets and started off the pier.

Matt Payne had already started to open his door as Jim Byrth brought the SUV to a skidding stop in the casino parking lot. They both jumped out. Then Byrth gave Payne a thumbs-up gesture as they heard the faint *wop-wop-wop* of the rotor blades of the police helicopter coming from the direction of Northeast Airport.

When Payne had called in for backup, Kerry Rapier said he also would alert the Aviation Unit to have Air Tac One circling nearby.

"That helo will light up the place like it's daytime," Rapier had said.

Byrth and Payne, guns drawn and staying in the shadows, began running toward the river. As they'd planned in the SUV after pulling away from the Fishtown dive bar, Byrth moved southward, to the far side of where the pier went out from the boardwalk, and Payne to the north.

After a ten-minute circle of the parking lot, Dmitri Gurnov flicked the butt of his third cigarette into the dog park.

And then he noticed a man standing on the boardwalk. The man held one of the casino's bags.

And then Gurnov recognized what was tied to its handle.

I will be damned! He has the money!

He reached into his jacket pocket, pulling out the Sig 9mm.

As he approached the man, he raised his pistol.

He heard someone behind him yell.

He quickly fired two shots, then a third.

The man went down. He rushed to him and knelt to grab the bag.

Then he saw the man's face. It was that of a swarthy, fortyish Latino. Bright red blood flowed down his hard face from the hole in his forehead.

Who the hell are you? Gurnov thought.

As Gurnov stood, he heard running on the boardwalk. Another man was rushing him, holding a Kalashnikov at hip level.

He saw his face as bullets fired.

"Ricky?"

Matt Payne watched the man in black clothing and the gray fedora raise a pistol at another man on the boardwalk.

Payne speed-dialed Rapier.

"Send the damn helo, Kerry!"

"On its way, Marshal."

"Police!" Payne shouted. "Drop the gun!"

There were two shots. With each muzzle flash, the man on the boardwalk staggered back a step. Then a single shot followed, causing his head to jerk backward. He dropped the bag he was holding, and then his knees buckled.

The man in the gray fedora grabbed the bag.

Then a third man ran up. He was firing an AK-47 from his hip. The man in the gray fedora fell backward. The third man knelt briefly by the first man, then bolted down the boardwalk.

Payne heard Byrth shout, "Stop!"—and fire a two-shot burst.

Payne, pounding down the boardwalk, heard the *wop-wop-wop* of Air Tac One's rotor blades growing louder. He looked over his shoulder and saw the beams of the floodlights from the helo's belly sweeping the surface of the dark river.

Payne ran in the direction he'd seen Byrth's muzzle flashes.

A moment later, a floodlight beam washed over him, then moved up ahead. It lit up the man, who was still up and moving fast.

Byrth took another two-round volley at him. That caused the man to suddenly turn back.

He was now running straight for Payne.

The helo hovered, its lights now brightly illuminating the entire boardwalk and most of the park. The pitch of its rotors changed with the wind gusts. Payne saw Byrth moving in his direction but away from the boardwalk.

Then Payne saw the dot of a red laser bouncing wildly across the boardwalk near the man.

Too damn windy for the sniper . . .

The man suddenly looked up and fired a half-dozen shots at the helo, then continued in Payne's direction.

"Police! Stop!" Payne yelled, taking aim.

The man took two wild blind shots in his direction.

Payne squeezed the trigger. His first round hit the shooter in the shoulder. But he continued running. Payne squeezed off two more rounds, the shots hitting the man in the left chest.

He was now within thirty feet—and still advancing.

Payne squeezed off his next five rounds in rapid succession, and when the slide locked open, he smoothly thumbed the magazine release, replaced the empty mag with a fully charged one, then thumbed the slide release, chambering a new round as he brought the sights back on the shooter.

Just as he was beginning to squeeze the trigger, the man collapsed at his feet.

Five minutes later, with more backup units arriving, their sirens screaming and lights flashing, Matt Payne waved off Air Tac One. Just as the helo's floodlight went dark, the Texas Ranger flicked a small black bean on the dead shooter's back.

Byrth turned and saw that Payne was staring at his hands. And that they were trembling.

"That was good work, Marshal. Sometimes these bastards—full of adrenaline, drugs, whatever—just won't go down."

Payne nodded. "Someone once told me, 'Always, always, always empty your mags.'"

[FIVE]
Off Key West, Florida
Thursday, November 20, 10 A.M.

The Viking, its engines at idle speed, skimmed almost silently across the glass-slick Atlantic Ocean. Matt Payne, at the flybridge helm talking on his cell phone, turned the wheel as the sleek Sport Fisherman passed the outer markers of the Boca Chica channel. That put the bow just to the right of the sun on the horizon, its golden rays glowing brighter and brighter.

"Yeah, Tony, last night Amanda got a nice photograph from Maggie McCain. It's of her and her parents on the sailboat leaving Saint Thomas."

"Speaking of Saint Thomas," Anthony Harris said, "I got a call from one of the DEA guys. He reported that they found Captain Jack floating in the harbor. And it wasn't pretty."

"How so?"

"You know boats have those emergency signal guns . . ."

"Sure."

". . . well, someone wanted to send a signal, all right. They fired a twenty-five-millimeter white phosphorus one into his chest."

"Damn! That's an illumination flare. Once it starts burning it doesn't stop until it burns out. That's fifteen, twenty minutes."

"Yeah, and apparently he lit up the harbor pretty good. They said folks from a cruise ship got video of it and put it online, thinking it was part of some celebration."

"Well, in a warped way I'm sure it is cause for celebration. For Garvey at least. But what about the coke?"

Tony chuckled. "Damnedest thing, Matt. You know the men's room over the evidence room? Night before last, a waterline to one of the shitters broke loose. Initial blame went to maintenance—or lack thereof. Then someone said it looked like the line might've got cut. Who knows? Regardless, the result was three feet of standing water. Flooded the shitter and, a floor below, all the evidence brought in during the previous forty-eight hours."

Matt heard steps and turned to see Amanda approaching the helm with a cup of coffee and a copy of *Cruising Guide to the Bahamas*. She slipped the cup into the holder on the console, then put the book in with the towels that were in a beach bag at Matt's feet.

Matt smiled at her and said, "Well, Tony, I guess once in a great while there is a little justice in this screwed-up world. Talk to you later."

He broke off the call.

Amanda tugged the phone from his grip. She turned it off.

"No more talking," she said, then tossed it into the bag. It disappeared under a towel. "Enough with the phone."

She then turned up the sound system.

Bob Marley was singing "Is This Love."

She put her arms around his waist and leaned in. They kissed.

"Now the fun begins," Amanda said, putting her hand on the throttles and shoving them forward.